— Lyonesse —

"Her Excellency, The Honorable Elenia Yakin."

Everyone present climbed to their feet and assumed a respectful stance, except for the three officers, who came to rigid attention. Yakin swept into the hall and, with Logran holding her chair, sat at the midpoint between the table's far ends, facing Morane. As if on cue, everyone else imitated her.

"Good afternoon," she began. "At the request of Lyonesse's Estates General, I convened this plenary so Captain Morane of the Navy, Lieutenant Colonel DeCarde of the Marines and Sister Gwenneth of the Order of the Void may explain the reasons for their unannounced arrival, what they propose, and why. For the edification of our visitors, the Estates General of Lyonesse is composed of the Colonial Council, whose leaders are at this table and whose members are sitting behind me; the mayors of Lyonesse's communities; the chancellor of the Lyonesse University; representatives of the Lyonesse Mercantile Association; senior administrators of the Lyonesse government; and representatives at large of trade unions, citizen's groups, and professional associations. The Estates General are called into a plenary only on rare occasions when the government is faced with grave decisions concerning the colony's future. This is one of them."

Morane nodded once to acknowledge Yakin's explanation. "Thank you, Your Excellency."

"So far, only a few heard what you told us and saw your evidence, Captain, though everyone knows the gist of your purpose. And of course, everyone on Lyonesse knows of the debt we owe you and your people," she continued. "If I could impose on you to repeat your story and answer any questions. My secretary is prepared to display the recordings of those unfortunate colonies." Yakin pointed at a giant screen dominating the one wall not pierced by transparent doorways.

"Certainly, Madame." Morane stood and let his gaze roam over the assembled colonists, meeting their eyes without embarrassment or nervousness, no matter how hostile they might seem.

Then he spoke in slow, measured tones about a subject few seemed able to grasp and even less accept as fact — the violent end of a social and political order that had lasted longer than a dozen lifetimes.

And how they could salvage humanity's future along with their own.

IMPERIAL TWILIGHT

Ashes of Empire # 2

ERIC THOMSON

Sanddiver
Books

PART I – LAST LIGHT

—1—

Mykonos (Coalsack Sector)

The trap door at the top of the basement stairs opened with the suddenness of a guillotine blade dropping on its victim's neck. Dust fell in random patterns like tiny star drops over the crude concrete steps and onto the ancient polished stone floor.

Marta Norum's gut clenched with a now all too familiar dread. She pulled her children deeper into the filthy alcove giving off the ruined building's ancient cellar, conscious they were trapped.

Petras, the capital of Mykonos, a planet settled long before the old Commonwealth died, was replete with stone dwellings built a thousand years earlier on foundations sunk deep into the living rock. Yet someone had stumbled into their hiding spot.

"Hello?"

A woman's voice, neither gentle nor harsh, wafted down among the shimmering motes. It seemed ageless, yet familiar. Marta Norum's mother might once have used such an intonation.

Or perhaps her mentors, women appointed *in loco parentis* during her extended stays with various monastic communities while her parents, Uther Norum, the Marquess of Cascadia, and Lady Cecilia searched for their next step up the greasy staircase of nobility ascendant.

In theory, the closer one came to the Ruggero throne, the safer one would be from any purges driven by imperial paranoia. Then, Dendera succeeded her father and pulled the fabric of empire from its shaky framework.

Marta suppressed a shiver of fear and clutched at the boy and girl huddled on either side of her. A faint whimper escaped the latter's quivering lips. The sound barely reached Marta's ear a few centimeters away, yet somehow the woman above them caught it too.

"I am Heloise, of the Mykonos Abbey, or what's left of it. This place is unsafe. Soldiers are combing through the ruins, searching for those on the run from Jorge Danton now that he no longer worries about the loyalty of the 84th and 91st Guards Regiments."

A pause.

"The usurper's troops show no mercy, even to widows and children. A quick, clean death is the best their victims can expect, although such a fate is unlikely. They consider killing Danton's enemies an enjoyable task, one which should be drawn out to prolong the entertainment."

A pair of scuffed, black, calf-high boots, size small, appeared on the top tread. They took one step, and Marta Norum could make out the loose black trousers preferred by Sisters of the Void tucked into them.

The rush of blood filled her ears while a thudding heart sent vibrations along every limb and through her skull. Marta's first words came out as a hoarse croak.

"How did you know we were here?"

Another step, this time revealing the hem of a knee-length dusty, black cloak.

"I sensed the children's terror. Their minds are not yet sufficiently developed to repress strong emotions."

"Sensed?"

Norum released her daughter and fumbled for the blaster tucked into her overcoat pocket. It was once part of her deceased husband's ceremonial attire, but no less deadly for that.

The Sister of the Void took another step.

"Some of us have a heightened awareness of others, especially when they broadcast powerful feelings." She chuckled dryly. "It makes us better healers than many, even though the Order would rather we don't discuss the matter with outsiders. But in the present circumstances... Besides, we were looking for you, Lady Marta. For you, Sigrid and Stefan."

"How do you know who we are?"

Marta raised the weapon with a shaky hand, her thoughts almost drowned by the roar of incipient panic.

"And why are you looking for us?"

"I wasn't a hundred percent sure of your identity until just now, but thank you for the confirmation. I'll be happy to explain why, but later when we're out of danger. We don't have much time to escape unnoticed."

"Escape where? Danton owns this planet."

Heloise took the remaining steps without saying another word and stopped at the foot of the stairs, in the rectangle of light created by a wan, late afternoon sun shining through a wrecked roof. She faced the shadows where Marta and her children hid and allowed them to take a good look at her.

Of average height, she appeared lean, almost rangy beneath the voluminous cloak. Short, iron-gray hair topped a face seamed by long decades of privation and service. Dark eyes beneath black brows searched Marta Norum's indistinct features as they acclimatized to the cellar's gloom, and for a moment, she fancied they could pierce through her skin and see her naked soul.

A shiver ran up Norum's spine at the notion, but it vanished almost at once, replaced by a sudden and unaccountable feeling of incipient relief which, in turn, seemed as if it might give way to bone-numbing fatigue.

"For now, we must leave Petras and find refuge. Though he might wish it were otherwise, Danton's grasp is still restricted to the capital's immediate surroundings. He'll need more time to make himself the undisputed master of Mykonos, even with the surviving military forces now under his command."

"Traitors to the Crown." Marta Norum's weary tone took the sting from her accusation.

"Realists. When he placed your husband's head on a pike, Jorge Danton became the most feared man in this star system. Despite their officers' conditioning, the Imperial Guards were always more loyal to naked power than the Ruggero dynasty. And now that the entire sector has slipped from Dendera's grasp it's better to join forces with rebellious units than fight and die for a distant ideal. But we can discuss the philosophy of rebellion later. Please come with me. We must get away before darkness falls."

The urgency in Sister Heloise's voice drove Marta to obey without conscious thought. She dropped the late Governor General Hachim LeGris' ceremonial blaster into her overcoat pocket and stood on shaky legs. Stefan and Sigrid, staring wide-eyed at the apparition in black, followed her movements without prodding, as if mesmerized.

"Why should we trust you?"

"Because my remaining Brethren and I are probably the only sapient beings in this star system who wish you well. Anyone other than us aiding you in the smallest way risks a horrible death at the hands of Danton's chosen executioners."

"And you don't fear him?"

"Since Danton ordered the massacre of the Mykonos Abbey Brethren on suspicion of loyalty to the Crown, we few survivors are the walking dead. Fear of the usurper has no bearing on our decisions. Now come, and don't forget your bags."

Heloise turned on her heels and climbed the stairs one by one without looking back.

Marta Norum briefly hugged her eight-year-old son and daughter, meeting eyes dulled by the indelible memory of their father's cruel execution and the long days of terror as they dodged Colonel Jorge Danton's murderers through the ruined quarters of Petras. Then, Marta motioned at them to precede her up the staircase and, after a final glance at the cellar that sheltered them for the last day and a half, she followed suit.

Five more dark-cloaked figures stood by the half-demolished restaurant's gaping windows and doors, peering out at the rubble-strewn streets. Two women and three men.

If Marta understood Sister Heloise correctly, they were the last of a once thriving monastic community devoted to medicine, learning, and charitable works in the name of the Almighty. Six survivors from among the thousands who once populated the abbey and countless priories scattered across the planet's surface.

Heloise thrust a dark bundle at Marta.

"Put this on and raise the cowl. Your appearance is too well known, but few will look twice at another Sister of the Void fleeing Danton's killers. There's no profit in denouncing us."

"What about my children?"

Heloise turned her eyes on the bewildered twins.

"You were careful to keep them from the public eye during your husband's rule. Dirty as they are now, no one will think them anything more than a pair of lost souls under the Order's protection."

"And I'm not sufficiently filthy?" She ran long, slender fingers through matted, shoulder-length blond hair framing a heart-shaped face prematurely aged by fatigue and fear.

"It would take more than mere grime to disguise you."

Norum shook out the bundle and obeyed Heloise's instructions. When her face was partially obscured by the baggy hood, Heloise nodded with approval.

"Good enough." She turned to one of the men. "Is the way clear, Sandor?"

"It appears so," the friar replied. "If we leave now, we'll escape Petras before predators come out to feed on the unwary."

"Where are we headed?" Norum asked.

"To the Port of Tiryns. We cannot risk taking what little air or suborbital service still connects Petras with Thera. It might take forty-eight hours or more to cross the Boetian Sea by ship, but few independent operators ask inconvenient questions when the money is right."

"Why Thera?"

"It is, for us, the safest place on Mykonos with a functioning spaceport." When understanding briefly sparked in Marta's eyes, Heloise allowed herself a tight smile. "Yes, we're hoping to find passage on a starship headed away from the Coalsack Sector."

"I see. But it still doesn't tell me why you choose to encumber yourself with a widow and two kids on the run from a mad Guards colonel."

"I'd like to know that as well," a disembodied male voice said from the shadows of a collapsed veranda. All six Void Brethren whirled toward it while Marta Norum reached for her children, eyes wide with renewed fear.

Heloise gestured at Sandor.

"Quickly, take them and go. Gellert and I will stay behind to cover you."

The man chuckled, though Norum's ears picked up undertones of amusement rather than menace.

"You're not going anywhere without my say so, Sister. Look into the street. If you squint hard enough, you might see a few of my men near the intersection. Several more are tucked away among the rubble, waiting for orders."

Norum glanced over her shoulder but saw nothing more than dusty walls, piles of stone and broken pavement.

"My men are wearing chameleon armor, and they know how to blend in."

"What do you want?" Heloise asked. "Quickly now. It's not healthy to stay among these ruins after dark, and the sun is about to kiss the horizon."

"Funny you should mention that, Sister."

—2—

Yotai (Coalsack Sector Capital)

"I'm not sure I share your pessimism, Admiral." Grand Duke Devy Custis, a powerfully built man in his sixties turned away from the three-dimensional projection depicting the Coalsack Sector and speared Pendrick Zahar with a hard glare. "Or did your battle group commanders experience a moment of panic?"

The imperial court's languid drawl colored Custis' words, but Zahar didn't mistake it for the affectation of a Wyvern buffoon.

"Your Grace?"

He tilted his head to one side and returned the duke's stare without fear or embarrassment. In contrast to Custis' broad, almost sensual features, the 16th Fleet commander's face was that of an ascetic — narrow, with a long patrician nose, sunken cheeks, and hooded eyes. His expression, even at rest, betrayed the predatory nature of a man who lived to exercise power.

Custis gestured at the hologram.

"Withdrawing your forces to Micarat seems a bit rash. It leaves Arietis and its wormhole junction in the hands of whoever gets there first, not to mention Peralka, Parvi, and Mentari, and *their* wormhole junctions."

"With the losses we suffered putting down several uprisings after Viceroy Joback's death, such as that led by the idiot Santana on Ariel, I no longer enjoy the luxury of spreading my forces along the frontier, Your Grace. Arietis is of limited use at the best of times and not intrinsically worth defending. The systems beyond have been or shortly will be overrun by invaders, making the Micarat wormhole junction their main entry point into this part of the sector."

As he spoke, Zahar pointed at various stars outlined in purple and red, showing they were no longer under 16th Fleet control.

"I took every precaution to make sure no inbound ship passes the wormhole traffic control arrays without permission."

"I wonder whether killing Joback while he still enjoyed the loyalty of so many star systems was a mistake."

"If I'd waited longer than I did, Your Grace, my losses would have been worse. I regret not slitting his throat the moment he declared himself for Dendera. It would have avoided us temporarily losing control of Ariel. Retaking that system proved costly in large part because one of the 168th Battle Group's commodores pledged herself and more than two dozen warships to Santana's service. Both are now dead, of course. Executed. Yet the damage is done, leaving us with losses we can ill afford."

"You couldn't have known about my plans," Custis replied in a conciliatory tone. "What about Parth?"

He pointed at a star outlined in green near the sector's outer edge.

"Barbarians coming via Arietis can reach it without passing through your Micarat choke point by the simple expedient of transiting through the Yin and Takeshi systems. Not that I'm overly fond of Parth, considering Dendera wanted me to end my days in one of its unhealthy death camps, but the system still belongs to this sector."

"I'm reinforcing Rayder Ostrow, who you might recall commands the 164th Battle Group, so he can fortify Parth to the same extent as Micarat and make it another choke point between us and the frontier. A few patrol ships will keep watch in the Yin system, enough to scare off the odd reiver wolf pack. If they find themselves at a serious disadvantage, their orders are to withdraw. Neither Yin nor Takeshi is worth fighting over."

"And the colonists?"

Custis ran a hand through his luxuriant silver hair, bound into a queue at the nape of the neck by a silk ribbon.

"With the empire collapsing and no immediate source of replacements, my ships are more valuable. If the colonists fear reivers, they're free to move."

Custis let out a soft snort.

"You're all heart, Admiral."

"Hard times demand hard decisions, Your Grace."

"Indeed they do. Rayder Ostrow, eh?" The grand duke tapped his chin with an elegantly manicured fingertip. "Isn't he the idiot who let — what was his name again — take *Tanith* and vanish?"

"Jonas Morane, of the cruiser *Vanquish*, sir." One of Zahar's aides helpfully offered. "Though it wasn't the name he used at the time. A Monokeros class transport by the name *Narwhal* carried *Tanith* away. Both ships were part of the 197th Battle Group, 19th Fleet, Shield Sector."

"Right. Thank you, Captain." Custis turned his gaze back on Zahar. "And you think this Ostrow is the man to defend Parth against barbarian incursions? Surely you can name another to take his place, someone who won't let the ragtag survivors of a loyalist battle group bamboozle him."

"In fairness, sir, Morane took his ships through what Ostrow discovered was a rogue wormhole. We're fortunate his command made it back to Parth unharmed. I would have relieved him if he'd continued the pursuit through an unstable part of the network beyond the empire's frontiers. As I may have mentioned, our ships are well-nigh irreplaceable these days. Could I ask why you're concerned about a prison transport carrying nobles Dendera couldn't execute out of hand?"

"Yes, but in private."

Custis nodded at the officers standing behind Zahar.

The admiral glanced over his shoulder.

"Please wait outside."

Once he and Zahar were alone, Custis said, "I found out shortly before going into stasis that Dendera's unloved sister Corinne was traveling with me in one of the prisoner pods under a secret identity. Had the prison ship's crew not sabotaged its antimatter fuel system, I would have brought *Tanith* with me to Yotai, and we would be decanting each stasis pod right now until we found Corinne."

"Why the interest in a Ruggero whelp, Your Grace? I thought you wished to make yourself regent of the Coalsack and use it as a springboard to reunite the empire under your rule."

A cold smile played on Custis' lips.

"Just because Dendera's madness is breaking the empire apart doesn't make her dynasty illegitimate in the eyes of many, perhaps even most of her common citizens. I intend to rule, yes, but with a legitimate monarch as a constitutional figurehead, and that means someone whose name is on the succession list, such as Corinne."

The smile vanished as quickly as it appeared. "Which means we need to find her."

"That may well be impossible, sir." When Custis opened his mouth, Zahar raised a conciliatory hand. "Nevertheless, I will order my intelligence people look for the prison ship or the ships that took it out of the Parth system — without mentioning Corinne's name. I have a fairly extensive web of operatives covering the Coalsack and beyond, but the wormhole network is vast."

Zahar paused as if digging up a distant memory.

"There might be another option if we cannot find Corinne."

Custis' dark eyebrows crept up a few millimeters. "Oh?"

"I'm sure Your Grace is familiar with the name Marta Norum, the Marquess of Cascadia's daughter. Though she's not a Ruggero like Corinne, Norum might be equally suitable for your purposes. I understand she's a direct descendant of Kal IV, Stichus Ruggero's predecessor, and thus not tainted by Ruggero blood. Granted, during Kal's day, the crown didn't pass down familial lines, but his name might suit those of who prefer to shake off the Ruggero dynasty. Norum was married to Hachim LeGris, the late governor general of Mykonos, another loyalist. LeGris kept his support for Dendera hidden until he made the mistake of confiding in his senior aide, an Imperial Guards colonel by the name Jorge Danton."

"I'm indeed familiar with Marta Norum. In fact, I met her long ago, well before Dendera's psychopathic tendencies surfaced. And this Danton — one of yours?"

Zahar dipped his head once.

"Pledged to me, yes, and no sycophant of the imperial court. I met Danton before the first star system rebelled and discovered his disaffection with the old order. Dendera's hand-picked generals declared Jorge unfit for promotion beyond colonel and sent him to serve as an aide to a provincial governor general with little by way of a family pedigree other than through his spouse. Since the Imperial Guards declined to make him a general officer, he did me a favor and gave himself a political promotion."

"His conditioning failed?" Astonishment tinged Custis' voice.

"So it seems. Or perhaps it never took. Not all minds can be bent to serve the empress with unquestioning fanaticism."

A frown creased Custis' forehead.

"Interesting. I'd heard rumors about officers feigning to be conditioned, but never met one. And now this Danton, a former Guards colonel, rules over Mykonos in my name? How amazing."

"Yes, though he didn't seize power without shedding a lot of blood, naturally. Parts of Mykonos, especially around the capital, were devastated. But he convinced the star system's two Imperial Guards regiments they'd be better off on our side once they suffered one too many defeats at the hands of Marine Corps and Mykonos militia units pledged to the rebellion."

"Just as you did here, Admiral. Nicely done, by the way."

Zahar bowed his head in acknowledgment.

"Thank you, sir. But the task wasn't particularly difficult. It merely required removing every loyal senior officer via assassination, which is what Danton did as well. With most of the system's military forces in hand, Danton assumed control, purged the government, destroyed the Order of the Void on Mykonos, and stomped out any signs of loyalty to Dendera. Jorge ordered Hachim LeGris' execution by beheading after trying him before a summary court-martial. But LeGris' widow and children escaped."

"Then please send word to our new governor general on Mykonos telling him I want Marta Norum found, detained, and sent to Yotai forthwith. Unharmed, it goes without saying. Should anything happen to her at the hands of Danton's troops, I will hold him personally responsible."   Custis' smile returned.   "Well done, Admiral. If Corinne remains among the vanished and we can find no one with a greater claim, Marta Norum will be my constitutional figurehead, the one around whom I will reunite the empire."

Zahar indicated the closed door.

"May I recall my aide and give the order, Your Grace?"

"Yes, but no mention of why I'm interested in Norum."

While Zahar obeyed, Custis turned back to the holographic projection of his truncated realm, wondering how soon he should announce it as the legitimate heir to the old empire and declare himself regent instead of viceroy. A green-tinged system well away from the others under his control attracted his attention.

It seemed almost submerged in a sea of purple and red-rimmed stars, those abandoned by the 16th Fleet or known to be under barbarian control. He quickly counted the wormhole connections from Micarat and grunted. Five transits away. Too far for subspace radio in the absence of relays — Zahar had ordered them removed when his units withdrew — and up to a week's travel in the fastest aviso.

"What's this?" He asked when Zahar rejoined him.

The admiral squinted at the projection, then stuck his finger into it and touched the unnamed star. Almost at once, a wall of text appeared to their left.

"Lyonesse." Custis grunted. "Never heard of it."

"A self-governing crown colony, sir. The last large imperial unit stationed there, the 77th Marine Regiment, withdrew almost ten years ago, leaving nothing more than a minor supply depot with a skeleton crew.

Lyonesse is effectively a wormhole network dead end with its sole exit at Arietis and sits in an isolated area of the galactic arm not easily reachable from inhabited star systems via hyperspace. Evidently, Fleet HQ did not believe a permanent naval presence was necessary."

"But since we don't hold Arietis anymore, shouldn't Lyonesse at least be marked in purple to show it slipped into the badlands and is no longer under Coalsack Sector control?"

"Indeed, Your Grace. It's probably nothing more than carelessness by the operations staff. Lyonesse rarely came to our attention before the rebellion, and nowadays?" Zahar shrugged. "It has no strategic, economic, or military importance whatsoever."

"Who governs it?"

Zahar peered at the text again.

"The Honorable Elenia Yakin, daughter of Baron Hengist Yakin."

Custis nodded knowingly.

"No fans of Dendera, the Yakins. Now you've jogged my memory, I believe Elenia's appointment as governor of Lyonesse was at her husband's behest, so he could work his way up to general in the Imperial Guards by bedding Dendera's favorites at court."

"Sounds like a charming fellow." Zahar's tone dripped with acid.

"I suspect Elenia got the better part of the bargain. One night in the wrong arms will undo years of pleasing bored noblewomen eager to reward attention with patronage. It wouldn't surprise me if he already met an unpleasant end. The court was rather unsettled by the time Dendera cleaned house and packed her closest advisers off to Parth for a few years of suffering before a nasty death."

Zahar grimaced.

"And yet she's stuck in a system which no longer enjoys our protection. I'm not sure her fate will be any better than that of the cad she married."

Custis took another look at the green-rimmed star representing Lyonesse, lost among a sea of red and purple.

"Perhaps."

The admiral waved his fingers at unseen controls, and Lyonesse lost its comforting glow, taking on the same menacing hue as every other star between it and Micarat.

"I'm sure Your Grace will not object to my declaring Governor Yakin's domain beyond our sphere of responsibility."

A sigh.

"No. I suppose it's inevitable."

"And no great loss."

— 3 —

Lyonesse

Captain Jonas Morane, commanding officer of the former imperial cruiser *Vanquish*, and acting commodore of the 197th Battle Group's remains fell silent, drained by the effort of speaking to an audience that seemed carved from stone.

A thickset, middle-aged man with a stubborn cast to his square features and a skeptical gleam in his eyes stood. He let his impassive gaze roam over the principal members of the Lyonesse Estates General surrounding the table before glancing at the other audience members seated behind Governor Elenia Yakin.

"I'm Anton Kell, president of the Lyonesse Workers' Cooperative." Kell's voice was rough, his tone challenging. "With all due respect, Captain, what proves to us you're not just a bunch of deserters from the imperial services looking to leech off hard-working people while hiding from justice in one of the empire's remotest star systems? Those recordings of Coraline, Palmyra, Arietis, and Lorien could easily be fakes."

He gestured at Gwenneth.

"It's well known that her kind are master manipulators. And those reivers who conveniently attacked just as you arrived could have been mercenaries in your service."

Morane knew questions of the sort would eventually come up. A few nodded in agreement, if not with Kell's words then with the sentiments behind them.

"You are free to analyze our recordings in any manner you wish. I can give you copies of the raw feeds if you want. We brought survivors of the Palmyra massacre with us. They can tell you about the attack, and I'm sure Chief Administrator Logran will arrange interviews through the crèche authorities.

"I know Colonel DeCarde would be pleased to let you speak with members of her unit about what they experienced on Coraline and Palmyra, just as I am willing to let you speak with members of my ships' crews. As for the growing civil war inside the empire, Her Excellency can attest to hearing about it from several sources well before our arrival."

He glanced at Yakin, who nodded.

"And of course you witnessed the reivers' attempt to raid Lyonesse, proof the Imperial Navy no longer controls the Arietis wormhole junction which guards the Lyonesse cul-de-sac."

Kell shrugged dismissively.

"Raids happen. We may be at the bottom of a triple transit dead end, but this is still the imperial frontier. I don't think it's enough evidence if you're asking the citizens of this colony to pay for your bizarre project and your salaries while you defend us from minor threats well within our militia's ability. We already see enough wealth squandered by stupid decisions made in the name of a so-called higher purpose when it could be used to improve our society through new programs."

"Why is my project bizarre, Mister Kell?" Morane asked in a mild, almost friendly tone. "Civilizational collapse is a recurring feature of human history since the dawn of time. We have the chance to preserve several thousand years of knowledge against the day humanity loses interstellar travel and becomes a fragmented scattering across this arm of the galaxy, unable to even remember its origins. And at relatively little cost, other than maintaining the ability to defend this world against forces who would pillage it and ruin everything you've worked for and everything we can still build. Make no mistake. The recent raid may have seemed small, but it was only the first of many. Once word of a star system untouched by civil war spreads, the barbarians will return, and in greater numbers."

A tall, slender woman in her fifties stood, cutting off Kell's reply. She wore her dark red hair in a short bob framing elfin features dominated by large dark eyes.

"Captain Morane has a point, Anton." Her clear orator's alto filled the large space, commanding everyone's attention. "Our existence as a civilized society isn't always about how much money we can throw at new entitlements to keep your members happy. If we slide down the technological ladder, as so many civilizations have done before us, be it through neglect or thanks to the depredations of savages from beyond the empire's borders, those entitlements won't matter a damn. Hunter-gatherer societies can't afford work-related benefits, let alone pensions, since that sort of lifestyle is nasty, brutish, and short, to quote Thomas Hobbes."

A smattering of subdued applause greeted her words. She turned to face Morane.

"I'm Emma Reyes, Chancellor of Lyonesse University, Captain. And as my friend Anton will tell you, I rarely hesitate to speak my mind, which has cost me more than one appointment during my career."

"A pleasure." He paused. "I think."

His quip earned him a few smiles, including an ironic one from Reyes.

"Likewise. One of my degrees is in history, Captain, so I can well believe humanity is ripe for another tumble, a big one. The more advanced a civilization, the harder it falls and the longer it needs to recover. I've been monitoring political trends for quite some time and noticed the same developments you did. Even if the empire isn't royally screwed, many people will die, and we will lose a lot of colonies. There's no getting around that fact. The best-case scenario is a truncated empire surviving in the Wyvern Sector, one too weak for anything more than keeping barbarians at bay. That doesn't help us. If we're not yet deep inside the lawless badlands, it's only a matter of time."

She gave the assembly a cold, hard stare, daring anyone to dispute her words.

"I'm chagrined I didn't think of something as elegant and fundamentally vital as Captain Morane's human knowledge vault. Challenge him on the details if you must argue, even on cost, but the idea is sound, and using the Order of the Void as part of an effort to preserve what we, as a species, have learned is equally elegant. Monastics of every faith have historically kept the spark of civilization alive in times of darkness. Why not use them once more?"

A louder round of applause greeted her impassioned declaration.

"If expenditures concern you," Morane said once the room quieted, "then consider this. My three ships face a limited lifespan. We'll keep them operational until we run out of parts. After that, I'll find a way to preserve them somewhere sheltered on one of the moons. The only cost to Lyonesse will be feeding and paying the crews. And once my ships are no more, the government can decide how much to invest in keeping a space worthy naval force, be it sublight or FTL.

"Colonel DeCarde's troopers will entail similar expenditures, plus keeping them equipped. Since Lyonesse already funds a colonial militia, it would make sense to merge the two and create a single full and part-time ground defense force, something neither Lorien nor Palmyra could field against barbarian raiders."

Morane glanced at Major Kayne as he spoke, but the former Marine sergeant's face remained expressionless. However, many in the room seemed to approve of his words, not least Emma Reyes.

"Or we could dispense with defense forces," the latter said in a conversational tone, "and either cut taxes or increase social spending, which would please many here. Although it'll do everyone a fat lot of good once reivers pour through our gates, and they will."

Reyes gave Kell a scornful glance.

"As Captain Morane pointed out, the godless bastards can choose to come the long way via hyperspace hoping to find low-hanging fruit or wait until the Arietis wormhole junction falls under their control and pour into our branch. No matter how they do it, without the ability to fight back, money won't mean a damned thing; enhanced early retirement benefits won't matter, and reduced work hours won't improve your lives. Nothing will."

Hecht chuckled.

"That's our esteemed chancellor. Eloquent to a fault."

"And what's your opinion, Speaker?" A man in the audience asked.

"I spent my life as a businessman before entering public service so I could give back to the community that made me successful." A few amused snorts greeted the declaration. He smiled back with false bonhomie. "And I've always believed in insurance. Captain Morane is offering just that, and at a price Lyonesse can afford. Granted, the devil is always in the details, but we can agree on basic principles."

Though still smiling, Hecht gave Morane a hard glance, letting him know that his support would come at a price, or at least with conditions.

Morane remained standing and let his eyes roam over the attendees again. But this time, he saw little, if any hostility, though he noticed plenty of worried faces. Some even returned his gaze with frank curiosity.

When no one else stood to question Morane, Governor Yakin asked, "Nothing else? In that case, I believe we can adjourn the Estates General. If anything arises, please contact my secretary. He'll make sure the matter is passed to the right person."

She stood, imitated by everyone else present, and left the room with Logran and Hecht on her tail.

Once the governor was gone, a tidal wave of voices made hearing any individual almost impossible. Reyes tried to attract Morane's attention as she pushed her way around the table through the crush of fellow representatives eager to leave, hoping she might intercept Morane. But it proved to be in vain. Major Kayne quickly ushered him, DeCarde and Gwenneth through the nearest door and down the steps where his staff skimmer waited.

As they sped off toward the depot, Kayne asked, "Permission to speak, Captain?"

"Certainly. What's on your mind?"

"You spoke of merging the colonial militia with the 6th Battalion. May I ask what you mean by that?" He sounded wary, but his eyes showed a spark of curiosity.

"Certainly. If Lyonesse is to create armed services, they'll need a unified command structure. And under that principle, if Lyonesse is to create a ground defense force, it too will need a unified structure, unified recruiting and training systems, standardized techniques, tactics, and procedures, organization, etcetera. There can't be a 6th of the 21st existing apart from the Lyonesse Colonial Militia. Don't you agree?"

Kayne seemed to hesitate before nodding.

"Makes sense."

"Good. Then perhaps you and Colonel DeCarde can put your Marine Corps heads together and come up with how it should be done. I wouldn't presume to interfere with matters I barely understand."

DeCarde and Kayne exchanged glances.

"Will do, sir. How soon would you like proposals?"

"No need to come up with an answer today." Morane smiled. "Tomorrow will do. Or the day after if you need more time."

When neither spoke, he said, "I was speaking in jest. Take a few days, sound out your command teams, wargame tables of organization and equipment. That sort of thing."

"Blank slate?" DeCarde asked.

"Sure. Why not? We won't see an inspector general from Fleet HQ show up any time soon, or ever. If we can invent a better way of doing things, unhampered by centuries of ossified tradition..."

"So basically," Kayne dragged out the words as he parsed Morane's order, "you want the colonel and me to invent our own organizational paradigm."

DeCarde gave him a broad grin.

"Yep. And please call me Brigid. Since we're about to be joined at the hip, there's no point of standing on ceremony. At least not in private."

Morane studied Kayne for a few heartbeats.

"I'll go out on a limb here, Matti, since we've not yet discussed the whole defense force structure with Governor Yakin, but as senior officer on Lyonesse, I'm promoting you to lieutenant colonel effective immediately. Considering the size of your command, it seems only right."

Kayne's eyes went from DeCarde to Morane and back.

"Thanks. I think. Our situation's convoluted legalities or lack thereof are giving me a headache. A few days ago, I was running a sleepy colonial militia, an ersatz Guards unit with just enough capacity to block landing reivers long enough so civilians could run for the hills. Suddenly, my militia is being brigaded with a genuine Pathfinder battalion to form the nucleus of a proper defense force. All of it with zero authority from either Wyvern or Fleet HQ on Caledonia. Unreal. Just unreal."

Morane chuckled.

"Hang on tight, Matti. It's just the beginning. I want to make Lyonesse impregnable, an oasis of civilization able to repel the coming darkness."

"So," Kayne gave Morane a speculative look, "does that mean you're to be our chief of defense staff?"

"If Governor Yakin wants me. And she would be commander-in-chief."

"I think she probably will, sir. I've done my best to organize what I could when the 77th left, but I'm still a command sergeant at heart, an infantry platoon leader. We need someone who graduated from all the right schools to get us organized."

DeCarde gave him a friendly nudge.

"I'm still an old sergeant at heart too, Matti. But we're both lieutenant colonels now, each with our own battalion. We will not only make this work but by the time we're done, it'll be a thing of beauty, the finest little combat formation in known space."

Morane gave them a mock blessing, then glanced at Gwenneth, who'd remained silent throughout the assembly.

"You seem rather tired, Sister."

She lifted a face seamed with fatigue and gave him a wan smile.

"We monastics find crowds wearying. That's partly why we join the Order, I suppose. You did well in there, Jonas. I should think we will see a groundswell of support build over the next few days as word gets out and people understand the full import of your words. I'd wager even now, transcripts and recordings are already circulating. Soon, everyone on Lyonesse will recognize your face."

"From your lips to the Almighty's ear, Sister. Well, perhaps not the recognition thing, but the Almighty is bound to listen more closely when one of his servants speaks."

"You'd be surprised, Jonas."

—4—

Mykonos

"You called for me, Excellency?"

Jorge Danton, governor general of the Mykonos system, turned away from the transparent aluminum doors leading to the gubernatorial palace's second-floor balcony. He'd been watching his capital slowly fade into night under a gray sky that matched his mood. All too many parts of Petras remained dark, especially on the western edge, where the worst of the fighting took place before the remnants of the loyalist 91st Imperial Guards Regiment surrendered to his rebel forces.

"I just received orders from Viceroy Custis."

"Ah. I was wondering why the urgent summons."

A mocking grin tugged at Danton's thick lips.

"Are you telling me the communication center's duty officer didn't alert you to the grand duke's missive, Harvey? Standards must be slipping."

General Harvey Marat waved Danton's comment aside with an amused air.

"Of course he called and told me about the message. But sensibly, he kept the contents to himself. Offering to read your mail, now *that* would prove standards are slipping."

"And you didn't ask?"

"I knew you'd tell me soon enough, sir. Orders from Yotai always seem to involve my command these days. It's the nature of the times in which we live."

Danton studied the Mykonos system's senior military officer with undisguised, though partially feigned suspicion.

"If I didn't know better, I might think you were mocking me."

"Perish the thought, sir. I saw your ruthlessness first hand. It gives me the motivation I need to stay on your good side. I prefer my head on my shoulders rather than on a pike like your predecessor's."

"And you'd rather keep enjoying the emoluments of a flag officer."

"It beats the alternative. What does Yotai want from us now?"

"The late Hachim LeGris' widow."

A quizzical expression twisted Marat's angular, rough-hewn features.

"I beg your pardon, sir?"

"The orders say find Marta Norum and send her to Yotai under tight guard." Danton's thick lips twisted in a dismissive moue. "Before you ask, our new viceroy didn't see fit to share why. But I've been assured of his displeasure should we fail."

"We don't even know whether she's still alive. No one's seen Norum or her brats since shortly before we captured LeGris and executed him."

"Nevertheless, we must find the delightful Marta, and deliver her or evidence of her death to Yotai."

A grimace replaced Marat's habitually sardonic expression.

"Why do I think serving Grand Duke Custis could make us long for Dendera's gentle touch?"

"Keep talking about that feeling, and you might find out, Harvey. Not everyone is as tolerant of your quirks as I am because not everyone knows what you did to help me seize Government House. Many in our military forces would love to wear your stars."

Marat cocked an ironic eyebrow.

"Tell me their names, Excellency, and I shall try to purge them from your administration before any covetous eyes land on your chain of office once they finish ogling my stars."

"So you can eliminate your competition for my job? Perish the thought. But enough persiflage. I know your troops are keeping an eye out for Lady Marta, but they must take on a more active role in finding her. If she's still alive, Marta can't have gone far. Not with two eight-year-olds in tow. And not with that recognizable face of hers."

"Should I divert my intelligence hunters from tracking down loyalist holdouts who escaped the purge? I ask because the latest reports show there's enough of them hiding in the wilderness to start a serious insurgency. And that's not even counting those who don't love the Crown but aren't happy a former Guards officer who pledged loyalty to Yotai is now running this star system."

Danton didn't immediately reply as he weighed the risks. Until matters were settled, Marat's intelligence service would be stretched beyond the breaking point. The rebellion and subsequent coup left them with too few trustworthy operatives.

"Divert your resources," he finally said. "The faster they find Norum or evidence of her death, the sooner they can go back to flushing out enemies of the state.

"As you wish." Marat sounded dubious but didn't seem inclined to argue.

"We all bow before a higher authority, Harvey. You to me, and I to Custis. Besides, we might get lucky and she'll walk right into the cordon you deployed on the far side of the Petras greenbelt to intercept stragglers."

"It won't be hermetic since I can't deploy enough troops. We control the obvious crossing points but the ground between them will only be covered by roving patrols. That still leaves plenty of bypass routes for anyone able to navigate through truly rough terrain."

"I doubt a courtier such as Lady Marta can do so, Harvey. If she's fleeing the city on foot, she'll stumble into one of your checkpoints or patrols. Just make sure she doesn't slip through because a half-asleep trooper didn't carry out a proper identity check."

Marat let out a mirthless bark of laughter.

"With the number of loyalist fighters still unaccounted for, they'll be thorough, don't fear. As motivators go, the bounty you put on enemy heads by far surpasses the thrill of killing despised enemies. Might I suggest you put up a substantial sum for Lady Marta? If the grand duke is that eager to see her, he won't mind you digging into the treasury."

"Excellent idea." A quasi-feral smile briefly lit up Danton's puffy face. "I wonder what the daughter of a marquess is worth."

"It depends on where you're selling her, I suppose. She's a bit old and lacking in skills to fetch a good price on one of the barbarian slave markets."

Danton snorted.

"To Grand Duke Custis, I mean."

"Fifty thousand should be enough to motivate anyone without making it seem like you're plundering the tax account."

"Done. Pass the word among your troops I'll pay fifty thousand to whoever finds Lady Marta Norum or ten thousand for her remains. And if she's alive, we need her unharmed."

"What about the children?"

"There was no mention of them in the message from Yotai, so I don't really care."

"You're a true humanitarian, sir." Marat came to attention. "Was there anything else?"

"No."

Marat snapped off a salute, turned on his heels and left. When he was alone once more, Danton returned to the balcony doors and stared out at the city. His city, now. On his planet, in his star system.

He had a good idea of why Custis might be interested in Marta Norum. She wasn't merely his predecessor's widow and the Marquess of Cascadia's daughter, she was also a direct descendant of Emperor Kal IV. It gave her claim to the crown a veneer of legitimacy the Ruggero line had lost, even if it was mostly false because of the succession rules in Kal's day.

"What are you up to, Devy?" Danton murmured. "Is Lady Marta your way of establishing a reborn imperial court on Yotai, with her as figurehead empress and you as the true power? And if so, why shouldn't I consider doing the same thing but build a new empire centered on Mykonos instead?"

— 5 —

"Why is mentioning the dangers of this area after dark funny?" Heloise asked.

A chuckle came from the shadows.

"Because my people and I are extremely dangerous, Sister. But we won't harm any of you."

"Then why are we speaking?"

"You may find this hard to believe, but we have a few things in common."

"And they would be?" Her eyes searched the collapsed veranda.

"Mainly a desire to get away from this shitty star system without suffering further casualties, and it sounds like you might have a ride waiting at the Thera spaceport."

Vague movement disturbed the darkness as if a ghost was taking shape just beyond the visible spectrum, or so it seemed to Marta Norum's tired eyes. Then a face, swarthy and angular, appeared when the mysterious speaker removed his helmet.

"My name is Anders Proulx. We've been tracking you since your little troop of refugees entered the ruined quarter."

Though his voice was steady, Proulx's seamed features struck Norum as those a man on the verge of exhaustion. He had what her Uncle Olav, an Imperial Marine Corps veteran, used to call the thousand light year stare of someone who's seen too much death.

"Why?" Heloise asked.

"That, Sister, is the second thing we have in common. We're both on the run from Colonel Danton's jackbooted thugs. I was curious to see why a group of monastics would risk passing through what has become the refuge of many who found themselves on the losing side, hunted by the new regime. Now I understand."

Proulx nodded at Norum.

"My respects, Lady Marta, and my sympathies for your husband's death. The good sister has a valid point. Your face is too well known. If anyone around here other than my troopers and I recognize it, your clerical escort might not live long enough to offer the Almighty a final prayer. Besides, the sisters and friars themselves will face a brutal death if they're spotted by Danton's soldiers or betrayed by someone who has a bone to pick with the Order of the Void."

"The Void giveth, the Void taketh away," Friar Sandor intoned in a low voice.

A wry grin flashed across Proulx's face.

"Blessed be the Void. But dying still sucks horse bollocks."

"You're a believer?" Heloise asked.

"In a sense. I believe in survival, though not at the cost of my soul since I won't make war on innocents, especially children, which is why we're hiding from Danton's troops and looking for a way off Mykonos."

Heloise gave him a suspicious glance.

"Care to explain that comment?"

"It's a long story and time is short, Sister. I refused an order because obeying would have meant committing a crime against humanity. Danton's savages slaughtered most of my unit in retaliation. We twelve are the sole survivors of almost two hundred men and women. And like you, we face immediate death if captured. I want to offer your party the protection of a dozen highly trained troopers, retired Imperial Marines, in exchange for berths on the ship you intend to take in Thera."

"*Retired* Imperial Marines?"

"We're private military contractors."

"Mercenaries," Sandor spat out the word as if it was poison.

"Security specialists, Friar, hired by the Mykonos Merchant Guild to protect their commercial interests when the admirals' rebellion reached the Coalsack Sector. After Danton seized power, he decreed that all military forces in the star system were answerable to his government and forced my unit to work alongside his troops. We said no to an illegal order a few days ago, and here we are, running for our lives."

"Why should I trust you?"

Proulx's lips twitched with amusement.

"Look into my heart, Sister. You'll see that while I'm no paragon of virtue, I am honest and wish you no ill. Or is your Order's reputation for producing adepts capable of searching sinners' souls vastly overblown?"

Heloise gave the other two sisters, Averyl and Maya, brief glances before saying, "Reputations rarely reflect the truth, Anders Proulx, but I think you're an honest man, at least according to your own lights. And since we're not only outnumbered but outgunned, I see little choice other than agreeing to your proposal."

Proulx's eyes lost their focus and wandered to one side for a moment, in what Marta recognized as the automatic reaction of someone listening to an invisible earbug. He muttered an almost indecipherable acknowledgment while a grim expression hardened his features. His gaze met Heloise's again.

"Glad you made the right decision, Sister. One of my troopers just reported movement by a platoon-sized body of armored soldiers three blocks north of here. Either Danton finally decided to flush his remaining enemies from the ruins and string them up, or they caught your spoor. Considering Admiral Zahar wishes to see the Order of the Void extinguished, I doubt Danton will rest until he cleanses Mykonos.

"Either way, it's time. You mentioned the Port of Tiryns. A good choice. We worked the docks for a few weeks before everything went to hell on this planet. I might still be in good enough odor with a few shipmasters who sail the Boetian Sea to secure us a few bunks behind false bulkheads, no questions asked."

"Smugglers?"

"Entrepreneurs who live by the motto don't ask, don't tell. A few of them owe me for squinting at their load manifest instead of insisting on an inspection." Proulx smirked when he saw Sandor's expression. "Don't worry, Friar. It wasn't for personal gain. I earn my keep through hard work, not peculation. Once we're out of danger, I'll tell you about it. Check the street for moving, rubble-colored lumps. Those would be four of mine."

Norum squinted through the ruined door, trying to make out the chameleon-armored mercenaries when one of them removed a gauntlet and waved. Watching a disembodied hand float above the ground struck her as nonsensical, but then it was as if a switch flipped in her brain and she could see four out-of-focus shapes that didn't quite mesh with the background.

"There you go," Proulx said. "The hand belongs to Hartwood Cahal. He did twenty years in the 77th Imperial Marine Regiment and is now my second in command. Please follow him. I'll bring up the rear with my remaining troops so that if the soldiers my sentry spotted get too close, I can divert them. We'll stop for the night when we're beyond Petras city limits."

Proulx and Sister Heloise held each other's eyes for a few seconds, then the latter nodded once before gesturing at her Brethren to form a protective circle around Lady Marta Norum and her children.

"Do you think trusting them is safe?" Marta murmured while Heloise guided them through the ruined building's gaping doorway.

"Nothing is truly safe in this universe," she replied in the same tone, "but our choices are limited. If we meet Jorge Danton's troops or his sympathizers along the way, we'll find out for sure whether Anders Proulx is telling the truth."

"At which point, it will be too late, Sister."

Marta took her children by the hand as they emerged from the half-demolished house.

"True, but only if he lied. If he told the truth, we will thank the Almighty for putting him across our path."

"I wish I had your faith."

A tight smile briefly lit up the sister's face.

"This isn't a matter of faith. Although I trust the Almighty will not give me more challenges than I can handle, I rely on my intuition and knowledge of human nature as guides."

"And they tell you we should go with these mercenaries."

"They tell me we need not fear them right now."

"That doesn't sound like a ringing endorsement."

"Give me enough time to study them, and I'll tell you whether my opinion changes."

When they were within a few paces of the waiting troopers, Hartwood Cahal raised his visor so they could see his face clearly and asked, "Do you have a preferred way out of Petras, Sister, or will you let me guide you to Tiryns?"

The overwhelming sorrow Marta Norum saw in Cahal's tired, blood-shot eyes touched something deep within her, and in that instant, she understood why Sister Heloise accepted Anders Proulx's offer.

No human could fake the expression of someone who, by a mere twist of fate, escaped a brutal massacre that claimed the lives of almost two hundred comrades.

"Please guide us. I won't pretend to know the best ways of avoiding Danton's patrols."

"As you wish, Sister." Cahal gestured at two of his troopers, sending them ahead. "They'll scout the way for us. Just follow me and obey my orders, especially if I tell you to duck or change direction. I'll let you keep an eye on your charges, but tell me if we're moving too fast for the wee ones."

"If need be, we'll carry them," Sandor said.

"Good." He pointed at the remaining mercenary. "Colyn will be right behind you."

"Do you think we'll encounter anyone else fleeing Danton's soldiers?" Norum asked.

"Perhaps. A lot of folks are hiding out in this area, waiting for things to settle before they go home. Or find new homes. If you're worried about coming across people who might do us harm, remember you got this far on your own with two bairns. I doubt many would challenge armored mercs."

"It wasn't without trouble." Norum produced her husband's weapon. "I shot a couple of predators during our first night among the ruins."

"Then keep it handy, Milady. I'm not one to refuse an extra gun in case things go sideways." He paused, as if listening, then made a sweeping motion toward the west. "The next three blocks are clear. Let's go."

Cahal set a swift, but measured pace, as if he knew instinctively how fast a pair of tired, hungry, and scared eight-year-olds could move without needing their mother's encouragement.

The acrid tang of burned flint filled Marta Norum's nostrils as they passed a heavily damaged section where loyalist troops made their last stand against the rebels. Hardly any walls remained, never mind roofs. Piles of blackened stone replaced structures in what was once the heart of Petras' original settlement, built over twelve centuries ago.

Without warning, the nauseating miasma of rotting flesh swamped every other odor. Marta instinctively blocked her nostrils and breathed in through her mouth, but Stefan wasn't quick enough. A strangled gasp escaped the boy's throat. His sister was even less fortunate. She skidded to a halt, retching miserably, though nothing came up, not even bile. Marta held the girl until her breathing steadied.

"Sorry about that Milady," Hartwood Cahal said in a low growl. "We figure there's a mass grave beneath the old town hall." He pointed at a large pile of disjointed rubble to their right. "It's not the only one around here either. Once the 84th Guards went over to the rebellion and defeated their former buddies of the 91st, they lost their ever-loving minds. The bastards killed anyone they suspected of loyalty to the Crown, no questions asked, no quarter given."

"Don't apologize. It's not your fault."

Cahal grunted.

"We could have pulled out from under Danton's thumb faster and put ourselves between his goons and the poor sods who thought remaining loyal was a political disagreement, not a death sentence. Not to mention avoid getting most of us killed in our sleep by the evil fucks."

Heloise and Marta exchanged a knowing glance. Survivor guilt.

"Hindsight is neither perfect nor useful," Heloise replied in a gentle tone. "The fallen won't come back, and no matter what we believe, they won't blame us for living."

The mercenary didn't reply right away. When he spoke, it was to apologize.

"Never mind me, Sister. You lost twenty times more good comrades than we did. That gives you a greater right to speak about the dead."

"We have an equal right, Hartwood Cahal. Grief is not a game of numbers. My burden of remembrance is no greater than yours because the souls of the departed only weigh heavily if we wish them to do so."

A grunt.

"Fair enough, Sister. I may be a simple warrior, but I know better than to debate one of you on spiritual matters." His left hand shot up. "One moment. Anders just lit up the company push."

Cahal listened for a few seconds, then said, "That platoon the sentries spotted are Danton's troops all right, and they're definitely on the hunt rather than making a random sweep of the ruins. Looks like guardsmen from the 84th but there's no way of knowing whether they're after us, you, or Lady Marta. Anders will try leading them south while we make a run for the west. Better that than try an ambush against two dozen trained soldiers when he has only a third of their strength. He gave me a rendezvous point west of here and says that at worst, we'll regroup in Tiryns."

Though Cahal didn't say so, Marta Norum heard the addendum nonetheless: *if he can break clean.*

— 6 —

Lyonesse

Morane and DeCarde were inspecting one of the depot's cavernous warehouses with Lieutenant Grimes when his communicator buzzed softly for attention.

"Morane here."

"Centurion Haller, sir. An Emma Reyes called. She said you'd remember her from, and I quote, *the command performance in the Great Hall of the People,* unquote."

"Is she on the net right now?"

"No, sir. She left her coordinates and invited you to join her for cocktails and dinner at the College Club, along with directions on how to get there. Madame Reyes suggested nineteen hundred hours but left it up to you if that time isn't convenient."

Morane raised his eyes only to see DeCarde smirk.

"A date already? Nicely done. But then you squids are rumored to find companionship in every port of call."

He gave her a half-hearted glare, which turned the smirk into delighted laughter.

"Centurion, please inform Chancellor Reyes I would be delighted to join her at nineteen hundred hours."

"Will do, sir. Haller, out."

Morane pocketed his communicator.

"What do you know about this College Club, Lieutenant?"

"Not much. I've never been there since I don't know anyone at the university," Grimes replied. "But the College Club is known as the most exclusive place in Lannion, sir. I hear even Governor Yakin needs a member's invitation before she can enter, and they're apparently hard to obtain."

"Oh, dear." DeCarde made a face. "One of *those* places..."

"What do you mean one of those?" He asked, giving her a quizzical glance.

"You know." She made a dismissive hand gesture. "Filled with stuffy academics drunk on their own importance instead of overpriced rotgut. I'd give a week's pay to see their faces when an uncouth man of war walks in and soils the sanctity of the place."

**

That evening, Matti Kayne's driver dropped Morane off in front of a sprawling two-story stone building that seemed to have begun life as a farmstead before the growing colony established its one and only university around it.

A discrete sign on the wrought-iron fence surrounding the property stated College Club - Members Only. Morane, once more in dress uniform — his few civilian clothes were still in orbit aboard *Vanquish* — took the short flight of steps two by two and entered through a sliding door designed to resemble the farmhouse's original.

He found himself in a lobby that was all wood paneling, brass fixtures, and replica paintings. A holographic artificial intelligence cunningly programmed to look like an elderly Victorian porter materialized out of thin air before him.

"Are you perchance Admiral Jonas Morane of the Lyonesse Revolutionary Navy, sir?"

A smile tugged at his lips. Reyes must have fed that line to the AI along with his particulars.

"Merely a captain, I'm afraid, and my current allegiance is neither revolutionary nor to any particular entity, but my name is Morane."

"Then sir's promotion is obviously overdue. Chancellor Reyes has asked us to extend you every courtesy. She is running a few minutes late. If you would wait in the lounge, through the door to your left and enjoy a libation of your choice..."

Morane inclined his head.

"Thank you."

"The Club is always pleased to host Chancellor Reyes' distinguished guests, sir."

With those words, the hologram vanished, leaving Morane alone in the lobby. He tucked his beret into a tunic pocket and ran splayed fingers through his stiff dark hair before entering the lounge.

A large room with many nooks, booths, and private corners, it continued the dark wood and brass fixtures theme. A copper-topped circular bar occupied the middle, staffed by what looked like a pair of human beings in crisp white tunics and dark trousers. The curving shelves behind them boasted more exotic bottles than Morane had ever seen in any wardroom or officer's mess.

If interstellar commerce was indeed fated to break down as he expected, the contents of those bottles would soon turn into some of the most precious substances in the Lyonesse star system.

The background buzz of conversation momentarily died away when more than two dozen pairs of eyes turned toward him as if attracted by a powerful magnet. A few sparkled with curiosity, but many blazed with undisguised annoyance, confirming DeCarde's prediction. Morane ignored them and made a beeline for the bar where one of the attendants gave him a friendly greeting.

"Good evening, sir. You must be the chancellor's guest. Can I offer you something from our extensive collection?" He gestured at the shelves. "We also offer several types of beer from the best breweries on Lyonesse."

Morane's eyes stopped on a familiar greenish bottle, and he tried to hide a smile.

"Is that an eighteen-year-old Glen Arcturus I see behind you?"

"It is. Would you like it with a splash of water, soda on the side, or neat?"

"A splash, please."

His answer, which identified him as a connoisseur of fine single malts, seemed to please the attendant who handed him a tulip-shaped glass half full with a dark amber liquid. Drink in hand, Morane wandered around the lounge, nodding pleasantly at those who met his gaze, even if they didn't bother hiding their disdain, and studied the mementos hanging from walls that gleamed like dark honey. Before he could make a full circuit of the room, a female voice interrupted his meandering.

"Captain Morane. Welcome."

He turned to see Reyes, now wearing elegant evening clothes, sweep into the lounge as if she owned it. Which, in a way, she probably did as chancellor. Reyes held out her hand, smiling wide enough to reveal even white teeth.

"I'm so glad you could join me. After your performance in the Great Hall of the People, I simply needed to make your acquaintance."

Morane took her hand and smiled back. Reyes' grip was stronger than he expected, and up close he realized she was almost his height, though nowhere near as broad across the shoulders.

"Why do you call it the Great Hall of the People, Chancellor?"

"Please call me Emma. I believe you're a historian at heart. That was clear from the way you spoke to the Estates General. Are you familiar with pre-diaspora totalitarian political movements?"

"Vaguely. Weren't they responsible for most of the biggest genocides in human history before the Migration Wars that birthed the old Commonwealth? And please call me Jonas."

"They were. The folks espousing these philosophies often called their countries Peoples' Democratic Republics though they were neither of, nor for the people, nor democratic, nor republics. Many of them boasted great assembly spaces where they could pretend to be all three. I simply find it amusing that the Lyonesse government spent money adding a massive citizen's assembly hall to the Colonial Council building when we live in an increasingly despotic monarchy where the opinions of ordinary citizens are deemed worthless. Or at least we used to."

She waved a slender, long-fingered hand toward the timbered ceiling.

"Considering what's happening out there, who knows what fresh political horrors will emerge from the nuclear fires? What are you drinking, by the way?"

"Glen Arcturus."

Reyes' eyes brightened.

"A fellow worshiper of the finest whiskey ever distilled. Would you believe most of my fellow academics consider its taste in the same category as that of folk medicine?"

Without waiting for an answer, she headed toward the bar.

"Good evening, Klaus. Would you be so kind as to serve me what the captain is having, with just a tiny splash?"

"Sure thing, Chancellor."

"And then, Jonas, we'll repair to my private dining room upstairs where we can talk without the entire university reading a transcript tomorrow morning." Reyes grinned at a scowling, bearded man peering over a wooden partition. "Isn't that right, Professor Noughtly?"

The man's face vanished abruptly.

"I fear Rob is not one of my fans, and he's even less a fan of military uniforms and those who wear them. He would have felt right at home in one of those people's republics I mentioned, even though he professes to deplore our current regime's totalitarian tendencies."

Reyes took the proffered glass and gestured toward the door.

"Come, Jonas."

She led him into the lobby and up a stately, winding staircase where they found a small dining room with an oval table capable of seating a dozen, but set only for two at one end.

"This comes with the chancellor's office, though I try not to abuse the privilege, lest the Rob Noughtlys of the world find more to criticize about me. Heaven knows they've already accumulated volumes." When he gave her a quizzical look, Reyes laughed. "Has someone ever told you why academic disputes can be so bitter?"

"No."

"Sayre's law. In any dispute, the intensity of feeling is inversely proportional to the value of the issues at stake."

"I think the Marines coined a corollary to that law, something Brigid DeCarde told me over tea during a long night watch while we were FTL between wormhole termini. The dumber an officer, the more he or she will focus on useless chickenshit."

Reyes snickered.

"Priceless. I must invite Colonel DeCarde next time so she can regale us with a Marine's earthy wisdom." She gestured at the chairs. "Please sit."

They studied each other in silence for a few moments.

"Tell me, Jonas, how did you conclude humanity faces a civilizational collapse catastrophic enough to call for a human knowledge vault on a planet lost at the far end of our senescent empire's wormhole network?"

"That's a long story and mightily bored you'll be."

"Try me. I'm a lifelong academic and hold several degrees in history. What others consider boredom I see as my intellectual lifeblood."

At that moment, a human waiter came in unannounced with a tray holding two wine glasses, a tall green bottle covered with condensation beads and two plates.

"The appetizers, smoked longfish, and a Pinot Gris from the Dereux Vineyards in Trevena," he announced in a solemn tone. Then, with a flourish, he put a glass and a plate before each of them.

"Thank you, Horace. I'll pour."

"My pleasure, Chancellor."

He nodded once and withdrew.

"Perhaps we should finish these before attacking the first course." Reyes held up her whiskey glass. "Smoked longfish is too subtle for a peaty single malt. You were about to bore me with a long tale."

"I suppose I was."

—7—

"There's not much to tell. The distant past always fascinated me, especially eras when long-established civilizations faced rapidly increasing decay and collapse. My interest was perhaps even a touch morbid. In my younger days, I devoured dozens of ancient textbooks describing the effects of entropy on long-lived classical empires, accounts written long before humanity's diaspora. Gibbon's *Decline and Fall of the Roman Empire*, Oman's *The Dark Ages* and his treatise on the Byzantine Empire were a few of the most influential."

Reyes gave him an appreciative look.

"Ancient indeed, but still among the finest accounts of that troubled first millennium of the Common Era, and in my opinion, the most relevant to our current situation. The later accounts of post-industrial empires collapsing in the century before the first faster-than-light starships simply can't compare. I'm impressed a naval officer found value in Gibbon and Oman when most of my learned colleagues teaching history wouldn't know either from a black hole."

"There's little to do aboard a warship when you're not standing watch and I've always been a bookworm."

"A vice we both share. But please continue."

"Several years ago, maybe as much as ten, I realized we were living in a rerun of the fifth century. Our empire's golden age died when Stichus Ruggero subverted the constitution and swept aside the careful balance that gave us eight centuries of political and social stability. I also came to understand how Dendera, in her attempts at becoming an absolute monarch, was finally pushing us over the edge. Not in two generations, not in one generation but within a few short years. The decline of the Western Roman Empire isn't even a best-case scenario for us, let alone the Byzantine Empire's long twilight.

"When I decided there would be no way to arrest the decline, I read every theory on the collapse of complex societies I could find. It led me to the belief a human knowledge vault, hidden away on a planet far from the galactic mainstream, might offer a shortcut from collapse to rebirth, and see us reform a new interstellar polity in a matter of centuries, not thousands of years."

Reyes nodded.

"The Long Night of Barbarism, a term popularized by Professor Nikolai Tchang, though I don't think he coined it. I know the theory well. We seem to read the same books, you and I. Except I neither saw the imminence of the empire's collapse nor did I think of preserving what we could here on Lyonesse. To my eternal shame."

Morane gave her a rueful shrug.

"My first officer, Iona Mikkel, used to call it my monomania, but after witnessing the Fleet turning against itself in an orgy of fratricide in the two years since Admiral Loren gave Dendera the finger, she became a believer. As did everyone aboard my three remaining ships after we narrowly escaped rebels who turned most of my battle group, including over four thousand crew members, into so much dust without a shred of remorse or comradely feeling.

"All of us understood we were destined to die at the hands of men and women wearing the same uniform as ours if we kept fighting for either side, along with millions, if not billions of our kind. The only way out was implementing my plan and fleeing for sanctuary."

"Perhaps that makes you a prophet of sorts. One who led his people to a promised land." She raised her glass in salute and drained it, imitated by Morane.

"You'd need to ask the Void Brethren. Prophecies are in their bailiwick." Reyes poured the wine, then invited Morane to eat. He took his first bite, then a sip, and smiled with delight. "Very nice. This place is growing on me."

After another bite, he sat back and examined her.

"Not that I'm a suspicious sort, but to what do I owe an impromptu dinner invitation from the Lyonesse University's chancellor, the planet's de facto top academic authority? We met for the first time only a few hours ago and didn't actually exchange words, though I'm grateful for your support. I'm sure it helped sway many opinions in that, what did you call it again? Hall of the People?"

"Are you wondering whether I have ulterior motives?" She gave him a coy smile that was only partially feigned. "Of course I do. I want the university to be at the heart of your proposed knowledge vault initiative. Consider this the first move in my campaign to make sure that the ever-scheming Hecht or Logran and their bureaucratic gnomes don't screw up everything. Knowledge is power, and they live for power over there in the halls of colonial government. Besides, I need to tackle a challenge that doesn't involve soothing ruffled academic feathers."

Morane took another sip of wine.

"Why do you call Hecht a schemer?" He asked, remembering the man's hard stare earlier that day, the one promising his support would come at a price.

"How else does someone like him become Speaker of the Colonial Council, Lyonesse's head legislator, so quickly after being appointed as a councilor? He vaulted over members with decades of honorable service and a better claim to the speaker's chair when the previous incumbent retired. Since then, he's been steadily working to increase the council's authority at the chief administrator's expense and has become an almost permanent fixture in Governor Yakin's salon."

Morane finished his dish and dabbed the cloth napkin on his lips.

"That was excellent, especially after months of eating standard shipboard food. Could I ask if you've been on Lyonesse long?"

"You can ask me anything. Whether I'll answer it is another matter." That coy smile returned for a few seconds. "I arrived here six years ago to take up the chancellor's job. Like our dear governor, my accepting a post in the empire's furthest backwater wasn't entirely voluntary. It was this or an end to my academic career. People with extensive, high-powered connections decided my outspokenness as vice-chancellor of Sanctum University on Caledonia was becoming a liability, and I needed to go in a way that kept the university's reputation intact.

"They thought it amusing to give me the chancellor's job here, at a much smaller institution that exists in almost total isolation. I could have lodged a formal protest but decided to consider this appointment a new challenge, though I didn't know then my move to Lyonesse would be permanent. But becoming chancellor here made me a pillar of the community, barely one step lower than Hecht or Logran on our fussy little social ladder. And that means I see and hear a lot."

"You said Elenia Yakin isn't here voluntarily either..."

At that moment, Horace returned, bearing the next course. He removed the empty fish plates and replaced them with soup bowls before topping up the wine glasses. When they were alone once more, Reyes nodded.

"A bizarre story, that. I earned my ticket to Lyonesse for being too mouthy, but Elenia earned hers for not being mouthy enough, in a sense. She's a baron's younger daughter, hence her title as an honorable. She married an ambitious man, an officer in the Imperial Guards keen on raising his social status. He had a general's stars in his eyes, but apparently in the Guards, unless you're either titled or part of a noble family, you won't make it past colonel."

"That would be true. It's well known among the Imperial Armed Services the Guards place pedigree above competence at the higher ranks."

"Just like livestock breeders. When he realized Elenia wasn't the sort of social climber he thought she might be, this charming specimen went on a hunt for a mistress with the right connections. Apparently, he's a handsome, roguish sort, with no sense of morality. Keep in mind what I'm telling you right now comes from Elenia. One night, after a party at Government House broke up, I stayed behind at her request for a few more drinks, and she unburdened herself. It was mostly the booze talking, though I suppose she felt a bit lonely as well, surrounded as she often is by sycophants, suck-ups, and grifters.

"I suspect Matti Kayne is her only real friend, though they're commendably discreet. Anyway, our rogue found himself a titled paramour, but she didn't wish to marry, nor did she want the lawful spouse around in case Elenia discovered the liaison and took public umbrage. So, as in my case, they found a suitably plausible excuse to ship her as far as possible from Wyvern, one that wouldn't alert Baron Yakin to his son-in-law's shenanigans. But enough gossip. Try the soup."

When Morane, who pronounced himself once more delighted, finished his dish, Reyes asked, "And who is Jonas Morane?"

He took a sip of wine, then gave her a half shrug.

"I'm just a simple Dordogne boy. Unlike Brigid DeCarde, who I suspect was born already wearing Marine battle armor, my family doesn't have a history of military or naval service. By a miracle, I won a place at the Imperial Armed Services Academy, and upon turning twenty-one, became a clumsy, callow ensign in need of mentoring by wise, long-service chief petty officers. They must have succeeded because I climbed up the ranks with monotonous regularity and finally got my own command five years ago. Since the navy isn't particular about titles of nobility, I might even have become a commodore, were it not for the Fleet falling into an orgy of self-destruction."

She smiled at him. "And yet, there's much more to the man behind the uniform than that, I daresay, especially if you not only read Gibbon and Oman but understand what lessons they tried to impart. You might be the only imperial officer who saw this disaster looming and came up with the idea to salvage our history."

"I'm only what you see, Emma. Perhaps more bookish and inquisitive than my peers, but I'm no visionary."

"He says with unabashed modesty." She raised her glass in salute. "You may not be a prophet or a visionary, but if you succeed, future historians may well consider that you triggered a black swan event. Are you familiar with the term?"

Morane shook his head.

"No."

"A twenty-first-century thinker by the name Nassim Nicholas Taleb, coined it, though he's not widely known outside academia nowadays. Swans, an avian life form common on Earth, were normally white, and the birth of a black swan was considered impossible, though they supposedly existed. A black swan event is a metaphor to describe an event that occurs as a surprise and has a major effect on the course of history. An extreme outlier if you like. Of course, that's a simplistic overview. If you want to read Taleb, the university has copies of his works."

"I would, though I doubt my actions come under this black swan event heading."

Reyes gave him a speculative gaze over the rim of her wine glass.

"That's not for us to say, Jonas. We merely need to make sure there will be future historians capable of looking back at today and deciding whether your arrival here fits the theory. Now tell me more about your knowledge vault and those mysterious Void Brethren you brought to Lyonesse."

— 8 —

Mykonos

Lengthening shadows chased the ragged band of fugitives through the city's worst ruins. They saw no other humans among the debris, but Marta could feel countless eyes watching them, their owners choosing prudence at the sight of armored men and grim, black-cloaked monastics.

After the first kilometer skirting rubble mounds, bomb craters and the occasional stench of mass graves, Sigrid and Stefan, exhausted by days on the run, faltered. At a gesture from Sister Heloise, the two burliest friars, Gellert and Alden, picked the children up and swung them over their shoulders without breaking stride.

No one spoke, not even in a whisper, as if the sound of human voices in this place might attract more than just predators picking through what little remained of a once vibrant district. Ghosts, perhaps. The spirits of those buried where they died, murdered by either faction at the height of the fighting.

Hartwood Cahal, grim determination writ large on his homely face, glanced back at them from time to time, though he provided no further sign of his commanding officer's success in drawing off Jorge Danton's soldiers. However, Marta found reassurance in the fact they heard none of the sounds she associated with a pitched battle between opposing troops.

Nothing other than the low whistle of a chilly breeze passing through wrecked buildings and the distant hum of Petras' undamaged section reached their ears. If not for the latter, Marta might believe the entire planet now looked like her immediate surroundings, the image of a civilization lost, perhaps forever.

She wondered whether similar scenarios were playing out on every human world across the empire. The last subspace news packet from Wyvern before her husband lost his struggle against Jorge Danton hadn't been encouraging despite the imperial propaganda service's obvious slant. When Dendera's bullshit artists couldn't even find the heart to make their good news missives believable, things were worse than anyone might imagine.

The detritus of a once vibrant city petered out as they reached the semi-wild forest which had replaced most of the farms surrounding Petras years ago in an unsuccessful attempt to give Mykonos' capital a greenbelt. Designed by a long-dead governor general to imitate the one encircling the imperial capital on Wyvern, it had cost a fortune and created so much ill-will that her successors let it revert to native flora and fauna rather than spend a single cred on maintenance.

But Norum found the time to bless that nameless governor general when her creation finally swallowed them. Hartwood Cahal led their party through the tree line and down an almost indiscernible game trail with the ease of one equipped to operate in complete darkness. Even the Void Brethren moved with soundless assurance though Marta could barely see her feet, let alone anything beyond Friar Sandor's back two paces in front of her.

Within minutes, the ruins were nothing more than a bad memory, a nightmare conjured by the savagery of Danton's rebels.

Then, the distant buzz of the city's undamaged quarters faded away, absorbed by dense thickets which quickly gave way to towering trees. And a lot of nothing for someone without night vision gear or heightened senses. Marta stumbled on an exposed root and almost fell, but a steadying hand grasped her upper right arm.

"You're doing fine," Heloise whispered. "Just a little more, then we can rest. The greenbelt's center is so filled with life that our spoor won't stand out on military sensors."

Norum offered the unknown governor general from another era a second blessing. If agricultural land still surrounded the city, their chances of hiding within a single night's march would have been slim.

After a week with little to no food — most of the scraps she found had gone to Sigrid and Stefan — what remained of her stamina was rapidly evaporating. And she was not an eight-year-old, small enough to ride on the shoulders of a fit, healthy friar.

Then, just as Marta thought she couldn't take one more step, Friar Sandor stopped walking. Since she'd not seen or heard a signal from their mercenary escort, Marta couldn't figure out why until Hartwood Cahal's face emerged from the darkness.

"We make camp here for a few hours," he whispered. "My men and I will stand watch, but this deep inside the forest, Danton's killers won't find us. Not with the hooting and howling from nocturnal critters. Some of the herbivores are almost human-sized and will give even the best sensing gear false positives."

"How long?" Heloise asked in the same tone.

"Four hours minimum, but no more than six. It's almost twenty-one-hundred now. I'd like to reach the river before sunrise, which is just after oh-five-hundred. Then, it's another three hours to the rendezvous point south of the Lysistrata Bridge. If the boss broke clean, that's where we'll meet up."

"And from there?"

"We either beg, borrow, buy, or steal a boat in Pheia and ride to Tiryns on the Celadon River, or we hike through the Lysistrata Forest which could add days to the journey. Assuming Lady Marta and the wee ones can manage a long trek."

"What about food?"

Cahal grimaced.

"We'll share our rations, but it's not much. Certainly not enough for a long walk to Tiryns. If you folks carry funds or trade goods, we can see what's available in Pheia when we look for a boat."

"Isn't a shopping expedition risky? Even a tiny village will have its share of informants eager to ingratiate themselves with Mykonos' new rulers."

The grimace vanished, replaced by a knowing smile.

"That's where you come in, Sister."

"I'm to be the buyer."

"We two will be the buyers. The others stay hidden. You can pass off as a harmless matron making her way west to rejoin family in Tiryns after escaping the last of the fighting in Petras, and I'll be your security guard. Between us, we don't look dangerous enough to harm a baby howler lizard."

Heloise considered the plan for a few moments, then nodded once.

"Agreed. Although if Danton's people were proactive and distributed images of my Brethren and me, it might become a tad risky. He'll have seized the Mykonos Abbey database by now."

"Which will help them only if they can tally up the Brethren they murdered and decide half a dozen are still on the run instead of simply rotting in a ditch the soldiers forgot to check. And they can't. I'm pretty sure of that. Danton might be a ruthless sonofabitch, but his intelligence analysts aren't the cream of the crop. No one knows you survived the rebel killing fields. So long as you don't behave like a sister..."

"Fair enough."

"Now try to catch a few hours downtime. There's a bed of native moss to your left. Lady Marta, the bairns, and your Brethren should be reasonably comfortable there, under the circumstances."

A few murmured orders later, Norum settled into a hollow between tree roots, Sigrid snuggled under her left arm and Stefan under her right. She tried to empty her mind, but in vain, and not only because of physical discomfort.

Fear, never far from the surface, kept her nerves on edge, as it had since narrowly escaping her late husband's fate. The twins were equally restless, battling their own demons, and it felt as if only five minutes had passed when Heloise, kneeling beside them, gave her a gentle shake.

"It's oh-one-hundred. Hartwood wants to move out."

"A bit more, Sister?" Marta asked in a sleepy tone, slurring her words.

"We were fortunate to get five hours, my dear." Heloise held out a small packet. "Survival rations. They might not seem like much, but even the smallest bite will give you a boost of energy. Hopefully enough to see us reach Pheia."

Norum shook off the last cobwebs of sleep and almost wished she hadn't. The details of their precarious situation swam back into clear focus, along with despair at ever living a normal life again.

"Any news of Anders Proulx and the others?"

"Hartwood didn't say. He merely told us it was time to move. I suspect we'd already be on our way if it weren't for your little ones. Hartwood and his troopers are still operating on sheer adrenaline. The Almighty only knows how they'll feel when it finally washes away, and their bodies go on strike." Heloise paused as if studying Marta with her piercing eyes. "As will yours, no doubt."

"And you?"

"Don't waste a thought on us. We Void Brethren know many ways of dealing with mental and physical exhaustion, though we pay the same price as anyone else at the end since we're only human. But we try to make that end come when the main peril has passed." She sighed. "It doesn't always work."

Heloise held out her hand to help Marta stand. She, in turn, pulled her sleepy twins up and gave each of them a hug and a kiss, murmuring reassuring words that sounded horribly false to her own ears. Nothing would ever be right again. Not with their father's head on a pike outside Government House and their lives destroyed by Jorge Danton. Even if they escaped Mykonos, would they find safety elsewhere in a galaxy gone mad with violence?

Marta doled out the survival rations and handed her children back to Friars Gellert and Alden, who'd appointed themselves as guardians, before their little column resumed its trek.

This time, Heloise took Marta by the hand and led her through the night, but she still regularly stumbled, as much because of roots and rocks as from sheer exhaustion. A few hours of fitful sleep wrapped in the borrowed cloak, waking whenever Sigrid and Stefan so much as twitched, left her almost as tired as before.

Growing up among the imperial nobility before pair-bonding with a star system governor general didn't prepare her for physical hardship. The dawning realization she and the twins would never have escaped Petras without Heloise, her Brethren and Anders Proulx's troopers, added to her burden of despair. Perhaps the Void's Almighty was more than a metaphysical answer to that which humanity couldn't understand and had bestowed blessings of survival on them.

Few among the empire's aristocracy held any beliefs beyond their own inalienable right to wealth, respect, and power. Marta had been, until recently, not much different from the rest of her social class. However, the last few days were forcing her to reassess everything she believed.

Escaping Danton's killers seemed almost like a miracle, but being found by Heloise and her little band of survivors and then by Anders Proulx's retired Imperial Marines defied any reasonable human's idea of coincidence, let alone probability. Perhaps there was a higher power watching over them.

Yet one part of her mind was conscious she might be suffering from what her Uncle Olav called the oh-dark-thirty blues, a condition many experience at the lowest point of the circadian rhythm when the cloak of night and profound fatigue make life seem too much of a chore.

After what felt like an eternity, the ghostly sense of nearby running water, a combination of increased moisture in the air and subliminal, aquatic sounds distinct from those of the forest pulled Marta from her dark thoughts. They had to be approaching the Celadon River which connected Petras with the coastal Port of Tiryns.

It was enough to encourage hope they might escape capture, and she pushed back at her overwhelming melancholy. Moments later, Hartwood Cahal stopped them for another of their regular, hourly breaks just short of where Marta noticed the darkness lose its oppressive quality. The outer edge of the greenbelt forest, perhaps?

It meant they were nearing the Lysistrata Bridge and the village of Pheia where they could rest while Heloise and the mercenary searched for Anders, a boat, and food.

When more than half an hour passed without resuming their trek, Sister Heloise climbed to her feet and unerringly found Cahal, standing guard with his winger. The other two mercenaries had gone ahead to scout their trail, as they did during every halt.

She returned after speaking with Cahal in a whisper so soft it was swallowed by the gentle breeze rustling through the forest's canopy and sat beside Marta once more.

"Hartwood's scouts spotted soldiers near the Lysistrata Bridge."

"Are Danton's troops looking for us?"

"Possibly, but I doubt it, and so does Hartwood. He figures they're running security patrols along the main route between Petras and the coast, looking for signs of loyalist activity."

"What happens now?"

"We wait until the patrols leave."

"What if they make a move in our direction?"

Heloise shrugged.

"We retreat into the forest and find another path."

— 9 —

A hint of dawn was filtering through the trees when Hartwood Cahal materialized beside Marta and Heloise. They'd been waiting in silence for over an hour since first hearing about military activity beyond the greenbelt and Cahal's grim expression told them immediately that he came bearing unpleasant news.

"Change in plans," he said without preamble. "It looks like soldiers from the 84th Guards are running a fixed checkpoint by the Lysistrata Bridge and mobile patrols covering the open terrain north and south of the Celadon. I think we're facing a cordon designed to intercept anyone fleeing Petras."

"People on the losing side, such as us," Heloise said in a flat tone.

"Yep. We can't let them spot us because they'll know right away what we are and who Lady Marta is. And that means the best we can pray for is instant death."

"The *best*?" Marta asked.

"Aye. Ever since going over to Danton, the 84th has been inventing new forms of torture to prove it's more ruthless than any other unit on this planet. It means captured loyalists usually experience a living hell before they die. Please don't ask me for details, Milady."

"I won't."

"The new plan is to skirt Pheia and head south under cover of the woods until we reach rougher ground where their patrols can't easily see us. A day's march, perhaps more. Once we're far enough west of the Guards cordon, we'll turn north and rejoin our intended route further downriver."

"What about Anders and the rest of your comrades?"

Cahal grimaced.

"They'll need to figure it out for themselves. To use the radio now and send a warning would be suicide."

"So we won't see them again before Tiryns for sure?" Marta asked.

"Unless we meet up by pure luck, no. We can't cut back to the Celadon and look for a boat until we're well past the rendezvous point."

"You still intend to find transport on or near the river?"

"Without it, whether on land or on the water, we won't reach the coast. Neither you nor your children have the stamina for such a long trek, Milady. My men and I might make it, and perhaps the Brethren would — *if* we find food." He glanced at Friars Gellert and Alden. "Besides, they can't keep carrying the wee ones for days on end."

"Don't worry about us," Gellert replied with a dismissive gesture. "We're used to hard labor. Not all servants of the Almighty spend their days in contemplation and prayer. Many, like Alden and I, do the manual work that keeps abbeys and priories in good shape. In fact, we escaped the massacre because of our duties. I figure the Almighty has plans for us, and they might just include carrying these precious treasures to safety."

An easy smile softened Alden's square, lean features.

"Let the little children come to me, and do not hinder them, for the kingdom of heaven belongs to such as these."

When she saw Cahal didn't know what to make of the friar's words, Heloise said, "Scripture, from one of our holy books, though I suspect Alden is being a tad facetious."

"Mischievous, Sister," he replied.

Friar Sandor rolled his eyes.

"And clearly unrepentant."

Alden sprang to his feet with athletic vigor.

"I shall offer the Almighty proper penance once we reach a place of safety. And if we want to get there before Gellert and I grow so old we can no longer serve as beasts of burden, shouldn't we be on our way?" He reached out toward Stefan, still sitting on a fallen tree trunk at his mother's side. "Ready to resume the journey, my young friend?"

The boy, who'd been as mute as his sister throughout the night, nodded shyly as he stood.

**

As the day advanced, their path into the depths of the greenbelt turned increasingly more arduous as animal trails became scarcer and harder to spot. By midday, Marta's entire body was screaming for mercy. A litany of complaints rose from her empty stomach, several of them embarrassingly loud, while insect clouds gave the party no respite.

A few hours later, she almost sobbed with joy upon realizing the late afternoon sun filtering through the dense canopy no longer came from straight ahead. Though she hadn't noticed the change of direction, Cahal was now leading them toward the Celadon once more, hopefully far enough behind the cordon to escape notice.

The Brethren, even Gellert and Alden, seem unaffected by their exertions. Marta barely heard them pant as they struggled through dense thickets, over fallen trees, and around fetid mires.

When dusk threatened to smother the forest once more with impenetrable darkness for anyone who didn't possess the mercenaries' night vision visors or the Void Brethren's eerie sixth sense, Cahal called a halt. He made his way back along the narrow trail to where Heloise, Marta, and the others waited.

"We're about two kilometers south of Elis, the next settlement downriver from Pheia. With the soldiers' eyes on the Petras greenbelt, we shouldn't attract much attention, but I've decided to spend the night here and wait until dawn. A large group traveling at night is bound to raise questions. Two of my men will head out around midnight and quietly check the area for enemy activity. If it looks clear by daybreak, Sister Heloise and I will enter Elis to look for food and a means of transportation. Settle in, eat, and sleep. We'll stand watch over you."

After a quick meal of emergency rations, Marta settled into a leaf-filled hollow among the roots of a tall, native tree, Sigrid and Stefan clinging tightly to her on either side. Sister Heloise sat beside them in the lotus position and appeared to enter a trance-like state.

"Will we ever stop running away, Mommy?" Stefan asked in a small voice, the first words he'd spoken all day.

"Eventually, love. Once we're far from the bad people who want to hurt us."

"Like they hurt daddy? Is that what will happen?"

"Trust in the Almighty, child," Heloise said in a soft voice without opening her eyes or so much as twitching. "You, your sister, and your mother were spared for a reason, though we cannot as yet understand why, just as Hartwood Cahal and his soldiers were spared. And we Brethren. But it should become clear in time. Tomorrow, we will find an easier way to the sea. And from there, a place where the bad people won't find us. In the meantime, try to rest and regain your strength. We're safe here. No one will disturb us."

Heloise's voice seemed to exert an almost hypnotic effect because Marta felt Stefan and his sister relax in her arms, their breathing rhythms taking on the regularity of sleep.

"Do you believe what you told them?" She asked in a whisper.

"Of course."

"I'm not particularly religious, Sister."

"Most humans aren't particularly religious, but everyone places faith in something. The urge to believe is a vital part of what makes us the sapient beings we are."

Marta exhaled softly. "It makes me wonder what the likes of Jorge Danton and Harvey Marat believe. Especially since they seem bound and determined to eliminate every single servant of the Almighty in this star system."

"Power. Political ideology. Amassing wealth. Any of the seven deadly sins will do. Mind you, it's more complicated than mere human appetites running amok. Many of our greatest thinkers believe those who reject the notion there might be a greater power holding the universe together often replace the emptiness in their souls by elevating the human to the status of the divine. But since the divine must be perfect, ideologues of various stripes have bedeviled our species for a long time with the notion we can be perfected. Sadly, they end up carrying out genocide after genocide to force an ideal on creatures inherently incapable of attaining it."

"I wouldn't think Danton and Marat are political ideologues, Sister."

"And you'd be correct. But their souls are afflicted by an emptiness, a craving they can't understand, and thus they try to fill it by amassing power without consideration for basic decency."

Marta digested Heloise's words before asking, "Why destroy your Order?"

"I wish it were because we represent their antithesis, but few humans possess that level of self-awareness. No, we're being persecuted because our Order bows to no secular authority. We're beyond the control of lawmakers, admirals, viceroys, and governors general, and thus perceived as dangerously powerful in our own right, even though we abstain from interfering in secular matters. As a result, those who overthrew the existing political and social construct through illegitimate means consider us a threat."

"So Danton and his master, Admiral Zahar, aren't persecuting you on religious grounds but because they believe your spiritual power, whatever that is, might imperil their temporal power? Considering what I know of either man, it makes sense."

"That's my conclusion as well, though I could be wrong. But we Void Brethren have studied human nature since well before the empire's birth, and basic human behavior patterns haven't changed since we first gained sapience."

A grim chuckle escaped Marta's throat.

"So much for the notion we can be perfected if only we'd adopt the proper way of thinking."

"And neither of us will come closer to that goal if we don't sleep." Heloise abandoned the lotus position and stretched out on the spongy moss at Marta's feet, wrapped in her cloak. "Good night."

— 10 —

Lyonesse

"Good morning, Sister. Thank you for joining us." Morane, at the head of a scuffed conference table, waved Gwenneth toward the last empty chair. DeCarde and Kayne were already seated, while a display on the far wall showed Acting Captain Mikkel aboard *Vanquish* as well as Commanders Ryzkov and Sirak from the tactical transport *Narwhal* and the frigate *Myrtale*, respectively.

She inclined her head by way of greeting, then sat.

"It would be churlish of me to refuse, considering the burden you're shouldering on our behalf."

"Speaking of burdens, I don't think I've formally thanked you yet for taking charge of the political prisoners. Please accept my and everyone else's gratitude, Sister. How are they doing?"

An unguarded flash of exasperation crossed Gwenneth's face.

"We do not seek gratitude, but to serve others, though a few of the recently decanted are causing several Brethren to reconsider their vows. We will be pleased

73

once Colonel Kayne's training camps are ready to receive them."

DeCarde snorted.

"Ungrateful little sods, eh? Figures. We save their useless, titled butts from a nasty fate on Parth but it's not good enough. What do they want? A ticket back to Wyvern? Their own palaces on the shores of the Middle Sea? Government sinecures in Lannion?"

Gwenneth speared the Marine with emotionless eyes.

"There are more complex psychological issues at play, Colonel. Few of them grasped what exile meant when Dendera pronounced her sentence. They were not given any time to reflect on their changed circumstances before entering stasis, and it is only now, here on Lyonesse, that the realization is striking them with full force. Many, perhaps even most are not equipped to deal with changes of such magnitude after a cosseted life of privilege and power. However, the dramatics a few put on thanks to their deeply disturbed states of mind can try the patience of a saint."

"Wait until they find out we actually expect them to find jobs and work for a living, like the rest of us peasants."

Morane raised a hand to stop any further banter and turned to Gwenneth once more.

"Should you like me to speak with them and lay the situation out in a clear military manner, just say the word."

"Perhaps that will become necessary, though I daresay a few of the higher ranked among them will demand to see you soon enough, anyhow."

"Thank you for the warning, Sister. Now on to other business. I'd like all starships to top up their antimatter fuel containment units at the cracking station. One at a time, please. I always want two ships guarding the high orbitals."

"You think someone might take out the cracking station?" Mikkel asked.

"It's the most vulnerable target in the system, Iona."

Vanquish's acting captain nodded in agreement.

"True. What about shore leave for our crews?"

"That was my next item. Once you're fueled up and back, you may go to two-thirds crewing and send one-third down for liberty. Through the depot, if you please, not the civilian spaceport. I'd like to keep a modicum of control." The three starship captains signified their understanding. "I'm meeting with Governor Yakin, Speaker Hecht, and Chief Administrator Logran this afternoon to present our initial ideas for the Lyonesse Defense Force, so we can regularize our presence here and integrate with the colonists. Once that's out of the way, we'll turn our attention on building the knowledge vault. Chancellor Reyes told me Lyonesse University is keen to help spearhead the effort."

Commander Ryzkov raised her hand.

"Where will the physical repository be, sir?"

"Warehouse D right here in the depot. It's the deepest of the chambers, large and armored to boot. Lieutenant Grimes and her people will empty it once we decide how the starship spare parts should be distributed. I asked around, and no one could think of a better place. Sealed up, it'll resist just about anything, including the ravages of time."

"Meaning we might vanish, but our works will live on forever. Good to know."

"The goal is to make sure we, as a star-faring civilization, don't vanish, Lori, but I understand what you're saying."

After running through a list of administrative points, Morane glanced around the table and at the displays. "That's everything. Questions?"

"Yes, sir," Mikkel said. "A few of the ratings asked the cox'n whether we'll allow them to resign and settle on Lyonesse as colonists."

"Certainly. This is now home. And since our little navy will not play an expeditionary role, the ships can function with reduced crews until we're forced to store them because we run out of fuel or spare parts. You can pass the word. Chief Administrator Logran assured me there's work for everyone. Some involves hard labor such as clearing out new settlements and opening up new farmland, but the effort comes with land grants. And those who resign from full-time service are welcome to join our reserve. We already have a reserve ground forces unit under Lieutenant Colonel Kayne, and I'm developing plans to create a naval reserve unit."

"Okay, good to know, sir. Be prepared to approve a slew of resignations in the next few weeks. A lot of the older crew members can't see themselves spending the next few years living aboard a starship in orbit or on patrols to the wormhole terminus and back."

"Understandable. Most of us signed up to see the galaxy, and it's unlikely we'll leave this star system ever again. Anything else, Iona? No? Lori? Nate? Brigid? Matti? Sister?"

Gwenneth nodded.

"You mentioned land grants. Is there any news on our request for a parcel to build the Lyonesse Abbey?"

"I intended to speak with you after the meeting, Sister, but yes. Since the colonial government is dragging its feet, Chancellor Reyes offered to lease a portion of the university's land endowment for a nominal sum. She would like to explore how your Brethren can help the university and the colony at large by using their skills in the areas of medicine, agriculture, teaching, et cetera. The land in question sits about ten kilometers outside Lannion and is suitable for animal husbandry and growing comestible crops. If you accept, we can move empty shipping containers out there to build your temporary abbey."

What Morane didn't add was any land grant at Speaker Hecht's behest might have come with strings attached, the sort the Order would find onerous after a while.

The ghost of a smile softened Gwenneth's ascetic features.

"I am most grateful to Chancellor Reyes for the offer. Living in close quarters with outsiders is difficult for many of the Brethren. I will accept on their behalf, though I must put it to a vote in Chapter. But I should like to meet with the chancellor in person before we formally take possession."

"She wouldn't want it any other way. If that was it, thank you. We'll do this again next week, same day, same time."

"Sir, can I speak with you alone afterward?" Mikkel asked.

"Sure, Iona."

They waited until the feeds from *Myrtale* and *Narwhal* faded, and the conference room emptied. Then, she said, "You're not coming back aboard *Vanquish,* are you?"

"No. I wanted to wait until Lyonesse's ruling triumvirate accepts my proposal and puts it to the Colonial Council for a vote before saying so, but *Vanquish* is yours now. I'm swallowing the anchor to become something similar to an acting chief of the defense staff. That way, I can best supervise the construction of the knowledge vault and deal with the inevitable politics that will bedevil it each step of the way. The promotion to captain will come once we sort out the legalities."

"You know Lori is senior to me, right? She might not be happy."

"I know, and I have plans for her. Worry about picking the right first officer and how you'll rearrange crewing protocols once the resignations trickle in."

"Aye, aye, sir. May I assume you'll be putting up a commodore's stars?"

"If that is the governor's wish. A well-regulated defense force needs a legal commander-in-chief, and as Lyonesse's ruler, she's it."

—11—

Mykonos

An eerie silence seemed to hang over Elis even though agricultural settlements usually bustled with life at sunrise, let alone almost two hours later. Sister Heloise and Hartwood Cahal exchanged worried glances as they left the woodland trail and crossed the deserted main highway before entering the riverside village proper.

Empty streets bordered by ancient houses and overgrown yards greeted them. Irregular gusts of wind gently blew dried vegetation debris this way and that, while a faint hint of damp, rising from the Celadon River, tickled their nostrils. Though they saw no living creature beyond a few native insects, Heloise could sense life, both animal and human, behind blank stone walls erected before the old Commonwealth became an empire.

She'd come through Elis years earlier, on one of the abbey's regular community outreach tours, and remembered it as a quaint, almost antiquated rural community which had remained virtually unchanged over the centuries, its inhabitants content with their pace of life. Most worked on one of the many surrounding farms, growing crops to feed the always ravenous star system capital and its surrounding districts. Heloise also recalled meeting people who'd moved from Petras to live in less frantic surroundings, though with a hard cap on growth, the settlement could only absorb so many outsiders.

"Something's not right," she muttered in a tone pitched for Hartwood Cahal's ears only.

"Ya think?" He murmured back. "I've seen livelier cemeteries."

They reached the town square without meeting another human being. In Heloise's memory, a granite statue of the empire's founder used to dominate the square's grassy center. The inhabitants must have destroyed it in recent weeks, along with every other imperial symbol when the rebellion reached Mykonos. Not even the ruins of a plinth remained.

Heloise nodded toward a covered arcade lined with shops.

"Someone in there is watching us. Perhaps we should ask why the town seems dead."

"How do you know we're being watched?" Cahal fell into step beside her.

"Instinct. I thought Marines could feel unseen eyes studying them." She glanced at him with an impish smile.

Cahal let out a soft snort.

"It doesn't always work. And in these screwed up times, you can't tell friend from foe without a program."

The arcade's shadows swallowed them while they slowly studied darkened windows and shuttered doors. When they came within two paces of one with a simple sign reading Elis Emporium, it opened a few centimeters, just enough to reveal a narrow, worried face.

"What are you doing outside?" A rough man's voice asked. "Don't you know about the curfew?"

Heloise and Cahal briefly looked at each other, then the former shook her head before meeting the storekeeper's hooded eyes.

"No. We've only just arrived and aren't aware of a curfew. I am Heloise, and this is Hartwood, my guide and protector. We're on our way to the coast and wish to buy food as well as inquire about road or river transport possibilities. What's going on in these parts?"

The man's gaze switched between Heloise and Cahal, his expression conveying he couldn't quite believe their lack of awareness.

"The Guards set up an exclusion zone on this side of the greenbelt two days ago, to catch anyone leaving Petras without authorization. Early this morning, at daybreak, the authorities put us under a curfew. We're forbidden from leaving our homes until further notice. Us, the folks in Pheia up by Lysistrata Bridge, and every other settlement in the area. They didn't tell us why, but anyone caught breaking it will end up in the Petras military prison under charges of treason against Danton's government. How is it you're here, in Elis, and you don't know?"

"A question easily answered, but since staying out in the open seems perilous, could we call on your hospitality and come in?" Heloise asked in the same gentle, quasi-hypnotic voice she'd used on Stefan and Sigrid the previous evening. "We would be glad to buy our supplies from you while we're here."

After a moment, the door opened wide, and the man stuck his head out. He looked left and right, then stepped back to wave them through. With the door shut behind them, he said, "The name's Jed Lormand. Welcome to the Elis Emporium."

Heloise inclined her head.

"Thank you for allowing us to enter, Mister Lormand."

He shrugged, though not without a touch of irritation.

"I'd be a lousy merchant if I turned away customers because the governor general has a comet up his ass for some reason. The damned rebellion should be over now that the last loyalists surrendered. Well, not so much surrendered as been shot. But you know what I mean. Things should settle, what with a new Coalsack Sector viceroy on Yotai running things independently of Wyvern. A grand duke by the name Devy Custis who gave Dendera the finger."

"You don't sound like a fan of our new rulers."

"Bah." Lormand made a dismissive gesture. "We traded one pack of power-hungry thieves for another. Give it a year or two and we'll wonder why so many people died just so we could rip the imperial crown off our public buildings."

"Dangerous words to use in front of strangers," Heloise said in a light tone.

"If Danton were to shoot everyone in this star system who thinks like me, he'd be ruling a planet-wide cemetery soon enough. Besides, you don't strike me as friends of the new regime. Otherwise, you wouldn't be heading for the coast on foot." When he saw alarm in Cahal's eyes, a cold smile appeared. "You learn to read people in my line of work, especially those merely passing through town."

"And you don't know why they imposed a curfew?" Cahal asked.

"No. But the officer who laid it on us said we should report any sighting of Lady Marta Norum to his command post at the Lysistrata Bridge and keep our eyes on her until he gets here. The governor general wants Norum unharmed."

"Just Lady Marta? I thought she had kids?" Cahal asked in an easy-going tone.

"The officer only mentioned her."

"Did he mention a reward?"

"No." Lormand shook his head.

Cahal grunted.

"Funny. Danton put a bounty on loyalist troops. Why not on her?"

"Never heard of him putting a bounty on loyalists, which makes me think if there is one on Lady Marta, the soldiers will want to keep it for themselves. Mind you, the 84th Guards are the greediest bastards in uniform you've ever seen. Joining the rebellion didn't improve their honesty. They might even be a bad influence on the rest."

"It'll be a cold day in hell before Marines take their cues from the damn Guards," Cahal replied, growling. "Even if the motherless bastards rose up against Dendera instead of dying for her."

"You're a Marine?" Lormand tilted his head to one side as he studied Cahal.

"Retired since before the rebellion started, so I got no dog in this fight. I swore an oath to the Crown a long time ago, and the Crown released me from that oath the day I hung up my uniform. Madame Heloise claims my service now."

"I see." Lormand turned to Heloise once more, and a slight frown creased his forehead. "Did you pass through Elis before? Something about you seems vaguely familiar. I not only have a good nose for people, but my memory for faces is also pretty decent."

"Sorry, no." Heloise shook her head as she held Lormand's gaze with guileless eyes.

"Ah, well. Maybe you remind me of someone else." He tapped the side of his head with an extended index finger. "Age is doing my memory no favors. Now, what can I do for you?"

Neither Lormand nor Cahal seemed to remember Heloise inferring she might explain why she and her guide were out in the open during a curfew. Or if the mercenary did, he was wise enough to stay silent.

"We need portable food, Ser Lormand. Something compact, easy to carry, yet nourishing for folk traveling on foot. Enough for a week or more."

"What you want are laborers' day packs. Popular in these parts. I can—" A woman's voice from the back room, behind the counter, interrupted him.

"Fay just called. She said a Guards combat car turned off the highway and is heading into town, Jed."

Heloise and Hartwood Cahal exchanged glances.

"Maybe they put ISR floaters aloft and saw us enter Elis," the latter said. When he saw a puzzled expression on Lormand's face, Cahal added, "Intelligence, surveillance and reconnaissance drones."

"Or they're checking up on the curfew," the sister said. "Let's not borrow trouble."

"If the buggers are showing up because they caught you two via aerial surveillance, they won't know anything beyond your disappearing into the arcade. There are twelve stores, along with private doors to another two dozen second-story apartments."

"Still, we shouldn't put you in danger, Ser Lormand. We'll take as many of your laborer's day packs as we can carry and leave. If your store has a discreet rear exit, so much the better."

The merchant studied Heloise through narrowed eyes. As his face lost its intensity, the Sister of the Void could almost see him mentally shrug.

"Best I don't ask questions. That way you won't tell me lies. And I can't tell the soldiers what I don't know. There's an old smuggler's tunnel leading from my basement to the river. The far end is well hidden. It gets you out of Elis unseen, though after that, you'll need to see to yourselves. We'll grab the day packs from my storeroom downstairs along the way."

He turned toward the inner door and made a follow me gesture with his right hand.

"Why are you trusting us with your smuggler's tunnel?" Heloise asked.

"Let's just say you bring to mind a kind person belonging to a group that did good work in my little town many years ago, people Danton fears so much he ordered their murder. Now come."

Lormand led them past the counter, through the back room, where a silent, elderly woman watched them pass, then down stone steps leading to the store's basement. He stopped at shelves loaded with small, foil-wrapped cubes, each stamped with a manufacturer's logo and a list of items.

"Help yourselves."

Cahal and Sister Heloise filled their bags in silence under Lormand's watchful eyes. If he thought it strange they were taking so many ration packs, he didn't comment. When they had enough for everyone to last five days, she glanced at Lormand.

"How much do we owe you?"

He named a figure Heloise thought might be closer to the wholesale than the retail price, but she dug a handful of anonymous cred chips from a pouch beneath her cloak without argument. The Rule governing her Order forbade its members from accepting charity, but under the present circumstances, she wouldn't refuse Lormand's kindness.

Heloise and her Brethren carried limited funds, only the little they could save when Danton's soldiers attacked the abbey and its outlying priories. And it had to last until they reached safety, if such a thing still existed.

The woman's voice echoed down the staircase moments after Lormand pocketed the chips without even counting them.

"That combat car is entering the town square, Jed."

"Our customers are leaving via the back way."

Lormand crossed the basement and stopped at a shelving unit filled with wine bottles lying on their side. He touched an unseen control pad, and it shifted to one side with a tired groan, revealing a dimly lit passage carved into the rock by laser drills long ago. Perhaps even before the ravenous flames of empire rose from the Commonwealth's dying embers ten centuries earlier.

The tunnel ended at a hidden door which opened on a natural cave cut into the steep riverbank at a time when the Celadon was a raging torrent several kilometers wide, channeling meltwater to the sea at the end of Mykonos' last ice age. Thick vegetation covered the outer exit, though enough light seeped through to let them study their surroundings.

"There's a path on the left. It follows the river for a while before heading into the woods. You'll eventually come out on the highway. From there, you'll be able to loop back and find the rest of your party."

Lormand, eyes fixed on Heloise, was clearly looking for a reaction to confirm his suspicions. He would have been better off to watch Cahal. The retired Marine wasn't quite as self-possessed.

Heloise inclined her head.

"Thank you for your help."

"Consider it a good deed for a good deed, Sister. May the Almighty watch over you and yours." Lormand vanished into the tunnel without waiting for a reply. The camouflaged door swung shut, turning the cavern wall back into an unbroken granite surface polished by flood waters.

Cahal grunted.

"Let's hope our overly perceptive storekeeper can keep his mouth shut. Nothing will get Danton's troops excited like the idea of hunting Void Brethren who escaped Danton's night of the bloody knives."

"I daresay finding traces of Lady Marta and her children might." She seemed to tense for a fraction of a second and laid a restraining hand on Cahal's arm as he took his first step toward the cavern's mouth. "Wait. I think we should stay here for a bit."

"Soldiers?"

"Perhaps."

"Then it's best if we pull back as far as possible to foil their sensors into believing our life signs are nothing more than those of whatever passes for gophers on this damned planet." Cahal turned his head away from the opening and examined the shadows before pointing at a section darker than the rest. "It looks like there's a branch heading back toward Elis."

Moments before entering the natural tunnel, Cahal thought he could hear the characteristic hum of a military skimmer patrolling the river.

"You called it, Sister," he murmured.

— 12 —

Lyonesse

Wickham Sanford, Governor Yakin's secretary, led Morane to Government House's small conference room. Since his first visit, he'd come to know it almost as well as his own back at the Lyonesse Imperial Fleet Depot, which desperately needed a better name now they were dozens of light years beyond the empire's outer reaches. Logran and Hecht were already there. As usual, Yakin would show up last, as befit her status.

Morane nodded at them.

"Speaker, Chief Administrator."

Hecht's calculating eyes seemed to shine with more than the usual anticipation as he replied, "Captain."

"Gentlemen," Sanford announced in a formal tone from the open doorway, "Her Excellency, The Honorable Elenia Yakin, Governor of Lyonesse."

They stood as one when Yakin swept in, trailed by the subtle sandalwood scent Morane now associated with the colony's reserved, almost enigmatic ruler.

"Please sit." She turned a courtly smile on Morane. "And how is the Lyonesse captain general today?"

"Captain general, Your Excellency?"

"If we're to create a defense force from whole cloth, why not revive ancient titles? Didn't the Imperial Ground Forces resurrect the rank of centurion at one point?"

"Early in the empire's history, yes. To replace the rank of Army and Marine Corps captain so there would no longer be any confusion with the rank of navy captain, which is equivalent to that of a ground forces full colonel. Considering centurions commanded company-sized units in another, much more ancient empire, adopting it seemed appropriate."

"Then why not captain general of the Lyonesse Defense Force?"

She appeared to be in a bantering mood, so Morane replied in kind.

"Because I'm a spacer and not a ground pounder, Madame. The title captain general was reserved for soldiers."

Yakin's lips formed a perfect moue.

"I suppose that is true, and since you're about to propose a structure with yourself as senior commander, you must also propose a proper rank designation. Please go ahead."

Morane touched the conference table controls, and an organization chart appeared on the main display.

"The Lyonesse Defense Force will be composed of two operational elements, a naval battle group, and a ground forces brigade. Our naval battle group will include *Vanquish*, *Myrtale*, and *Narwhal*, and any other ships Lyonesse might take into service. Our ground forces brigade will include two infantry regiments, one full-time, and one part-time with a full-time cadre. The 6th Battalion of the 21st Pathfinder Regiment will be our full-time unit. We will keep the regimental title but drop the battalion designation and simply call it the 21st Pathfinder Regiment. The part-time regiment will be formed from the Lyonesse Colonial Militia and, at their request, take the name Lyonesse Rifle Regiment."

"No surprise so far," Hecht said. "Who commands what?"

"If you'll allow me, Speaker, I'll broach the proposed appointments after I finish with the structure."

Hecht gave him a grudging nod.

"Thank you, sir. As you can see from the chart, we will also field a joint support group, responsible for logistics, training, command and control, etcetera. We will create the support group using the Lyonesse Imperial Fleet Supply Depot and elements taken from both the starships and the ground units.

"I'm withdrawing most of *Narwhal*'s shuttles and pilots to form a transport squadron based at the depot. Additionally, I intend to cull parts of each ship's crew and both ground units to form an aerospace defense unit, a logistics battalion, as well as a battle school to provide basic training. That, in a nutshell, is how I propose to organize with what we can field today. The ships will be able to function with reduced crews since we don't expect them to leave this star system. And the ground units will begin recruiting to increase numbers as soon as the battle school is up and running."

"You're the expert, Captain," Logran said. "But it seems to make sense."

Yakin nodded. "Agreed."

"What about cost?" Hecht asked.

"I can give you the preliminary budget once we finalize our structure and sort out the legal status of the Lyonesse Defense Force, Speaker."

"Ah, yes," a cold smile crept up Hecht's face. "The legal status. I was hoping you'd broach that subject. And what are your thoughts?"

He speared Morane with a hard stare that said it was time to repay the Speaker of the Colonial Council for his support.

"We take the original imperial constitution as our model, sir. The governor is titular commander-in-chief, but the head of the defense force reports to the legislature, in this case, the council."

Logran reared up from his usual slumped posture.

"Now wait a minute. The defense force will be a department of the Lyonesse government, and its commander should report to the chief administrator via the head of public safety."

When Hecht didn't immediately reply, Morane understood the speaker expected him to defend the doctrine of legislative supremacy in matters concerning the armed services. It would allow Hecht to avoid participating in a jurisdictional squabble.

The next words he spoke would make one man an enemy. If that man was Logran, his enmity would percolate throughout the administration. And if it was Hecht, whose power on Lyonesse transcended that of a speaker, Morane could well imagine the mischief he could cause the knowledge vault project. Even Emma Reyes wouldn't be able to resist Hecht's wrath, much less his influence over every facet of Lyonesse society.

"We cannot afford the mistakes that allowed Stichus Ruggero to seize the throne, Chief Administrator, and thereby suffer the empire's fate." Morane kept an even, no-nonsense tone. "The imperial bureaucracy's encroachment on both the senate's and the Crown's authority diluted their control of the Fleet and gave Ruggero an opening. We now know, four long generations later, what the catastrophic consequences are. The Lyonesse Defense Force must report to the legislature, as specified in the original twenty-sixth-century imperial constitution."

"I disagree." Logran glared at Hecht, suspecting the speaker had put Morane up to it.

"As is your right, Chief Administrator. But to make sure Lyonesse has a future while the empire crumbles, the legislation creating its armed services must specify the council's supremacy."

"If that's your way of thinking, Captain, then perhaps you're not the best choice as chief of staff. We should ask that colonel of yours, DeCarde, to whom she believes the head of our defense force should report."

"You will hear the same answer from every officer under my command, and from Lieutenant Colonel Kayne and his officers. They understand what's involved."

"By the way, Morane, who or what gave you authority to promote him?"

With Logran veering off on an inconsequential sidetrack, Morane knew they'd settled the point. For now.

Yakin raised both hands.

"Speaker Hecht, I expect the council to prepare and pass the proper legislation."

"Yes, Your Excellency." Hecht's face showed no emotion, but his eyes, when he glanced at Morane, held a spark of triumph. "And now perhaps we can discuss the key appointments? I'm sure our new chief of the defense staff has suitable proposals for our consideration."

Morane understood he would get what he wanted, at least while Hecht held sway. But this wasn't the start of a beautiful friendship. It was that of a patron-client relationship steeped in politics.

Yet if it meant the knowledge vault would see completion before a fresh wave of marauder raids struck this system, then his conscience would gladly bow to the greater good. The real question was how to mollify Logran.

No matter how Hecht couched his legislation, Lyonesse's chief administrator would still exert a certain amount of influence over the defense force's destiny, and that of the vault. Perhaps even a critical amount. And now he'd earned Logran's displeasure...

"Shall we discuss appointments?" Governor Yakin asked. "I take it no one objects to my promoting Captain Morane to the rank of rear admiral forthwith?"

A pained look briefly crossed Morane's face.

"Under the old imperial constitution, promotion to flag rank was subject to a vote in the legislature. Mine should be as well."

Yakin held his eyes for a moment, then acquiesced with a nod.

"Certainly. We should start in the manner we intend to continue and do things in proper form. Speaker Hecht, I hereby submit Captain Morane's name for promotion to rear admiral. Wickham will draft the letter for my signature the moment this meeting has ended."

Hecht bowed his head in what struck Morane as a surprisingly formal gesture.

"I will present the nomination to a full council vote at the earliest opportunity, Madame. In the meantime, I will take it upon myself as speaker to sanction Captain Morane's proposal ahead of a formal council vote so he can go ahead. Do you agree, Madame? Chief Administrator?"

"I do."

Logran waited for a heartbeat before shrugging. "Sure. Let's make it happen."

— 13 —

Mykonos

Once the sound of the riverine patrol craft faded away, Heloise and Cahal left the cavern and returned to the deep woods after crossing the highway at a spot with plenty of overhead cover from ancient trees. Colyn Skurka intercepted them close to the hide where the others were waiting.

"Everything is good here. How did things go in Elis, boss?"

"We bought food for several days, but forget about taking a boat. Guards skimmers are patrolling the Celadon, and they probably have ISR floaters up. Plus, they put a curfew on the area. Murderous bastards aren't taking any chances. This is a serious cordon, not some half-assed exercise to intercept loyalist survivors just for shits and giggles. Apparently, there's a call out from Danton to find Lady Marta and bring her in, which might explain the extra activity."

"Crap. Are you going to tell her ladyship? She's already fragile as it is."

"Can't see where I have a choice, Colyn." Cahal patted his winger on the shoulder. "Besides, I figure Lady Marta is tougher than she looks. Remember, she kept herself and her kids hidden from Danton's pigs for almost a week before we found them."

Skurka nodded. "True. What now, if riding the Celadon is out?"

"Stay in the forest and keep using animal trails to head west until we're beyond the Guards' cordon."

"How will we know?"

An amused expression crossed Cahal's face.

"Take a peek at every village, town, and settlement along the river until we find one which doesn't seem like it's under a curfew. That'll be our clue."

Skurka grunted with embarrassment.

"Right. I deserve a slap on the head for missing the obvious. In my defense, beauty sleep is hard to come by these days. When I don't get enough zees, my brain turns to mush. What about Anders and the others?"

"We best write the rest of the unit off as casualties and proceed under the assumption we're the only ones left. If we meet up along the way or in Tiryns — good. If they don't make it, and we sail into the sunset on our own, I'm sure Sister Heloise and her fellows will join us in prayer for their souls."

"You think they might not make it through the cordon?"

"Could well be."

"Why is that?"

"No Void Brethren to help keep them safe from Danton's evil."

Cahal's sibylline statement seemed to puzzle Skurka, but after a quick glance at Heloise, he chose to let the matter slide.

"Shall we inform the others and head out?" Heloise gestured toward a dense thicket where another mercenary, quasi-invisible to anyone without the sister's heightened perceptions, stood guard. "The sooner we're away from this area, the better."

**

"They're looking for me, specifically?" Marta Norum frowned at Hartwood Cahal. "Nothing about Sigrid and Stefan?"

"That's what Jed Lormand, the shopkeeper said, Milady. No mention of the wee ones."

"Then it probably isn't because Danton wants to wipe out what's left of my late husband's family in this star system. Otherwise, why wait until now to spread the word among the civilian population that I'm wanted? Me, without mentioning my children. He was content enough to ignore us ever since his troops stuck Hachim's head on a pike." She paused, then nodded to herself. "Though I can guess why he's might suddenly be interested."

"Milady?"

Norum ignored Heloise's warning glance and said, "Perhaps he belatedly decided my bloodline could be useful to him. Or if not Danton, since he's known about my family tree for a long time, then whoever he now serves."

"Viceroy the Grand Duke Devy Custis, according to our friend Lormand. Apparently, Custis isn't one of Dendera's fans, which means he intends to rule the Coalsack Sector independent of Wyvern."

Understanding sparked in Norum's eyes.

"And there's our answer."

"Milady?"

"I'll bet Custis is the one who wants me unharmed, not that vile creature Jorge Danton."

Cahal let out a soft grunt.

"Can't say I understand what you're talking about and if you'd rather not discuss matters openly, fine by me. Yes, Sister, I caught the significant glance you gave Lady Marta. Whatever it is, I can smell the stinking rot of imperial politics from here, and an honest Marine always tries to avoid getting splattered."

"What about dishonest Marines?" Norum asked with a mischievous expression in her eyes.

"They're either drummed out of the service or encouraged to join the Imperial Guards. We should be on our way. The Port of Tiryns won't come to us."

**

"Forget the river, boss," Skurka whispered. "That old farm transporter sitting by the storehouse should take us to Tiryns without breaking a sweat."

Cahal studied the darkened district agricultural cooperative spread out below their hilltop aerie.

"The owners might object enough to call the damned Guards."

"The owners are in bed already and won't know it's missing until morning. They sure as shit won't be able to track it, not with over ninety percent of the planet's satellite constellation trashed in the fighting. No global tracking system means no way to find the truck except by hunting for it on the ground, and the Guards are otherwise busy these days. Such as making sure no escapee from the Petras massacres can plot against Jorge the Impaler." When Cahal didn't immediately reply, Skurka added, "You know you want to, boss. It'll be tight and dank in the back of that thing, but we'll be in Tiryns before daybreak."

"And I suppose you'll sweet talk the transport's AI into letting us steal it?"

"Me and one of the sisters — Averyl. I've been chatting her up during breaks, and one of her jobs at the abbey was taking care of their artificial intelligence array. She's what you might call a holy programmer."

"Try not to confuse the sisters with your usual sort of female friend, Colyn. Besides, the job of liberating that transport is something for a real hacker, not a programmer, holy or otherwise."

"Don't worry. I'm sure Averyl can take care of herself around our sort. And keep in mind holy programming might cover a lot of sins. The Void Brethren are said to wield strange powers. Why shouldn't they apply to artificial intelligence as well?"

Hartwood Cahal could almost see Skurka's smug smile behind his blank helmet visor.

"No life signs in the vicinity. I'll bet they leave that old heap there overnight all the time. We've been looking at the area long enough to know it's not under a curfew. That proves we're past the Guards' lines so there shouldn't be any regular patrols in the area. Besides, it's a perfect night for a raid thanks to the cloud cover. No moon or starlight to give us away. I doubt we'll get a better chance of finding transport between here and the coast."

"I'll pass it by Sister Heloise. With Lady Marta on Danton's most wanted list, she might not want us to rip off a truck and potentially alert the bad guys."

"We're hardly alone in running away from Petras. Besides, the Guards are so full of their own bullshit, they'll figure no one got through the cordon. Some dumbass officer from the 84th who'd never make it in the Corps will write off the transport's disappearance as pure thievery and leave it to the cops, who won't care because they're too busy bashing heads. Sister Heloise will be game, especially with Lady Marta twisting her ankle when we crossed that damned creek this afternoon."

Cahal knew his winger was right. If they could hack into the transport's controls and drive it off to a prearranged rendezvous, they'd spare themselves another week of walking. If not more, considering Lady Marta's ankle injury.

"Let's go back to the hide and talk it over," he finally murmured.

**

"That was almost too easy," Skurka said when a bend in the road swallowed the cooperative's lights.

"The Almighty always offers a way, provided we keep our faith and search for it."

When the mercenary glanced at Sister Averyl, sitting beside him in the transport's control cabin, he saw the glow of the instrument panel light up one of those mysterious smiles which first attracted his attention.

"I prefer keeping faith in my skills, Sister. And in yours. That was impressive. Easy or not, we did good. So long as the cops don't stop us."

"Trust in the Almighty, Colyn Skurka."

"I'm not a big believer, unlike the boss back there," he jerked a thumb over his shoulder at the transport's cargo compartment. "Hartwood seems to have adopted Heloise as a combination of commanding officer and oracle."

At Heloise's suggestion, Cahal had led everyone as close to the cooperative as they dared, keeping to the shadows. Meanwhile, Skurka and Averyl had hacked the vehicle's AI so they could be on their way sooner than if they made a detour to load up in a secluded spot off the main road. The sister seemed so confident no one questioned leaving the forest this close to a human settlement.

"That's okay. The Almighty believes in you."

Something in her tone caused him to glance at her again, but this time, he saw mischief gleaming in her dark eyes.

They spent the next few hours in companionable silence, the mercenary at a loss for safe topics of conversation, and forced to concentrate on driving through the night along an unlit road. Averyl had disabled the self-driving functions since they couldn't risk the AI changing its mind or a traffic control node that survived the rebellion seizing control of their vehicle.

Tiryns' outskirts eventually materialized from the pre-dawn gloom, and it quickly became plain that portions of the port city had suffered as heavily from the fighting as the most devastated parts of Petras. Piles of rubble littered the outskirts, casting strange shadows under widely scattered light globes still in working condition.

Skurka, his concentration focused on navigating through the debris, missed Averyl's gasp of alarm and by the time he realized they'd come within sight of a checkpoint, it was too late. Backing up now would make things worse.

He switched his radio to send on the short range unit frequency.

"We got problems, boss. Checkpoint. Can't see if it's Guards, cops, or someone else. Too late for evasion. Standby."

— 14 —

Lyonesse

DeCarde's head whipped up from the map projection she was studying with Kayne the moment she spied Morane in the hallway of what they now thought of as Lyonesse Defense Force Headquarters.

"And?"

"I got everything we wanted." Morane entered the conference room adjoining the operations center and gave them a weary grin. "Congratulations, *Colonel* DeCarde. Please be so kind as to hand the 21st Pathfinder Regiment to Lieutenant Colonel Salmin and stand up the 1st Brigade."

"And you?"

"By common accord, we decided appointing a defense force chief and making promotions to flag rank will need a Colonial Council vote, as per the old imperial constitution."

"Surely in your case, that's a mere formality."

"But an important one, Brigid. We don't want to repeat the empire's mistakes. If you'll pardon me, I need to call what will soon be the Lyonesse Navy and announce a few promotions and reassignments. Lori Ryzkov has a lot of work ahead to form the Defense Force Support Group. And the sooner we turn our plans into reality, the harder they will be to undo if people in the colonial government get second thoughts."

He nodded at Kayne.

"And part of that means regularizing your unit, Matti. You're no longer in charge of a colonial militia but a reserve regiment."

"Yes, sir. Might I suggest we hold formal ceremonies marking the creation of the Lyonesse armed services?"

"With Governor Yakin as reviewing officer?" When both DeCarde and Kayne nodded, Morane said, "Done. I'm sure it will please her excellency to receive full military honors as commander-in-chief."

A loud shout echoed from the far end of the hallway. Morane turned to look for its source and saw a figure in green tussling with a man wearing a prisoner's gray single piece garment by the staircase door.

"Let go of me, you cur," the man shouted in what Morane recognized as a distinctly nasal version of the courtly Wyvern drawl. "I will speak with whoever commands this asylum for congenital morons."

Morane gave DeCarde a sardonic glance and muttered, "Gwenneth warned me."

Then, in a louder voice pitched at the Marine guarding the headquarters entrance, he said, "Please escort that individual to my office."

The sentry released the intruder and stamped to attention. "Yes, sir."

**

Morane's office, previously that of the 77th Imperial Marine Regiment's commanding officer, was as bleak and sparsely furnished as a prison cell. Its austerity didn't escape the political prisoner's attention, judging by his disdainful expression.

After examining the room, still closely watched by a visibly annoyed Marine lance corporal, he turned a cold stare on Morane. An unattractive sneer distorted his patrician features.

"You run this place of perdition, do you, *Captain*?" He made Morane's rank sound like an insult.

"Why don't you sit?" Morane gestured at the field chair in front of his desk. He nodded at the lance corporal. "Please wait in the corridor."

The Marine stiffened.

"Sir."

He saluted, pivoted on his heels, and left.

Morane studied his unexpected guest before speaking. The man seemed to be in his late fifties, with silver-dusted black hair and a sculpted face that could only come from genetic engineering, but his eyes seemed much older and held no more warmth than interstellar space.

"My name is Jonas Morane, and I am the senior armed services officer in the Lyonesse system. My battle group rescued you and your fellow political prisoners from certain death at rebel hands."

"And you're expecting me to shower you with gratitude? After keeping us penned up like animals since we woke?"

"Your living conditions are no worse than those of my Marines."

"Really? Do you know who I am?"

Morane's lips twisted into a deliberately mocking smile.

"A rude individual who trespassed and imposed himself on me in a most discourteous manner. I expected more from a former nobleman of the imperial court."

The man leaned forward with what he likely believed to be a threatening expression.

"I'm Severin Rembert Downes, Count Hallibrank, and you will show me proper respect."

"Or what?" Morane's reply seemed to a catch Downes by surprise, and he blinked twice. "We are no longer in the empire. Titles of nobility hold no sway on Lyonesse. However, we still expect common courtesy. Especially from someone who might right now find himself dying by millimeters in a Parth jungle or, if the rebels had decided to not bother with another batch of useless courtiers, be so much space debris.

"We gave you and the rest of the political prisoners a chance at a new life. Find some gratitude before my patience runs thin, and I carry out Dendera's sentence. Lyonesse has a place of exile called the Windy Isles, from which no one can escape. The worst of the common criminals who traveled with you are already there, building their own settlements and growing their own food, lest they starve. We can easily send you and any other obnoxious lordlings to join them."

Downes stared at Morane in shock, momentarily robbed of his ability to form words. Finally, he said in a hoarse voice, "No one ever dared speak to me in this way."

Morane cocked an ironic eyebrow.

"Not even Dendera when she dispensed with your presence at court because she suspected you of plotting her overthrow? Hard to believe. Or do you mean no one you consider inferior has ever dared?" Morane let out a derisive snort. "Get used to it, Severin. You're on a new world with different rules. We will shortly resettle you former political prisoners in the community at large where we expect you to do honest work and earn a living under the supervision of someone who doesn't give a damn about dusty old titles."

"You wouldn't dare," Downes hissed. "I'm a member of the imperial nobility, not a damned commoner with grubby hands and a dull mind."

"Please don't waste my time with useless posturing, Mister Downes —"

"*Count* Hallibrank, or My Lord, if you please," the man snarled. "I was the secretary to the imperial chamberlain. I've squashed more insolent officers of your sort than I care to remember."

Morane ignored the outburst.

"Why did you force your way into my office, Mister Downes? Other than to show your lack of manners?"

"Who is governor of this planet? I demand to see him or her."

"That would be The Honorable Elenia Yakin, who has no interest in speaking with any of the political prisoners."

"I'm personally acquainted with Elenia's husband, Brigadier General Quimper of the Imperial Guards. Take me to her now, you ill-bred lout."

"She won't waste her time on useless drones, especially those who claim friendship with a thoroughly dishonorable man like her former spouse."

Downes lunged forward as if to grab Morane by the lapels and shake him. Morane reached up, wrapped his hands around the count's wrists, and pushed back.

"Trying to assault me was a terrible idea, Mister Downes. You are on an installation belonging to the Lyonesse Defense Force and thus subject to military discipline and military law. This conversation is finished. Lance Corporal?"

"Sir," a loud voice responded from the corridor. The man appeared in the doorway seconds later.

"Take this individual to the brig. He'll stay in solitary until tomorrow morning, on short rations. Spending time alone might give him a chance to reflect on the wisdom of adapting to his new life.”

When Downes began to sputter, Morane said, “Legally, you and the rest remain convicts until a Lyonesse court vacates your sentences. Since your sort is largely responsible for the empire’s decay and collapse, you’ll not find any sympathy if you continue to display this level of arrogance and entitlement. No one here will lose a moment’s sleep if the court sends you to the Windy Isles instead of setting you free. There’s no room on this planet for parasites, troublemakers, or anyone who won’t pull his or her own weight. Good day, Mister Downes.”

When the former count and his Marine escort vanished down the stairwell, DeCarde stuck her head into Morane’s office.

“Nasty customer? We heard raised voices.”

Morane pinched the bridge of his nose with the thumb and index finger of his right hand and sighed.

“Make a note Brigid. We must quash any attempt to set up a nobility in exile on Lyonesse with utmost ruthlessness, including summary execution. Otherwise, we won’t survive for long.”

“Isn’t our governor one of them?”

“Technically, but I doubt she has much sympathy for those who used to be her peers at court, let alone those who thought themselves her superiors.” When he saw DeCarde’s quizzical look, he made a dismissive gesture with his left hand. “Something Emma Reyes said when I was at the College Club, but don’t ask. It’s not my story to tell.”

“When do you want Matti and me to brief you on our preliminary plans?”

“Since the Rifle Regiment companies are already dispersed throughout the main settlements, may I assume you intend to spread out the 21st Regiment’s squadrons as well?”

"Yes. We're ready for you in the operations conference room unless you'd rather we do this later."

Morane climbed to his feet.

"Anything to help calm my irritation after meeting Severin Downes, formerly Count Hallibrank. Lead on."

**

When the daily command conference broke up the morning after Morane's run-in with Downes, Gwenneth lingered until only the two of them remained in the room.

Morane gave her a curious glance.

"Is there something on your mind, Sister?"

"News of the treatment you gave Mister Downes has spread through the political prisoners like wildfire. I'm not sure incarcerating him was wise."

Morane sighed.

"You may be right. But the damn idiot not only got up my nose the moment he opened his mouth, he and his ilk also represent everything that's been wrong with the empire since Stichus Ruggero usurped the throne."

"Downes described the incident in a most inflammatory manner and is stirring up no end of unrest among his fellows. Unfortunately, the deeply negative atmosphere he's creating causes my Brethren further distress. We will persevere, but I must ask how long before we may at least move some of the political prisoners to Matti's camps if we can't yet send them into the community? Since the Brethren voted in favor of Chancellor Reyes' offer, the land is ours, and Lieutenant Grimes has begun to set aside shipping containers we can transform into housing. Thus, everything is in place to found our new abbey. We would like to resume a monastic life, yet we cannot leave this place until you free us of our duty to the prisoners. Void Brethren do not walk out on their commitments."

"Perhaps I should send the entire lot to the Windies. Get them out of our hair while the colonial government helps us prepare the training camps to receive semi-permanent residents. I don't care about forcing the politicals to live in austere conditions, but food, medical care, and the like must come from Gus Logran's administration. We don't have the resources, and it's not as if the buggers can work for a living before the courts vacate their sentences."

Gwenneth grimaced.

"That will be another point of contention. Half of the politicals expect the sort of sinecure they enjoyed at court, while the other half hopes to live off the first half's sinecures."

"The Windy Isles it is then. Leave the useless bastards there for a year and teach them a lesson they won't forget. It'll save us converting Matti's training camps into holding facilities."

"As much as I'd like to agree with you, such a sentiment would come from the part of me I strive to keep in check. Still, it would be a blessing if you could give the colonial administration a little shove and move some of them out of the barracks."

"Such as Downes and his cronies. Understood." He gave her a crooked grin. "I will do my utmost to hasten the chief administrator at our next meeting, but the moment I put forth the principle that our armed forces must report to the council, not the administration, I lost most, if not all of his goodwill."

"A shame. At least the public safety people were diligent in removing the common criminals destined for work farms. I believe the last of them left yesterday."

"Small mercies."

"The criminals were never our concern. Those I spoke with were happy they landed on a better world than Parth."

"The politicals might not once they fully understand their situation, but I can't see the Windies being any worse than Parth's Desolation Island."

Gwenneth gave a small shudder at hearing the name of humanity's harshest and deadliest open-air prison, a place of exile from which no one returned.

"May the Almighty look kindly on the souls marooned there."

"Indeed. Because no one else will."

— 15 —

Mykonos

Skurka let the transport glide to a silent stop a few meters before the checkpoint, a horizontal metallic pole running across the street. Its ends sat atop dented cubic shipping pods. He could make out half a dozen figures on either side, all armed. More probably lurked behind scabrous, battle-scarred walls on either side.

One of the figures, wearing castoff armor and carrying a military issue carbine, approached the driver's side. A single glance told Skurka the man didn't move or hold his weapon like a trained soldier. He stopped a good two meters from the cab and gestured at the mercenary to open his window.

When Skurka complied, the man asked, "Crown or freedom?"

"Neither, friend. We're ordinary folks trying to survive."

"What's your business in Tiryns?"

"We want to find a ship heading west, to Karinth, where people hopefully aren't killing each other because of fucked up politics."

The man studied Skurka for a moment.

"You look like a soldier," he said in an accusing tone.

"I was a private military consultant working for the local merchant guild before the rebellion. Now I'm just another displaced person trying to keep his head attached to his neck."

A grunt.

"What's in the back of your truck?"

"Eleven more tired people who want to escape the madness with my friend and me." When Skurka glanced at Sister Averyl, he saw her staring intently at the shadowy figure. "I'm not carrying any cargo or other valuables. Feel free to check. Just so you're aware, a few worked with me on the merchant guild contract, meaning they're armed and armored, but only for self-protection. None of them owe allegiance to either the Crown or Jorge Danton."

"Then you won't mind us looking."

"Nope. Let me warn my passengers."

Instead of replying, the man made a gesture toward his comrades at the checkpoint, then indicated the transport's back end. Two figures broke away from the group.

Both also wore mismatched castoffs, though they carried civilian pattern weapons, reinforcing Skurka's suspicion these were either concerned citizens trying to keep their part of the bombed out town safe, or predators looking for easy marks.

He heard the rear door open with a soft squeal and glanced back in time to see Cahal jump out, carbine slung at a lazy, downward angle. Yet he held the pistol grip in a way that would allow him to raise the barrel and fire almost instantly. A military professional would recognize the stance, but neither of the men took notice.

"I'd consider it a favor if you tried to avoid making a lot of noise," Cahal said in a conversational tone. "There are two terrified wee ones inside, and it's taken us this long to calm them."

Neither of the checkpoint guards replied, though they silently stuck their heads through the opening before one of them turned to the first man.

"Eleven with the big guy here, including a pair of kids, Jake. Three armed. No cargo. Want us to frisk them?"

Jake, eyes still on the control cabin, met Sister Averyl's intent gaze.

"No. They can go."

Moments later, the transport came to life again, and they passed the checkpoint.

As a gray dawn chased away the night's last tendrils, it quickly became plain that apart from the suburbs, Tiryns had suffered less than Petras. Compared to the star system's capital, half ravaged by rebel and loyalist troops over the previous weeks, the port city seemed only superficially wounded.

Once a bustling center of commerce, Tiryns appeared to exist in a sort of stasis, unable to greet the new day. But soon Skurka and Sister Averyl saw movement in the shadows, lights coming on behind curtained windows, and doors opening furtively, proof many citizens hadn't fled into the countryside, or worse yet, died at the hands of the warring factions.

The main docks were on the banks of the Celadon River, a kilometer or so upstream from where it merged with the waters of Tiryns Bay and two kilometers beyond the town center.

Surprisingly, the port itself was more or less intact, as if the combatants had tried to spare that particular piece of critical infrastructure from the wider orgy of destruction.

However, where a dozen ocean-going vessels would fill most of the berths at any one time, they found only two smallish, beetle-shaped cargo ships, one in the process of off-loading, the other taking on containers. Both were skimmers, built to rise above the waves once out on the open waters, and capable of reaching the western continent of Karinth in under two days.

The port's perimeter fence and security gates were casualties of war, allowing Skurka to reach *Laertes*, the on-loading ship, unhindered. He parked the transport near one of the gangways, careful to avoid blocking any of the autonomous cargo handling bots scurrying back and forth between the ship and the nearest warehouse, itself scarred by gunfire.

The tang of salt air greeted them when they climbed out, a pleasant change from the faint miasma of burned polymers, pulverized stone, and smoldering hydrocarbons that hung over downtown Tiryns even this long after the last skirmish.

Sister Heloise and Hartwood Cahal teamed up to negotiate the group's passage while the remaining mercenaries and Void Brethren clustered around the truck, nervously eying their surroundings for any signs of Danton's soldiers or what remained of the Tiryns police battalion. Marta and the children stayed inside the transport, out of sight, as ordered. Moments after Heloise and Cahal vanished into the black maw at the top of the gangway, a soft rain started falling.

They reappeared almost half an hour later. Although Heloise seemed as impassive as ever, relief shone on the mercenary's tired features.

"By the shit-eating grin you're wearing, boss, I'll guess we're sailing the ocean blue in a few hours," Skurka said in a low voice once Cahal and the sister rejoined the group. "Am I right?"

Before Cahal could answer, Heloise nodded.

"Indeed. We may go aboard now and settle in. *Laertes* is due to leave in ninety minutes."

"It won't be a luxury cruise," Cahal warned. "*Laertes* doesn't normally take passengers, but it's sailing short-handed, thanks to the rebellion, so there's one crew cabin available. But she'll take us away from this place and hopefully to a saner part of Mykonos. Besides, half of us will stand guard, so we don't need racks for everyone."

"Mind you, it cost us most of our remaining funds," Heloise said, "so we must stretch our rations. The price of our passage doesn't include food or drink other than water."

"Stand guard, boss? You don't trust the boaties?"

"I trust no one I don't know, Yann." Cahal indicated the gangway, then Dufour's winger. "You and Raynor lead the way. There's a boatie up top waiting for us. Colyn, you and I will hang around here until we're about to leave. Let's put her ladyship, the bairns, and the Brethren aboard. We're almost clear, folks, but not quite."

"What about Anders and the others?" Skurka asked.

A grimace creased Cahal's face.

"He knows where we're headed, Colyn. And he knows the deal. We see the civilians to safety. Everything else is in the Almighty's hands."

******

"Shit."

Colyn Skurka's heartfelt curse yanked Hartwood Cahal from his contemplation of a silent loading gantry looming over the pier. Frozen into place since before the rebellion, it seemed like an oversized industrial sculpture underlining Tiryns' reason to exist. Both troopers stood in the entry port's shadows at the top of the gangway, weapons slung, waiting for the moment of departure.

"What?"

"My sensor detected a combat car near the port's main gate."

"A routine patrol?" Cahal checked his carbine out of habit, to make sure it was ready, then glanced at the readout in his helmet's heads-up display. "Lousy timing. If the boaties are on schedule, we cast off in just over five minutes."

"I can't think of any other reason for the poxed Guards to show up so early on this fine morning, boss. But if they're patrolling Tiryns, why were civilians working that checkpoint?"

Cahal grunted.

"Your guess is as good as mine."

He opened the unit push and sent a terse warning to Yann Dufour and Raynor Day, standing guard at the cabin door.

"What should we do?" Skurka asked.

"Make them believe we're just honest citizens about to take a cruise. What else? I doubt they'll immediately figure us for being survivors of Danton's mercenary massacre."

A pair of low-slung, gray, ground-effect combat cars with 84th Guards Regiment markings slowly made their way around the warehouse and onto *Laertes'* pier. They stopped short of the ship and idled silently for more than a minute. Cahal knew the soldiers inside were scanning them with military-grade equipment and couldn't fail to notice two armed and armored men at the entry port.

One of the cars settled on the cracked concrete. Its aft ramp opened to disgorge half a dozen soldiers in full fighting gear led by a centurion. Cahal stepped out onto the gangway and waited for them to approach.

"Can I do something for you, Centurion," he shouted when the soldiers were within earshot.

"You can drop your fucking weapon and put your hands on your head, asshole," the man replied. "Your fire team buddy as well. I know who you treasonous vermin are."

The naked aggression in the centurion's voice caught Cahal by surprise, but instinct took over in a flash. He fell backward, through the entry port, and took cover to one side, opposite Skurka.

"Let's not make this harder than necessary, Centurion. We're leaving in a few minutes, and it would be a shame to spoil our peaceful departure with a shootout nobody wants. Neither my winger nor I are your enemies or the enemies of Governor General Danton."

"You mistake me for someone who gives a shit. A fugitive wanted by the star system government is aboard this ship. We will find her, and those who oppose us will die on the spot. It's in everyone's interest to cooperate. Now drop your weapons and surrender, or I will open fire."

Cahal was aware the Guards could force their way in, but not before he and Skurka gave them a hard time, something the centurion must have figured out as well, hence threats instead of a direct attack. But even if they fought, two against a platoon backed by combat cars wouldn't last long.

And then what? They'd take Lady Marta and the bairns, and massacre the Brethren on the spot. Besides, any moment now, *Laertes'* captain would figure out it was better to expel his last-minute passengers so his ship could escape Tiryns unscathed.

"What fugitive are you talking about, Centurion?" Cahal asked, temporizing while he desperately searched for a solution.

"Lady Marta Norum, you idiot."

"What the fuck makes you think she's here?"

"Because your late commanding officer, Anders Proulx, told us under field interrogation she intends to take a ship in Tiryns, and what do I find when I check the one preparing for departure? More mercenary scum of his sort."

A vicious curse escaped Cahal's lips unbidden.

"You fuckers killed him?"

The centurion made a hand gesture at an unseen watcher inside his combat car. Seconds later, a bloody, naked body was tossed out the aft opening. It landed on the grimy concrete with a dull thud. By the angle of Proulx's neck, Cahal figured it was broken and the man dead.

"He took a long time to die. Longer than his men. You and your winger are the last survivors. Give me Norum, and I might let you escape. She's the only one I want."

The fact he was still talking meant the centurion definitely didn't want to fight his way aboard if he could help it.

A soft voice from inside the ship, one filled with sorrow and resignation, startled Cahal.

"I heard everything, Hartwood. I'm sorry for Anders and the rest of your comrades, but this is the end of our run together. More innocents will needlessly die if you try to fight them off for my sake."

"What do you mean, Milady?" The mercenary asked in a gruff tone, though he already knew what her answer would be.

Instead of replying, she shouted, "I am Marta Norum, Centurion. What is your purpose?"

"Governor General Danton ordered we bring you to him unharmed, Lady Marta."

"Only me?"

"He mentioned no one else."

She took a deep breath before stepping into view.

"If I surrender, will you let everyone else sail away aboard *Laertes* in peace?"

"No!" Cahal hissed. "Stefan and Sigrid need their mother, Milady."

Norum gave the mercenary a sad smile.

"I want them to live, Hartwood," she said, pitching her voice for his ears only. "And if I don't negotiate everyone's safe departure, I will find myself the sole survivor. The needs of the many must triumph. Danton wants me alive for a reason, and it won't be to stage another public execution so he can further consolidate his grip on power."

"Nothing prevents him from killing us after he has you in his custody."

"Indeed. That's why you will shoot me if the Guards try to keep this ship and everyone else aboard from leaving Tiryns unharmed. Surely you can kill an unarmored woman from a great distance. After all, you're a Marine, a veteran of the 77th Imperial Regiment."

"But—"

She raised a restraining hand.

"This is how it must be. My life for that of my children. If we're to convince the Guards officer I will die should he play us false, I need your undying pledge you'll obey me without reservations. Anything less and the bastard might suspect we're bluffing. Promise you will shoot me if he shows any signs he might prevent this ship from sailing away."

Cahal searched her face but saw nothing more than grim determination. He inclined his head.

"I hear and obey, Milady. If the Guards bastard tries anything, I will take your life and leave him with nothing."

"And for that, please accept my undying thanks." She raised her voice once more. "Centurion, I surrender. In exchange, you will allow *Laertes* and my companions to leave in peace."

"I give you my word," the Guards officer replied after a moment of hesitation. "Your surrender in exchange for their escape."

"Your word means nothing, Centurion. Not after your regiment forswore its oath and rebelled against the star system's legitimate ruler."

She felt satisfaction at watching his cheeks redden with a mixture of anger and embarrassment.

"Here is how it will be. I will leave this ship and stand on the pier, unencumbered, while my companions leave. Should you try to fire on *Laertes* or otherwise keep it from sailing away, First Sergeant Hartwood Cahal, Imperial Marine Corps, retired, and a better man than you'll ever be, will shoot me. One round, one death. Needless to say, Governor General Danton won't forgive you for such a blunder. Your own demise won't be quite as swift or as painless, I'm sure. That is my proposal. Take it or leave it. Should you refuse, we will fight, and I will die one way or the other, as will you."

Another pause while the officer digested her words, then, "Agreed, Milady."

She glanced at Cahal again.

"Take care of Stefan and Sigrid, Hartwood. See they're safe and make sure they know their mother loves them beyond words. They don't know I'm leaving. We had no time for goodbyes."

"Promised, Milady. I give you my oath as a Marine. I'll make sure the wee ones suffer no harm, even if it means my men or I die trying."

She reached out and touched his cheek with her fingertips.

"You're a good man and a good friend. Perhaps we will meet again, and I can thank you properly for everything you've done."

"I'm sure the Almighty won't leave your bairns without a mother for long," he replied in a hoarse voice.

"The galaxy is full of orphans these days. Farewell, Hartwood."

Heloise, who'd remained unheard and unseen until now, said, "I will come with you, Marta. Not as one of the Brethren, since revealing I belong to the Order of the Void would mean instant death, but as your personal attendant, a sworn liege woman if you wish."

Marta turned to face her. "Why?"

"Because this is my path, set by the Almighty, now that you chose to sacrifice your freedom for the lives of the others." Heloise sounded so confident, so serene, both Norum and Cahal were struck speechless for a few seconds.

Marta met the sister's impassive eyes and understood any attempt to dissuade her would be futile.

"Thank you."

After a final nod at Cahal and Skurka, she stepped out onto the gangway.

"Centurion, I am bringing my personal attendant with me. I'm sure the governor general understands a lady of my rank cannot travel without one."

"As you wish," he replied. "Whenever you're ready."

Both women walked down the shallow ramp slowly, with the sort of stately poise befitting a noblewoman of the empire and her lady-in-waiting.

Shortly after that, a glum Cahal, now stretched out on the ship's upper level, his weapon pointed at Norum's back, watched her and Heloise shrink in the distance through his gunsight while the soldiers waited patiently by their combat cars. He kept his aim until *Laertes* reached the Celadon's ever-widening mouth and they finally disappeared from view.

Cahal left his perch and headed for to the berthing deck with a heavy heart, knowing his next and exponentially more difficult task, would be explaining to Sigrid and

Stefan why their mother left them in his and the Void Brethren's care.

— 16 —

The Guards centurion proved to be surprisingly courteous, enough so Heloise figured Jorge Danton had put a substantial bounty on delivering Marta Norum unharmed and healthy. The trip back to Petras in the combat car's rear compartment seemed stunningly brief and made a mockery of their long, painful trek from the capital to Tiryns.

Laertes would surely still be within sight of the coast as they climbed the bloodstained steps of Government House. Marta stopped on the veranda and turned to the western horizon, wondering what sort of life awaited her children.

The centurion coughed politely to attract her attention.

"Milady, Governor General Danton is waiting for you in the reception room. If you'll please follow me."

She turned a cold stare on him.

"Since this was once *my* residence, I shall dispense with your services and find my own way to the reception room. You're dismissed."

The centurion snapped to attention and saluted out of sheer reflex at her commanding, aristocratic tone, proof he remained an imperial creature by training beneath a rebel's veneer.

"Of course, Milady."

Once inside the opulent foyer, Heloise said, in an amused voice pitched only for Marta's ears, "Some might suggest you were rather unkind to the centurion, my dear."

"How so?"

"He clearly hoped to bask in Jorge Danton's gratitude as well as his riches. You deprived him of the honor."

Marta let out a soft and rather unrefined snort.

"Tough. I didn't surrender to flatter the ego of a treasonous subaltern who murdered a dozen private security consultants guilty only of helping innocents escape a vile creature such as Jorge Danton, may the Almighty damn his soul."

"Danton damned his own soul a long time ago."

"Which doesn't do much for his victims, since he's still among the living."

"Danton's turn will come."

Watched closely by armed soldiers standing guard at regular intervals along the main corridor, Marta led them unerringly to the reception room where, in better times, her late husband would formally receive envoys, senior officials, and other notables.

They entered without knocking, let alone announcing themselves only to find Jorge Danton seated on the throne-like chair Marta's husband had disdained as overly pretentious. Guards officers resplendent in silver-trimmed black uniforms, their right shoulders dripping with the twisted gold cords appropriate for aides-de-camp to a star system governor general flanked him. Danton was clearly expecting his prisoners, though when he noticed they weren't accompanied, a frown creased his broad forehead.

"Lady Marta." Danton gave her a polite nod when she stopped in the middle of the room and looked around as if he were not present. "Thank you for accepting my invitation without causing a fuss. Now who is this woman, and where are Sigrid and Stefan?"

Norum's cold stare finally settled on her husband's murderer.

"Where my children are is none of your concern, Jorge. Neither you nor I will ever see them again, though I expect they're about as safe as possible on Mykonos these days, especially with your incompetent thugs running the show. And this is Heloise, my lady-in-waiting."

Danton's eyes narrowed in disbelief.

"I don't recall you ever taking a personal assistant, Lady Marta. When did you hire her?"

"That is also none of your concern. I decided the circumstances called for a companion sworn to me. Where I go, Heloise goes, end of story. Now why did you send your rabid curs to fetch me, and why such concern for my welfare?"

Danton raised a thick hand to rub his chin as he considered her. Marta noticed the gleam of a governor general's large gold ring on his thumb — her late husband's property.

"Grand Duke Devy Custis, who now rules the Coalsack, commanded me to find you and send you to Yotai unharmed."

An air of disdain settled over Marta's tired face.

"What does that overweening sociopath want with me? Or did he not share the reason with his oversized lapdog? Tell me, Jorge, how long do you expect to keep your own head on your shoulders with someone like Custis as ruler of this sector? I can't see him trusting a former Imperial Guards officer who forsook his oath to seize absolute power on Mykonos for himself. You should expect a battle group from the 16th Fleet to appear in orbit any day now, escorting Devy's own choice of governor general. If you're lucky, Custis might exile you to Parth instead of pronouncing a death sentence."

Danton waved her words away with a dismissive hand gesture.

"Doubtful. Admiral Zahar backed me when I triggered the rebellion on Mykonos, and he's not a man who'll allow anyone to double-cross those who served him well."

"Whatever helps you sleep at night. Why does Custis want me on Yotai?"

"He didn't say, but I can guess. Can you?" A sly smile tugged at his thick lips.

"I'm not interested in playing forty questions. Humor me."

Danton turned to the senior of the two aides, a colonel Norum couldn't remember seeing before today.

"I'll speak with Lady Marta in private now, Axel. Please leave us."

When the colonel, trailed by his junior, closed the reception room door behind them, Danton sat back and said, "It's simple, Milady. Emperor Kal IV's blood flows in your veins via your mother's branch of the family tree."

"So?"

"You still can't see it?"

"I can see many things, but I want to hear what fevered dreams your diseased brain can produce."

"Grand Duke Custis plans on raising a new imperial flag over the Coalsack Sector as a prelude to reuniting human worlds under a fresh crown. And to do so, he needs a figurehead sovereign with a legitimate connection to an imperial bloodline, no matter how tenuous, such as the descendant of Kal IV."

"Nonsense. Devy can play emperor among the ashes as much as he wants without a puppet empress to give himself legitimacy."

"Only if he keeps his ambitions confined to the Coalsack. Convincing other sector viceroys to acknowledge Yotai as the imperial capital will be easier under a sovereign who can not only trace her bloodline back to the last of the legitimate emperors but isn't tainted by Dendera's lunacy."

Norum rolled her eyes.

"Speaking of lunacy. Does little Devy believe he can put out the fires Dendera started and glue the shattered pieces of her realm together again? He'll be lucky to keep the Coalsack intact. Human history is replete with examples proving that once an empire begins to crumble, it can't be saved, especially after outlasting its natural lifespan by a wide margin, like ours."

Danton seemed taken aback by the venomous scorn in her voice.

"I don't know his intentions, Milady and was merely theorizing based on the available evidence."

She scoffed.

"Perhaps. I wouldn't put it past Devy Custis to confuse his fantasies with reality. Since he can't marry into the Ruggero bloodline, why not set up a rival court, complete with a new empress to claim Dendera's crown? I suppose watching him try will keep me amused until the scheme comes crashing down around his ears, along with what remains of centralized government in this part of the galaxy. When do Heloise and I leave for Yotai?"

As he visibly hesitated before answering, an evil smile pulled up the corners of Marta's mouth.

"Oh, dear. Are you thinking of stealing Devy's plan for galactic domination and becoming the Coalsack Sector's regent with me as your figurehead empress?"

The flash of anger in Danton's eyes confirmed Marta's suspicions, and her smile turned to derisive laughter.

"Don't even think about it, Jorge. You'd need Admiral Zahar's backing, and he's more likely to make himself regent of Devy's stillborn second empire than let you become his lord and master. To him, you're nothing more than a crude, but useful tool.

"Besides, where Devy might have the faintest of chances to succeed if the Almighty, fate, and every god in the galaxy smile on him, you have no chance whatsoever. Oh, don't worry, Devy need not find out about our conversation. As you indicated, this is speculation. Of course, a promise you won't hunt for my children and their protectors will go a long way to ensuring my silence. Better yet, consider them dead and buried. But it would be in your interest to send us on our way as soon as possible, lest Devy suspect you might hold me back for nefarious reasons."

Danton's jaw muscles worked for a few moments as he chewed on his anger at being found out so quickly. Thank the Almighty he'd sent his aides out of the room. Otherwise, one or both of them might get the bright idea of telling Harvey Marat, who'd delight in proving his loyalty to Custis by seizing power and executing his predecessor.

"I'd like to do so, but Grand Duke Custis specified he would send a ship once I informed him of your detention. You'll be my guests until it arrives, which could take a week or more if the 16th Fleet's Yotai battle group is otherwise occupied. In the meantime, my junior aide will take you to the guest quarters where you'll stay under guard."

"No need for that preening popinjay to bestir himself, Jorge. I know the way. If you haven't emptied out the residence's wine cellar yet, would you be a dear and tell one of your flunkies to bring us a bottle of the Stark Castle fifty-five with our lunch? I think after this morning's events, Heloise and I deserve to put on a decent buzz."

She gave Danton a mocking bow before turning away and leaving the reception room, Sister Heloise in tow, without waiting for a response, let alone his permission.

"Wow," Marta said in a soft voice once they were in the guest suite. "I can't recall the last time my mouth ran away from me like that. It was — exhilarating is the right word, I think."

"And entertaining." Heloise gave her a weak smile.

"Though I'd gladly slit his throat with a knife instead of using mere insults to wound his pride. And yes, before you say it, I'm aware our every word is being recorded for Danton's benefit. I don't mind letting him know how I feel."

"I was not about to remonstrate with you, Milady. And since Jorge Danton's days are numbered, it doesn't matter in the slightest," the sister said over her shoulder as she examined the suite's amenities.

"Why do you say that?"

"The shadow of death is already reaching for his soul. He'll not see another summer solstice." Heloise paused before adding, "Nor will those surrounding him."

A shiver ran up Marta's spine, triggered in part by the contradiction between Heloise's prophetic words and her matter-of-fact tone.

"What do you mean?"

"Precisely what I said. Don't ask me to explain because I cannot, but I know Mykonos' tribulations are only beginning, and when they end, little will remain."

The grim finality of Heloise's words stilled any further questions. Instead, Marta asked, "Could my lady-in-waiting perhaps draw me a bath? I haven't washed in so long, I'm not sure what cleanliness feels like anymore."

"Of course."

— 17 —

Lyonesse

"Good morning."

Governor Yakin swept into the conference room with her usual energetic grace and settled into the carved, throne-like chair at the head of the table.

"You'll be pleased to know I just signed off on the legislation creating the Lyonesse Defense Force and approved the Colonial Council's nomination of our first chief of staff. That was quick work, everyone. It shows how much we can do if we're of one mind."

She smiled at Morane.

"Congratulations on your appointment. Are you sure you don't want to be titled captain general?"

He inclined his head respectfully.

"No, Your Excellency."

"Rear admiral it is, then."

"I was thinking commodore would be high enough, considering the size of our armed services, Madame."

Yakin gave him a mock frown.

"Herewith an impromptu executive order for you, Admiral. No more arguments about your rank. I am now the commander-in-chief, and even if the title is mostly ceremonial, I expect a certain amount of deference on your part." She reached into her pocket and withdrew something. "Hold out your hand."

Morane complied, and Yakin dropped a rear admiral's two stars into his palm.

"I suppose we should have done this more formally, but since you've been an admiral in everything but name since before your arrival here..."

"Thank you." Morane removed the gold captain's bars from his battledress collar, tucked them in a pocket, and replaced them with the twin silver stars as if such a promotion was an everyday event. "Would now be the right time to ask that you preside over the Lyonesse Defense Force's official stand up ceremonies at Base Lannion?"

"It would, and I accept with great pleasure. Shall I find a suitable uniform to wear?"

"If Your Excellency so wishes. I'm sure we can fabricate something to your specifications. With a vice admiral's three stars and a viceregal representative's gold cords, I should think." Morane turned to Hecht and Logran. "You are, of course, invited as our principal guests of honor, gentlemen."

The speaker beamed at him, though his joviality didn't reach his cold, calculating eyes.

"Thank you, Admiral."

Logran, on the other hand, gave Morane a silent, grudging nod, arms crossed, proof he still smarted at losing the argument on civilian control of the armed services.

"Unless you'd like to discuss other items related to these matters, Admiral, we should go on with the day's business."

"Certainly, Madame. I have nothing else."

Yakin turned her gaze on the increasingly ill-tempered chief administrator.

"The floor is yours."

Logran straightened in his chair and gave Morane a squint promising trouble.

"Thank you, Your Excellency. It pains me to bring up a matter concerning the political prisoners."

"I hope you're about to tell us the courts voided their convictions and the social service agencies stand ready to integrate them into the community, Gus," Morane said. "We can't keep them penned up for much longer, never mind the strain on defense force resources when we should be rebuilding."

Logran pointedly ignored his intervention.

"Madame, when we approved our chief of the defense staff's plan to resettle the politicals in colonial militia training installations, we weren't informed conditions would almost resemble those of concentration camps."

"No one thought they'd live in the lap of luxury, Gus, but concentration camps? That's more than a little dramatic." Morane shook his head. "Our own troops spend several weeks per year in those installations, and as free citizens of Lyonesse, they're hardly the sort to accept mistreatment without saying a word. Besides, it's only until your folks sort things out and we can set them loose. It's not like they're being worked to death."

"Why you think we have a problem on our hands?" Hecht asked.

"Because of the appalling conditions in those camps, Rorik. My office has received complaints from the politicals accusing *Admiral* Morane of neglecting their welfare, abusing their rights, and generally treating them without compassion or consideration."

"In the space of a few days? They're quick to complain." Hecht shook his head, eyes aimed at the ceiling, as if beseeching the universe for sanity. "But then, they're pampered Wyvern nobles and not frontier colonists like the rest of us."

Yakin raised a restraining hand to forestall any further back and forth.

"Could the chief administrator's allegations contain a hint of truth, Admiral?"

"Certainly not, Madame."

Morane repressed an urge to give Logran the stink eye. He could well imagine who made the complaints, and how they filtered up to the chief administrator's people.

"The politicals live in the same conditions as our defense force members when they're occupying the training camps, and are fed the same rations, courtesy of the Colonial Administration. We also added amenities the troops don't enjoy such as entertainment suites, book repositories, expanded sports facilities and more, as well as spiritual support courtesy of the Void Brethren. The troopers assigned to provide security treat the politicals with the same respect and consideration they show any citizen of Lyonesse.

"Are they as comfortable as if they were in their fine mansions on Wyvern? No, but we're not talking prison camp hardship, let alone what they'd be enduring on Parth if it weren't for my battle group. Perhaps what the detainees find objectionable is the fact we're making them take care of their own food preparation, cleaning, and other domestic duties rather than turn my soldiers into servants."

Hecht let out a bark of derisive laughter.

"Figures."

"What I don't understand," Morane continued, "is how word reached Gus' office, and from whom. The detainees are supposed to stay incommunicado until we regularize their status."

When Logran didn't respond right away, Yakin cocked a carefully sculpted eyebrow at her chief administrator.

"Would you care to explain?"

"The most serious complaint came from Severin Count Downes of Hallibrank, but there were others, from other camps. The how is through employees of the Department of Government Services working for the defense force as maintenance staff. Count Hallibrank's complaints, in particular, came to me via a sanitation engineer at the Caffrey Training Camp who noted the prisoners' plight and did the right thing by informing his superiors."

Morane couldn't entirely hide an air of profound irritation at hearing Downes' name.

"I'd say it's more likely Downes somehow impressed your sanitation engineer with his noble rank and promised him or her future preferment once he gains a position suitable for a count in our society. The engineer in question is to be removed from Camp Caffrey, Gus. At once. And never be employed to support the defense force again. The same applies to anyone else agitating on the politicals' behalf."

Logran glared at Morane.

"That's not your decision to make, *Admiral*. You uniformed people may be answerable to the council, but civilian personnel still belong to my administration."

"Very well. As chief of the defense staff, I'm ending our contracts with the Department of Government Services effective midnight today. I will not allow dissemblers, climbers, and assorted lackeys who suck up to dishonest, arrogant, high-born sociopaths like Downes on any military installation. We will see to our needs. I'm confident many private businesses would be glad to offer the necessary services."

A dismissive sneer twisted Logran's face.

"And pay for them how? Your budget covers only military salaries and expenses."

"Perhaps the council will vote an amendment to our respective budgets and give me the funds you'll no longer need now that the maintenance and support of military installations is my direct responsibility."

Logran turned to Yakin. "Governor!"

"Admiral Morane is within his rights," she said in a soft tone.

"But Count Severin was the secretary to the imperial chamberlain," Logran protested. "Surely we should investigate his complaints, rather than punish people who felt they were doing their duty as compassionate, law-abiding citizens."

Yakin didn't raise her voice, though her face hardened enough to show Logran was treading on dangerous ground.

"Severin Downes was an acquaintance of my husband. They were members of the same social circles on Wyvern, circles I didn't care to join. He is anything but honest and upstanding, Chief Administrator, like many of the so-called noble born. I can well believe he and others are trying to manipulate easily impressed Lyonesse citizens with promises of future consideration once they regain their rightful places."

"Could I make a suggestion, Madame?" Morane asked, as much to diffuse the sudden spike of tension in the room as to avoid offending Logran any further.

"Go ahead, Admiral."

"We four should conduct an impromptu inspection of the Caffrey Training Camp and see for ourselves that the conditions, while austere, are humane and in keeping with the politicals' status as detainees waiting for the courts to process their release. We could leave now in one of your aircars, so our chief administrator can't accuse the defense force of covering up misdeeds."

Logran's caustic expression at hearing the suggestion caused Morane to suspect he was a recipient of Downes' promises.

Morane saw the governor hesitate and suspected the idea of speaking with a man who abetted her husband's betrayal might be too much. But then, she nodded.

"An excellent idea, Admiral. And as legal ruler of Lyonesse, even one with limited executive powers, I order the following. Titles, including my own, are henceforth forbidden, and the nobility abolished on this planet. Speaker Hecht, if the council could find time to debate my executive order and pass an appropriate act to enshrine it in our laws, I would be grateful."

"We will make room on the calendar as soon as possible, Madame. I'm sure the motion will pass with little debate."

And with those words, Morane thought, Yakin had cut the last few strands keeping Lyonesse attached to the empire. Whether anyone else in the conference room realized it, they were now indeed an independent star system, unfettered by a dying empire and a thousand years of ossified tradition.

— 18 —

Governor the no longer Honorable Elenia Yakin climbed out of the aircar and studied her surroundings. As Hecht, Logran, and Morane joined her on the rammed earth parade ground, a Marine command sergeant in green battledress uniform and brimmed field cap emerged from the headquarters building and headed in their direction. Political prisoners by the dozen converged on the open space, curious about this unexpected break in their monotonous day.

The noncom came to a precise halt six paces from the aircar and saluted.

"Command Sergeant Anno Leung, D Squadron, 21st Pathfinder Regiment, sir. I'm the duty officer."

Morane returned the compliment.

"At ease, Sergeant. Governor Yakin, Speaker Hecht, and Chief Administrator Logran wish to tour the resettlement camp and see how our former political prisoners are doing."

"Yes, sir. Certainly." Leung turned to Yakin. "Your Excellency, gentlemen, what may I show you?"

Before Yakin could answer, a loud voice suffused with the nasal Wyvern twang that set Morane's nerves on edge called out, "My dear Elenia. It is you. Thank the Almighty someone heard my entreaties."

Severin Downes broke through the throng and hurried toward the visitors, arms outstretched. A pair of Marines armed with nothing more than holstered blasters made as if to restrain him, but Morane raised his hand, stopping them. The deadly gleam in Yakin's eyes should suffice to deter Downes.

"My dear Elenia?" She parroted. "We were never formally introduced."

Downes stopped in his tracks, momentarily nonplussed by the arctic chill in her voice.

"Severin Count Downes of Hallibrank, Elenia. Your husband Wade is one of my good friends."

"My former husband, who proved to be an utterly despicable cad worthy of the imperial court's cesspool, and I do not share friends, Mister Downes. In fact, I can't recall a single friend of Wade's I didn't consider vile. And you will please address me as befits the office I hold. An ex-courtier such as yourself should know the proper forms."

Anger blazed in Downes' eyes.

"Forms? I beg your pardon, but did you forget a count outranks an honorable, especially the daughter of a minor baronet, and that a secretary to the imperial chamberlain outranks a colonial governor?"

"I am well aware of court hierarchies, Mister Downes. But we are not on Wyvern, we are in the Sovereign Star System of Lyonesse, which is no longer part of the empire. I issued an executive order abolishing titles and making the idea of a noble class anathema. Therefore, I am no longer an honorable, and you are not a count. As for being the chamberlain's secretary." She waved her hand to indicate the camp. "Your presence here is evidence enough you lost that post when Dendera condemned you to exile. Besides, your erstwhile master died before Admiral Morane found and salvaged the prison ship taking you to Parth."

Downes' jaw muscles clenched as he fought to restrain his fury.

"Are you insane? You can't simply abolish the nobility because you're annoyed at being exiled on a shitty backwater colony with no future. I can see why Wade set you aside for someone from a better bloodline."

"Mister Downes," Morane growled in a tone so menacing the man took an involuntary step back. "You will show Governor Yakin the respect she deserves, or you will find yourself in the Windy Isles before this day is out. The proper terms are 'your excellency' when you first address her, then madame afterward. Is that clear?" When Downes didn't respond, Morane raised his voice. "Is that clear, Mister Downes?"

By this time, complete silence had fallen over Camp Caffrey as everyone stared at Yakin, Morane, and Downes in astonishment.

"And so we understand each other," Morane continued, "the empire's writ no longer extends to this system, and hasn't since the Coalsack Sector rose in revolt against Dendera. Lyonesse is a self-governing, independent world, empowered to write its own laws. No one here gives a flying fuck about Wyvern, the court, or the empress. You will be simple citizens once you're released from custody. Simple citizens who will make their own way in life, without sinecures, political connections, patronage, or nepotism."

"Now listen here—"

"Shut up, Downes. Just shut up. I am beginning to regret salvaging *Tanith* and saving your worthless hides. Lyonesse might be better off if I'd left that damn ship to drift forever. The next time you wish to lodge a complaint about your living conditions, you will speak with the camp duty officer who will pass it up the chain of command for consideration. Do not try to suborn employees of the Lyonesse government again, or I will see that you're charged with corruption. Perhaps a year or two working a prison farm upcountry will force that lazy aristocratic lump you call a brain into realizing your life has irrevocably changed."

Downes' eyes shifted to Logran, but the chief administrator was staring out over the perimeter fence at the green fields surrounding Caffrey.

"Are you going to let this jumped up space rat with fake stars on his collar speak with me like that, Chief Administrator? I thought your Department of Public Safety was in charge of our well-being."

"The defense force is responsible for your welfare, Mister Downes," Logran finally muttered. "Best do as the admiral says."

Downes gave both Yakin and Morane a final poisonous stare, then turned on his heels and stomped off, pushing his way through the stunned throng.

"His sort makes me happy I'll never see Wyvern and the court again and confirms abolishing the nobility is the right thing for our planet." She lost most of her icy countenance and essayed a smile. "I'd love to see the camp now, Command Sergeant Leung."

**

Emma Reyes chuckled as Morane recounted the visit to Camp Caffrey later that evening in the Chancellors dining room at the College Club.

"I always figured our Elenia hid a reinforced titanium backbone beneath exquisite manners and the patience of a saint. She just needed the right encouragement. Finally letting out a bit of that repressed anger must have gone far to lance the old boil. The poor thing's been sitting on it for eight long years, pretending nothing could touch her. And good riddance to that aristocratic nonsense. Few will mourn the fact they can never become a lordling or grandiose lady now. And those who will regret the nobility's abolition are the sort undeserving of honors. You'd be surprised how many of my most insufferable academic colleagues dream of adding a title of nobility to their pedigree." She snorted. "As if it would hide their many character flaws."

Morane took a sip of his wine and nodded.

"But I fear once we set Downes and the other former aristocrats loose, a few of them will stop at nothing to regain what they believe is theirs by right of birth. Logran might turn his back on Downes for the moment since he sees there's nothing to gain by sucking up, but our friend Severin will try again. His sort never stops because they never learn."

"Probably. The important thing is we cast off the last trappings of empire and stepped into political adulthood, ready to find our way in the galaxy."

"Just keep in mind that while adults can call for help from their parents, star systems who declare independence, not so much. Even if our imperial or rebel parents don't yet realize we left the family home."

Reyes raised her glass in salute.

"Making sure we keep what's ours would be your job, Admiral. Though I'm of Elenia's opinion. Captain general is an elegant title for someone commanding both ground and naval forces. What happens when Brigid DeCarde succeeds you?"

"Then she becomes a major general." He emptied his glass and accepted Reyes' offer of a refill. "You'll attend the defense force inauguration ceremonies?"

"I wouldn't miss them for the world. We see little pageantry in these parts, and it'll give me an occasion other than graduation to wear a chancellor's full fig."

"I'm sure you look fetching in it."

Amused self-mockery suffused her delighted laugh.

"I look like a tall, strangely colored mushroom, thanks to the oversized Tudor bonnet *de rigueur* for Lyonesse University officers. But since change is in the air, perhaps I can force through an amendment to the faculty's ceremonial dress code. Though not in time for your parade, I suppose. The council of deans will probably argue about such a proposition for months on end without resolution."

"Sayre's Law again?"

"Yep." She toasted him and drained her glass. "It's one of the universal constants, like gravity or entropy."

"I'm sure the professors in your physics department would object to that characterization."

"Doubtful. They show no patience for petty infighting. At worst, they might say my metaphor makes no sense, which would technically be true."

"Not to change the subject, but how goes our knowledge vault project?"

Reyes sighed.

"I think I've finally convinced every last department head of the need to create repositories for their respective knowledge bases and put the necessary time and effort into producing a durable physical output we can store in your underground warehouse. I fear processing the data dumps from your starships is still pending while we search for volunteers. However, Sister Gwenneth promised me two or three dozen Brethren to help once she settles the Order into its shipping container abbey. They'll work here on the university grounds, which should thrill those among the faculty and student body who profess to be militant atheists. But that's always good for a few laughs since they don't appreciate the irony of their zealously held belief in being non-believers."

"And you?"

"What do I believe, you mean? I'm firmly in the mushy middle. Hedging my bets, so to speak. But I don't mind the Order of the Void or others like them. They serve a useful purpose beyond matters of faith, and unlike the most militant of my faculty atheists, they don't proselytize. Beyond that, I don't give it much thought. You?"

"Some days I'm part of the mushy middle, other times, I either fiercely want to believe in a higher power or strongly reject the notion. But I admire those whose faith appears unshakable, like Sister Gwenneth and her colleagues. They always seem so peaceful, so reconciled with the universe. Except when the political lordlings got the best of them. That was the first time I saw Gwenneth struggle to keep her composure. Which tells us something."

"And before we delve too deeply into metaphysics or the mysteries of the universe, could I interest you in a twenty-year-old Glen Arcturus Special Reserve? I'm reliably informed it's the only bottle left on Lyonesse, and with the empire cut off, the last of its kind in this part of the galaxy."

Morane returned her mischievous smile with a broad grin.

"Which of the political lordlings must I kill with my bare hands for such nectar?"

"No one need die for this, my dear admiral. But the nectar is hidden away in the university chancellor's official residence. Shall we scandalize faculty and student body alike by pretending to carouse behind hallowed doors?"

— 19 —

Mykonos

The door to the guest quarters opened without warning, as it often had since Danton locked Marta and Heloise into their gilded cage. Unable to cause her direct harm for fear of attracting Grand Duke Custis' wrath, he and his staff contented themselves with small irritants such as invading their privacy at the least opportune moments. Thankfully, Danton didn't even make a pretense at hospitality and kept well away from both women, which suited Marta. She didn't think herself capable of verbally assailing her husband's murderer again like on the day of their arrival, let alone sit across from him at the dining room table without using her fork as a weapon.

But worry about her children and her own future took an emotional toll. After a few days of watching Marta sink into what could soon become a crippling depression brought on by terminal hopelessness, Heloise quietly began to teach her the basic mental discipline exercises every Void postulant learned in the first few weeks after entering an abbey. Marta proved to be an apt student and not only snapped out of her funk by the middle of their second week of confinement but showed the beginnings of a Void Sister's composure in the face of difficult situations.

Both women were sitting in the lotus position on the day room's bare floor, eyes closed, spirits soaring through the universe, or at least, so it seemed to Marta's spinning visions when Danton's junior aide burst into the room.

"Your transport to Yotai has entered orbit, Milady. One of its shuttles will shortly land on Government House's private pad. Please make sure you and your lady-in-waiting are ready to leave by fourteen hundred hours."

"Understood," Marta replied in an absent voice, her inner sight, what Heloise called the third eye, still fixed on the Void.

After giving her and Heloise a strange look, the Guards officer retreated into the corridor.

A few minutes later, once both surfaced back into the here and now, Marta said, "It would be nice to know whether the others reached safety before we leave Mykonos."

Marta now knew, from late night whispers in her ear, after she began Heloise's mental discipline training, the Brethren were hoping one of the Order's starships would pass through the system and hear Sister Averyl's distress beacon. Hence the attempt at reaching Thera on the western continent where, far from the heart of Danton's thuggish administration, they could wait in anonymity.

"If I might get a few minutes of access to a communications node still in contact with the rest of the planet, I might be able to check for a message."

A crooked smile banished Marta's serious expression.

"Maybe I should make doe eyes at that commissioned Guards idiot when he comes to fetch us."

"It might be better if we wait until we're aboard the ship. Her captain will probably be more amenable to your wishes considering the importance Viceroy Custis places on your welfare."

"So I make doe eyes at him or her and hope I buy you time at a communications terminal. No problems. I'll play the future ruler of a reborn empire under Devy's wise guidance until my brain leaks from my ears if that's what it'll take."

They packed their few belongings — toiletries and clothes which once belonged to Marta and escaped destruction when the rebels took Government House. Since Heloise was approximately her size, she'd chosen a few of the more sober items, in keeping with her assumed status as a noblewoman's companion.

At fourteen hundred hours precisely, the door opened again, and an impatient-looking aide gestured at the corridor.

"Time, Milady. The shuttle is on final approach."

"I gather Jorge isn't seeing us off?" Marta asked as she swept into the corridor.

"His Excellency is otherwise occupied, Milady, but he sends his best wishes for a pleasant trip."

As they passed through Government House's back door, a pinnace-sized shuttle scarred by decades of hard use flared its thrusters one last time before gently settling on a cracked pad scoured by countless landings and liftoffs over the centuries. The craft still wore Imperial Navy crown and anchor markings even though its registration number started with the prefix identifying it as belonging to a starship from the rebellious 16th Fleet.

Moments later, the aft ramp dropped, and an officer in blue battledress uniform emerged. She stopped at the ramp's edge and raised a gloved hand to her brimmed cap in salute.

"Lady Marta Norum? I'm Lieutenant Ari Tosh of the Rancor class frigate *Vindicta*. Viceroy Custis sent us for you."

Marta inclined her head.

"I am Marta Norum, Lieutenant, and this is Heloise, my companion and lady-in-waiting. We're honored the viceroy spared one of his frigates to convey us, especially in these trying times."

Tosh seemed to accept Heloise's unplanned addition to the passenger list without question.

"The star lanes are no longer as safe as they once were, Milady. Viceroy Custis did not want to take undue risks with your welfare."

"How considerate of him," Marta murmured, glad she was able to refrain from uttering a more sarcastic reply.

"If you and your lady-in-waiting are ready to leave..." Tosh's tone turned her words into both a question and an invitation.

"We are, Lieutenant."

Marta walked up the ramp and into the passenger compartment, choosing a window seat. Heloise settled in beside her.

The shuttle lifted off without further ado, giving Marta a good look at Petras from above before the clouds swallowed them. Though the devastation left by the fighting lost its immediacy from such a distance, she could finally appreciate how widespread it was.

Cut off from the world, Marta never discovered how many died at the hands of the warring factions or as collateral damage. But the numbers must be astronomical, especially if the rest of the planet's major settlements were as damaged as its capital. She could not help wonder what sort of safety Sigrid and Stefan might find in a galaxy bent on self-destruction if Mykonos' recent descent into factional violence was an example.

Heloise must have sensed Marta's sinking mood because she reached out and gently squeezed her hand. Though the gesture didn't dispel the gloom enveloping her, it reminded Marta she was not alone, and that mere thought gave her spirits a small but welcome lift.

As they reached the upper atmosphere, she caught a glimpse of Karinth, the planet's second largest continent, though not the coastal city of Thera where, the Almighty willing, her children waited for a ship from the Order of the Void. What chances did she have at seeing them again in this life if she was headed to Yotai and they to parts unknown?

She'd been raised in an old-fashioned noble household, where stoicism was prized above almost everything else, yet silent tears rolled down her cheeks nonetheless as she clutched at the memory of happier days to ward off a renewed surge of despair.

"Take heart, my dear," Heloise unexpectedly whispered into her ear. "The Almighty would not set us on this path without a purpose."

"My heart is being sorely tested these days." A pause, then, "Will I see them again?"

"I don't know."

She looked at the sister with a teary smile, "Thank you for not lying to me."

"Avoiding the truth never ends well, even though we often wish otherwise."

**

The frigate's captain, a careworn, fifty-something woman with sad eyes met them on the shuttle deck shortly after landing.

"Welcome aboard, Lady Marta, I'm Rika Weever," she said, holding out her hand. "Viceroy Custis sends his best."

"How kind of him. Thank you for your welcome and for transmitting the viceroy's greetings. I gather you weren't warned I was traveling with my lady-in-waiting, Heloise."

"Indeed, not." Weever turned to the sister. "Welcome. Please accept my apologies in advance. I'm afraid we only prepared one VIP berth."

Marta waved Weever's apology away.

"No worries, Captain. Heloise and I will gladly share a cabin."

"Very gracious of you, Milady."

"But if I could ask for a favor?"

"Certainly, if it's in my power to grant."

"Before we break out of orbit, Heloise briefly needs access to an undamaged planetary communications node so she can make sure her relatives are settling into their new homes.   We weren't able to find a working connection before leaving. Dendera's loyalists destroyed much of the planet's vital infrastructure during their futile resistance."

Weever's eyes went from Marta to Heloise and back again, as if she sensed something unusual in the request, but didn't want to deny someone traveling in her ship at the orders of the Sector's overlord.

"The CIC will set up a link and route it to your cabin."

Weever was true to her word, and Heloise wasted little time wending her way through a cybernetic labyrinth to find a sibylline message left by Sister Averyl.

All is well.

"Averyl posted the notice three days after we parted ways. It means they reached Thera without issues and settled in to wait. Since there are no further missives, I can only assume nothing has changed."

It was the best news to reach Marta's ears in almost two weeks, and a tentative smile touched her lips. But moments later, she realized this might also be the last time she heard of her children, and the brief spark of joy vanished.

The next day, at Heloise's suggestion, Marta joined her in a deep meditative trance shortly before *Vindicta* crossed Wormhole Mykonos One's event horizon and left the star system. Though she let the tears run freely when they resurfaced, the moment of peak emotional crisis was behind her. Not for the first time, Marta wondered whether she'd have gone mad without the gentle yet surprisingly tough Sister of the Void as her companion and spiritual guide.

But Heloise seemed distant, almost lost in herself, as if something had chased away her accustomed aura of serenity. When Marta gave her a questioning look, a sad smile briefly lit up the sister's pale features.

"It's nothing. I'm overtired. Perhaps I should take a nap."

Heloise climbed into her bunk, stretched out, and closed her eyes. Within moments Marta heard her breathing fall into the regular rhythm of sleep. How she envied Heloise's ability to cut herself off from the cares of life and regenerate.

— 20 —

"Your Excellency?" General Marat stuck his head through the half-open door to the governor general's private office.

Danton's eyes broke away from the latest, and so far dismal report on the campaign to cleanse this continent of any remaining loyalist strongholds as he glared up at his military commander.

"What is it?" The acid of unrestrained irritation dripped from his tone. "If you're here to tell me *Vindicta* left the Mykonos star system, en route to Yotai as per Grand Duke Custis' orders, it could have waited until the daily update conference."

Then, the dismay on Marat's face registered and Danton waved him in.

"You look like a man who caught his most trusted subordinate in a plot to replace him."

"If only it were that," Marat carefully closed the door behind him and took one of the chairs facing Danton's desk. "*Vindicta* left, thankfully. Shortly before she crossed Wormhole Mykonos One's event horizon, Wormhole Three's traffic control buoy reported twenty-one starships crossing over from the Cascadian Sector. Their transponders identify them as belonging to the 27th *Imperial* Battle Group."

Marat's emphasis on the word imperial did not go unnoticed.

"Are you telling me a loyalist naval unit entered my star system?" Incredulity transformed Danton's sour face.

"It seems so. At last count, the 2nd Fleet was among those who didn't rebel against Dendera."

"But the Cascadian Sector is home to the 10th Fleet, and they're on our side."

Marat replied with a helpless shrug.

"Perhaps Wyvern finally realized this rebellion isn't just a few discontented admirals and viceroys indulging in a fit of pique and sent out expeditionary forces to bring them back into line. The fleets protecting the Home Sector field almost twice as many capital ships per battle group as the outlying ones."

"And their officers' devotion to the Crown is unquestionable," Danton added in a thoughtful voice. "They're as deeply conditioned as any Guards general. We can't fight off that many, Harvey."

"Indeed, Your Excellency. One doesn't need Commodore Sekine's spacefaring acumen nor her congenital pessimism to discern the obvious."

Danton scowled at Marat's openly sarcastic retort but took it as a sign of the general's nervousness. Dorean Sekine, flag officer commanding the 166th Battle Group's Mykonos Task Force was Marat's naval counterpart, though she took her orders from Yotai, not the star system governor general.

And faced with a force twice the size of hers, not to mention heavier in capital ships, Sekine might simply decline to fight and follow *Vindicta* through Wormhole One. After all, Mykonos wasn't a strategic junction, nor did it boast infrastructure vital to Grand Duke Custis' ambitions, and hard to replace starships were better used as a fleet in being, not thrown away for little gain.

"She'll bug out," Danton said.

Marat inclined his head.

"That goes without saying, which leaves us almost wide open. We have next to no long-range ordnance left and the few remaining orbital platforms won't survive a cruiser's guns for long."

"I'm open to suggestions."

"Surrender and beg for mercy? Bullshit them into believing we're loyalists who are fighting off rebel scum? Beg Dorean for space on her ships to evacuate anyone whose head will adorn the Government House gates once imperial forces land?"

"Speaking with you never fails to cheer me up." Danton's thick fingers tapped the marble desktop in an irregular rhythm as his scowl deepened. "Bullshitting them is probably out. LeGris fired off a message naming me as the leader of the Mykonos rebellion. Whether it reached Wyvern is open to question, but every damned subspace relay along the way has kept a copy since it went out as class one priority. Gambling that an expeditionary force from the Wyvern Sector won't query functioning relays is on the same level of stupid as a player who bets his entire fortune when he holds nothing more than a pair of deuces."

"Now who's being cheerful?"

Instead of replying, Danton stabbed at the screen embedded in his desktop.

"Contact Commodore Sekine."

More than a minute passed in tense silence before the miniature hologram of a naval officer sitting in her CIC command chair materialized above the screen.

"What is it, Your Excellency?"

Never one for pleasantries to begin with, Commodore Sekine, a woman well in her sixties, with a pinched face and pursed lips stared at Danton through emotionless, dark eyes.

"You're aware of the incursion from the Cascadian Sector, Commodore?"

Sekine nodded.

"Twenty-one warships are hard to miss, especially when they're not bothering to dampen their ID beacons. Since they were nice enough to let the wormhole traffic control buoy contact us before destroying it, I can only surmise the 27th Battle Group's commander wants to make sure everyone is aware they're coming at Mykonos. Otherwise, they might have tried a stealthier approach, such as sending one ship through an hour or two earlier than the rest to take out the buoy."

"The buoy is gone?"

"That's what I said. If they use standard imperial tactics, their commander will dispatch ships to Wormholes One and Two, so you can expect their traffic control buoys to vanish within the next day."

"What are your intentions, Commodore?"

"Withdraw through Wormhole One before ships from the 27th blockade it. My orders give me discretion if I face vastly superior enemy forces. My commanding officer and Admiral Zahar would rather I didn't sacrifice ships needlessly."

Danton and Marat exchanged glances.

"You're leaving us defenseless, then."

"My recommendation is surrender before they sterilize the surface with kinetic strikes. Our most recent intelligence reports suggest the empress directed loyalist commanders to show no mercy. Anything other than instant submission results in devastation. Dendera would rather rule over depopulated star systems than put up with a single spark of dissent, and the officers of the Home Sector fleets are happy to oblige."

"But they'll execute everyone in the Mykonos government and military forces if I surrender."

"Without a doubt, but by sacrificing yourselves, you can at least avoid subjecting the population to further horrors. Kinetic strikes from orbit leave lasting scars, and if they're aimed at critical infrastructure, Mykonos will go from thirty-sixth-century living standards to those of the eleventh century in less than an hour."

"Take my staff and me with you, Commodore. If we're gone, the imperials will see no reason to bombard the planet." The words came out in a rush, propelled by a sudden vision of his own head on a pike beside that of his predecessor.

A humorless cackle greeted Danton's entreaty.

"My ships are already well on their way to the hyperlimit, Your Excellency. I can't afford to turn back and waste hours taking on evacuees. If you can't stomach surrendering because you're almost certain to face summary execution, may I suggest suicide? Perhaps someone with more intestinal fortitude can hand control of the Mykonos system to the 27th Battle Group's commander in the hope your troops suffer nothing worse than forced labor in exchange for rebellion ringleaders facing imperial justice."

"I find it incredible one of Admiral Zahar's flag officers is peddling defeatism." Danton's indignant tone didn't quite mask his growing fear.

"Things will get worse for everyone before they improve. *If* they improve. I'd rather fight to save a single star system and make it secure against anyone so we can rebuild instead of wasting ships trying to protect everything against the empire's inevitable entropy. As for your fate and that of your people, we have a saying where I come from, Excellency. You made your bed. Now lie in it. After what you did, you'll get no sympathy from the spacers in my task force. Sekine, out."

The holographic projection faded away, leaving a stunned Danton to stare at his blank screen. He finally shook himself and glanced up at Harvey Marat, only to see the barrel of a high-powered blaster looking back.

"What—"

"Since I know you'll try to pull a twilight of the gods scenario and take Mykonos into the abyss with you instead of surrendering, I'll implement Commodore Sekine's suggestion. Except instead of suicide, we'll do this via murder."

Before the governor general of Mykonos could reply, Marat's blaster coughed once, and a neat black hole appeared between Danton's eyes. He remained seated upright for a few seconds, an almost comical air of astonishment on his florid face, then he fell forward onto the marble desktop with a loud thud.

"Time to disband Mykonos command, the planetary government, and any hint of military or civil authority, then head for the hills," Marat muttered to himself. "Let the imperials find a planet without leaders, without defenses and with nothing that might threaten the resumption of Dendera's misrule. But by all means, why don't we let the imperials find you, Your Defunct Excellency. It might go some way to assuage their wrath."

Marat holstered his weapon.

"You know, I never could stand the Imperial Guards, and you were one of their least appetizing specimens."

— 21 —

Lyonesse

"Lyonesse Defense Force, atten-SHUN." Rear Admiral Jonas Morane's voice echoed across the Lannion Base landing strip, converted to a parade ground for the occasion.

Fifteen hundred right feet came up off the tarmac and stamped down next to fifteen hundred left feet in unison with a mighty thump.

"Shoulder ARMS."

A disembodied voice wafted over the thousands of spectators, including, in places of honor on either side of the reviewing stand, Chief Administrator Gaspard Logran, Speaker of the Colonial Council Rorik Hecht and Lyonesse University Chancellor Emma Reyes. Quasi-invisible news drones floated overhead, transmitting live video of the ceremonies to every corner of the planet and to the starships in orbit.

"Please stand for the arrival of Her Excellency, Elenia Yakin, Governor of Lyonesse, and Commander-in-Chief of the Lyonesse Defense Force."

A silent, open-topped staff car adorned with plates bearing the governor's seal, a golden, double-headed Vanger's Condor on a green background clutching a banner with the defense force's newly proclaimed motto 'We Shall Prevail' entered the parade ground.

Elenia Yakin, resplendent in a vice admiral's dress uniform, complete with gold bullion aiguillettes hanging from her right shoulder sat in solitary splendor on the bench-like back seat. The sky blue beret on her head was the same model worn by human military forces since before the Commonwealth's formation, but it sported the Lyonesse Defense Force's condor, anchor and crossed swords emblem rather than the old, crown-topped Imperial Armed Services badge. Though they had broken with the rest of humanity, Morane wanted to keep a few links to the past, and the beret was one of them.

Her aide, Lieutenant Hetty Grimes, formerly the supply depot's commanding officer, sat up front beside the driver, a corporal from the Lyonesse Rifle Regiment. Both were in the dress uniforms of their respective branches, though Grimes also wore gold aiguillettes over the right shoulder.

The car came to a smooth stop precisely in front of the reviewing stand. Both Yakin and her aide-de-camp got out, the former climbing up the stand's steps while the latter took position beside it.

"Lyonesse Defense Force, to your commander-in-chief, present ARMS."

Fifteen hundred weapons, mostly carbines and rifles, along with the swords carried by officers and command non-commissioned officers, came up. The Rifle Regiment's band burst into 'Ruffles and Flourishes,' and the gubernatorial flag unfurled on a traditional navy mast to the reviewing stand's rear.

Yakin received the Lyonesse Defense Force's salute with the aplomb of a veteran flag officer, thanks to time well spent in practice under the sharp eye of Regimental Sergeant Major Bedros Havel, the Lyonesse Rifle Regiment's top kick.

When the music died away, Morane called the shoulder arms and invited Yakin to inspect the troops, formed into four battalion-sized units. The 21st Pathfinder Regiment, as the most senior unit present, held the right of the line. Next came the Lyonesse Rifles, who'd been granted the status of an Army regiment as per traditions predating the empire. The Lyonesse Defense Force color party occupied the center of the formation, followed by a naval contingent, under the command of Captain Mikkel and formed by spacers drawn from the three ships in orbit. The fourth and final unit, holding the left of the line, was the Lyonesse Defense Force Support Group under Captain Lori Ryzkov, *Narwhal*'s erstwhile commanding officer.

The band struck up a traditional slow march as Yakin, with Morane on her right, slowly marched down every row, meeting the eyes of each Marine, soldier, and spacer.

The march past that followed the inspection was, for the vast majority of spectators, one of the most stirring displays of martial pomp and pageantry they'd ever seen. Fifteen hundred officers, non-commissioned officers, and junior ranks passed the reviewing stand in perfect step to the sounds of a full military band augmented by the Marines' beloved bagpipes.

Once the troops were back in line and standing at the parade rest position, Governor Yakin's clear voice rang out over Lannion Base as her gaze swept the ranks.

"I don't think I've ever witnessed such an impressive display of discipline, professional pride, and esprit de corps. Certainly not from the Imperial Guards I saw on Wyvern. And I know your fighting abilities far outstrip theirs as well. I don't think it would be exaggerated to say you are probably one of the finest planetary defense forces in existence, one not only born for these troubled times but specifically created to protect what will one day become the cradle of humanity's rebirth among the stars.

"And I daresay my fellow citizens are in complete agreement. Know that I am honored beyond words to be your commander-in-chief. It is therefore with great pleasure I formally proclaim the creation of the Lyonesse Defense Force. In the name of the people of Lyonesse, I charge you with our safety and the safety of our precious knowledge vault." She raised her hand to her brow in salute. "We Shall Prevail."

When Yakin fell silent, a deep-throated roar of approval erupted from the assembled battalions, joined seconds later by the audience's enthusiastic applause. Morane, facing Yakin from twenty paces away, saw her eyes widen in surprise before a delighted smile softened her serious expression. Sergeant Major Havel might have helped her look and act like a flag officer, but nothing prepared the reserved former noblewoman for the cheers of troops who'd gleefully adopted her as their own.

After that, the rest of the ceremony went by in a blur, but when Morane marched the defense force off the parade square, they were treated to the thumping clap of spectators accompanying the rhythm of the band. Just as the troops had adopted Yakin, it seemed the citizens of Lyonesse had adopted them.

— 22 —

Yotai

"Lady Marta!"

Grand Duke Devy Custis, Regent of the Coalsack Sector, rose from behind his gilded desk and crossed the opulent viceregal office to greet Norum, hands outstretched while the silent aide who'd guided her from the palace's shuttle pad withdrew.

Norum dipped her head in the greeting typically exchanged between social equals at court.

"Devy."

Both the gesture and her use of Custis' first name without title or honorifics were designed to annoy him while showing she in no way considered herself his inferior. But Custis' broad, welcoming smile never wavered. He took Marta's hands and studied her face.

"Some might think you're less than pleased to exchange Mykonos for Yotai." He released her and waved at a settee group to one side. "Please, let us sit and get reacquainted. I believe we last saw each other well over twenty years ago when your father presented you at

Emperor Karlus' court along with your brother Madoc during that decade's gathering of the Nobilitas."

"Why should I be pleased?" Marta asked in a lazy tone as she took a deceptively comfortable chair across from Custis and crossed her legs.

"I suppose you haven't heard the latest yet. Can I offer you something? Coffee? Tea? Or perhaps one of Yotai's fabled medicinal spirits?"

Marta shrugged. "Coffee is fine."

Custis made a hand gesture which she assumed was for an unseen aide watching them.

"Minutes before your ship crossed the wormhole event horizon and left the Mykonos star system, a strong imperial task force emerged from the wormhole connecting Mykonos to the Cascadian Sector. Imperial as in loyal to Dendera. Twenty-one ships, none of them smaller than a cruiser. If our intelligence reports are correct, they're operating under orders to devastate any rebellious world which does not instantly submit to the Crown and turn over its senior political and military leadership for automatic execution as traitors. Since my own naval forces would have been annihilated had they stayed behind, I evacuated them and left Mykonos to the imperials. You made it out just in time. Judging by what Admiral Zahar told me about this Jorge Danton who took over, it doesn't look good for the planet's civilian population, never mind anyone connected to his regime."

Marta struggled to keep her bland expression against an overwhelming surge of despair. Judging by Custis' unchanged demeanor, she succeeded. But the news might explain Heloise's somber mood in the days following their departure. Could she have sensed the arrival of forces planning to punish Mykonos' treason with utmost violence in the moments before the wormhole swallowed *Vindicta*? Custis was still prattling on while she felt her heart sink into a black hole from which it might never escape.

"Pardon?" When he stopped talking and gave her a questioning look, she said, "My apologies. I'm a bit fatigued by travel and news that countless more innocents might pay for our so-called betters' feckless pursuit of absolute power."

"It is I who should apologize. Perhaps letting you rest for a day or two before we met would have been kinder, especially since you're safe under the 16th Fleet's protection."

A frown creased her forehead. "What about that imperial task force?"

Custis waved the question away.

"I doubt they'll go beyond Mykonos. Besides, their commander will know they cannot hope to enter the Yotai system with impunity. Twenty-one ships, minus those detailed to guard the formation's withdrawal route, won't make it past the wormhole defense arrays, let alone come within firing range of Yotai itself. You're perfectly safe here."

A serving bot, carrying a tray with two cups, a carafe, and various small bowls, entered the office via a hidden side door. At Custis' silent signal, it placed the tray on the low table separating him from Marta and vanished.

"Since we're among friends, my dear, I think we can help ourselves." After they'd done so, Custis took an appreciative sip and sat back in his chair. "I'm not sure whether I should ask, but the records show you and your late husband had two children which should be around eight years of age. Did they also fall victim to the unfortunate turbulence that took poor Hachim's life?"

Marta kept her eyes on her cup while she ran through one of Heloise's mental discipline exercises. Otherwise, she might chuck the hot coffee in Custis' face. Unfortunate turbulence indeed. A parade of increasingly mortal insults in a dozen human languages crossed her tongue, though none dared escape lips clamped together by main force.

Instead, she gave him a faint, almost helpless nod, though a feeling as irrational as it was pervasive told her Sigrid and Stefan still lived under the protection of Hartwood Cahal, Sister Averyl, and the rest of their small party. If the invading imperial task force commander felt compelled to sterilize Mykonos in retaliation for Danton's defiance, it would have happened by now. But Custis needn't know.

"I'm so sorry, Marta."

He almost sounded sincere. Almost. Perhaps finding out she had no living offspring fit with his plans. Or maybe, like many of the aristocratic sociopaths who spent time in Dendera's orbit, he never entirely developed the ability to feign empathy. It wasn't a useful survival skill around an empress unable to show the slightest feeling for others.

"Apologies won't bring them back, Devy. Jorge Danton was Admiral Zahar's creature, though the Almighty only knows how Zahar turned a Guards officer. If I'm to blame anyone on Yotai for losing my family, he's it." She finally looked up at him, sure her emotions were under control once more. "Now tell me, why am I here, and not dying under the empire's kinetic strikes along with the citizens of Mykonos?"

"Perhaps we should save that discussion for another time, once you've recovered from your ordeal."

"We will discuss the matter now, Devy."

Custis' reaction to the steel in her voice — back straightening, eyes hardening, and the beginnings of a scowl creasing his high forehead — seemed almost comical.

"I beg your pardon?"

"You need me for a nefarious scheme, otherwise, why send a precious frigate to Mykonos. I don't carry great military or political secrets in my head, nor do I own riches beyond imagining. And as for social climbing, the daughter of a marquess hardly constitutes a step up for a grand duke, especially one with a spouse and offspring of his own. Besides, I doubt the concept of an imperial nobility will survive the downfall of Dendera's empire."

She gave him a smile where mischief warred with contempt.

"It has to be important. You've been letting me overstep the bounds of familiarity with nary a peep. The Devy Custis I knew would never countenance such behavior from the likes of me while he was still scheming for greater power at the imperial court. Time to cut the crap, as my Uncle Olav used to say."

"Your Uncle Olav sounds like a colorful figure."

"He was a colonel in the Marines and didn't have much use for your sort, Devy, or for anyone else who wasted their life on Wyvern. He never used his title as far as I can remember or even acknowledged owning one. I can't imagine what he'd make of the current situation if he were still among the living. Probably wish a pox on everyone and find himself a quiet wormhole cul-de-sac with a pleasant, habitable planet."

Custis chuckled.

"If your uncle were still alive, he'd be too late, unless his appetite for adventure outstripped his self-preservation instincts. There was one such dead end star in the Coalsack Sector, but with frontier systems slipping out of our reach, the wormhole junctions to get there are no longer under the 16th Fleet's control."

"Oh?"

"A place called Lyonesse. Not that it matters. Star systems without strategic value aren't worth the expenditure in precious, quasi-irreplaceable ships and crews."

"That sounds a tad callous," Marta replied in an arch tone. "The inhabitants remain human beings and citizens of the empire."

"We've entered a new era of realpolitik. Practical objectives to save what we can before regrouping and rebuilding are the only things that matter. Unfortunately, it means Lyonesse, among many marginal systems, will be forced to fend for itself until a reborn empire can once more assert suzerainty."

"If they survive long enough. The empire isn't merely in the throes of another unpleasant realignment, Devy, it's dying and has been since Stichus Ruggero seized the throne. When he transformed the imperium into a hereditary monarchy, he injected a fatal virus into the body politic. Dendera is the ultimate manifestation of that disease. This time, I fear we face collapse on an interstellar level, and that means centuries, if not millennia of darkness."

A smirk creased Custis' face.

"How dramatic! But then, I understand you hold a doctorate in political history. Perhaps you're applying the wrong lessons of the past to interpret current events. Our empire is the first polity of its kind, which means we're on a path humanity has never taken. Parts of the empire are collapsing, but much of it will survive. Disunited, yes, yet capable of coming together again under more enlightened leadership."

"Your leadership, no doubt?" She allowed herself a sly smile. "Or is this where I come in? Am I to give your reborn empire the legitimacy of Kal IV's bloodline, one free from the Ruggero madness? Legitimacy without power, no doubt. As my regent, you'd be the actual ruler, the *éminence grise* behind the throne, *n'est-ce pas?* Where star system governor generals and the military's flag officers might balk at a viceroy making himself dictator for life, they would welcome the stabilizing influence of a constitutional sovereign. Especially one with impeccable credentials and not a hint of Ruggero DNA in her family tree. How am I doing, Devy?"

Custis greeted her deduction with ironic applause.

"I see you won't be the easiest of figurehead rulers, Milady. Or should I say, Your Majesty?"

"I've not agreed to play a part in your scheme yet, Devy, and I see no reason for my participation. Let history take its course. If the Coalsack Sector is destined to survive as a beacon of civilization during the long night of barbarism, it can do so without me."

"No sense of *noblesse oblige*, Marta? Your father would be sorely disappointed. You and I can reverse the empire's decline. First here in the Coalsack, then in neighboring sectors, until we reunite humanity and set the foundations for a new polity, at peace with itself and free of any Ruggero poison."

Norum made a great show of indecision, biting her lower lip and letting her eyes roam everywhere, but she'd made up her mind back on Mykonos. Though she would suffer the fate of all figureheads and live in a gilded cage, with Heloise's help, she might be able to track down her children. Besides, to borrow another of Uncle Olav's favorite expressions, what else would she do with her time? Play endless games of pinochle?

"I'll go along with your scheme, Devy, but under one condition."

His eyebrows crept up.

"And that would be?"

"You treat me as your partner in this, not as your puppet. That means you listen to my views and treat them with the consideration they deserve. I know more than you do about successful and unsuccessful forms of government, and more importantly, the history of those few polities who survived civilization-level disruption to endure another few centuries of growth, stagnation, and decline. Take it or find a descendant of Kal IV who didn't complete post-graduate work in political history."

Custis studied her with amused eyes for a few seconds, then leaned forward and stretched out his hand.

"Deal." A pause. "Your Majesty."

Though she shook hands with him, Marta knew full well he'd renege at the first clash of opinions. Devy Custis didn't suffer opposition gladly, one of the many character flaws which no doubt contributed to his expulsion from Dendera's court.

The bigger question hanging over Marta, and in no small extent, Heloise, was whether she would genuinely go along with his scheme or only until they could find Sigrid and Stefan? The historian within her knew instinctively the empire was past the tipping point, and no amount of shoring up would help. Its time was over. And then what? Would there be safety, for her children, for her, and for Heloise? And how long before Dendera's demented vengeance reached Yotai to turn the rebellious sector capital into a depopulated ruin?

Marta knew Heloise would tell her to trust in the Almighty's plan, but if such a thing existed, it seemed remarkably nebulous to her mortal eyes.

PART II - TAPS

— 23 —

Lyonesse

The communicator's insistent buzz cut Rear Admiral Jonas Morane off mid-sentence. He stabbed at the device and said, "Morane."

"Operations, sir, Centurion Haller. We received an urgent call from the Government House guard detail. Severin Downes and eight other former politicals trespassed on the grounds and are attempting to push their way in so they can petition Governor Yakin. So far, the troops are keeping them away without resorting to force. But they refuse to leave and are becoming agitated. The NCO in charge is asking for instructions. His rules of engagement don't cover this sort of situation."

Morane gave Colonel Brigid DeCarde a disgusted look.

"Why didn't we let the useless buggers stew a few weeks longer in the camps?"

DeCarde raised her hands, palms outward.

"Don't look at me, sir. I was all in favor of sending them to the Windy Isles for a year so they could learn about true hardship from confirmed criminals."

"Did the sergeant of the guard call the Lannion Police Service?"

"He did, but since the incident is occurring on star system government premises, they said it was for the military to sort out."

Morane rolled his eyes while stifling a groan. This was Chief Administrator Logran's doing. No wonder the incident landed directly on his desk instead of being dealt with by civilian authorities. The municipal police forces were answerable to the Department of Public Safety, which in turn worked for Logran. And the Lyonesse Defense Force didn't, as yet, field a military police unit.

"How about I take a troop from the rapid reaction squadron and deal with *Mister* Downes," DeCarde suggested. "In a peaceful manner, needless to say."

"A full colonel backed by the empire's former elite troopers to quell a minor intrusion? Seems like overkill."

"Sending one of my centurions or a platoon leader might end with Downes bleeding from various orifices seconds after he opens his mouth. But don't worry, I intend to work my charm on the little lordlings and convince them annoying me would be a terrible idea. The Pathfinders are coming as muscle if I need to arrest them."

"Understood. Thank you for taking care of this, Brigid."

"I need my entertainment, sir." She jumped to her feet and snapped off a salute. "But the governor needs to rip those twits a new one. They've only been loose for a couple of weeks, and this is what? The fourth incident?"

"Fifth. They seem to be slow learners for folks who once sat on the highest councils of state."

"Which explains why the empire is fucked up beyond belief."

DeCarde turned on her heels and left Morane to fume at Severin Downes' incurable sense of entitlement.

The former Count Hallibrank had been militating for aristocratic sinecures the moment the Lyonesse courts voided all political convictions and Logran's community services folks moved him and the others into various communities where they could find work. At first, his arrogant whining was a minor irritant, but Downes quickly convinced the chief administrator to resettle him and his family in Lannion instead of Trevena, as Morane had urged. At least there, he would have been far enough away to discourage impromptu attempts at pestering Yakin face-to-face.

However, the governor's ingrained sense of courtesy so far prevented her from telling Downes where to stick his demands. Unsurprisingly, he took her reticence as a sign of weakness and therefore believed he could get his way through sheer persistence. That the Lyonesse Colonial Council enshrined the nobility's abolition in law meant nothing. Downes wanted to recreate the Wyvern Court in miniature around Yakin so he could scheme, peculate, and peddle influence with impunity, a far better use of his time than honest work. Not that he'd admit it in so many words.

Ostensibly, he wanted to serve the governor as a trusted aide, an adviser, or perhaps even a chamberlain, someone to help relieve the incredible pressures of ruling a star system. Never mind that Elenia Yakin could manage easily with the counsel of her chief administrator, the head of her armed forces, and the speaker of the council.

Fortunately, a majority of the politicals took what Lyonesse offered without complaint and kept a low profile within the community, aware their fate would have been much worse if it weren't for Admiral Morane's rescue and Lyonesse's welcome. But Downes nevertheless managed to assemble a small, yet vocal group of dissidents comprising those who'd been most influential at Dendera's court before her paranoia led to their sentencing and exile.

Morane forcefully expelled Severin Rembert Downes from his thoughts and called up Sister Gwenneth's latest progress report on the knowledge vault, moving from the utterly useless to the most vital thing on Lyonesse.

**

DeCarde left Command Sergeant Tejko and Number Five Troop, B Squadron, to wait aboard the rapid reaction squadron's combat carriers parked outside Government House's walls, where Downes and his cronies wouldn't see them unless necessary. She drove in with her staff car, a silent, civilian pattern skimmer painted dark green and bearing Lyonesse Defense Force markings in black on either side.

As she came around the curved driveway, DeCarde spotted a group of civilians milling about at the top of the grand stairs leading to Government House's main entrance. They were blocked from entering by a rank of uniformed guards from the Rifle Regiment's full-time component. The soldiers held their carbines at the port, across the front of their bodies, ready to repel intruders without opening fire.

Downes' grating nasal voice assaulted her ears the moment she climbed out of the car. He was haranguing the guard detail's sergeant mercilessly, using every insult in the upper crust dictionary. The noncom, standing stiffly in the parade rest position, face blank, did his best to ignore the former count. His composure impressed DeCarde sufficiently that she made a mental note to tell Matti Kayne the man deserved a letter of commendation.

"And what's this?" DeCarde asked in a loud voice after plowing through the lordling cluster without a word of apology. "Mister Downes, will you kindly stop abusing my soldiers?"

Downes abruptly fell silent as he turned his head toward the source of the interruption. His eyes widened when he took in the oak leaf wreath and three diamonds of a full colonel.

"At last. The organ grinder," he sneered. "Your monkey here doesn't seem to understand a man of my rank has automatic access to a mere honorable, though she is a star system governor."

"And what rank would that be?" DeCarde asked in a tone so dripping with honey that a faint smile relaxed the sergeant's tense features. "As far as I'm aware, you're neither a member of the defense force nor any of the municipal police forces or the Lyonesse government."

"I'm a count, you bloody uniformed imbecile." Downes' outraged glare was almost comical. "No Guards officer would dare address me in such a manner. They're much too professional. But then Imperial Marines were never known for their couth."

"Aha," DeCarde drawled, "I think I know the reason for this little misunderstanding. Would you like me to share my theory with you?"

"The only thing I want to hear is you ordering these," he waved his fingers at the guards in disgust as he searched for an appropriate epithet, "creatures to step aside and let me in."

"So I take it that's a no? Shame, it's such a good theory." She glanced at the guard detail noncom. "Are you interested, Sergeant?"

"Yes, sir," he barked out.

"See, I think Mister Downes is suffering from severe delusions. He seems to believe he's a count even though there's no such thing as titles of nobility on Lyonesse. He also appears to be under a misapprehension I'm an Imperial Marine Corps officer when this star system isn't part of any empire. And, to top it off, he used the word Guards and professional in the same sentence when everyone knows doing such a thing violates every law of nature. What do you figure, Sergeant?"

"I think you're right, sir."

DeCarde turned a cold smile on the nonplussed ex-nobleman.

"So, Mister Downes, am I right? Are you suffering from delusions or are you merely an insufferable twit who can't take no for an answer? Think it over for a moment. If you're deluded, my troopers can bring you to the Lannion General Hospital for observation in the mental ward. If, on the other hand, you're an insufferable twit, I can toss your entitled ass out into the street, along with of your similarly disagreeable cronies. Or you could leave under your own power and never again enter Government House grounds unless invited or summoned. If Governor Yakin were prepared to receive you, her secretary would have let the guard commander know. Since that didn't happen, I daresay you're not welcome."

Downes snorted with derision.

"I'd like to see you lay your hands on me, Colonel. Facing a court-martial will be the least of your problems."

"Not that I can't pick you up by the scruff of the neck and give you the bum's rush, Mister Downes, but here are your choices. Leave now and stay away or face arrest." She let her eyes roam over the assembled former political prisoners. "A troop of Pathfinders is waiting by the gate for my signal to incarcerate you in the Lannion Base stockade until the Lyonesse attorney general decides whether charges for trespassing and threatening the governor's safety are warranted."

Downes locked eyes with her in a futile struggle for mastery before snarling, "You'll regret this, Colonel. Mark my words."

"I already regret bringing *Tanith* to Lyonesse, as does Admiral Morane. Don't make us shove you back into stasis and send you off toward the galactic center at sublight speed."

After a final, albeit silent sneer, Downes turned to his friends.

"I think we made our point. Hopefully, Elenia will find the courage to reconsider the foolish notions these colonial yokels forced down her throat."

DeCarde turned her eyes heavenward at his unthinking words. She couldn't think of anything less likely to make Yakin take Downes seriously than an accusation she lacked courage. And since it was a given she'd been watching this little drama via the security system...

Or was Downes really so arrogant he didn't think belittling the woman he wanted to petition would be held against him?

"There's a difference between hope and fantasy, Mister Downes. Try to stay with us in the real universe." DeCarde adopted the parade rest position beside the guard detail sergeant and watched them leave.

Once the former nobles vanished into Lannion proper, Government House's main door opened and Wickham Sanford stuck his head out.

"Colonel, the governor would like to offer you a cup of tea and bend your ear for a few minutes. She understands if duty calls you elsewhere."

DeCarde glanced at him over her shoulder.

"If I can beg the governor's indulgence for a few minutes, I'd like to speak with the guard detail before accepting her kind invitation."

"Of course. She's in the small conference room and asks that you join her when you're ready."

Sanford disappeared into Government House's shadows.

DeCarde stepped back so she could take in the entire guard detail.

"Stand easy, folks. What you did this morning was solid. Holding your ground without resorting to force was precisely the right thing to do, unpleasant as it might be. And Sergeant, kudos for making it seem as if you couldn't even hear Severin Downes' foul language. Decking the filthy sonofabitch would have been more satisfying, I know, but when we're exercising police functions, we can't go around beating up on civilians."

"Thank you, sir. It wasn't easy. My parents came here to escape jerks like him and his buddies. But I figure the sergeant major would chew me a new one if I indulged in a bit of asshole bashing. Can I ask why the Lannion Police didn't come to deal with this? Hauling in civilians who are trespassing and threatening to riot is their job. The only thing they told me when I called was it's on star system government premises and not their problem. When we were briefed, the centurion told us local law enforcement dealt with anything short of direct threats to the governor and Government House."

"No idea, Sergeant, but I'm sure the admiral will sort it out."

"Yes, sir. Maybe he can set up a military police unit if this is how it'll be. We're infantry, not cops trained to deal with unpleasant citizens."

"I wouldn't be surprised if that's what he does. Any more question or comments?" When the noncom shook his head, she checked with each of the Rifle Regiment soldiers, but they imitated their leader. "Then I'll let you get back to your duties. Until further notice, report any issues to the Lannion Base operations center directly, since the local cops don't seem to give a damn."

"Yes, sir. Detail, atten-SHUN."

The sergeant and DeCarde exchanged salutes before she entered Government House.

— 24 —

Morane glanced up from the weekly logistics report the moment he spied movement outside his office door.

"So?"

DeCarde grinned. "Problem solved with no injuries other than to Severin Downes' damnable pride, sir, though I doubt I made much of an impression on him. The governor asked me in for tea and biscuits afterward. Seems like a lot of politicals are slamming Government House with petitions, requests, demands, pleas, and whatever since we released them into the community. Unacceptable lodgings, unpalatable food, demeaning work, impolite government officials, you name it, they complained about it.

"Even we valiant defense force troops get our fair share of abuse. Yakin showed me a few of the more colorful messages. For example, you're a tyrannical, self-promoted sadist with delusions of adequacy while I'd be rejected as a Guards private on grounds of congenital cretinism. And that was one of the least insulting among them."

Morane rolled his eyes and sighed.

"Wonderful." He gestured at the chair in front of his desk. "Tell me everything."

"The only ones not targeted for abuse are Her Excellency, Gus Logran, and Speaker Hecht, though a few apparently hinted they consider Yakin a traitor to her social class." DeCarde sat before continuing with an air of distaste. "Setting the politicals loose gave them access to public communications nodes, and they're vomiting up every single grievance accumulated since day one. Downes and his closest followers are merely the most vocal and active of the lot. They represent the tip of the garbage dump as Madame Yakin put it, which should tell you she's quickly shedding her legendary politeness. She asked me to tell you she wishes we'd left *Tanith* to her fate in the Parth system."

"The governor, you, me, and everyone one else forced to deal with the whiny buggers. Except there were a few aboard who deserved rescuing, such as Friar Locarno and the abbey's newest novice." Morane sat back in his chair. "You know, maybe we should offer to move the lordlings and their families to an offshore island where they can set up their own little kingdom and call each other duke, earl, count — whatever tickles their fancy — and pretend the empire is eternal."

"Those useless twits would starve within a week. It's a nice idea, though. But back to this morning. The governor asked if I thought her gathering the politicals together and laying out the facts of life might help."

"I trust you told her she shouldn't acknowledge the complaints in any way? Petitioning a star system governor should be reserved for important matters, not the mewling of entitled layabouts unhappy they can't live it large on the backs of ordinary citizens anymore."

"In the most direct Marine fashion I could muster and stay within the bounds of decorum. I also suggested we shift the guard post to the main gate and thereby avoid another mini-riot on the veranda. She agreed. I've asked the supply section to make a nice-looking gatehouse from a spare container, so the troops don't stand out in the rain. As you may have noticed, this place is rather damp a lot of the time."

"Part and parcel of living a few clicks inland from a subtropical ocean. Good thinking, though."

She gave him an ironic, albeit seated bow.

"I'm not just a scary face. One thing the governor mentioned worries me, though. Gus Logran's been hinting he could hire a lot of the lordlings into the colonial administration — not exactly no-show jobs, but appointments with grandiose titles, a living wage, and little by way of menial work. Create several committees, commissions, advisory boards, that sort of thing."

An involuntary groan escaped Morane's throat.

"It's all we need. Bureaucratic bloat, Wyvern-style. As soon as you make someone like Downes chair of an advisory board, he'll damn well try to advise you. By force if necessary. Since the council needs to vote on enlarging Logran's budget so he can pay for those not exactly no-show jobs, I trust Speaker Hecht opposes the idea?"

DeCarde grimaced.

"The governor says that so far, Hecht has been suspiciously quiet and why would he object if supporting the scheme means Logran owes him? Hecht is big on snaring people into his web via unspoken political favors, something I'm sure you noticed." A mischievous smile lit up her face.

"Logran and Hecht better not dream up a defense oversight committee staffed by Downes and company, because that's where I draw the line."

"I doubt the governor would allow something that egregious, not to mention the elected council members who won't accept a committee of appointees interfering in matters reserved for the legislature. But there are probably plenty of less visible areas where they can cause no end of mischief. And yes, I told the governor you'd react this way upon hearing about Logran's idea and Hecht's lack of visible opposition."

"Good. The last thing we need to do is resurrect the empire's mistakes in miniature just so Gus Logran can please a handful of blowhards for reasons I can't fathom."

"He's a career colonial office man, Admiral. A creature of the metastasized imperial administrative apparatus. He doesn't believe, in his heart of hearts, that the empire is crumbling, leaving us alone, cut off and free to choose a different path. I'll bet good old Gus, Colonial Office drone that he is, figures kissing up to people who once wielded real power on Wyvern and might again someday, could help his career."

"You think Logran's that deluded?" Morane cocked a skeptical eyebrow.

"Yep. And he's not the only one on Lyonesse still wondering whether we're deserters from the Imperial Armed Services who exaggerated the situation for personal gain, now that memories of the reiver raid are fading."

"Where are you getting this, Brigid? Last time I checked, building an intelligence service was way down on our list of action items."

A smirk accompanied DeCarde's conspiratorial wink.

"You don't need an intelligence service if half of your troops are part-timers who live and work among the civilian population. Matti Kayne likes to pass along the local gossip when my brigade's command team gets together for coffee once a week. I presume he picks it up at happy hour in the company canteens after a training weekend or from shooting the bull with his own command crew."

"And when were you going to share this with me?"

She gave him an unrepentant look.

"There's enough on your plate without you wasting brainpower worrying about local yokels, conspiracy theorists, those who are nostalgic for the trappings of empire and other strange creatures infesting our little corner of heaven."

"Thank you. I think."

"On a related note, are you seeing Emma Reyes tonight?"

Morane's eyes narrowed in suspicion.

"Not that my private life concerns you, but yes. Why do you ask?"

"Since we're discussing unofficial intelligence gathering—"

"You mean gossip."

"Call it what you want, admiral. Some younger Rifle Regiment part-timers still studying at the university picked up evidence that more than a few faculty members are deeply unhappy with Order of the Void Brethren working on the knowledge vault."

"Not surprising. Emma mentioned a number of her professors view monastics with extreme suspicion. They'd rather we leave the knowledge vault entirely to the university, never mind it doesn't have even a fraction of the spare capacity for such labor-intensive work."

"That's well known, sure. But I just remembered something Matti mentioned the other day in passing and with what we just discussed, I wouldn't be surprised if there's a connection. It seems those disgruntled academics are talking about a cabal to challenge Emma's chancellorship so they can remove her and appoint someone less favorable to the Void Brethren. Someone who'll exercise greater, if not absolute control over the knowledge vault rather than let, and I quote, a bunch of damned mystics and military morons mess around with humanity's legacy. That comes verbatim from a cabal member overheard by one of our soldier students the other day. She also overheard the same academic, in a separate incident, mention former Wyvern officials who might be inclined to help."

"Not wise to discuss such matters within earshot of students."

DeCarde made a face.

"I get the feeling Emma's opponents believe everyone shares their enlightened opinions."

"A failing common among the self-righteous. Doesn't the Lyonesse University's Board of Trustees control who is named chancellor and aren't the trustees appointed by Governor Yakin on the advice and recommendation of the Colonial Council? I don't see how disgruntled professors can threaten her."

"And what happens when the lordlings weasel their way onto the board, thanks to back-scratching between Gus and our esteemed and rather Machiavellian speaker of the council? They replace Emma and allow the university to seize control of the knowledge vault project from those whom the dissident professors consider heretics."

Morane's eyes took on a thoughtful expression.

"Sister Gwenneth warned me early on about Hecht's ambitious character, and since knowledge is power..." His voice trailed away.

"What better way to deprive the Void and us of control over the vault than filling the Board of Trustees with those who owe Hecht a debt of gratitude. Remember, Elenia Yakin is no despot with unlimited powers. She's the closest thing to an early empire constitutional monarch we have, and that means she only has the last word on matters of interstellar, star system, and defense policy. In everything else, the council can override her with a two-thirds majority vote, which I'm sure Hecht can cobble together at need."

"Let's hope we're a pair of pessimists merely borrowing trouble."

"Sure, but I'll keep my power packs charged and my copper disks pure. You may wish to speak with Gwenneth and Emma."

"I'll do so. And tell Matti to keep the informal intelligence service in high gear."

"Already done. In return, how about you give the support group a military police company, so my grunts aren't stuck playing substitute cop with rules of engagement more suited to reiver raids?"

"Are you ready to cough up a platoon or two of volunteers?"

"I can't refuse if I'm asking, right?" DeCarde jumped to her feet. "If there's nothing else on your mind, a few administrative issues await me."

Morane returned DeCarde's salute and watched her leave his office. Why did crass politics always intrude, even on work undeniably for the common good?

Perhaps because the seven deadly sins were one of the universe's few constants, afflicting humanity until it succumbed to entropy and vanished into the mists of time. And if that was the case, did the daunting task he'd put in motion, that of preserving the best his species could offer, even matter?

— 25 —

Yotai

"Have you given any further thought about how we might ease you into the public consciousness as the reborn empire's legitimate sovereign, my dear?" Grand Duke Devy Custis handed Marta a cup of tea before settling into a chair across from her. "Please let me know how you like this blend. It comes from the south slopes of the Gandamack Range. Have you ever been there? If not, perhaps I could take you. It is one of this planet's most scenic regions."

She repressed a shudder of disgust at the man's false bonhomie.

"No. This is my first time on Yotai."

"Then we'll plan a little tour in the next few weeks, shall we?" He took a sip of his tea and smiled. "Wonderful. I can easily see you decreeing this the new imperial blend, by appointment to her majesty, Empress Marta, first of her name."

She tasted the tea before giving Custis what she figured was a suitably regal nod, though she found his brew rather ordinary, perhaps even too tannic.

"A thought worthy of contemplation, in time. I'm not yet Empress Marta, first or last of her name."

"Of course. What about my original question?"

"Did I come up with fresh ideas of how you could crown me without giving rebellious star systems royal indigestion?"

It was a matter she'd discussed with Heloise for appearances' sake, conscious Custis' intelligence people or at least their AIs were listening in. Marta had no intention of becoming Custis' figurehead in what she knew would be a doomed attempt at rebooting the empire.

"Indeed."

The insistent chime of an incoming communication saved Marta from answering. An irritated expression briefly creased Custis' forehead as he waved his hand in a pattern signifying he accepted the link. Within seconds, Admiral Zahar's foreshortened hologram appeared above the low table between them.

"I trust this is important, Admiral. Lady Marta and I were about to discuss future constitutional arrangements."

"It could be, Your Grace. One of my intelligence teams may have found the trail of that mysterious battle group from the 19th Fleet which salvaged *Tanith* in the Parth system."

"The 197th, under a Captain Jonas Morane, if I recall?"

"That would be the one. It passed through the Arietis system several months ago, not long after I withdrew our forces and just before your arrival here. According to my operatives, the 197th turned back a reiver wolf pack intent on raiding Arietis, then stuck around while its Marines, a battalion from the 21st Pathfinder Regiment, trained the local militia. They left in somewhat of a hurry to pursue the wolf pack when it returned and slipped down the Lyonesse wormhole cul-de-sac. Neither the reivers nor the 197th have been seen in the Arietis system since, though the few merchant vessels who ventured to Lyonesse afterward claim that system is now home to a handful of former imperial warships and ground units."

"So Elenia Yakin gained a two-ship navy and some Marines."

"Three ships. Besides the cruiser *Vanquish* and the tactical transport *Narwhal*, which carried *Tanith*, Morane also has a frigate by the name *Myrtale*. When the 197th passed through the Arietis system, a civilian ship called *Dawn Trader* accompanied it. According to Lloyd's Register, *Dawn Trader* belongs to the Galactic Dawn Corporation, which we suspect is either owned by the Order of the Void or works for it."

Custis rubbed his chin as he pondered Zahar's report.

"Interesting."

"It gets even more so, sir. Although Morane probably destroyed the reiver wolf pack, a ship we believe was *Dawn Trader* emerged from the Lyonesse branch a week or so later. We've not yet been able to track it through Micarat or any of the sector's traffic control nodes."

"Should I be worried about a naval force with unknown allegiance in our immediate neighborhood, Admiral? One which is friendly with the thrice-damned Order of the Void or seized *Dawn Trader* from the meddlers and is using it as what? A spy ship? A privateer? Or something worse?"

"Compared to battle groups from Dendera's 2nd Fleet probing the Coalsack Sector's border systems? No. Not in the slightest."

"How did this information reach you, Admiral?" Marta asked. "I thought your forces removed the Arietis subspace relay when they withdrew."

"I deployed scout ships to keep an eye on the wormhole junctions we abandoned, Milady, both to listen for reports from intelligence teams traveling aboard civilian ships and to warn us of incoming threats."

"Has one of your scouts been watching Mykonos since you withdrew the naval units stationed there?"

A guarded expression appeared on Zahar's holographic face.

"On and off, Milady. Why do you ask?"

"I'd like to know what happened after Dendera's forces arrived, yet I can't find anything in the 16th Fleet's operations log. After all, Mykonos was my home for several years."

Custis couldn't quite restrain a frown.

"You've been delving into naval affairs, my dear? Best we leave such things to the admiral and his people, don't you think?"

She turned eyes colder than the depths of space on him.

"As sovereign, I'm also the commander-in-chief of our armed services, Devy. Or will be once we set a date for my ascension to the imperial throne. I shall, therefore, ask Admiral Zahar any question I please and expect straightforward answers."

He raised his hands in surrender.

"Certainly."

"Admiral?"

Zahar's hologram sketched a slight bow.

"Yes, Milady. From what we pieced together, someone eliminated Jorge Danton and his government, then attempted to surrender. Dendera's forces nonetheless wrecked the orbitals, then bombarded the surface, destroying spaceports, ground control nodes and anything else that might enable space travel. In effect, the planet is now back at a pre-diaspora level of technology. We assume that if Danton's replacement hadn't surrendered, the imperial forces would have bombarded population centers as well, reducing the survivors to something like the Stone Age."

Marta nodded, stomach roiling with an unexpected surge of acid at Dendera's casual cruelty, and at what it meant for those she and Heloise had left behind because no one knew why Danton wanted her. If she'd known it was to give Custis' scheme a veil of legitimacy, she'd have taken the children with her.

"Not quite *Carthago delenda est*, but the spirit is similar." Her inner scholar, analytical to a fault, warred with deep disgust at the military leaders carrying out their psychopathic ruler's decrees. "Take away a rebellious star system's capacity for further warfare if it surrenders, and salt the earth if it resists. Then, once you've created a wasteland, raise the imperial banner and call it peace. After a suitable interval, let the grandchildren of the survivors rejoin humanity's interstellar civilization."

"That's what my analysts said, Milady," Zahar replied, "but not in such eloquent terms."

Custis nodded with more enthusiasm than her words merited.

"This is why we must create a new empire, Marta, to keep other star systems from suffering Mykonos' fate. And if we can't prevent the destruction of their infrastructure, we will help them rebuild much faster than they ever could on their own or under Wyvern's thumb."

A sarcastic smile twisted her lips.

"What you, Dendera, and everyone else seems to forget is the fact we're not in a closed environment, with only pro- and anti-Wyvern factions. The rest of the bloody universe gets a vote, and after our species dominated this part of the galaxy for over a thousand years, it will vote to feed on the empire's carcass. There won't be anything left for Dendera or her heirs to reclaim.

"We, here in the Coalsack, might hold on to a rump state which in time could venture forth to sow the seeds of revival. But for those planets laid waste by Dendera's admirals, the worst is yet to come. The millions who've died so far will become countless billions, especially if no human star system keeps the capacity for interstellar travel and we enter an era of barbarism capable of completely erasing civilization as we know it."

Both Custis and Zahar stared at Marta, astonished by the anger and passion behind her words. Neither of them knew her vehemence stemmed mainly from the deep-seated terror the orbital bombardment killed Sigrid, Stefan, and their caretakers. And yet a tiny and to her logical self, irrational spark of awareness almost smothered by fear whispered they still lived.

"Surely it won't be that bad, Milady," Zahar ventured when she composed herself.

"No, Admiral. It will be worse, much worse, now that Dendera has chosen a scorched star system policy instead of letting the empire peacefully fracture more or less along the stress lines her dynasty created. Better twenty-five quarreling sectors united here and there through shifting alliances than thousands of planets where time flows backward until the survivors of formerly advanced societies can sink no further."

An embarrassed silence greeted her final outburst. Then, Custis said, "I think we should resume our conversation at another time, my dear. Perhaps resting before tonight's reception is advisable." He turned his eyes on Zahar's hologram. "Back to the 197th, Admiral. What else did your intelligence operatives tell you?"

"They plan on taking the next available ship to Lyonesse, sir. Considering how long it took for their report to reach Yotai, the team might already be there."

"What is your interest in Lyonesse?"

Custis seemed about to dismiss her question, but something in Marta's eyes caused him to change course.

"The prison ship my family and I were on, *Tanith*, also carried others condemned to exile on Parth by Dendera. Admiral Zahar's forces rescued my family and me, but the prison service crew sabotaged *Tanith*'s antimatter fuel system, rendering it unable to travel FTL. Among the hundreds in stasis pods aboard, there are many I'd like to recover and bring here. Since it seems this Captain Jonas Morane piggybacked *Tanith* on his tactical transport and took it to Lyonesse, I must search for my lost companions there."

For reasons she couldn't explain, Marta knew Custis wasn't speaking the whole truth. There was more to his interest than just friends from the imperial court.

"We hardly need more idle layabouts, Devy. I don't want useless nobles cluttering up my capital, and neither do you. Let Lyonesse enjoy the privilege of high-born drones leeching off their society." When he didn't reply, she asked in a commanding tone honed by countless hours of training under Heloise's strict tutelage, "What is your true interest in tracking down a lost prison ship?"

"Dendera's sister Corinne was aboard, hidden under the identity of a common criminal, but none of us knew her assumed name," Custis replied, inexplicably unable to keep from telling Marta the truth.

"Is it because she was your first choice as a puppet ruler, or are you afraid she might become someone else's puppet, one with a more immediate claim to the imperial throne reborn in exile?" Marta studied Custis for a few seconds before allowing herself a cold smile.

"Both, am I correct? Initially your first choice but now a potentially dangerous competitor to your current candidate, as in what if Corinne establishes a competing empire? How soon will we hear news from the operatives heading to Lyonesse, Admiral?"

"It could be weeks or even months, Milady. Regular traffic between star systems we don't directly control has all but ceased, and Lyonesse is five wormhole transits past Micarat, our last defended outpost on that part of the network."

Marta rose to her feet.

"Please keep me appraised. In the meantime, I will take your advice, Devy, and rest before tonight's dreary business."

A vaguely annoyed expression crossed Custis' face.

"You may consider hosting provincial nobility a dreary affair, but such receptions are part and parcel of our strategy to legitimize you taking the imperial crown."

"Indeed. And I will play my part to perfection, have no fear."

With that, Marta turned her back on Custis and his military commander, leaving them to contemplate her assessment of their precarious situation. The urge to tell Sister Heloise of an Order of the Void starship by the name *Dawn Trader*, now on the loose somewhere in the Coalsack Sector or perhaps even beyond, had become overwhelming.

— 26 —

Lyonesse

"Another new arrival at the wormhole terminus, Centurion. Freighter by the name *Avadora*, ten crew under a Captain Makeda Krengel," Petty Officer Harkness announced, raising his hand to attract the attention of the operations center's duty officer, Eve Haller. "*Condor* confirms she's a merchantman, lightly armed with no indications she might be a reiver in disguise. Captain Krengel advised *Condor* he carries two hundred and sixty-four migrants from Arietis."

Condor, the Lyonesse Navy's fourth and newest ship was little more than an ancient, sloop-sized freighter impounded by the government a few weeks earlier and fitted with naval-grade improvements culled from the Lannion Base supply depot. Its former captain, a shifty-eyed Peralkan, figured it would be an excellent idea to cheat his way out of paying for the outbound cargo he'd taken aboard. Instead of lifting off on schedule, he'd found himself on a prison farm for his pains.

Now crewed by former Imperial Navy personnel under one of *Vanquish*'s lieutenants, the sloop was taking her turn as guard ship at the wormhole terminus, to screen incomers. Though few civilian vessels made their way down the Lyonesse cul-de-sac nowadays, those who showed up invariably carried migrants with enough wealth to pay the extortionate fees demanded by greedy captains.

Since the 197th Battle Group's arrival in the Lyonesse system, word had filtered back to Arietis and other places abandoned by the 16th Fleet that the little known planet no one cared about while the empire still owned the Coalsack Sector was a safe harbor. If you could reach it.

And though the trickle of migrants remained small enough to present few problems on what was still a mostly virgin world, many on Lyonesse, Morane among them, worried they might admit settlers who could present a danger, perhaps not now, but at a later juncture.

"Warn the Lannion harbormaster, PO," she replied, referring to the man responsible for Lyonesse's main civilian spaceport. "He can let Social Services know a fresh batch of customers is on the way. Once we have the ETA, activate the rapid reaction squadron so it can greet *Avadora* upon landing, in case the people aboard don't come from frightened masses yearning to breathe free."

Harkness gave her a skeptical glance.

"Two hundred and sixty-four bodies crammed into a tramp freighter doesn't make for much of a raiding party, sir, unless they didn't get the message this place has more bite than bark."

"Agreed, but why take chances?"

"True."

Haller typed out a brief log entry, then routed it up the chain of command with the tag *important, but not urgent.* Admiral Morane and Colonel DeCarde want to hear about anything unusual in what they now considered their star system, and a new arrival, even if it was peaceful, qualified.

Then, she transmitted the data on *Avadora* to *Vanquish*, currently in orbit, though she figured the cruiser's communications chief would have intercepted *Condor*'s report and warned Captain Mikkel by now. No doubt she would send one of her other ships to intercept *Avadora* at the hyperlimit and confirm the freighter's peaceful intent.

**

When Morane's office communicator chimed, he glanced down at the screen and grimaced.

"Gus Logran. I bet I know why he's calling."

Sister Gwenneth gave him a commiserating smile.

"Among his many characteristics, our esteemed chief administrator is predictable. Please feel free to answer, Admiral. Our discussion has run its course anyhow. Let him know the abbey is aware of the incomers and as always, stands by to help."

"Thank you, Sister." Morane stabbed his communicator. "Gus. What can the defense force and, since Sister Gwenneth is with me, the abbey do for you today?"

"Send those inbound migrants back to Arietis," the choleric chief administrator replied without preamble. "That makes what? Close to two thousand since your lot showed up? We're not equipped to absorb a surfeit of immigrants unable or unwilling to clear out new settlements in the hinterland."

"Oh, I don't know that we're getting more than our fair share of layabouts, Gus. The new farming village on the Otnabog River seems to do fine, thanks to the abbey's help."

"Sure, but the administration still has to feed and lodge newcomers, as we're still doing for too many of those damned politicals since they don't seem able to work. If we continue taking in every one who shows up, it'll soon turn into a flood we can't handle. What happens to keeping the light of civilization burning bright if Lyonesse can't stay afloat?" A stubborn expression replaced his earlier air of irritation.

"We're hardly a life pod. Lyonesse is a big planet, with plenty of usable landmasses, and there's not even a million of us who call it home."

"What about undesirables?"

"They can open new settlements in the Windy Isles." Before Logran could reply, Morane added, "We'll be on hand to help your people, Gus, as will the abbey. I doubt everyone on Arietis and in the surrounding star systems intends to come knocking on our door. Most people will either stay on their native worlds and fight it out or pray any new overlords treat them with kindness. I daresay we're getting the more enterprising and far-sighted of the bunch. Besides, once we run out of arable land on Tristan, you can offer bounties as an encouragement to brave the wilds of Isolde and open it up for settlement."

Logran scoffed. "You always have a glib answer for everything."

"Unfortunately, no. Otherwise, I'd be able to propose a way of getting those lazy aristo buggers off their butts and out of our hair."

A humorless bark escaped Logran's throat.

"You're not the only one with ideas around here. I should probably let Rorik make the announcement, but he's stolen my thunder often enough." A short pause, then Logran added, in a low grumble, "Among other bits of thievery."

Morane and Sister Gwenneth exchanged a puzzled glance. Other than offering the politicals work in one of the Hecht family's myriad business enterprises, neither could see how the speaker of the council might solve the problem posed by Severin Downes and his cronies' intransigence.   Even employment in a managerial capacity remained beneath their dignity. They wanted nothing less than to spend their days in the corridors of power, lording it over the hoi polloi.

"I'm listening, Gus."

"You'll love this. He arranged, through his son Gerson who heads the Lyonesse Chamber of Commerce as well as the family consortium, to put the most senior among the politicals on various corporate and business association boards of directors, with healthy honorariums. Severin Downes himself is slated to become the chair of the Hecht Enterprises' board once the shareholders vote him in. Seeing as how the Hechts between them hold fifty-one percent of the voting shares, it's a done deal."

When Logran saw the look on Morane's face, he burst into laughter.

"Oh yes, my dear Admiral. And it's not just one appointment per former aristo. They'll each hold enough to make a healthy living. And the back-scratching will be epic. Those politicals will owe Rorik a debt they'll never fully repay, or at least he'll never consider it repaid for as long as he lives. In return, he — or rather Gerson, since Rorik's business interests are held in a blind trust for the duration of his term as member of the council — will have a finger in every little pie on Lyonesse."

"Ingenious," Morane said in a dry tone.

"Anyone who thinks the younger Hecht operates with no supervision from his father is deluded enough to buy a hundred hectares of virgin Isolde jungle, sight unseen."

Morane studied Logran's image for a few seconds before giving Sister Gwenneth another quick glance. Her sphinx-like expression told him he was on his own.

"You seem even less happy with Rorik than usual, Gus. Care to share?"

"Asks the man who owes him a favor because he supported the principle of legislative rather than administrative control over the armed services."

"I owe only three things — a duty to protect the citizens of Lyonesse, submission to the will of the Colonial Council in plenary session, and obeisance to my commander-in-chief, the governor."

"Rorik won't see it that way."

"I'll ask my question in a different form since you and I have been at odds for months. Why are you confiding in me now? I get the feeling you didn't just call to complain about a fresh shipload of settlers."

When Logran didn't immediately answer, Sister Gwenneth spoke for the first time since Morane accepted the call.

"Perhaps our chief administrator feels the balance of power between his office and that of the speaker might be upset by Rorik Hecht drawing ex-courtiers hungry for a taste of power into his web."

An embarrassed silence greeted her statement.

Finally, Logran let out a rueful sigh.

"You don't mince words, do you, Sister?"

"I never saw the point in tiptoeing around an issue when acknowledging uncomfortable truths is clearly in everyone's interests."

"What happened, Gus?" Morane asked. "I thought you and Severin Downes were pals."

"Once he realized I could only offer ordinary civil service jobs within the administration, he stopped being chummy."

"And here I thought you were whispering suggestions in Elenia Yakin's ear about appointing lordlings to sinecures on the Government House staff."

"I tried. Once. So they'd shut up and stop bothering her. She told me to never raise the subject again. Otherwise, she'd speed up the legal changes transforming my job into that of a prime minister appointed by her on the advice and consent of the Colonial Council."

This time, it was Morane's turn to laugh.

"Then Rorik Hecht, the man who could influence whether you become our first prime minister, proposed a solution to the problem of finding jobs the politicals would accept. And you saw no choice but to back his move, even though you understood the dangers of increasing his influence over Lyonesse."

"It won't do the defense force or your knowledge vault any good if Rorik gets his fingers into either."

"So all is forgiven, and we're friends again? Or to be blunt, allies against Hecht's schemes?"

Logran gave him a hard stare, jaw muscles working while he chose his words.

"I still disagree with the military being answerable to the legislature instead of the executive, but yes. You and I have more things in common than either of us have with Rorik."

When Morane glanced at Gwenneth, she gave him a tiny, but encouraging nod he interpreted as meaning 'go with it.'

"What would they be?" He asked in a neutral tone.

"We were servants of the empire, imbued with the notion of duty to our sovereign and fellow citizens. Sure, we might be tempted to enhance the power of our positions so we may better serve or even gain plaudits, promotions, and honors, but not to line our pockets."

"And Rorik Hecht isn't so imbued?"

Logran snorted with disdain.

"He talks a great game about selfless public service, but his eye is always on the main prize, and that's Rorik Hecht's standing on Lyonesse. You won't find him breaking any conflict of interest rules. He's exceedingly scrupulous and careful to obey the letter of the law. However, his family and those indebted to him one way or another will always make sure everything they do meets with Rorik's approval. Once he's taken every advantage he can from serving on the Colonial Council, you'll see him back in private life, richer, more influential, and more powerful than before."

"Meaning he's like every other politician throughout human history, while you and I are not."

"Precisely."

"Tell you what, Gus. I'm glad to work with anyone whose interest is for the greater good of Lyonesse, its people and the precious treasure we're slowly accumulating under Lannion Base. But only if they behave lawfully and ethically."

"Which would exclude Rorik."

"Has he behaved unlawfully or unethically?"

Morane's question gave Logran pause. Then, he replied in a grudging tone, "Not that anyone can prove. But he's one of those people for whom they invented the term trust but verify."

"Fair enough. I'll be glad to work with you as a colleague and friend, provided you deal honestly with me and mine. Needless to say, I'll return the favor. Things will worsen over the coming years, including the inflow of displaced persons. If we can't pull together as a society, we will surely crumble to dust."

— 27 —

"Are you still having doubts?" The team leader asked his winger in a low voice as they walked from the freighter *Avadora*'s grounded belly ramp to the Lannion Spaceport terminal. They were careful not to stare at the armed, battledress-clad Marines making sure no one strayed from the path leading to immigration control. "Those jarheads are wearing 21st Pathfinder Regiment cap badges, though I don't recognize the formation patch on their shoulders."

"Seems to match the flag flying over the terminal. Some sort of double-headed avian critter. I guess the folks on Arietis weren't lying. Otherwise, I'd be really pissed by now."

The chaotic trip from Arietis aboard a tramp well past its prime and carrying more breathing human bodies than the designers of its environmental systems ever contemplated had strained the 16th Fleet's intelligence operatives' patience.

"It's worth checking this place out in any case," the third of the team's four members said, "even if we don't find what we're looking for. It feels different from everywhere else we've been, and they'll want to know about it at home."

The leader glanced over his shoulder at her.

"What's so different?"

"When was the last time you saw the cream of the Marine Corps running spaceport security to make sure newcomers don't cause trouble? They're the real deal, Kamaal, minus the imperial crown on their badges, not a hick star system militia playing dress-up or cops with a paramilitary fetish. They have the stance, the moves, and that look in their eyes. A full squadron's worth too, I'd say.

"Whoever's running this place isn't taking chances on folks skipping immigration checks. That says something compared to every other damned star system in the sector, including the ones we still hold. And you might have noticed there's not a single imperial emblem or flag in sight."

Kamaal Bouras — it wasn't his real name, but after months working undercover, the fake identity felt eerily natural — knew better than to challenge her assessment. She was not only a Marine command noncom with Special Forces experience, but she'd also actually served in the same regiment as these troopers many years before. Jaimee Markov — not the woman's real name either — would undoubtedly recognize her own kind better than anyone else in their team.

"Jaimee's right about the atmosphere around here," the fourth member of Bouras' team, said. "I can't put my finger on it, but it feels like the citizens of Lyonesse declared their independence from the empire and the sector, and told no one outside this star system. Every other place we visited either clung to a hope imperial forces would return, or trumpeted its loyalty to Grand Duke Custis."

"To be more accurate, the viceroy of the Coalsack Sector, Ty," Bouras' winger, Cerys Orobio replied with a sardonic grin. "Most of those we spoke with didn't know Custis from Joback or the little green man who owns Tortuga Station."

Their banter ceased by unspoken accord as they came within earshot of a squad from the 21st Pathfinders guarding the door, but their eyes never stopped moving.

Once inside the terminal's spacious arrivals hall, more of the silent, hard-faced Marines funneled them into orderly lines, though Bouras managed to keep the four of them together as a group. It surprised him to see human immigration officers in law enforcement blue at each of the counters, instead of the AI holograms common across the empire.

They too sported a green patch with a gold, double-headed avian on their tunics' upper sleeves, but instead of crossed swords with a numeral like those of the Marines, theirs displayed the ancient portcullis symbol long associated with gatekeepers. It was yet another sign Lyonesse might have unilaterally seceded from both empire and sector, and was prepared to enforce its sovereignty.

The large portrait of a solemn, dark-haired woman on the far wall where that of the empress should hang, did nothing to dissuade Bouras of his growing certainty. She wore a navy dress uniform with a vice admiral's stripes on the cuffs and the intricately twisted, gold bullion aiguillettes reserved for an imperial viceroy on her right shoulder. But instead of the Imperial Armed Services insignia, her sky blue beret bore yet another version of the golden double-headed creature, this time with crossed swords and anchor.

It had to be Elenia Yakin. The woman in the portrait matched the image from the mission briefing pack implanted into every operative's memory. But according to the data, she was a mere colonial governor who never held naval rank, let alone that of a flag officer.

The four agents slowly made their way to the head of the line until Bouras stood behind a yellow stripe etched into the stone floor. Eventually, the immigration officer made the universal hand signal to approach, and Bouras gestured at his teammates to follow.

"Are you a family unit?" The officer asked when he saw the four move in unison. "If so, you may approach together. Otherwise, it's one at a time."

"We're related and traveling together, sir."

He gave them the skeptical stare of someone who's seen and heard it all but didn't demur. They placed their identity wafers before him while he studied their faces one at a time, then asked, "Are you requesting permission to land on Lyonesse as immigrants, refugees, or visitors?"

Bouras knew pretending to be anything other than visitors would see them corralled by whatever passed for social services because a world which presented such an organized face to newcomers wouldn't let prospective settlers wander off by themselves.

"Visitors."

The immigration officer's eyebrows rose by a few millimeters, as if in disbelief.

"We don't see many of those nowadays, Mister..." he glanced down at the ID wafers, "Bouras. There's little to see or do and no regular starship traffic since the troubles started. Most who show up want to remain permanently. How long do you intend to stay?"

Bouras shrugged.

"A few weeks to scope out the commercial possibilities, then jump on the next available starship."

"Merchants, are you?"

"We represent Universal Exports' Coalsack Sector Division, sir. The recent political rearrangements are forcing our employer to rethink trade routes."

The officer seemed to parse his memory for a few seconds, though his eyes never left Bouras.

"I don't think I heard of Universal Exports carrying out business on Lyonesse when this was still part of the empire. I trust you carry enough funds to support yourselves because visitors can't take local employment without the chief administrator's permission."

"We carry enough imperial creds and precious metals to keep us comfortable for several months, sir."

"Good. We still use imperial creds as currency, though you may find prices on imported items much higher than expected. And while this is no longer an imperial star system, civil and criminal laws remain the same, so take care you avoid infractions. We have prison farms and for longer sentences, an isolated archipelago that makes Parth's Desolation Island seem like a vacation spot."

"We are law-abiding people, sir. You need not worry on that account."

"Glad to hear it. Welcome on Lyonesse." He touched something beyond Bouras' line of sight. "I gave you three-month visas allowing you to live here as visitors and recorded them on your IDs. Please make sure they remain there until you leave, so you're not picked up and detained as illegals during a routine police check. If you either plan on staying beyond three months or are forced to do so because of shipping issues, you must visit the immigration office in downtown Lannion before the visas expire to get them extended. Otherwise, you'll be arrested and detained until we can deport you."

Bouras politely inclined his head.

"Understood, sir."

"You may recover your IDs and exit immigration control."

Once out in the terminal's main hall, Cerys Orobio muttered, "An isolated archipelago that makes Parth's Desolation Island seem like a vacation spot? Charming.

What does it say about a planet when its immigration officers feel the need to mention something dismal like that?"

"I don't know offhand," Bouras replied absently, his eyes on the hall's far end. There, officials in business suits guarded by another half dozen armed Marines were herding immigrants burdened with heavy bags and cases out a side door toward a line of busses bearing municipal transit markings. "But I'd say this star system is ruled by serious people who want no one to disrupt what they're building."

As they stepped out of the terminal to search for transport, Ty Renlinger nodded at the many scorch marks etched into the road and neighboring buildings.

"Looks like someone tried them on, and not that long ago. A few months, maybe. Less than a year. Those scars still look relatively fresh."

"That reiver wolf pack the 197th Battle Group chased up the Lyonesse branch most likely," Markov said. "I'll bet they were ambushed right here on their way to raid downtown Lannion, which means the ships landed. And that means the reivers arrived before the 197th. Otherwise, something like *Vanquish* would have turned them into orbiting wreckage. Interesting."

"How come?" Orobio asked.

"This place hasn't seen an Imperial Armed Services garrison, beyond the naval supply depot, in almost a decade. Ergo, the local police and militia probably fought off those reivers by themselves without self-destructing in the process. Think about that."

"Oh."

"Oh, indeed. This place is getting more interesting by the minute." Markov nudged Bouras. "Worth the trip on its own, right boss?"

Bouras grunted in agreement.

"Let's walk into town and see how far the fighting went."

Thirty minutes later, the team stopped within sight of Lannion's central square.

"Looks like they contained most of the reivers at the spaceport, though from the odd shot hole, a few escaped and ran. I wonder what happened to the ships and why they didn't bomb the shit out of this place once they realized the attack was going sideways."

"Must be because the 197th finally entered orbit and didn't give them time to strike from above," Renlinger suggested. "Whoever remained aboard must have lifted off and tried to run the moment it looked like the jig was up. Badlands barbarians don't give a shit about that no one left behind business."

— 28 —

"Major Gelbar reports no issues at the spaceport, Centurion," Sergeant Rodion Kuryakin, the duty communications tech said once he'd caught Haller's attention. "Final tally is two hundred and sixty migrants from Arietis asking for asylum and four visitors here on a three-month visa. The migrants are at the processing facility where the debriefing team is getting ready. Gelbar is standing A Squadron down and returning to base."

The processing facility, formerly known as Camp Lannion, used to be the Lyonesse Rifle Regiment's training installation on the city's outskirts. Morane turned it over to the administration when it became clear they faced a small, but steady influx of arrivals and likely would until starship traffic through the Lyonesse branch of the wormhole network ceased entirely. The Rifles' Headquarters and A companies now used a section of Lannion Base instead, which suited Lieutenant Colonel Kayne and his troops.

"Four visitors?" Haller turned away from the operation center's panoramic window and glanced at the communications station. "Did we get any details from immigration control?"

Kuryakin, a Rifle Regiment noncom who'd served a hitch as a starship communications rating in the Imperial Navy before settling on Lyonesse, nodded.

"Visual from the checkpoint and the screening officer's notes."

"Good. I'm glad the colonial administration has taken Admiral Morane's advice on increased security to heart."

"You think they could be persons of interest, sir?"

"When did we last see visitors on a three-month visa, Sergeant? As opposed to immigrants and starship crews taking shore leave?"

Kuryakin scratched his short salt and pepper beard, lost in thought.

"Couldn't say offhand, but if it happened while I was on shift, I'm sure I'd remember. Want me to check the database?"

Haller shook her head.

"No need. We haven't seen actual visitors to Lyonesse since I started working operations. Show me the visual."

"Coming right up." Kuryakin pointed at the main display.

Haller, along with the other six operations center watchkeepers, studied the video of four humans, two men, two women, moving as a group through the immigration lines until they reached the immigration officer's counter. They listened to the interplay, then watched them leave the arrivals hall.

"Comments?" She asked once the video faded away, replaced by four columns listing the personal data on the visitors' ID chips. "Take your time."

"If they're trade representatives, I'm a Void Sister," Sergeant First Class Eddy Craddoc, one of the veteran 21st Pathfinder noncoms assigned to Defense Force HQ, said.

"Why?"

"Their eyes are everywhere, and they move like fighters. Especially the dark-haired woman." Craddoc glanced at his terminal. "Jaimee Markov. If she walked into the sergeant's mess tonight, I'd ask her which regiment. Maybe even flash my challenge coin."

"Are you sure?"

"Call it gut instinct. The other three, no, but they're not career civilians."

"Anyone else?" Haller asked.

"Now that Eddy mentioned it, yeah, the buggers don't strike me as merchants," Sergeant Kuryakin said. "But don't ask why. It's just a feeling. Perhaps because they don't act like wide-eyed tourist or worried migrants wondering whether we'll let them stay."

Of the four petty officers culled from the 197th who filled out the rest of the duty shift, none added anything, though the senior among them, Vlad Harkness, tentatively agreed with his buddy, Craddoc.

Haller gave the ID data readout a last glance.

"So be it. Sergeant Kuryakin, tell the Lannion Police, the immigration section, and the public safety coordination center those four should be considered persons of interest. They should be watched but not approached until further notice."

"Wilco, sir."

Seized by momentary indecision, Haller nibbled on the inside of her lower lip before coming to a decision. She dropped into the duty officer's throne-like command chair and stroked the screen embedded in its right arm. Compared to most military organizations throughout history, the Lyonesse Defense Force functioned with a vanishingly small staff cadre and a dizzyingly vertical command structure.

As operations center duty officer, she enjoyed direct access to the admiral and his three immediate subordinates, but Haller knew better than to go beyond entering noteworthy events in the daily log unless necessary.

However, something told her that while this wasn't on the same level as a reiver wolf pack emerging from the Lyonesse wormhole, it might be noteworthy enough to ring up Colonel DeCarde, the defense force second in command.

DeCarde's smiling face appeared on Haller's private screen moments later.

"What's up, Eve?"

"We may have welcomed visitors of interest among that last batch of migrants, sir."

"Visitors? As in they came, they'll look around, and they'll leave?"

"Four, purporting to be trade representatives looking for opportunities. Immigration gave them three-month visas. Our records show no other tourists since the admiral convinced Mister Logran to set up strict entry controls, and that wasn't long after we arrived, so it's been a while. Immigration sent us a video along with their ID data. We figure they might be something other than they claim."

"In that case, I want to see what you saw. Send everything to my terminal."

DeCarde looked away while the video played on her office display. When she glanced up at Haller again, her face wore a puzzled frown.

"You did well to pass this on right away. There's something off with those tourists. The dark-haired woman—"

"Markov."

"Yes, that one — she seems vaguely familiar."

"Eddy Craddoc figures Markov wouldn't seem out of place in the sergeant's mess and might even carry a challenge coin."

"He thinks she wore a winged dagger at some point?"

Haller nodded.

"And the others, while not in the same class as Markov, probably answer to service numbers. I doubt they represent a company called Universal Exports. Not only has it never done business on Lyonesse, but who in their right mind would troll for commercial opportunities at the far end of a wormhole cul-de-sac cut off from whatever's left of imperial space?

"Based on the latest migrant debriefings, the Arietis wormhole junction might not be a reiver's paradise yet, but if I recall correctly, ship owners stand to lose their insurance coverage if they go into star systems no longer under navy control. That's why we're seeing nothing but scummy tramps these days instead of company freighters."

DeCarde tapped her chin with an extended index finger.

"Then why would these fake tourists come here?"

"I guess the only way to find out is see what they do. We notified the police and civilian authorities to keep an eye on them as persons of interest."

"Good. And I should probably ask Matti Kayne to sic his informal intelligence network on them."

Upon hearing the name of the Rifle Regiment's commanding officer, Haller gave Sergeant Kuryakin an involuntary glance. He and the other watchkeepers were listening in on her conversation with DeCarde, and when their eyes met, Kuryakin gave Haller thumbs up, then pointed at himself.

"An excellent idea, sir. Perhaps the operations center should be appointed as an information clearinghouse for Colonel Kayne's spies. I have just the man for the job — Sergeant Kuryakin."

"Done. Thanks for the heads-up, Eve, and keep me apprised of developments. I'll let the admiral know. DeCarde, out."

Haller climbed out of the command chair and walked over to the panoramic window overlooking Lannion Base from the operations center's clifftop aerie. She could easily make out Lannion itself, strung along the banks of the broad, muddy brown Haven River, including Government House, a bright white rectangle at the center of a lush, walled-in park.

Further south, high above the Middle Sea's hazy shoreline, thunderheads were building ahead of the usual late afternoon downpour. At this time of the year, it left the air so muggy Haller often thought she'd be better off with gills.

A soft rumble drew her eyes to the civilian spaceport a few kilometers east of downtown Lannion. *Avadora*, now rid of her human cargo, was firing thrusters to prepare for takeoff. Haller idly wondered whether she was carrying anything worth selling back in the big, wide galaxy or returning to Arietis with empty holds, and whether she'd land on Lyonesse again one day. *Avadora* could even be the last starship to visit if rumors about the Coalsack Sector government losing its grip on one star systems after another were true.

The growl of overworked thrusters grew, though the sound remained muted by both distance and the armored window. Moments later, Haller watched a tiny black shape rise on columns of brilliant light. She followed the freighter's progress until it vanished from view, swallowed by the towering clouds.

When Haller turned back toward the room, she noticed Eddy Craddoc was once again studying the video, eyes moving between it and the ID pictures on a side display.

"Tell you what, Centurion," Craddoc said when he felt Haller watching him. "The more I think about it, the more I figure they either bleed Marine green or Navy blue. Except for Markov. She bleeds Pathfinder gold. I can feel it in my bones. How about me and a few buddies hang out where they end up staying and try to make friends? Unless they show up at the recruiting office asking to join us, they're here on someone's orders. We probably want to figure out whose."

Haller considered his proposal for a few seconds, then shook her head.

"Let's leave that job to the Rifle Regiment's street runners for now. If you're right and Markov used to be one of us, she'll figure you out within the first ten seconds. Best if she and her friends don't know we're paying them any attention."

Craddoc put on a crestfallen expression and sighed.

"I didn't think of that, sir. Never mind."

— 29 —

Yotai

The reception, one in a long series designed to heighten Marta Norum's profile among the Coalsack Sector's notables, seemed even drearier than any of its predecessors, despite the lavish pomp and circumstance usually seen only at the imperial court on Wyvern. This time, Custis had summoned the star system high commissioners, governors, and governors general who owed him allegiance, sending his fastest ships to convey them through the wormhole network.

After being informed Lady Marta was a direct descendant of what Custis now publicly called the last legitimate emperor, Kal IV, every noble, politician, and senior officer wanted to bask in her imperial glow. That Custis gave himself the title of regent shortly before and announced Marta was destined for greater things didn't help. Sadly, most were tedious creatures when they weren't oozing venality and greed.

If it weren't for Heloise's silent, yet steadying presence as her lady-in-waiting, Marta would gladly give each of them a piece of her mind. Then, she would march off to the 16th Fleet HQ senior non-commissioned officers' mess in the viceregal palace basement for a few shots of whiskey in the company of salty veterans unimpressed by the nobility. The latter was a habit everyone in the palace from Custis and Zahar on down deplored, but none dared forbid the future empress from visiting her loyal troops.

What they didn't realize is that she used the noncoms' network to stay informed of military and naval matters without Zahar or his officers being any the wiser. Among the many bits of wisdom she learned from Uncle Olav was one most senior officers either never learned or forgot once they wore stars.

If you want to know what's really going on, ask a Marine command sergeant or a navy chief. And she'd shamelessly traded on Olav's good name and standing among old time Marine Corps noncoms to run her own informal intelligence service. Much of what she heard never even made it to Zahar's ears, let alone those of Grand Duke Devy Custis, Regent of the Coalsack Sector. He enjoyed next to no respect among members of the senior NCO's mess, especially those from the 55th Marine Regiment assigned as palace guards, a job they found demeaning.

Marta, standing beside Custis in the place of honor, let her eyes roam across the immense ballroom, brilliantly lit by hundreds of floating crystal candelabras and filled with almost a thousand of the sector's highest ranking officials. The military officers were resplendent in dress uniforms dripping with gold bullion, medals, and other martial devices. Their civilian counterparts variously wore the civil service uniforms proper to their appointments or the sort of formal clothes rarely seen in a frontier sector. A Marine band, arrayed on a balcony overlooking the dance floor, played lively tunes with verve and élan, creating a harmonious counterpart to the dissonant drone of too many conversations.

Yet beneath the shining veneer, she sensed an almost desperate urge to recreate what existed before Admiral Loren rose against Dendera's rule and triggered the civil war now tearing apart the mightiest empire in human history. The smiles were too bright; the conversations were too animated, and the formal bows of those approaching her and Custis as they stood in isolated splendor at the heart of the ballroom were too enthusiastic.

Marta sensed a yearning for safety and stability permeating the overheated atmosphere. Yet it seemed tainted by an unconscious, almost primal fear that no matter what, their future was bleak, that the old empire could never be reassembled, and that the certainties of the past were gone forever.

Animals knew instinctively when catastrophes were in the offing. Humans did as well, though few could translate feelings of uneasiness into the realization they faced mortal danger, both as individuals and as a civilization, and thus ignored them.

Where Custis and Zahar dreamed of a reborn empire growing and prospering under their leadership, Marta saw nothing other than *Ragnarök*, the end of all things which must come before humanity can regenerate and repopulate the galaxy. Tonight's reception, splendid as it was, presaged *Götterdämmerung*, the twilight of the gods, not their entry into a new Valhalla.

Those thoughts and feelings weren't new. She'd come to Yotai already convinced Custis' scheme was a forlorn hope. Her visions of the end, however, were strengthening with each passing week, each gathering, reception, and formal dinner, and with each step closer she took to the throne. Though Marta couldn't quite pinpoint why, she suspected Heloise's teachings were doing more than just opening her inner, third eye. Whether by accident or design, she couldn't tell.

"You seem lost, my dear," Custis murmured in Marta's ear. "Is everything all right?"

"I felt someone walk over my grave, Devy, nothing more."

In truth, it was over humanity's grave. But she wasn't about to discuss the matter with Custis. Especially not in the middle of Yotai's most prominent social gathering since well before the rebellion, when a young Dendera toured her realm and stopped off to be feted by the Coalsack Sector's nobility. He could see nothing beyond his ambitions and would laugh at Marta's mystical notions of a coming Armageddon.

Custis gave her a curious glance, then pasted a false smile as he saw the governor general of Micarat and her spouse approach them.

"Look sharp, my dear. Janae Gumbs and that idiot partner of hers want to make their manners."

Marta had met Gumbs the previous day when Custis introduced her to the assembled star system government heads after presenting his plan to reunite humanity under the protection of a constitutional government cleansed of the Ruggero dynasty. He'd referred to her as Kal IV's direct descendent, the light which would guide them to a new golden era of justice and prosperity.

Strangely enough, none of the men and women assembled in the viceregal reception room showed the slightest bit of amusement at Custis' overwrought language. There too, Marta had sensed an atmosphere of almost irrational hope.

Gumbs, a hatchet-faced former Imperial Navy commodore who'd seized control of Micarat with the help of her task force after Admiral Zahar murdered Viceroy Joback, bowed to Marta first.

In doing so, she acknowledged, as others had before her, that Lady Marta held higher implicit rank than Regent Custis. Instead of feeling insulted, Custis smiled, seeing the social demotion as a vindication of his plan to crown Marta and make her the figurehead empress in whose name he would rule.

"Milady. I trust you're well."

"Indeed, Excellency. Thank you for asking. And you?"

"Delighted." She gestured at her companion, a vacuous looking man who appeared to be twenty years Gumbs' junior. "May I present the Honorable Lucius Benasser?"

He bowed with formal stiffness. "Milady."

"Thank you for coming, Mister Benasser."

A smile of pleasure lit up his face.

"I wouldn't have missed it for the world, Milady. It's so," he paused, looking for the right word, "so splendiferous."

"How kind of you."

Gumbs nudged her partner when it looked as if he was about to reply, and both greeted Custis before wandering off to find the wine table.

"Where did she ever find him?" Marta asked in a low voice, not expecting anyone to answer.

"I understand she used to pay him for certain, um, services when she still commanded the Micarat Task Force. Since governors general with ambitions shouldn't be so crass, Janae formalized the arrangement."

"And when she tires of the boy?"

"That is a question best left unanswered."

"Why?" She smiled at a passing general as he dipped his head in an abbreviated, walking bow.

"Didn't you see there was no soul behind Janae's eyes?"

Marta thought back at their brief interaction, irritated at herself for missing something so obvious mostly because of her ruminations about the coming *Ragnarök*.

"I noticed. Charming."

"If it's any consolation, I intend to dispense with her services when the time is right."

"Don't kick out your friends on my account, Devy."

She nodded at a passing high commissioner who wore a silver-trimmed dark blue civil service uniform, complete with sash and every bureaucratic medal known to humanity. Marta figured the many awards proved he could compose a thoroughly useless memorandum using every ponderous word ever invented.

"We need to make this a clean start, my dear, and Janae is among those whose habits and competence won't stand scrutiny in the long run."

"That would describe pretty much everyone, don't you think? People who violently renounce their oaths and murder anyone who refuses to do so can't be relied upon ever again. Someone willing to betray once will always be willing to betray again should it suit their aims. If you wish to make a clean start, begin by replacing your favorite snake, Pendrick Zahar, then tear through the chain of command from there. Once you're done, replace the ruler of every star system, and tear through *their* chains of command."

"Leaving me with what? This sector and the empire we shall build need men and women with relevant experience. That means swallowing our distaste and wiping the slate clean for those whose usefulness transcends my immediate needs. The rest? I'll deal with them due course. Once I no longer need them."

"How Jesuitical of you, Devy. But why should I expect anything less from the man whose ambition is to be Cardinal Richelieu to my Louis XIII?"

"What—" Movement by the ballroom's grand entrance, where Marine sentries snapped to attention and saluted, swallowed Custis' puzzlement at her biting remark.

"Here come Baron and Baroness Romito, finally. Speaking of bad habits such as tardiness... Once they've made their obeisance, we can go on with the evening. Everyone else who matters is here. Smile, Marta. I'm about to make you the sole legitimate empress of humanity across the stars."

"And yet, in the end, I won't even be so much as Queen of Yotai," she murmured in reply as the vision of a burning viceregal palace briefly flashed before her mind's eye. Yet Marta felt no anguish at a future which might engulf her in fire and blood because she continued to feed on the irrational certainty her children would find a safe harbor against the coming storm.

After receiving the Romitos' greetings, Custis stepped up on the dais behind them and made the agreed upon signal to the bandmaster who wrapped up the piece they were playing. Four musicians put down their instruments, picked up heraldic trumpets, and stood.

As they raised the instruments to their lips, the audience could see the banners hanging from them. Blue squares fringed with gold tassels, they bore the imperial crown above a coat of arms few besides Custis and Marta could identify as that of Kal IV.

The bandmaster raised his baton, and the imperial fanfare rang out, killing all conversation instantly. At first, most in the audience looked at the trumpeters. Then, as the import of the music registered, they turned to the opposite side of the ballroom where Regent Devy Custis, head held high, waited for silence.

His exquisitely tailored black suit bore only a fraction of the medals, decorations, and adornments dripping off the various military and civilian uniforms surrounding him. Its severity now that he loomed over everyone else became plain enough to convey the message he intended. The platinum and gold regent's chain around his neck was the only badge of office he required. Once the imperial fanfare died away, Custis raised both hands.

"Governors general, governors, high commissioners, my lords and ladies, admirals, generals, officers military and civilian, thank you for attending this historic event."

His voice carried effortlessly to the furthest corners of the cavernous hall. And even though his thanks were pro forma considering tonight was a command performance — show up or give up your place in the hierarchy — not a single murmur of derision or dissension greeted them.

"As you know by now, human civilization is under siege. The madness of the usurper's blood, come to a full boil in Dendera's veins, has effectively ended our thousand-year-old empire. Billions have died, entire star systems are laid waste, and the scavengers our ancestors drove into the galactic badlands are coming back to take what is ours. But we will not let them."

He hammered out the last sentence, enunciating each word as his voice rose to a shout. On cue, the audience applauded, if not enthusiastically then with appreciation, and Custis inclined his head in a regal gesture of thanks.

"Tonight," he continued once the applause faded away, "I declare the empire reborn and cleansed of the Ruggero taint. From this moment on, Lena is no longer merely Yotai's largest city and the seat of the Coalsack Sector viceroyalty. It is also the new imperial capital."

Thunderous applause, this time filled with genuine enthusiasm, rolled over Marta like an ocean wave driven by gale force winds. In its wake, hope, something long absent from Yotai and its dependencies, seemed reborn.

Custis raised his hands again, appealing for quiet. When it came, he said, "A reborn empire needs a sovereign with impeccable qualities. In time, once we elect a duly constituted imperial senate, we will re-institute the ancient laws of succession. But here, today, we must acclaim a new ruler so we can begin our sacred task of rebuilding on the ruins of Dendera's catastrophic misrule."

He paused for dramatic effect, eyes roaming over the crowd, then held out his right hand to Marta, still standing at the foot of the dais.

"Citizens, it is my honor to present your future sovereign, a direct descendant of Emperor Kal IV, humanity's last legitimate ruler." Custis waited until she stood beside him, facing the crowd, then turned toward her and bowed his head. "Behold Lady Marta Norum, who will ascend the throne as Empress Marta, first of her name."

Yet another round of wild applause, this time punctuated by hundreds of throats roaring "Long live Empress Marta," threatened to deafen her. Custis glanced at the bandmaster again and nodded once. Moments later, the imperial anthem, which had not been played since the rebellion first broke out, smothered the assembly's enthusiasm with its rousing strains. Voices that called out Marta's name moments earlier now broke into song, belting out a familiar refrain.

Those in military uniforms stood stiffly at attention while civilians placed their right hands over their hearts. Even Custis sang with gusto.

Marta, as befit an empress-designate, remained silent and aloof since, by custom, a sovereign never uttered the words of the imperial anthem. She was, therefore, the only one to notice Admiral Pendrick Zahar twitch in the unconscious movement she'd long learned to associate with a message coming in on his earbug.

Zahar's face hardened moments later. His eyes switched between her and Custis, but there was no mistaking their unvoiced message. Bad news was in the offing, and at the moment of Custis' greatest triumph since setting foot on Yotai.

— 30 —

A welcome blanket of silence enveloped Marta when the door connecting the ballroom with one of the palace's hidden passageways shut behind them, cutting off the hubbub of voices celebrating her nomination as their next empress. Custis had pled affairs of state and excused them from the festivities, promising to return later for a champagne-fueled toast to her future imperial majesty.

Once in the regent's office, he invited Marta to sit in the place of honor while Heloise and the aides made themselves inconspicuous against the far wall. By now, everyone in the palace gave her the same status as Custis' military aide and where he went, so did she.

"I gather the news you wish to impart is bad, Admiral," Marta said in a flat tone before Custis could speak.

"It is Your Imperial Highness." Zahar glanced at Custis for an indication whether he was briefing the regent or the future empress. Seeing nothing to guide him, he kept his attention on Marta.

"The aviso attached to the Isabella Task Force emerged from Wormhole Yotai Two thirty minutes ago and broadcast on the emergency subspace channel. A battle group from the 2nd Fleet entered the Isabella system via Wormhole One and delivered the same ultimatum Mykonos received. Since the balance of forces is roughly equal, Rear Admiral Demeas Manard, who commands at Isabella, intends to ambush them at the hyperlimit as they drop out of FTL and convince his opposite number to withdraw."

Custis clenched his right fist in anger.

"We can't afford to lose Isabella, Admiral. She's more valuable to our plans than Mykonos."

"I know, Your Grace. That's why Manard will fight." Zahar glanced at the universal date-time readout by Custis' desk. "The engagement will be over by now. Unfortunately, we won't hear how it went for up to a standard day, if not longer. The aviso returned to Isabella the moment fleet operations acknowledged receipt of its message."

"What about subspace radio?" Marta asked.

"Considering the distance between Yotai and Isabella, and the absence of any booster relays in between, the nineteen hour round trip via the wormhole means news travels faster by aviso in this case, Highness."

Custis began pacing in front of his desk.

"Do you plan to send reinforcements?"

Zahar nodded once.

"I alerted the 161st Battle Group. It's accelerating toward the hyperlimit as we speak, but the trip to and through the wormhole will take at least twenty hours, so they'll likely arrive after the battle has already been decided."

"I hope whoever is filling in for Romito on Isabella has enough smarts to surrender unconditionally and evacuate potential target areas if Manard loses the fight."

"Mykonos' example should suffice to make sure your orders in a case such as this are obeyed, sir."

"One would hope," Marta said in a soft tone, "but humans rarely behave rationally under duress." She glanced up at Heloise's bland face.

Custis had made no moves at reclaiming the Mykonos system after orbital strikes obliterated its space-going infrastructure. With no direct wormhole links to the badlands, it was at little risk of a barbarian incursion, unless both Micarat and Yotai fell. Or invaders came via the Cascadian Sector, which appeared to still be in Dendera's hands, or at least part of her navy's hunting grounds.

Yet even the token ground forces Zahar eventually agreed to send didn't pick up any signs of surviving Void Brethren, their mercenary protectors, and two small children, orphaned by their father's murder and their mother's abduction.

Marta vowed to order a full-scale landing on Mykonos once she assumed the throne. It was the only reason she cooperated with Custis' scheme. She felt no desire to be the figurehead ruler of a rump empire destined, if her visions weren't the fevered dreams of encroaching madness, for an ignominious end.

"Shall I inform Baron Romito, sir?"

Custis gave Marta an involuntary glance. When she returned his unvoiced question with a minute shake of the head, he said, "Not yet, Admiral. Let's wait and see how it plays out. Tonight we celebrate a new empire. Setbacks, if any, can wait until morning. Besides, as you said, we're at the mercy of time and distance, and won't know what transpired until later."

"As you command, sir."

Custis ceased pacing and faced them.

"Shall we rejoin the festivities? Since there is nothing further any of us can do to influence matters in the Isabella system, especially if the decisive battle has already come to pass, perhaps it is time to cement the loyalty of our leading citizens with a formal toast to Her Imperial Highness."

A sardonic smile briefly crossed Marta's lips.

"How many out there do you think are wondering why they should bend the knee to an unknown daughter of a borderer marquess whose domain is on the other side of the old empire, solely because Kal IV's blood runs in her veins?"

"They bend the knee because they know the alternatives are unthinkable, my dear. You don't need everyone's unrestrained adulation. You only need enough followers able to make dissenters pay a price. And you have that."

"Unrestrained adulation?" She raised a skeptical eyebrow. "I doubt it. Otherwise, you wouldn't dare call me your dear, a practice I must ask you to cease forthwith."

Her regent seemed momentarily robbed of words. Jaw muscles moved as he chewed on words he could no longer utter, and after a few moments, Custis bowed toward Marta.

"Of course, Your Imperial Highness. I apologize for my inexcusable familiarity."

She silently held his eyes with a blank stare long enough to elicit a twitch of discomfort.

"No one out there adulates me, Devy. They feel relief at what seems like a return to normalcy. Most human beings prefer being ruled, not left to their own devices. The anarchy that demolished a thousand years of certainty has taken a toll on their psyches, and my ascension to a throne cleansed of the Ruggero stench soothes their inner turmoil."

"Your Highness is quite the psychologist." Custis gave Heloise a brief, but suspicious glance as he sat on the corner of his desk. "One could almost wonder if you received mind-meddler training from the witches who call themselves Sisters of the Void. A good thing Admiral

Zahar proscribed their Order on pain of death for meddling with minds to prop up Dendera."

"A good thing? No. A mistake," Marta snapped. "The Void does not exert control over others and certainly does not prop up any sovereign. But the sisters are useful as counselors because they understand *people*, something vital for everyone who aspires to govern. You cannot rule humans if you're unable to recognize what drives them. That, in large part, was the Ruggero dynasty's failure.

"A hunger for power impelled Stichus, not a wish to preserve the empire for the common good of an often fractious species. But he understood human nature sufficiently to seize the throne without shedding blood. His successors, selected because of lineage and not for their ability, didn't inherit even Stichus' minimal understanding. Each generation felt less empathy for its citizenry than the previous one until we found ourselves ruled by a sociopath who by now has ordered the murder of billions. Is either of you familiar with Sun Tzu? I'm sure you must be, Admiral."

"Indeed, Highness," Zahar replied when a frown of puzzlement creased Custis' forehead. "He remains required reading at the Imperial Armed Services Academy."

"Sun Tzu famously said, 'if you know the enemy and know yourself, you need not fear the result of a hundred battles. If you know yourself but not the enemy, for every victory gained you will also suffer a defeat. If you know neither the enemy nor yourself, you will succumb in every battle.' Do you recall?"

"Yes, Highness."

"Tell me, Admiral, do you believe the principle enunciated by Sun Tzu applies to more than just enemies and battles?" When he didn't immediately reply, she said, "let me change a few words, and you'll see what I mean. If a sovereign knows the people and knows herself, she need not fear for her rule. If she knows herself but not the people, then her rule will be uneven and often resented. If she knows neither the people nor herself, she will destroy her realm."

Zahar nodded.

"Understood."

"Devy?"

"I get what you're saying, Highness. I'm not sure how we ended up discussing this subject when we should be back in the ballroom, raising a glass to your health."

"You accused me of being trained by what you term witches, men and women massacred on Admiral Zahar's orders because the rebellion suspected they were Dendera's creatures. I pointed out if they were indeed her servants, their influence was nil. Dendera understands nothing of her responsibilities and cares not a whit for humanity because the concept of empathizing with others is entirely foreign to her nature. Exterminating the Order of the Void was a crime, not a good thing, or a regrettable necessity."

Marta saw Zahar's features tighten under her accusation, but he politely inclined his head.

"We shall remain in disagreement on that subject, Highness, considering the fact Sister Katlynne, who once led the Yotai Abbey, convinced Viceroy Joback to resist the rebellion. I witnessed it with my own eyes and had to strike him down. Besides, the deed is done."

"You mean she advised Joback that rebellion would entail nothing but negative consequences for the citizens of the Coalsack Sector. And she was right, as Mykonos proved. Not to mention the many star systems you abandoned to their fate, such as Arietis, Peralka, and Lyonesse. They too will suffer in due course, just as the original subject of our discussion might be suffering as we speak. Even if Rear Admiral Manard won the battle, many of his people will have died at the hands of their former brothers and sisters from the 2nd Fleet. Did you ever consider Katlynne might have been counseling Joback to consider a third option, one that involved neither rebelling nor proclaiming renewed loyalty to Dendera?"

Zahar's eyes briefly shifted to Custis while he fought off a sour grimace.

"And what could that have been, Highness?"

"Come now, Admiral. Surely a man who reached your high rank knows how to weave a path around competing interests without offending any of them. Joback had many weaknesses, but he took his responsibilities toward the people of this sector to heart."

Custis, who saw Zahar's patience was rapidly evaporating under Marta's scathing arguments, dropped to his feet.

"As do we, Highness. Debating the right or wrong of decisions made before you and I arrived on Yotai, while interesting in its own right, will remain nothing more than an academic exercise. We now carry Joback's burden and must do our utmost to stabilize what remains before correcting past mistakes. And part of that means rejoining our guests to seal the compact between our new sovereign and her people." He gestured toward the door. "Shall we?"

Knowing she'd crossed the line of propriety by goading Zahar about his guilt in ordering the deaths of many thousand Void Brethren, Marta agreed by rising from her chair. It would be unwise to antagonize the man who commanded the most significant naval forces for dozens of lights years in every direction.

"Certainly, Devy." She faced Zahar and met his gaze without a shred of embarrassment. "Admiral, please accept my excuses. I should not address you in such an inconsiderate manner."

He bowed stiffly at the neck, face still hard with suppressed irritation.

"Your Imperial Highness need not apologize for speaking her mind. It is a prerogative of her rank."

"And yet I must do so anyway, Admiral." Marta let a faint smile cross her lips. "A sovereign who knows herself should be confident enough to show contrition when necessary."

If Zahar noticed Marta's careful choice of words, he gave no sign, though she read approval in Heloise's watchful eyes.

"Thank you, Highness." Zahar turned to his aide. "Warn them we're coming back, Colonel. They're to pass out the champagne now."

— 31 —

The deafening cries of 'Long Live Marta' still echoed in her ears when she and Heloise finally entered their private apartments on the palace's top floor, which had become the future empress' exclusive refuge.

"If I never live through such nonsense again, it won't be too soon." Marta removed her crimson, gold-trimmed tunic and carelessly tossed it over the withdrawing room sofa. One of the housekeeping droids would take care of the garment in due time. She pulled a small sensor from a hidden pocket in her ankle-length skirt and glanced at its screen.

"We're clear."

The instrument, liberated from 16th Fleet HQ stocks by one of Marta's friends in the senior non-commissioned officers' mess, would tell her if someone reinstalled the surveillance devices she'd ordered removed a few weeks after their arrival on Yotai.

"It was a tad overwhelming, I agree," Heloise replied after dropping into one of the deep, sinfully comfortable chairs. "But the energy in that room... I can't recall ever

233

experiencing the like before tonight. How did you perceive it?"

"As waves of sound and emotion threatening to knock me over, if truth be told." Marta sat across from Heloise and sighed. "I can't help but feel sorry for them. Their hope I'm able to bring back that which vanished forever saddens me because nothing will restore what once was. At least not in our lifetimes and not even in those of our children's children. I don't know why I'm so certain of it, but tonight reinforced my fears Devy's scheme will end in fire and blood no matter what we try."

"You had visions during the evening." It was not a question. Somehow Heloise always knew when Marta experienced mental turmoil.

"Several."

She described them, ending with the brief flash of a planet, she assumed it was Isabella, under orbital bombardment.

"Why do I see these things, Heloise? And why always images of death and destruction, never of joyful events. Is my mind misfiring and showing me artifacts of my imagination born from a belief the worst is still to come? I remember reading somewhere a person's two brain hemispheres can go out of sync. Is this what's happening?"

"Are you asking me whether you're going crazy? Perhaps. Everyone has a breaking point. You saw your partner executed in a barbaric manner, you lost your children to an unknown fate on a world recently devastated by Dendera's navy. And now Devy Custis forced you to become his figurehead empress in a doomed scheme to revive the empire. Combined, those stressors can push many humans to the limit."

A wry grin lit up Marta's face.

"Wait until Devy figures out he's replacing Dendera with another psychotic bitch."

Heloise smiled back.

"Hardly. You're still far from madness, and you cannot ever turn into Dendera's species of sociopath, my child."

"Then what is my problem, O Wise Sister of the Void whose head is filled with eldritch knowledge?"

She studied Marta for a few seconds with compassionate eyes.

"It's simple. You're becoming one of us. The talent was always there, inside you, but the stresses of the last six months, coupled with my tutelage, is freeing it from the mental prison of your upbringing as an imperial noblewoman. And it is strong. Stronger than any I've experienced."

Marta did a double take.

"Um. What? Are you saying I should wear black robes now?"

A gentle sigh escaped Heloise's lips.

"No. Nowadays, wild talents aren't forced to choose between the abbey and having the ability wiped from their minds. Training is the preferred method for those who don't wish to become one with the Void, and you're learning faster than any other novice I've taught over the years."

After a brief pause, Marta said, "Do you remember telling me you were looking for us when we first met in the ruined quarter of Petras?"

"Yes."

"You said you sensed Sigrid and Stefan's terror?"

"Of course."

"Why were you looking for us?"

A knowing smile appeared.

"Finally, you think to ask the question. Because we already knew you were a wild talent. Sister Lioslaith, who led the Mykonos Abbey before her death, sensed it when she first met you, shortly after your husband became governor general. It is probable Sigrid will develop a form of it as well when she reaches adulthood, considering her emotions were so strong at the time that we could read them from a fair distance. You, on the other hand, already displayed an unusual amount of self-control."

Marta gave Heloise an exasperated look.

"That's nice and well, but it still doesn't tell me why you were looking for us, or how you came close enough to home in on our emotions."

"We track wild talents as a matter of policy, so we can intervene if they experience distress. When the troubles started, Lioslaith ordered me to watch you because she a vision, much like the ones you're experiencing. She could not tell us what or why. Only that it was vital you survived."

"This is getting a little too strange." Marta hugged herself and shivered. "Visions, talents, sisters with supernatural abilities. And now you're saying I'm a mystical seer like Lioslaith." A pause. "You know, I remember her studying me intently whenever she visited Government House, yet it didn't seem intrusive at the time. So this talent you keep talking about, what is it? Precognition?"

"There is no such thing. We cannot know the future because it remains in constant flux until the moment it becomes the present."

"Then it's not so different from the past," Marta replied in a droll tone. "Considering how often history is rewritten to support a particular social or political narrative. But—"

Heloise held up a restraining hand.

"Let me continue. Why do you think the Sisters of the Void are known as the best healers in history, especially when it comes to mental ailments?"

"Because you can sense emotions. You're empaths. Right?"

"Yes, but there's more. The abler among us can also project emotions. Not to override a person's own feelings, let alone their free will. Not only is it forbidden, but we've thankfully not produced a sister capable of violating another's mind in such a manner. Though we hear stories of a failed experiment, back before the empire was born..." Heloise's voice trailed off before she caught herself.

"However, we can strengthen another's resolve in the face of stress, anguish, despair, and any other mental hardship by sharing our own energy, though it can become dangerously tiring. We don't discuss this second ability outside the confines of the Order, as you might understand, but we often use it to speed healing."

"And I'll bet you used it on me."

Heloise nodded.

"In our early weeks together, before you opened your third eye and became able to gather your inner strength."

"So that's why you insisted on my learning and practicing a sister's mental discipline."

"For both our sakes. A talent as strong as yours without discipline would give me more than just headaches, and while we cannot override someone's emotions or free will, it is possible for an unrestrained empath to reinforce negative feelings in others, albeit unwittingly. Considering the mood around here..."

"I see." A contemplative expression relaxed Marta's features. "Does this mean Zahar was right when he accused Void sisters of meddling with Dendera or Joback's mind?"

"No. We can counsel, based on the emotions we read, and help those in need or distress, but the Order's Rule forbids attempting to influence behavior. Besides, less than one in a thousand sisters are strong enough to do anything more than reinforce a person's predispositions by helping strengthen his or her resolve. And those few become abbey healers who work with ailing fellow empaths — not an easy task at the best of times, as you might guess. When a psyche in pain broadcasts, the entire community hears."

A shudder ran down Marta's spine.

"It puts a whole new meaning on the expression clash of minds." She looked up at Heloise again. "Why did you wait until now to tell me?"

"I waited only until you asked the right question."

"A test, then?"

"No. The decision to ask that question was always yours to make. You chose this time, and I respect that choice."

"And if I'd never inquired?"

A knowing smile deepened Heloise's laugh lines.

"You would have. Eventually. Your awareness is still growing, and with that growth comes an urgent need to understand why."

Rather than a reply, the rumble of barely suppressed laughter rose up Marta's throat.

"Can you imagine the reaction of my oh so loyal Admiral Zahar if he finds out his new empress is a Sister of the Void in everything but name? He and Custis already look at you sideways."

"Which is why I spend a not inconsiderable amount of energy deflecting their suspicions."

Marta sat up.

"You can do such a thing?"

"Yes, and I shall teach you how once you've mastered the last of the basic disciplines. But for now, I suggest we rest. It may not seem as if you spent a lot of energy tonight, but trust me, simply deflecting the raw emotions in that ballroom took as much of a toll on you as it did on me. You'll sense it the moment your thoughts stop spinning in circles. Our talent comes with a cost, as such things do, which is why those who came before us locked themselves away in abbeys until they devised ways of dealing with the undisciplined minds of humanity at large."

The moment Heloise's words registered, Marta felt an irrepressible urge to yawn.

"Do sisters also possess the power of suggestion?"

"All humans do in a fashion. Individual effectiveness either depends on sincerity or acting skills, except for yawning. Inexplicably, the mere idea forming in one's mind is enough of a trigger."

Heloise stood with the grace and effortlessness of a gymnast half her age, joined her hands below her chin, and bowed at the waist.

"Good night — *Sister*. May the Almighty watch over your immortal soul."

Sensing Heloise's unexpected formality conveyed something more than just the usual polite exchange before they retired to their separate rooms, she stood as well, imitating her gesture and intonation.

"And I too wish you a good night under the Almighty's protection, *Sister*."

For a moment, Marta read approval in Heloise's eyes, and it warmed her heart to a surprising degree. She might not wear the Void's black, but she belonged nonetheless, and that simple realization nourished her hope the future might not be one of fire and blood.

When she was alone in the withdrawing room, Marta realized Heloise never explained the possible causes of her brief, but troubling visions. And for a moment, she wondered whether they were images of possible futures if not necessarily ones preordained by fate, rather than mental misfires.

Perhaps she didn't ask the right question, or Heloise thought her awareness needed more time to grow before it could encompass the whole truth. Or her statement there was no such thing as precognition *was* the only answer she'd hear. But it still both rankled and amazed her how easily Heloise deflected the subject.

— 32 —

Lyonesse

"Isn't that Count Hallibrank?"

Ty Renlinger nodded at a man in his mid-fifties entering one of Lannion's poshest restaurants. He was in the company of Speaker Rorik Hecht, easily identifiable thanks to prominently displayed portraits in various public places. They were accompanied by two expensively dressed, middle-aged women.

After Admiral Zahar's spies couldn't find any record of *Tanith* landing on Lyonesse, Jaimee Markov suggested they spend their evenings staking out restaurants and bars liable to be patronized by former members of the imperial nobility.

She and Renlinger were ensconced in a booth at the back of *Tristan's Table*, the fine dining establishment touted as Lyonesse's best. Befitting its status, *Tristan's* occupied one of Lannion's most exclusive street corners, within sight of Government House and many of the capital's more luxurious private residences, such as the one owned by Speaker Hecht. Their colleagues, Bouras and Orobio, were across town at the *Condor's Head*, another place favored by the colony's upper crust.

"Yep." Markov studied the foursome out of the corner of her eyes. "And the blonde woman is the former Countess Hallibrank — Cherelle Downes as she is now legally known. This place abolished the nobility, remember?"

"I remember, but the mission files they uploaded to our wetware memory banks list *Tanith* prisoners by their titles, and I'm having a hell of a time overriding the damned data feed with updated information."

He tapped the side of his head with an extended index finger.

"But congrats if you can do so. And for the idea of stalking high-end places. I was afraid we'd run through our funds in the space of a week with nothing to show for it. But here we are, the second day of Operation Gluttony watching the most senior of the condemned courtiers hobnobbing with one of Lyonesse's top citizens. It proves *Tanith* landed here and decanted at least a couple of stasis stiffs. They'll be pleased back home."

"A shame they didn't bother narrowing it down for us with a few names. They can't be concerned about the whole bunch, common criminals, and hard core jailbirds included."

"What's the plan, now we spotted Severin and his Cherelle?" Renlinger drained his wine glass and grimaced. The local plonk had a distinct earthy tang he found distracting. Best stick with beer. "Approaching him, considering his social circles nowadays, will be a bigger problem than making friends with Lyonesse Defense Force drinkers while keeping our covers intact."

"That's Kamaal's call. Our orders are to find *Tanith* and we just spotted two of its most important passengers." She paused as movement by the entrance caught her attention. "Make that four. The former Earl of Hadley, Brady Apostolos, and the former Countess Hadley, Verity Apostolos, just walked in. Looks like they're joining the Downes party."

"And our plates are coming."

Once the server left them to enjoy dishes picked from the menu's cheapest items, Markov pulled a small, boxy device from her pocket, placed it on their table, and aimed it at Downes, Hecht, and their companions. She waited for the sensor to calibrate, then instructed it to concentrate its audio pickup on them.

"There. We can listen to the conversation later." Markov picked up her utensils. "I hope this stuff is worth the price we're paying. The wine sure as hell isn't."

They lingered as long as possible without attracting undue attention after finishing their meal and paying the bill. Unfortunately, their targets seemed to be settling in for the long haul, downing bottle after bottle of a much better vintage than the operatives could afford. Finally, Markov pocketed her sensor and slid out of the booth.

"Let's go take a walk around the neighborhood to digest and find a nice bench from where we can see Severin and Cherelle leave," she muttered in a tone pitched only for her colleague's ears. "Kamaal won't thank us if we come back without an address."

"What about the other two? We each take a pair?" Renlinger asked once they were out in the humid evening air.

"I don't like splitting up, but perhaps this once it might be worthwhile. You take Apostolos, and I'll take Downes." Markov's leisurely pace faltered for a moment. "Shit."

"What?"

"Tall, dark, and handsome party wearing a centurion's diamonds over by the Government House gate, talking to the sentry. Looks like a duty officer doing her rounds. Keep walking, Ty, and don't stare."

Moments later, the woman climbed into a defense force staff car idling at the barrier. It slipped aside soundlessly and the car, wearing nothing more than a double-headed condor, crossed swords and anchor insignia instead of a registration plate, turned left on the quasi-deserted boulevard and headed north, toward Lannion Base.

"Talk to me, Jay," Renlinger said in an urgent whisper, sensing his winger's agitation as they walked away in the other direction with the languor of gourmets who overate.

"I could swear that was Adrienne Barca. We were together in the 2nd of the 21st long before she took a commission. We knew each other pretty well."

"So? You didn't show signs of heartburn when we studied the organization chart and saw a Centurion Barca, 21st Pathfinder Regiment, on the roster."

"I wasn't looking for old friends, Ty. Adrienne and me, it was long ago, and she's not the only Barca in the Corps, so I didn't make the connection. If I'm right and that was Adri, she can't see me up close. Otherwise, we're fucked because she'll ask questions I can't answer. They called her many things over the years, but stupid wasn't one of them. And she has a memory for faces like you wouldn't believe."

Intrigued by Markov's urgent tone, Renlinger asked, "How close were you two?"

"What business is it of yours?" She snapped.

Renlinger held up both hands in a gesture of surrender.

"Whoa, Jay. No need to rip my face off. Take a deep breath and relax. I'm just asking because if it's been a long time, why should Barca see through your disguise."

She took a deep breath.

"I suppose you'll bug me until I tell you." When Renlinger gave her a happy nod in an attempt to defuse the tension, Markov sighed. "Adrienne knows where I'm ticklish, and vice versa. Good enough?"

"So you fooled around. What's the problem?"

She took a deep breath and said, "I don't know why I'm sensitive about it. Maybe because of the way our relationship ended. Sorry I turned snarly on you, but seeing her again, here, spooked me. After the shit of the last eighteen months, all those regiments decimated if not wiped out and the empire gone to shit, I never figured to find Adri Barca here, where they sent us to search for a stolen starship."

"You going to tell Kamaal about her?"

"Do I have a choice?"

**

Bouras clapped Markov on the shoulder after she told him about seeing Adrienne Barca at the Government House front gate.

"Don't worry about it, Jay. The chances of you bumping into her are pretty damn low. And if you do, make like she's a total stranger. This is a big galaxy. Lots of complete strangers resemble each other in one way or another because of common ancestors in the distant past."

"They're called phenotypes," Cerys Orobio offered.

"Sure. Whatever." Bouras nodded agreeably. "Let's listen to Severin Downes, Brady Apostolos, and their dinner companions. If they're breaking bread with this Rorik Hecht character, it could be educational. Well done on finding where those former stasis stiffs live, by the way. We may need to visit one of them at some point."

The four operatives settled into the ancient, sagging easy chairs surrounding their apartment's living room table. Renting temporary lodgings by the week, dingy as they were instead of using one of the city's hotels turned out to have more advantages than just saving money. Chief among them was the other tenants in the rundown, ten unit building, subscribing to the credo of don't ask, don't tell.

It meant no one paid the operatives any undue attention. And since, unlike a hotel, the apartment's owners didn't offer cleaning services, it was easier to keep clear of surveillance devices and set telltales to detect intrusions.

Markov placed her sensor on the table and tapped its controls. A small holographic projection of the dinner party appeared above it.

"I think you recognize the people around the table, other than Speaker Hecht's partner."

When her colleagues nodded, she said, "Sit back and enjoy. This will be a long night."

After a few minutes, Bouras groaned.

"I was hoping to never hear that damn Wyvern drawl again. I don't know which of them annoys me the most."

Renlinger shrugged.

"Downes by a nose, though the other three are no better."

"Seems like the locals are onto a good idea, abolishing the nobility."

"Don't mention that to anyone at home, boss. Otherwise, our next mission might be to find Tortuga Station, and who knows if that place even exists."

A few minutes later, Bouras held up a hand.

"Pause the recording, Jay. Did this Hecht guy just mention something called a knowledge vault?"

Orobio nodded.

"That's what I heard."

"What the fuck is that?" Renlinger gave Bouras a puzzled glance.

"If we keep listening instead of yakking, we might find out," Markov replied in a biting tone.

Two hours later, Bouras suppressed a mighty yawn and stretched his arms over his head.

"Let's leave the rest for tomorrow. I think we heard the juicy parts, anyway."

"But we're still no wiser on this knowledge vault, except Hecht wants to take control of it away from the military and the Order of the Void," Renlinger said.

"Not quite." Markov climbed to her feet and paced around the room. "I'd say Hecht was feeling out Downes and Apostolos to see if they'd help him do just that. I got the idea those two are the top dogs among the exiled lordlings and can make the other stasis stiffs march in step. Downes seems to have a hate-on for the military. He practically quivered with anger every time Admiral Morane's name came up."

"Yeah, I noticed. That's when his accent became really hard to stomach."

Markov stopped in front of Bouras.

"What's next? We know *Tanith* landed here. The proof is in that recording. Do we find every other passenger, in case the bosses are looking for a specific stiff but won't or can't tell us the name, then bugger off? Or do we try to find out what this knowledge vault does when it's at home? If the star system's top politician is making like there's a power struggle over it, to the point of enlisting people pissed off at the Lyonesse government for stripping them of their titles, we probably should investigate."

"You could call your old girlfriend and ask her," Orobio suggested, winking at Markov. "If the military controls this vault, she'll know about it. A bit of pillow talk, a tickle or two, and we can write up the mission report."

Markov gave her the rigid digit salute, then groaned when she saw the thoughtful expression on Bouras' face.

"No, Kamaal. Not now, not ever."

"Let's not be too hasty. I know Cerys meant it as a tasteless joke, but she might be onto something."

"I got a better idea," Markov replied. "They said the Void Brethren were working with the university on this knowledge vault. How about we snoop around the hallowed halls of learning? Civilians are a lot more likely to let secrets slip than a veteran Pathfinder centurion who probably remembers why we weren't on speaking terms when I left the 2nd of the 21st."

Bouras remained silent for a moment, then he came to a decision.

"We work both angles of the mission so we don't miss something important. Admiral Zahar isn't exactly a forgiving guy. Jay, you and Ty will visit the university tomorrow. Cerys and I will tail Severin Downes and see if he can lead us to more of his friends. That way, he won't wonder why the cute couple he saw at *Tristan's Table* keeps showing up wherever he goes — in case the constipated asshole accent masks a keen sense of observation."

— 33 —

Yotai

Marta swept into the briefing room with stately grace, seeming to float above the polished marble floor as if on an antigrav cushion. As always a silent, yet watchful Heloise trailed her. Everyone rose, the military officers coming to attention.

"Regent, Admiral," she nodded at Custis and Zahar, standing side by side on the other side of the oval table. "I understand we received news from Admiral Manard at Isabella."

She slipped into her chair, the signal for everyone else to do likewise. Heloise took her place beside the principal aides along the wall. By unspoken accord, the officers who attended Custis and Zahar left her the senior position, conscious the lady-in-waiting to the future empress outranked them. Their deference, grudging as it was, privately amused Heloise since they didn't know what she really was.

"We have, Your Imperial Highness," Custis replied. He turned to Zahar. "Go ahead, Admiral."

"Protecting Isabella against the incursion of a battle group from Dendera's Retribution Fleet did not go as well as we hoped."

A sardonic smile briefly tugged at Marta's lips.

"Retribution Fleet, Admiral?"

"Apparently, that is what Dendera calls the formation engaged in destroying everyone who resists her rule. We took it from an intelligence intercept."

"Thank you. Please continue."

"Rear Admiral Manard used a retrograde maneuver after ambushing the enemy battle group as they emerged from FTL at Isabella's hyperlimit. Do you know what that is, Your Highness?" When Marta shook her head, Zahar said, "In short, it means Manard placed himself between the enemy and Isabella, withdrawing as they advanced, so he could keep engaging until they either break off or are neutralized."

"Or the enemy destroys Manard's ships."

"Just so. Retrograde maneuvers can devastate opposing forces if they're of equal strength since they remain in constant contact. In this case, Manard lost over half of his ships before the imperial commander decided he no longer had the strength or the appetite to continue and fled. But not before firing off a swarm of kinetic strikers from just beyond the orbit of Isabella's outer moon. Manard's ships and the orbital defense platforms destroyed many, with the ground-based aerospace systems taking most of the rest, but enough got through to cause, at a conservative estimate, almost fifty thousand civilian casualties.

"While Isabella's capital took the brunt of the strike, one projectile punched through the main orbital station, killing almost two-thirds of the skeleton staff aboard. Fortunately, the star system government evacuated it twelve hours earlier. The station will need significant repairs before we can once again use it as a transshipment facility for cargo and passengers.

"In total, the enemy killed three thousand, two hundred and fifteen naval personnel. We won't get a final tally of civilian casualties for a while because the strikers vaporized anyone near ground zero. The imperial battle group lost two-thirds of its ships with an estimated five to six thousand lives."

"More souls sacrificed on the altar of human greed and vanity for the sake of power," Marta murmured to herself, appalled as much by Zahar's report as by his clinical tone.

"Highness?" Custis gave her a questioning glance.

"Our species may have conquered the stars, but beneath the shiny veneer of a high-tech civilization, we're still the same fratricidal savages as our distant ancestors who roamed the plains of prehistoric Earth, unredeemed and perhaps unredeemable."

"And that's why we must hasten the rebirth of a just empire, capable of protecting its citizens from Dendera's apocalyptic nightmare."

"Are our forces strong enough to keep stopping this Retribution Fleet until it leaves the Coalsack Sector alone, Admiral?"

To his credit, Zahar grimaced as he shook his head.

"Since we can't tell when and where they might appear with enough lead time to muster our strength, imperial battle groups can more easily achieve local superiority for brief periods. And that is all they need since they aim to devastate a star system rather than retake it. And they appear to be showing a degree of fanaticism never seen before. Admiral Manard said his opposite number kept on coming long after naval doctrine would have dictated he break off the engagement and flee. I reviewed the battle logs and agree."

"So the Retribution Fleet can destroy us piecemeal unless we concentrate our forces in a few core systems where they'll be strong enough to deal with incursions."

Zahar's sour expression grew.

"In a nutshell, yes. Eventually, they'll run out of ships and crews through sheer attrition with the overly aggressive tactics Manard witnessed, but we'll run out faster. Our population base is smaller than the Wyvern Sector's, and our orbital yards can't produce capital ships at anywhere near the same rate as theirs."

"And offering resistance whenever they give a star system an ultimatum merely jacks up the death count, not to mention the destruction of critical infrastructure."

"An accurate assessment, Highness."

"Then our only choice is to not play Dendera's game, gentlemen."

"What do you mean?" Custis asked.

"If we cannot protect a star system from Retribution Fleet attacks without suffering unacceptable losses, we should withdraw from that system militarily but still keep political control in some manner. If and when imperial ships appear, the local government will surrender and declare its loyalty to Empress Dendera."

A vague air of surprise spread across Custis' patrician features.

"You're saying we shouldn't try to defend what's ours unless we establish overwhelming superiority?"

"It's better than picking a fight that can only end with unacceptable casualties. I'd rather see our people keep their critical infrastructure along with their lives. Dendera wants her admirals to salt the ground at the first sign of resistance. Let's not give them that pleasure, especially if they've become increasingly fanaticized. They wish to make a desert and call it peace. We want our peace to flourish."

"You realize what an order to surrender at the first sight of imperial warships will do for morale across the sector, Highness. The people threw off Dendera's chains. Asking them to submit meekly will not go over well."

"Leaving aside the fact that many, perhaps even a plurality, would have remained loyal given a choice, only the living can experience morale issues, Regent. I'd rather see my citizens unhappy but alive. We can cheer anyone up once the danger has passed. Resurrection, on the other hand, is beyond our capacity, unless you recently gained godlike powers. And you seem no holier than when we first met at court long ago."

Though she couldn't see Heloise, since the Sister of the Void sat behind her, Marta nonetheless fancied she could feel her smile of approval.

"Granted, Highness. Life is always preferable. Admiral Zahar and I shall take your suggestion under advisement and discuss the matter."

"You will do more than that, Regent."

Marta's soft tone didn't make her words less of a royal command. On the contrary. In the ensuing pause, most around the table and sitting against the walls were forced to reconsider whether Regent Custis was in control of the proto-empire's destiny.

"I would like to see a plan by the end of this week to consolidate our forces in formations capable of chasing off Retribution Fleet battle groups without suffering undue losses. Once we know which star systems will form our hardened core, we can decide how to exert political control over the rest while Dendera exhausts her resources."

An embarrassed silence fell over the briefing room. Marta knew the flag officers present, Zahar chief among them, were aware Custis wanted a figurehead empress, one whose role as military commander-in-chief would be limited to ceremonial functions, leaving important decisions to her regent.

Yet now he'd presented Marta as the future sovereign, silencing her voice in public fora was no longer an option. Whether they approved of her taking an active role remained unanswered, though based on the general atmosphere and the surreptitious glances around the table Marta sensed many of them thought her point was valid. Dendera's admirals might no longer care whether they lived or died, provided they pleased their empress, but the officers of the 16th Fleet didn't hold the same opinion.

"As you command," Zahar finally replied, bowing his head in submission. Custis, jaw muscles working as he digested Marta's orders, remained silent. "Would Your Highness agree to minimal forces, perhaps a few patrol vessels remaining in each border star system to act as tripwires, withdrawing the moment they make out the enemy's strength and intentions?"

"I would, Admiral. So long as their presence, be it ever so brief once Retribution Fleet starships arrive, doesn't provoke Dendera's mad admirals into declaring those star systems in rebellion against the Crown and imposing a Carthaginian peace. You may even keep control over planetary ground forces — reinforce them if necessary, as you did on Mykonos, so long as they vanish into the hills once the government surrenders and submits."

"Of course."

"Did you wish to discuss anything else, Regent?"

"No, Your Highness," Custis said, facial expression and voice once more under control after being forced to back down by a willful figurehead ruler who'd just demonstrated she was anything but.

**

Once back in the privacy of the imperial apartments, Heloise dropped into her accustomed chair, and studied Marta as she removed her tunic, folded it carefully over the sofa's back, and sat.

"Amusing as that was, I think you went just a bit too far in exerting your authority over Custis."

"If I'm going to be sovereign of this rump kingdom beset from every side and destined for a dismal future, I should take responsibility for the lives of my people, don't you think?"

Heloise inclined her head by way of acknowledgment.

"Just take care Custis doesn't rue making you his candidate and puts extra effort in finding Corinne."

"After publicly naming me? I don't think he can manage a switch, especially since he made such a big deal about my being a direct descendant of the last pre-Ruggero emperor. Replacing the empress-designate he toasted in front of the sector's star system rulers with a Ruggero won't do much for his credibility with the 16th Fleet. I'm sure you noticed Zahar isn't blindly loyal to our esteemed regent, and he's already murdered one viceroy. If the admiral sees issues with my directives from a military standpoint, I'm sure he'll say so. He might not be in full agreement, politically speaking, but I didn't order him to place his ships and crews at greater risk than they are now. On the contrary."

"I don't disagree. I merely wished to see if you understood the ramifications of your actions in the briefing room earlier."

A mocking smile twisted Marta's lips.

"What? You don't trust your star pupil? I'm crushed."

"You're my only pupil at the moment, so I have no basis of comparison to call you a star. But humor me. I've lived two lifetimes to your one, based on our respective ages, and seen many a novice let her newfound self-awareness and mental discipline lead her into trouble, particularly if she, just like you, was one of the rare sisters with the ability to reach out and not only receive.

"It is possible Custis bowed to your will because he accepted your logic, or perhaps he sensed Zahar and the other flag officers thought the plan a better one than scattering their forces and dying by degrees. After all, you alone from those present could call on extensive knowledge of the past to guess what might happen in the future."

"True, but I sense you're about to drop the other shoe."

"Only because you're becoming perceptive. The other possibility is that you may have unconsciously — and this is difficult to describe with mere words — projected your will at Custis and the military officers, overriding their desire to object. The effect would last only while you were in the room. By now, they could be wondering what happened."

"Oh." A thoughtful expression crossed Marta's face. "Do you think I may have done so?"

"I don't know, child. Since I also belong to the one in a thousand with heightened abilities, I'm immune to another's mental pressures. But at the time, it did seem they agreed rather more easily than I expected. We shall see in due course, I should imagine."

Before Marta could reply, her communicator chimed. She pulled it from her skirt pocket and glanced at the screen.

"One of my drinking friends tells me the latest dispatches from Mykonos might include an item of interest."

"Will you go to the senior non-commissioned officers' mess right away?"

"I can't. It's too early."

"Then I suggest exercise followed by meditation."

— 34 —

Lyonesse

"And our last item."

Centurion Eve Haller, who was chairing the weekly coordination conference, turned away from the briefing board and took her seat at the head of the table.

"Last week, four visitors claiming to be commercial representatives for a company by the name Universal Exports arrived aboard *Avadora* along with the most recent bunch of immigrants. I was on operations watch at the time and saw the arrival hall's video feed, as well as the visitor credentials. It was the duty crew's general opinion that the four behaved less like civilian merchants than current or former military personnel. One, of them, in Sergeant First Class Eddy Craddoc's opinion, might even carry a challenge coin familiar to those of us with service in Special Forces units."

She gestured toward Centurion Greff, the Rifle Regiment's operations officer.

"As Ian knows, Colonel DeCarde asked Colonel Kayne to put eyes from the Rifles' informal intelligence network on them. Yesterday, those sharp young troopers spotted our visitors behaving rather strangely for commercial representatives."

"She's about to drag out the suspense again, I can sense it," Centurion Adrienne Barca, B Squadron's executive officer, grumbled in a stage whisper.

Lieutenant Commander Ann Creswell's foreshortened holographic projection chuckled. *Vanquish*'s combat systems officer, like the other warship representatives, attended the weekly meetings remotely from orbit when they weren't on wormhole terminus picket duty.

"Be merciful. Working in a clifftop aerie doesn't give poor Eve much scope to stretch her acting muscles."

"Or any other muscles for that matter, and that's why you might find me in the HQ gym at oh-six-hundred every morning if you bothered to get up that early, Adri."

Barca gave her friend a wicked grin.

"Everyone with a shred of pity for Defense Force HQ chair warmers, raise your hand." When no one moved, she sat back and said, "There you go. Now speak so we can be about our business. Some of us are in the middle of field training exercises and need to return before our COs come up with ideas that'll give us XOs fresh stomach ulcers."

Haller raised both hands in surrender.

"All right. Two of the visitors were seen snooping around the university and showed a special interest in the library annex where the Void Brethren are working. The other two spent most of the day watching Severin Downes, whom you'll remember for his charming personality and larger-than-life sense of entitlement. They took up residence in a lease by the week apartment near the river docks."

"Which is both smart and dumb. They traded a hotel's surveillance suite for the beady eyes of wharf rats able to smell trouble a parsec away," Barca replied. "Perhaps the Lannion cops can chat up their informants. And since I'm probably not the only one who hasn't seen what those people look like, could you put their mugs and ID data up on the main display, Eve? Let's see if Eddy Craddoc can still dig up suspicious characters."

"You didn't read the relevant daily digest?" Haller asked in an arch tone.

"So I'm running behind. That's what happens when your CO's enthusiasm at planning an exercise on a new planet with plenty of unexplored potential for mischief needs reining-in."

"Want the full video from immigration?"

"Might as well," Barca said to unanimous nods of agreement.

When the video died away, and the foursome's ID pictures replaced it, Haller noticed something was bothering Barca.

"You recognize one of them, Adri?"

Barca bit her lower lip before shrugging.

"Only the dark-haired woman Eddy Craddoc figured might be one of our sort—"

"Jaimee Markov."

"Right. Her face is annoyingly familiar. She reminds me of someone I was close to years ago when we were both sergeants in the 2nd Battalion. Same phenotype, but with subtle differences. Moves like her too, or at least the way I remember her moving. Krystal Sandt. She left the 21st and transferred to a line regiment not long after our relationship turned sour. I've not seen her since that day."

Haller's forehead creased in a frown as she rifled through her memory.

"Krystal Sandt? The name rings a bell, for sure. But I can't remember much. Definitely not what she looked like. I was in the 4th Battalion before taking my commission and rarely spoke with anyone in the 2nd outside of the sergeant's mess." She glanced at the other Pathfinders around the table. "Any of you remember her?"

When they shook their heads in turn, Haller said, "Pass the picture around your squadrons, and see if anyone other than Adri comes up with a possible ID."

"Will you let the colonel know?"

"That's not optional. If four military-looking offworlders, one of them potentially a Pathfinder, are snooping around the university end of the admiral's knowledge vault and taking an interest in Lyonesse's biggest pain in the ass, we might have a problem."

A grimace twisted Barca's lips.

"If you ask me, there's no might about it. Those people are on a recon mission. I think they're looking for *Tanith*, considering the interest in Severin Downes."

"Tell you what, I'll make sure they're under constant observation," Centurion Greff offered. "Some of my budding counterintelligence agents can afford to skip classes for a few days. And I'll speak with the Lannion Police chief of detectives. He's an old drinking buddy of mine."

"Thanks, Ian. If there's nothing else, we're done here. Since you're about to head into the wild sierras where the condors roam, Adri, how about we see if the colonel has a minute. That way, you won't need to return from the backwoods when she decides your past relationship with someone who resembles a woman overly interested in the knowledge vault could be important."

Barca sighed.

"I suppose."

"Not a good break up?" Creswell asked.

"Are any of them?"

"I suppose not. Until next week, then." Her hologram winked out, along with those of *Myrtale*'s and *Narwhal*'s combat systems officers.

**

DeCarde sat back in her chair, fingers tapping the metal desktop in a rhythmic tattoo when Haller and Barca finished speaking.

"If we're indeed talking about Krystal Sandt, a former noncom in the 2nd Battalion, 21st Pathfinder Regiment, masquerading as Jaimee Markov, putative commercial representative, I agree we might have a problem. We need to find out why they're here and who they work for."

"There's one way of finding out, sir. I could always confront Markov and see how she reacts. If that's Krystal and not a distant cousin who shares her genetic makeup, she won't be able to hide anything from me."

"If we're at that stage," Haller said, "we might as well haul them in and ask Sister Gwenneth for one of her human lie detectors."

"On what grounds?" DeCarde's fingers stopped moving. "Did they break any laws?"

"National security?"

"That's a slippery slope, Eve. What waits at the bottom of it wouldn't be pleasant for the society we're trying to build. The admiral's vision might even take a hit if we turn Lyonesse into something that smells like Dendera's bloody police state. Our first and most important job is protecting the knowledge vault, and that means shielding the host planet from its own worst instincts."

"Then we're back to Adri's suggestion, sir. We can keep Colonel Kayne's irregulars on their butts from sunset to sunset and be none the wiser if they're here on a recon mission."

DeCarde stood and walked to her office's single window overlooking Lannion Base.

"You didn't part on good terms, I gather. Tell me the story."

"There isn't much to tell, sir. I was a command sergeant working as the A Squadron operations noncom and Krystal was a buck sergeant working as D Squadron's intelligence analyst when we met and hit it off. Same mess, different chain of command, no problems, right? We moved in together. But with the squadrons on different deployment schedules — you probably remember the entire regiment was busy eight or nine years ago — we spend half our time apart, the other half making up for lost time."

"Burning the candle four times as fast."

"Six or eight times, sir, if not faster. Krystal figured out pretty quick the Pathfinder lifestyle wasn't what she wanted in the long run. But leaving the 21st for a line regiment at the other end of the empire meant we'd never see each other again unless we transferred together."

"And you wanted to stay."

"Being a Pathfinder was my life, Colonel. Leaving the 21st wasn't an option, no matter how I felt about Krystal. She didn't understand, and the relationship flipped one-hundred and eighty degrees from really good to really ugly. We both felt a lot of hate, the sort that leaves a permanent scar. I moved back into the command noncom quarters on base, and she made like I no longer existed. Eight weeks later, Krystal transferred to the 55th Marine Regiment on Yotai."

Upon hearing the name of the Coalsack Sector's capital, DeCarde whirled around to face Barca.

"Yotai. That's where Grand Duke Custis ended up after his minions sprung him from *Tanith*'s stasis pod farm. Which means if Markov is Krystal Sandt, and she's still a member of the 55th, Viceroy Custis is her ultimate boss."

Eve Haller let out a low whistle.

"I think we just found a good reason for military spies to visit Lyonesse."

After a heartbeat, Barca whispered, "Corinne Ruggero, better known, or rather unknown as Sister Incognito of the Lyonesse Abbey. That's why they're interested in Downes. *Tanith* might be gone, but he's the most visible of the stasis stiffs who traveled with Corinne and Custis. Someone on Arietis told Custis' people about the prison ship mated to *Narwhal*, so here they are. Nice way to repay us for giving their militia a leg up."

"We didn't exactly hide *Tanith*, Adri," DeCarde dropped into her chair. "And if we're on the right track, Markov and company are trained operatives. Didn't you say Krystal worked as a squadron intelligence sergeant? She'll have learned the basics. And who knows what the others are behind those fake names and faces. Do you know what her assignment in the 55th was?"

"No, but since Krystal's secondary occupational specialty was battlefield analyst, she probably didn't end up humping a plasma rifle." An air of pained indecision crossed Barca's square features. "If you want me to chat up this Markov and find out if she's Krystal, I'll do it. Hell, if it's a matter of protecting the vault, I might even make nice to her. I might need to spend time with Sister Katarin afterward, purging my soul. But as they say, duty first."

"You can always apply to join the abbey as a novice when your time with the regiment is up," Haller said in a flippant tone.

Barca gave her a weary smile.

"A life of contemplation and service to others seems pretty damn good right now."

"I wouldn't have taken you for a believer in the Almighty."

She gave DeCarde a droll smile.

"I'm like most Marines, Colonel — I want the Almighty watching over me when I'm ducking enemy fire, not when I'm evading angry lovers. So what's the word?"

"If I may," Eve Haller said, "I can ask Sergeant Kuryakin to put you in touch with the Rifle Regiment's spook chasers. Do a couple of surveillance shifts and see if you get that feeling in your gut. You know the one I mean."

"Sure. When your heart drops into your stomach and splashes starship reactor acid all over your insides. What about the squadron field exercise?"

"I'm sure your squadron sergeant major would love to play executive officer and keep Bowdoin from having too much fun," Haller said. "What do you think, Colonel? As a first step, I mean? No laws broken, no slippery slope. If Adri doesn't feel weak in the knees, we switch to another line of thinking. If she does, then we can discuss an oblique approach."

DeCarde's eyes shifted from Haller to Barca and back, trying to gage the latter's reaction.

"Adri seems torn between a hearty yes and hell no. Am I right?"

Barca nodded ruefully.

"You are, sir. Some memories never go away, and Krystal's one of them. If she's hiding behind Jaimee Markov's identity, one look into her eyes will do the trick."

"That's all I need. Give me a yea or nay with ninety-nine percent confidence, and I'll bring it to the admiral. If we're being scouted by one of Grand Duke Devy Custis' recon teams, he'll want to make the final decision. Will you be okay letting Bowdoin know you're on temporary detachment at my orders? I'll speak with Piotr Salmin the moment we're done here to close the loop."

"No problems, Colonel."

"In that case, go make friends with Matti Kayne's irregulars. When this is over, I'd like your opinion on whether they're candidates for our proposed counterintelligence unit. So far, the admiral's been thinking about creating a military police company. But if the warlords of this galaxy keep sending us spies, we'll need more than just our own law enforcement."

Haller and Barca shot to their feet.

"Yes, sir."

"Enjoy."

— 35 —

Yotai

Marta, wearing loose dark clothes, made her way down one of the viceregal palace's service staircases, tailed by the ever-present Heloise. A rabbit warren of well-lit passages brought them to the senior non-commissioned officers' mess open side door. Marta stuck her head through and caught the eye of the nearest Marine command sergeant, a member of the 55th Regiment's guard detail, silently asking for permission to enter.

When he gave her the nod, she left Heloise in the corridor to stand watch and slipped into the mess. An assemblage of half a dozen large, interconnected rooms, it was paneled in dark, rich wood harvested from a species of Yotai tree analog similar to oak. A wall-length bar backed by mirrored shelves holding bottles of every alcoholic drink known to humanity dominated one side of the main room. The bar itself was topped by a polished sheet of metal supposedly taken from the hull of a downed reiver starship five hundred years earlier, though time and use had worn off any identifying marks.

Plaques, souvenirs, images, and bladed weapons of every sort covered the walls while old banners, many of them captured in battle, hung from blackened ceiling beams. The heavy furniture scattered in random groupings was milled from the same native wood as the wainscoting. But unlike the wall coverings, it shone under the soft lighting thanks to a varnish capable of resisting just about anything short of a blaster's plasma bolt.

A faint aroma of roasted meat mixed with that of stout ale tickled Marta's nostrils as she looked for her friend from the 16th Fleet HQ operations center, a Marine Corps command sergeant by the name Nadav Sodhi. He served under Uncle Olav in the 35th Imperial Marine Regiment on Peralka thirty years earlier, during the reign of Emperor Karlus, and held him in high regard.

She found Sodhi, wearing casual civilian clothes, sitting alone in the snug nursing a tall glass of beer while waiting patiently for her. He glanced up as soon as he saw movement from the corners of his eyes and gestured at the seat across from him.

"Please grab a pew, Milady. Can I offer you anything?"

"A Glen Arcturus, if the mess still has any, but it goes on my tab, Nadav."

When she first reached out to the noncom network shortly after arriving on Yotai, Marta had insisted they treat her as nothing more than a simple guest. It meant no standing when she entered a room, no paying for her drinks, or taking notice of her titles. And if her presence in the mess was no longer desired, she would respect that decision as well.

"No problems." Sodhi touched the edge of the tabletop. "Won't be but a minute. Not many customers left now that supper's done."

"Any reason?"

The old noncom shrugged.

"Wednesday evening is usually dead."

A serving droid entered the snug moments later, carrying a crystal tumbler filled with an amber liquid. The smoky, boozy aroma of a twelve-year-old single malt hit her nostrils seconds after the droid placed the glass in front of her.

She raised it in salute.

"Skoal, Nadav."

"To your health, Milady."

After taking a sip, Marta smacked her lips with appreciation.

"That's the good stuff. It'll be a sad day when we've emptied the last bottle in the Coalsack Sector."

Sodhi made a dismissive sound.

"Maybe for you, but I'm a beer drinker, and Yotai isn't about to run out of suds."

"Good thing I'm developing a taste for the local whiskey. That won't run out either."

A theatrical shudder ran up Sodhi's spine.

"Pass. Since Zahar razed the Yotai Abbey, there hasn't been any drinkable rotgut on this damned planet. Say what you want about the mind-meddlers, they were master brewers and distillers."

"How's duty these days?"

"Nothing changes much in the operations center, Milady, but my friends in the 55th and 56th aren't getting any happier with the increased spit and polish bullshit. It's almost like the grand duke is trying to turn us Marines into damned Guards. Is it true we're about to get our imperial titles back because of you?"

Marta nodded.

"That's the plan."

"Then I guess you won't be drinking with us lowly sergeants no more."

"And why would I stop? As the empress, I'll be commander-in-chief of the armed services. Doesn't that mean becoming an honorary member of every single mess, be it junior, noncom or officer?"

Sodhi half closed one eye as he rummaged through his memory.

"Can't say I remember offhand, but it sounds about right. The old-time emperors and empresses, before Stichus Ruggero, wore uniforms with no rank badges or fancy trim to show they were one of us."

The comment brought to mind pictures Marta had seen of Kal IV during his term as emperor. In them, he always sported a black Marine tunic no different from that of a private, adorned only with the medals and qualification badges he'd accumulated during a long career in the Imperial Marine Corps.

"At least they earned those uniforms," Marta replied after taking another heady sip. "I don't know what I'll be expected to wear."

"Whatever you damn well please, I figure." Sodhi gave her a complicit smile. He took a healthy pull at his beer and exhaled slowly. "Like I said in my message, I received news from Mykonos. My buddy Nate tracked the people you're looking for from Tiryns to Thera and from Thera to a tiny place called Issos, about fifty klicks inland, west of Thera. Issos escaped the imperial attack unscathed because it has nothing more than a dirt strip."

Marta nodded, her mind's eye calling up images of a village she'd visited with her husband during their first year on Mykonos when Hachim was still establishing himself as governor general.

"They lived in a house on the outskirts and didn't mingle much with the locals, though nobody in Issos said anything bad about them. The way Nate tells it, they don't remember much, other than there were two kids, four security guards — mercenaries, probably — and quiet folks who were good at medicine and farming."

"Lived?"

"That's the thing, Milady. About two months ago, give or take, a shuttle landed by the house one night and the next morning, the kids, mercs, and quiet folk were gone without a trace. No one in Issos saw the shuttle. Hell, most didn't even know one landed, so I'm afraid that's where the trail ends. Sorry."

Marta reached out and squeezed Sodhi's thick, muscular forearm.

"Don't be. Your friend Nate sent the most encouraging news I've received since leaving Mykonos. If a starship picked them up, then my children are safe."

A skeptical frown deepened the lines creasing his face.

"Really?"

"The people who promised to care for Sigrid and Stefan figured a ship would eventually come to pick them up. And it sounds like that happened."

"How will you find the wee ones now?"

"The Almighty will provide, my friend." Marta could almost hear Heloise's calm voice speaking in her head. "Besides, the man who appointed himself their protector will make sure nothing happens. He's a bit like you and a lot of the others around here."

She gestured toward the main room.

"No, scratch that. He's a lot like you, which shouldn't surprise me. Hartwood Cahal used to be a Marine noncom. He served in the 77th."

"Used to, Milady?" The amused glint in Sodhi's eyes told Marta she'd made a faux pas.

"Of course. I should know better. Former Marines are those tossed out of the Corps. Hartwood Cahal retired honorably."

"You want I should ask around if anyone knows this guy? It might give us an idea where they went from Mykonos."

"Please."

"Consider it done."

"Tell your friend Nate he has my undying thanks. If he ever comes to Yotai, I'd like to meet him and say so in person."

She raised her glass and swirled its contents around before swallowing them in one gulp. The whiskey burned a fiery path down her throat, yet in her heightened state, it was strangely soothing.

"And buy him as many drinks as he wants."

"Knowing Nate, he'll take you up on the offer and try to run up the biggest tab this mess has ever seen." Sodhi drained his glass. "And that's it, Milady."

"It was more than I hoped."

"Then I'm glad to be of service."

Overcome by the need to tell Heloise, Marta pushed her chair back and stood.

"Thank you again for everything, Nadav. I've kept you long enough. Be well."

"You too, Milady."

Conscious of the need to exercise self-discipline, Marta crossed the main bar at the same sedate pace she always used in public rather than bounce with glee like her roiling emotions demanded. She even nodded politely and smiled at the smattering of patrons when they glanced at her.

Heloise must have sensed a change in her emotional state the moment Marta stepped through the door because she gave her a quizzical look.

"Good news?"

"Yes. I'll tell you once we're in private." An uneasy feeling suddenly washed over Marta, threatening to dampen her spirits. "Let's go back upstairs."

"A good idea, Highness." Admiral Zahar's deep voice seemed to come from the shadows of a connecting corridor. "You shouldn't be — what is the expression among the nobility again? Slumming? This is no place for our future empress."

"On the contrary, Admiral, but now isn't the time for a prolonged discussion on the matter."

He stepped out into full view.

"It is nevertheless a discussion we must have at some point. For now, could I please ask you to stop using non-commissioned military personnel as your private intelligence service? Any of your needs can and will be satisfied via the proper channels. If you'll recall, I offered to assign an officer of suitable rank as your aide-de-camp, though you deemed it unnecessary. Perhaps Your Highness would reconsider if the aide also acts as your liaison with the 16th Fleet staff, empowered to find the answers to all your questions."

"I'll take the suggestion under advisement, Admiral. Thank you. Now if you'll excuse us, my lady-in-waiting and I will regain our apartments."

"Enjoy the rest of your evening, Highness."

Zahar bowed his head as Marta and Heloise vanished into the corridor warren.

Once back in the imperial apartments, still surprisingly surveillance free according to Marta's sensor, she turned a relieved smile on her companion.

"According to Nadav's friend in the Mykonos garrison, a starship shuttle picked them up eight weeks ago."

Heloise let out an unaccustomed sigh.

"Praise the Almighty. It could only have been one of our ships, answering the distress beacon Sister Averyl carried."

"One of *our* ships?" Marta parroted. "As in the Order of the Void?"

"We own the Galactic Dawn Corporation, which in turn owns a small fleet of armed merchant vessels crewed by Brethren, though we neither advertise their ownership nor the crew's status as members of the Order. The operational revenues help fund our abbeys and good works, and we travel on our own ships to the greatest extent possible for various reasons, not least of them being safety."

A guffaw escaped Marta's lips.

"The mind-meddlers have their own navy? Will wonders never cease?"

"In recent times, owning a navy, as you put it, helped save lives. When Galactic Dawn was formed, the then head of the Order established a formal Rule obliging our ships to rescue any Brethren threatened by invaders or local authorities. She also ordered that every abbey, priory, and mission keep beacons able to summon any Galactic Dawn vessel passing through their star system on hand. Averyl carried one, as did Friar Sandor. Evidently, one of the Dawn ships visited Mykonos."

"Where would it take them?"

"I couldn't say. The Order's home is on Lindisfarne. But that star system is at the other end of the empire and might be effectively out of safe reach, considering the wormhole network inevitably passes through star systems at war against either the Crown or the rebellion, or humanity itself."

"They're still alive and safe, I'm sure of it. But I don't know where they are."

A faint smile tugged at Heloise's lips.

"Consider this the Order's version of Heisenberg's uncertainty principle. Some of us can search our feelings and either sense another living spirit, though not determine where it is, or we can pinpoint the spirit's location and not know whether it lives or has become disembodied."

Suspicion gleamed in Marta's eyes.

"That sounds almost like an attempt at humor."

The sister's smile widened.

"Just a little joke among those of us with heightened senses. Our talent connects us with other living human souls. It is not a galactic positioning device."

"Too bad."

"The Almighty will provide."

An involuntary snort escaped Marta's self-discipline.

"That's what I told Nadav Sodhi word for word. I could almost hear your voice in my head when I spoke."

"Then my teachings *are* sinking in. I'm gratified."

"And now, you're also sarcastic."

"An unfortunate habit which excludes me from ever becoming a priory's leader, let alone the head of an abbey. But I don't yearn for a position of leadership, so it doesn't matter."

"Yet you're not unhappy with being a lady-in-waiting."

"We also serve who stand in the shadows and watch. Speaking of which, I trust you won't accept Zahar's renewed offer of an aide-de-camp."

"Certainly not. We both know a dog robber would be nothing more than Zahar's spy." When Heloise raised a questioning eyebrow, Marta said, "Dog robber is apparently an ancient nickname for military aides. Uncle Olav used the term disparagingly, though I found no mention in the historical records of its origin or derivation."

"Ah. So you'll continue to use the non-commissioned officers' grapevine?"

"I'd like to see Zahar stop me." When Heloise opened her mouth to reply, Marta raised both hands. "Yes, I understand. Don't push him too far. He's more dangerous than Devy Custis."

— 36 —

Lyonesse

"That tears it." Cerys Orobio backed away from the sitting-room window overlooking the street below. "We're not just being tailed, they're casing this building. Amateurs for sure, but it means someone made us. A pair of kids, no older than twenty, are sitting on a stoop across the way, having a grand old time. Problem is, I remember seeing both faces twice yesterday and once this morning while Kamaal and I were watching Severin Downes do his thing."

"Could it be a coincidence?" Bouras joined her and glanced out. "Lannion isn't what you'd call a big city, so seeing the same faces more than once wouldn't be as strange as if we were in Lena, which has ten times as many people."

"My gut tells me they're a tail, Boss."

Bouras turned to Markov and Renlinger, sitting at the dining table, sipping tea.

"Did either of you feel an itch between the shoulder blades in the last day or two?"

"Now you mention it," Renlinger replied, "I did feel as if a person or persons unknown were spying on us at the university, both yesterday and today. But I wrote it off as normal curiosity about strangers looking around, casually asking questions such as why a bunch of Void Brethren are working in the library annex. No particular faces caught my attention, so it might just have been normal paranoia. By the way, the answer is packaging data for the knowledge vault, which in its physical form is an armored chamber deep beneath Lannion Base, impervious to anything short of a planet-busting strike from orbit. The locals aren't exactly keeping it a secret."

"Did they also tell you why they're packaging data to store in an underground bunker?"

"Because this Admiral Morane, who led the 197th Imperial Battle Group here after it was damn near wiped out by rebel forces, convinced the locals that human civilization was going into the shitter. To give our species a head start, they're storing every bit of important knowledge in a safe space so Lyonesse can kick off a new cycle of technological progress even if it gets bombed or raided. Although since this place is a wormhole cul-de-sac, it should be a lot safer than a major junction like Arietis or Yotai."

"Or, since I don't buy the civilization collapse bullshit, it could be they want to make this star system the capital of a new empire," Markov said in a thoughtful tone. "They'll definitely want to know about this at home. No chance we can send a subspace message, is there?"

Bouras shook his head.

"While they're still operating a booster relay here, it doesn't do us much good since the Arietis system no longer has one. It means the only way to contact the rest of the galaxy from Lyonesse is via starship."

"I'd like to suggest that having spotted enough of *Tanith*'s stasis stiffs alive and well, we can safely report it landed here and offloaded the prisoners," Orobio said. "It could now either be in cold storage, orbiting a moon or one of the other planets, or scuttled because the sabotage wasn't repairable. Since no one told us to find a specific stiff, I'd say we met our mission objectives. We should hop on the next starship and head home. I'm sure news of what's happening here will interest everyone, including the top guys since Lyonesse intends to go its own way right on Yotai's doorstep."

Renlinger raised his hand.

"Seconded."

Bouras turned to Markov, who nodded.

"What Ty said. If the Lyonesse police or military placed us under surveillance, it's best to get the hell out with the information we collected so far."

"Okay. The next ship it is. But while we wait for one to show up, the mission doesn't turn into an unplanned holiday. We keep sniffing around. I'd still like to find out what happened after Morane stole *Tanith* from under the Parth Task Force's nose."

"And hear more about their plans to become the self-appointed guardians of humanity's legacy," Markov added. "Especially since it involves members of a religious group wiped out with the most extreme prejudice I ever witnessed. The big boss will really want to hear about them."

Bouras wandered over to the window again and glanced out.

"An older woman is talking with the kids Cerys thinks are watching us. Looks tough, possibly serving or ex-military."

Markov jumped to her feet.

"Let me see that."

But by the time she stood beside her team leader, the older woman was gone.

"What did she look like, I mean beyond generalities?"

"Nothing remarkable. Black hair, dark complexion, aquiline nose, one-seventy to one-seventy-five centimeters tall, strong build, angular face, in her forties. Like I said, she struck me as one of your lot, the way she stood."

"Shit. That sounds like Adrienne Barca. Or at least the woman I saw talking to the Government House gate sentry two nights ago. You know what that could mean?"

"The locals not only made us for a recon team," Orobio replied, "but somehow figured out what your real identity is if they're sending an old girlfriend to check.'"

Bouras shook his head.

"Maybe we're making a lot out of nothing, guys."

"That's not what my gut tells me, Kamaal."

"Your gut is doing backflips because of the fond memories," Orobio said, winking.

Markov glanced out at the street again.

"They left."

"Scan for a replacement team. If you don't spot one, then we're getting worked up about nothing. Watchers would know by now we go out to eat in the evening and wouldn't assume we don't need a tail because we're staying in until tomorrow."

"Nothing obvious," she said after a few minutes. "But that could mean squat. We'd better check our sixes on the way to the restaurant."

"And if we spot another set of familiar faces, then what?" Renlinger asked. "We invite them up for a drink and a chat?"

"Find a way to let them know we're neither blind nor stupid."

Orobio held up a hand.

"Hush."

"What?"

"Listen."

A distant, almost imperceptible rumble reached their ears.

"Starship on final approach," Renlinger said in a whisper. "Why didn't we know one was landing today? The spaceport would have received a warning from the wormhole terminus as early as last night."

"Because none of us checked the arrivals board. We decided to leave on the next ship only ten minutes ago, remember?" Orobio turned to Bouras. "We take this one, boss?"

"If there's room. Contact the spaceport now and try to reserve a four bunk cabin."

**

Barca's communicator buzzed for attention. She fished it from her pocket and glanced at the display.

Targets booked a berth on the incoming ship.

The recon team, which might or might not include Krystal Sandt, were leaving before she had a chance to study them up close.

"What's up, Centurion?" The Rifle Regiment reserve private, a nineteen-year-old student at Lyonesse University who moonlighted as a surveillance operative, asked.

"Looks like our targets found what they were looking for, or noticed we were watching and got spooked. They're lifting on the tub that just landed."

A disgusted grimace appeared.

"Shit. Begging your pardon, sir."

"No reflection on you or your mates, Loukas. We play this out and wave goodbye."

"Why don't we take them in and find out for who they're working?"

"No legal grounds. And here I thought you were studying law."

"That's Naioth — Private Virk. I'm a civil engineering major."

"Right. Practicality above all, eh?" Barca gave him a friendly smile to take any sting out of her words.

"I guess. What's the plan?"

Barca took a deep breath and looked down at the rental apartment building from her aerie at the top of the Haven Shipping Company's warehouse, one block away.

"They still need to pass through emigration control at the spaceport."

She called up the arrivals and departures schedule on her communicator's display. *Ekosia* was lifting in three hours — just enough time to offload another batch of migrants and take on a bit of cargo.

"And that won't be long now. I can do this myself, but you're welcome to tag along."

"If you don't mind, Centurion, I'd rather see this through to the end. I was one of the first tagged with watching them."

Barca clapped Loukas on the shoulder.

"That's the attitude I like from an engineer. The ones who don't see things through usually end up building crap capable of killing people. Come on."

"What happens when we see them at the spaceport?" Loukas asked, following Barca down the metal stairs to where an unmarked, dusty old staff car waited, hidden from curious eyes.

"If Jaimee Markov is the person I used to know way back when, I'll see if we can have a quiet talk. Otherwise, since none of them committed a crime on Lyonesse, they're free to go."

"Understood, sir."

Once at the spaceport, Barca identified herself to the senior immigration officer on duty and arranged to have

Markov pulled aside when she passed through departure control.   One of his people would bring her to an examination room unless Barca waved them off.

Then, she and Loukas took a seat near the gate where they could watch without being seen and waited. Less than an hour later, the regular bus between downtown Lannion and the terminal disgorged the foursome, each carrying a travel bag. They seemed preternaturally alert to their surroundings, as if suspecting, with good reason, they might be under surveillance.

Barca studied the black-haired woman who called herself Markov, and within a heartbeat, she knew it was Krystal. People age, their appearance may change, they might even modify it, but the eyes never lied, nor did a person's unconscious gestures. Both were as achingly familiar to Barca as her own. No need to wave off the immigration officers. She watched as they entered the departure control area before heading to the interview suite, Loukas in tow.

The senior officer, waiting by the door to the suite's observation room, said, "They gave us a bit of lip, but she came in the end." He patted the holstered needler on his hip. "The threat of arrest two hours before your ship leaves is a good incentive to cooperate. You want to examine our guest before speaking with her?"

"Yeah."

The observation room's door swept open at the officer's gesture. "Take your time. I'll hang around in the corridor with Private Loukas."

"Thanks."

Once inside, Barca examined Markov via the video pickup. She appeared composed, but there was an edginess to her movements as she slowly paced back and forth, ignoring the metal table and chairs in the center of the room. Now that Barca could see the woman up close, her conviction it was Krystal only deepened. Yet she hesitated at the thought of going next door to confront her in person.

Their acrimonious parting might have happened many years ago, on a world several hundred light years away, but a surge of anguish born from long-suppressed feelings made it seem like yesterday. Perhaps it would be easier if she simply told the immigration officer to release Krystal without a word of explanation.

Once she boarded *Ekosia*, chances were excellent their paths would never cross again in this life. But tempting as it was to avoid dealing with her emotions, Adrienne Barca was a Marine, a Pathfinder, someone who'd seen death up close more often than she cared to remember. Duty came before everything.

She took a deep, calming breath, then reached for the connecting door, knowing the next few minutes could reopen painful wounds. Yet with the empire imploding, this might well be her last chance to say all the things she'd been holding in for so long.

Jaimee Markov, born Krystal Sandt, abruptly stopped pacing as the door opened with the soft whine of infrequently used machinery and turned toward it. She unconsciously adopted the parade rest position, feet apart, hands joined in the small of her back.

When their eyes met, Barca felt a jolt of electricity run through her body until it reached every single nerve ending. Blood pulsed in her ears with the insistent ringing of a kettledrum while her skin tingled.

"Hello, Krystal. How are you?"

— 37 —

"My name is Jaimee Markov. Why am I being detained?"

"There's no use pretending, Krystal. You felt the same thing I did just now when we looked into each other's eyes. Don't deny it. I could tell."

Sandt crossed her arms in a defensive gesture and leaned against the wall at her back.

"Fine. What do you want, *Centurion* Barca? Unless you have grounds for arrest, I'm being detained without cause. There's a bunk waiting for me on that starship."

"What do I want? Come on, Krys, you show up on the planet where I've made my forever home, a place at the ass end of the galaxy, and you expect me not to reach out? The way things are nowadays, once you leave, that's it. I'll never get a chance to make things right, or at least say I'm sorry."

Sandt scoffed. "And you waited until the last second? Why even bother."

"I only saw your picture at this morning's briefing, Krys. Until then, you and your friends were nothing more than visitors of interest. But the moment Jaimee Markov's face appeared on that screen, I knew it was you. Some things are seared in your soul forever."

A faint sneer curled up Sandt's lip.

"Visitors of interest? How fucking quaint. What does that mean?"

"Only refugees fleeing barbarian raids and merchants looking to sell us stuff they figure we can't fabricate ourselves come here nowadays. It makes tourists, even if they're pretending to be commercial representatives, unusual enough to watch. Then you sniffed around the university library and certain former members of the imperial court exiled by Dendera whom we saved from a worse fate on Parth. Anyone with more than two brain cells will want to know what you're doing here."

"So? Isn't Lyonesse a free world, as in if you don't break the law or trespass, you're free to do whatever you want?"

Barca smiled.

"Not entirely. We're pretty careful with potential threats, seeing as how we'd rather not go down the toilet like so many star systems have since the rebellion started. That's the whole point of what we're doing here. Survive with our civilization intact, so humanity's entire history isn't lost forever."

"Ah, yes. That collapse bullshit. What do they call it? The long night of barbarism." Sandt smirked. "I'm not buying what you folks are selling."

"I saw it with my own eyes, Krys. The 6th of the 21st almost died on Coraline trying to prop up the imperial governor general. A few hours after Admiral Morane picked us up on his way here, Coraline was getting its ass bombed back to the Stone Age."

Barca drew a thumbnail sketch of their trek through a frontier abandoned by the navy and ravaged by reivers.

"You passed through Arietis on your way here and noticed it's no longer under imperial protection, right? A wormhole junction with six termini abandoned just like that. It means the 16th Fleet also cut star systems connecting to Arietis loose except maybe for Micarat. If that's bullshit, then I don't want to see what you consider a dire situation."

"We still hold Micarat," Sandt said before she could stop herself.

"Good to know, in case we send out for a few crates of Glen Arcturus. Who is this *we*, Krys? Are you part of Admiral Zahar's mob?" When Sandt gave her a stubborn glare instead of answering, Barca let out a sigh. "How about we restart this conversation? Hello, Krys, how are you? You're looking well. Believe it or not, I've missed you."

After a moment of silence, Sandt snapped, "What do you want?"

Her overt hostility twisted Barca's gut into a knotted mess.

"I want to tell you how sorry I am that we couldn't part as friends. When I saw your picture this morning, I realized my feelings for you still run deep and that this was probably our last chance to say goodbye. If you work for Zahar or whoever holds Yotai and the surrounding star systems, your home is at least five unprotected wormhole transits from here. Before long the only ships roaming the Arietis branch of the network will be those of barbarian raiders. Lyonesse is about to be cut off from the rest of humanity. You won't come back, and I won't be able to leave, even if I didn't swear to defend this place." When Sandt kept her gaze stubbornly on the floor instead of replying to Barca's impassioned entreaty, the latter whispered, "Please look at me, Krys."

"Do you know how bad it hurt when you put your precious Pathfinder career ahead of me? We could have transferred to a line unit together, but no, it was special operations and nothing else for you, even if it meant spending half your life on offworld missions. But I got over it — over you. The 55th is a good outfit with some of the best Marines I know. I even made command sergeant and assistant regimental intelligence officer before the rebellion broke out."

Sandt looked up at Barca with defiant eyes, but the moisture in their corners told a different story.

"How did you fare during the fighting on Yotai? The Void Brethren who escaped Zahar's massacre told us hair-raising stories."

"I — we did okay. Sure it was a bloody mess, but once we killed off most of the senior officers in the 19th Guards Division, the rest surrendered pretty quickly. A lot of them signed up with us as recruits. Probably figured joining the winners was the best way to survive. It was worse on places like Mykonos and Ariel, where the Imperial Guards outnumbered Marines."

"The Coalsack seems to have escaped the worst of it so far, from what we saw. But it won't last."

"Your collapse fairy tale again?" Krystal Sandt essayed a small, albeit sardonic grin. "We'll be fine. Grand Duke Custis is consolidating the sector. Once we're strong again, watch out. We might even reclaim Lyonesse."

Barca shook her head.

"No. It could take a few years, but my admiral is right. The slide won't stop until humanity hits rock bottom and billions more die. How many Coalsack Sector star system governors general told Zahar to stuff it?"

"What do you mean?"

"Zahar killed Viceroy Joback and told Wyvern to fuck off. How many did the same to him or Custis? It's a disease, Krys, one that won't stop until the host dies." She hesitated as a reckless hope surged through her veins. "Stay here. Let the others go back and report. Stay here with me. We can finally do what you wanted and serve in a line regiment together. There's nothing but death waiting for you on Yotai."

Soft laughter escaped Sandt's lips. At first, it sounded dismissive but then took on a hysterical edge. Barca feared she was losing what little rapport she'd made.

"*Now* you want me to stay? Too little, too late, lover. Much too late. Perhaps I won't ever come back to this quaint backwater star system, but if I do, it'll be with the 161st Marine Division to reclaim Lyonesse for the Coalsack Sector. Your knowledge vault scheme? Pathetic. The empire might be finished, but civilization is doing just fine in our corner of the galaxy, thank you very much. There will be no long night of barbarism. Not while we — my mates and I — do our duty. Now let me go. You've said your piece, and if it means anything, I no longer hate you as I did then, but I'm not sure indifference is an improvement. As they say, it's the opposite of love. But if you want my forgiveness, you have it. Now let me go."

Barca inclined her head in defeat.

"Should you ever need a safe harbor and can find your way back here, I will greet you with open arms. And if I'm no longer among the living, my comrades will do so."

Sandt let out what sounded like a faint sob as she inhaled.

"And *my* comrades are waiting for me, Adri. You've always been big on loyalty. I gave mine to the 55th long ago, and more recently to those three social menaces waiting out there who've become my only family. I'm sure you understand. What you and I had is part of our past, and it has to stay that way, especially now we're headed for radically different futures. You left the Marine Corps along with the rest of the 6th Battalion, 21st Imperial Pathfinder Regiment and became an officer of Lyonesse so you can protect this knowledge vault. I stayed in the Corps to fight for something I believe will be the heart of the next empire, despite your admiral's visions of disaster. We're on divergent paths."

"Fair enough. My offer stands. You and yours can claim shelter here." Barca hesitated. "What will you tell your superiors about Lyonesse?"

"The truth. Even if I wanted to withhold information, there are four of us, and we will each be debriefed separately."

"If I ask what that truth is, will you answer?"

Sandt locked eyes with Barca before nodding.

"Yes. For old times' sake. And for reaching out to say farewell. The four of us are a covert recon team. I'm the only Marine. Kamaal Bouras is a two-and-a-half striper from naval intelligence while Orobio and Renlinger are chief petty officers. Our mission was finding the Imperial Prison Ship *Tanith*. The ship — not a specific stasis stiff. The orders came with a list of the prisoners aboard. We traced *Tanith* to Lyonesse and found many of its passengers, though not all of them, living freely here. The ship itself appears to have vanished."

"*Tanith*'s fate is no great secret. Since we couldn't make repairs without risking a major antimatter explosion, we scuttled it into the sun. What else will you tell your superiors?"

"That Lyonesse made a unilateral declaration of independence and intends to chart its own course, separate from that of the empire. Our report will also detail what we found out about your knowledge vault project and your military forces, and the fact you're taking in refugees from Arietis." Sandt gave Barca a half shrug. "Everything comes from open sources, by the way. We're a recon team rather than spies.   And until something changes drastically, we're still fundamentally on the same side, you and us."

"I hope so unless your superiors take violent exception to our UDI. But since at least four star systems between here and Micarat are no longer under the 16th Fleet's control, we shouldn't look like a threat. Not with our small navy."

"Don't worry. The 16th took a beating during the rebellion. I don't think either Admiral Zahar or Grand Duke Custis will risk the defense of our border systems to send an expeditionary force here. Dendera's fleets are far from finished, and in time, the barbarians will become bolder and more aggressive, especially if they sense weakness."

"Spoken like a true battlefield intelligence analyst. But be honest, Krys. Do you believe Yotai can make itself the center of a reborn empire? Or are Custis and Zahar pissing into the wind?"

A sad smile softened Sandt's expression.

"Does it matter? If they can do it, I'll die knowing I did my part to keep civilization alive. And if not, I'll die knowing I tried."

Delighted laughter filled the interview room.

"You *have* changed. The old Krys didn't even know how to spell fatalism, let alone what it means."

"This isn't fatalism, Ari, but loyalty — to people and to an ideal — something you taught me."

When Sandt fell silent, they exchanged wistful smiles, knowing neither would deviate from her chosen path, just as before, during better days when the empire seemed eternal.

"This is becoming harder than I expected. You've awakened feelings I thought dead."

"Then stay with me. Let your colleagues report back to Yotai without you."

"No. But if your admiral is right and the universe goes to crap, perhaps I'll think about making my way back here somehow." Sandt pushed herself off the wall. "I should go now before we both lose our dignity by bawling like children. We're veteran Marines, dammit."

"One last hug?"

"Yeah."

After releasing her embrace, Sandt caressed Barca's cheek with her fingertips and said, in a husky voice, "Live well, Adri."

Barca touched the back of Sandt's hand.

"You too. I'll leave my porch light on. It might not be visible from Yotai, or even the next town. But it'll be there."

"I know." She dropped her hand and stepped back. "Please don't walk me to the ship. Otherwise, we will both cry, and I want this to be my last memory of you."

"In that case, goodbye, Krys."

When the interview room's door closed behind Sandt, Barca stared at it for a long time, lost in thought as she let her emotions settle before rejoining Private Loukas and heading home.

— 38 —

Yotai

Heloise unfolded her limbs and rose in a fluid movement, interrupting her meditation session less than halfway through. The sudden movement startled Marta, who'd been reading Zahar's proposal to redistribute the 16th Fleet's ships. She instinctively knew something was wrong.

But before she could ask what had disturbed her, Heloise pulled a palm-sized object, something like a large talisman on a metal chain, from her robe's voluminous folds and placed it on Marta's desk.

"Carry this on your person at all times from now on, child. It is my beacon. Should any of our ships pass through the Yotai system and hear the signal, its captain will do everything possible to find and retrieve you."

"What—"

Heloise held up a restraining hand.

"Take the beacon and keep it against your bare skin. It draws on the body's electric field and only transmits in the presence of a Void Brethren's brain waves. That's how our ships identify the wearer as one of us. You'll know what to do when the time comes. Just listen to your instincts."

"Explain yourself." Marta slipped the chain over her head and tucked the talisman beneath her shirt, out of sight.

"I sense danger approaching, and that means my time with you is ending. No matter what happens in the next few minutes, you must let events unfold as ordained. My Brethren and I survived the Mykonos Abbey massacre for a purpose. Since you're now as aware and capable as the strongest of us, I've completed the task given me and am no longer vital to your destiny."

"That's not an explanation, it's a suicide note."

"No." Heloise shook her head. "A manifestation of *memento mori*. I'm surprised I could keep Admiral Zahar from uncovering my true nature for so long. He is one of the rare untrained males capable of detecting our abilities. Some of them become deeply suspicious of our motives, to the point of considering us a dangerous enemy."

"You planned on telling me about this when?"

"The moment it became necessary. I couldn't risk you triggering Zahar's mistrust by accidentally brushing his mind. Your status as the empress-designate protects you, but that might not last. If a ship answers the beacon, promise me you'll escape."

"Of course I will. It could be the ship that picked up my children. How did you keep Zahar from suspecting?"

"I used the mind-dampening discipline I taught you whenever we were in his presence, to mask myself from his sixth sense. But it isn't perfect, and repeated interactions with me likely reinforced his initial dubiousness about my being a genuine lady-in-waiting." When she saw the surprise in Marta's eyes, Heloise nodded. "Zahar suspected something from the day we landed on Yotai."

"What is it you think will happen? And when?"

Heloise tilted her head to one side.

"The what is an end and a beginning. The when is—"

A menacing aura touched the edge of Marta's consciousness. She was startled for the second time when the main door to her apartments opened without permission. The sound of booted feet on polished marble filtered through from the foyer.

"—Now."

"They're in the office," a man's voice called out.

Moments later, Admiral Pendrick Zahar, tailed by two armed Marines, entered. He stopped a few meters in front of Marta's desk and bowed his head. The Marines spread out, one to each side and aimed their carbines at Heloise.

"Your Imperial Highness, pardon the unannounced intrusion, but I'm here on a vital matter of state security that cannot wait."

Marta put on a haughty expression and, in her best Wyvern Court drawl, replied, "Unannounced intrusion is putting it mildly, Admiral. You may not enter my private quarters without my express permission, even under the pretense of state security. This is *lèse-majesté*, and carries harsh penalties, even for a man wearing four stars on his collar."

"Perhaps, but I suggest you hear me out, Highness, because treason carries even harsher penalties, even for an empress-designate."

"What are you talking about?"

Zahar, unfazed by her tone, nodded toward Heloise.

"I have proscribed the Order of the Void throughout the Coalsack Sector on the grounds of high treason and its Brethren are condemned as threats to humanity. Which means your so-called lady-in-waiting is a traitor, a criminal liable for execution.”

“This is preposterous, Admiral. Leave my private quarters now, or I will dismiss you as head of my armed forces.”

“You are not yet legally commander-in-chief, Highness. No one will obey your orders, nor is Regent Custis inclined to grant you power over me or anyone else after your performance in the briefing room a few days ago.” He turned a baleful stare on Heloise. “You’ll be pleased to know I’m not acting on mere suspicion. I also asked my people on Mykonos make inquiries after your companion attracted my suspicions. You see, I can always tell mind-meddlers from honest people. But Heloise puzzled me until a few hours ago when a report came back confirming she’s a Sister of the Void who somehow survived the Mykonos Abbey’s destruction.”

“So? She is my personal retainer and thus under my protection.”

Zahar’s humorless laugh filled the room.

“Even a reigning empress cannot protect her personal retainers when they’re guilty of high crimes against the state. And you’re merely a designate.”

“Your assumption of guilt is not in evidence, Admiral.”

He pointed a finger at Heloise.

“She is a mind-meddler and therefore guilty. Since we are still under martial law, execution shall be immediate. Seize her, Sergeant.”

Marta sprang up.

“No!”

Heloise took her hand and squeezed.

“Sit, Milady.” Then, turning a defiant face on Zahar, she said, “Shoot me here and now, Admiral. The Almighty will recognize his own.”

Marta dropped back into her chair, instinctively obeying Heloise, though her entire being screamed in silent rage. Unable to move or even speak, she watched as Zahar pulled a long-bladed knife out from under his severe naval tunic and came around the desk at Heloise, his face a mask of unrestrained rage.

Helpless, Marta watched as Zahar drove his knife between Heloise's ribs, piercing her heart. At the same moment, she heard the sister's voice in her mind as clear as if she'd spoken aloud.

"I will be with you, always."

Then, one of the Mykonos Abbey's last surviving members crumpled to the floor and died.

Stunned, Marta kept her grip on Heloise's hand, feeling the life force fade away even as she sensed her third eye gaining unexpected strength. She was astonished at how little blood came from the wound once Zahar withdrew his blade and wiped it on Heloise's black robes, and even more so at the peaceful look on her face.

Zahar glanced at the Marines.

"Take her body to the incinerator and dispose of it at once. There will be no memorial service."

"I will see your head on a pike for this," Marta said in a preternaturally calm tone.

"I am more likely to see yours displayed in such a manner, *Highness*."

"Don't count on it. Evil never prospers, and you are one of the purest embodiments of malice I've ever encountered. The next time you cross me, I will kill you. Mark my words."

Driven more by a raw, primal instinct than conscious thought, Marta concentrated her body's energy and aimed it at Zahar. She ignored the eerie, Heloise-like voice at the back of her mind pleading with her to desist from making such a show of strength.

Zahar staggered, fighting to stay upright while his hands went to his temples as if overcome by an intense and sudden migraine. It vanished a fraction of a second later, leaving him to stare at Marta in astonishment after he regained his self-control.

"Do not cross me again, Admiral. Ever." She was pleased her voice remained steady even in the face of sudden and intense fatigue.

"You're one of them," he hissed. "A mind-meddler."

"No, I'm something much worse, as you'll come to understand in time. The sisters follow the Rule of the Order, which commands them to never harm another. I do not." Marta tapped the side of her head with an extended finger. "And Heloise lives on, up here, her abilities now added to mine. Make any move against me, and that little taste of agony will seem like bliss. Now go away and never forget I am your commander-in-chief, to be feared and obeyed."

"We'll see what the regent has to say about this," he replied through clenched teeth.

"Devy Custis?" Marta made a dismissive hand gesture. "He's no longer relevant."

She turned her gaze on the two stunned Marines.

"Take Sister Heloise to the morgue and make sure they prepare a proper funeral pyre in the main courtyard. I will see her soul sent into the Void by nightfall."

The sergeant, unable to process what he just witnessed, fell back on unquestioning obedience and snapped to attention.

"As you command, Highness."

"Neither you nor Custis need to attend, Admiral. In fact, I'd rather you stay away."

At a loss for words after such an unexpected reversal of fortunes, Zahar bowed, then turned and stalked out of her apartments, heels clicking on the foyer's bare marble floor.

Marta watched the Marines carefully pick up Heloise's body and carry it away. Neither dared look up as they left.

When the door closed behind them, Marta slumped in her chair, physically and emotionally drained. She let the last few minutes repeatedly play in her mind.

After reflecting on the incident for what seemed like a long time, Marta gained a better understanding what had happened and why. And that she now carried a part of Heloise within her, a spark of her consciousness, passed on through physical contact at the moment of death.

Heloise knew her demise was imminent but could only give Marta that ultimate gift if she was killed right there and then, while they touched each other. Goading Zahar into acting himself must have been child's play since he could sense a sister's mind touch and nursed an unreasoning hatred for the Order of the Void.

"What have you done, Heloise?" Marta asked in a soft, almost inaudible voice. "To yourself and to me?"

I did what was necessary, child. Your survival is more important than mine.

The words, the voice, and the intonation were so precise Marta could almost believe Heloise was talking to her from beyond the grave, albeit only in her mind.

"Are you in there with me?"

Of course not. I'm dead. And so will you be if you don't take care with Zahar. Attacking him out of pure reflex was understandable, but dangerously premature. You're strong, more powerful than I was, but not invincible.

The dry, exasperated tone reminded her so much of the times when she asked Heloise what were in retrospect dumb questions. Whether the words came from Heloise or her own subconscious, Marta couldn't deny their truth.

Lashing out at Zahar had been irresponsible, foolish even, and left her vulnerable. If he killed her before a rescue ship from Galactic Dawn passed through the Yotai system, she would never see Stefan and Sigrid again.

Work on your self-discipline, so you don't use your abilities to hurt someone without forethought. Better yet, obey the Order's Rule and do no harm.

"Easy for you to say," Marta muttered. "My witchy wits are the only thing left, and they won't be easy to keep in check if I'm suffering from a case of Void-induced split personality."

When her mind didn't answer, she shrugged.

"Be that way. Now pardon me while I meditate over my grief and figure out how to survive."

— 39 —

Lyonesse

The rap of knuckles on the open door pulled Admiral Jonas Morane from his quiet contemplation of Lannion Base and the star system's capital beyond. Late afternoon mist, blown inland by a southerly breeze blurred distant shapes and gave the city a ghostly air under the reddish light of a sun reaching for the western horizon.

"Got a minute, sir?" Brigid DeCarde's voice asked.

Morane turned around and gestured toward the chair in front of his desk.

"For my second in command, always."

"You seem preoccupied. I mean more so than usual."

He sat across from her and grimaced.

"Things might be heating up, but you go first."

"Adrienne Barca just finished briefing me about her conversation with one of the offworld visitors at the spaceport shortly before they left aboard *Ekosia*, the freighter that lifted ten minutes ago."

"After dropping off two-hundred-thirty-three additional migrants. I expect an earful of complaints from Gus Logran any moment now."

The Marine shrugged. "At least we refined the processing down to a science. They'll be at the Otnabog River settlement before sunset tomorrow, which means only a day's worth of work for Logran's people."

"Still a day too much for some. Tell me about Centurion Barca's foray into counterintelligence work. You know I'm seriously thinking about her as CO of the Defense Force Security Company, right?"

"I figured Adri was among the top three choices. You're aware we suspected one of the visitors was an old acquaintance of hers, right?"

"So you told me. And was she?"

"Oh, yes." DeCarde nodded. "Her real name is Krystal Sandt, and she's a Marine Corps command sergeant from the 55th working for Admiral Zahar's intelligence service." DeCarde repeated Barca's oral debriefing almost verbatim. "Adri will submit a written report by tomorrow."

"If Zahar, or more likely Custis, is looking for *Tanith*, it's because of Corinne Ruggero."

"Who no longer exists. Her cover identity was officially recorded as deceased in transit."

"We know that, but once those naval intelligence operatives return to Yotai, Custis will believe we're sheltering her. And he'll be aware of the knowledge vault project."

"Do you think he might send an expeditionary force? There are at least four star systems no longer under Yotai control between him and us."

"If he believes the prize is worth the risk, five transits by a task force capable of defending itself aren't much of an impediment." A pause. "Unless he's facing enemies coming from within the empire, as this Sergeant Sandt seems to have intimated."

"At least his operatives didn't scheme with Severin Downes and company to give us grief."

"Small mercies considering our next crop of problems."

"That's why you were staring wistfully out into the distance?"

Morane nodded.

"Rorik Hecht made his move earlier this afternoon. He rammed a vote through the Colonial Council to set up what he calls *The Knowledge Vault Oversight Commission.*"

"Oh, crap."

"Save your strongest cuss words for when I'm done speaking, Brigid. It gets worse."

"Naturally. Whenever life gets too easy, Fate flexes her fickle finger. How will she fuck us this time?"

"The Commission membership will include eminent citizens of Lyonesse, appointed by a Colonial Council vote after suitable hearings."

"You're on it, I hope."

"Yes. So are Emma Reyes and Sister Gwenneth. We three will be the ex officio commissioners, allowed to nominate stand-ins if we can't take part in deliberations. You're mine, by the way."

"Gee, thanks. I think."

"Including the chair, Hecht's latest brainchild will include eleven members. I already mentioned the three ex officio members. Of the other eight, four will be named by the Estates General and the last four by the council itself. Hecht has already made the council's nominations public. Severin Downes, Brady Apostolos, Mei Chiang, and Keita Fakaj, the most senior and most vocal among the former political prisoners. Hecht is justifying his choices by pointing at the experience they gained serving the imperial government. Never mind they were little more than useless courtiers fighting each other for the illusion of power in Dendera's Capitol of the Damned. Guess who's slated to become the commission's chair?" He gave her a significant look.

"Downes?"

Morane tapped the side of his nose with an extended index finger.

"Precisely."

A groan of dismay escaped DeCarde's throat.

"Why, oh why did we ever pick up that cursed prison ship? Is anyone working on a time machine so we can go back and tell our former selves to leave *Tanith* for the 16th Fleet?"

"Sorry. Traveling to the past is either impossible or requires a special rogue wormhole that doesn't allow you any control over time and space, depending on the physicist you ask."

"What powers did the council give this commission?"

"Inform and make recommendations to both the Colonial Council and the governor. But it's the skunk's nose under the tent flap. Give Hecht and his pal Downes a few years. They aim to take full control of the vault."

"Can we do anything about it?"

Morane shook his head.

"Not until Lyonesse has a new constitution. The current Colonial Council can create and fund any non-executive commission that strikes its fancy, provided doing so doesn't violate existing laws."

"And Hecht isn't looking to hold a Constitutional Convention any time soon, I'll bet. He likes things just as they are."

"He does because he knows many, if not most of the Estates General representatives don't want a legislature subservient to someone with his ambitions. However, Elenia Yakin can't stay governor forever, chiefly because she'd rather not become the next monarch by default, and without a mechanism to replace her, we're stuck. Governors are appointed by the empress on the advice and consent of the Imperial Senate. We have neither, and eventually, Lyonesse will need a new *princeps civitatis*."

"A what now?"

"First Citizen. It's Latin. Since we don't yet know what form Lyonesse's government will take, Elenia Yakin, Emma Reyes, and I use the term in conversation when we're discussing the future chief executive."

"How about the governor simply summon the Estates General and when they assemble in the Hall of the People, declare it a Constitutional Convention? I'd love to see old Rorik's reaction."

"Don't think we're not discussing it. But our governor is a stickler for propriety. She believes, as do I, that one cannot base a new social compact on even the slightest lie. Otherwise what we create will always carry a whiff of illegitimacy, and that's no recipe to nurture a spark of civilization against the coming darkness. Instead, Lyonesse will crumble just as the empire is doing nowadays because Stichus Ruggero founded his dynasty on a pack of lies."

"Then what's the answer?"

"To Hecht's commission? Gorge it with information, then let it spew advice no sane person would ever contemplate. And while they're distracted with cocktail parties, plenary sessions and public consultations, make sure they can never gain physical access to the vault itself. Thankfully, it's on defense force grounds, and no matter what Hecht might wish, I can bar anyone short of the governor from entering Lannion Base."

"If you ask me, shooting him and Downes now will save us a lot of grief."

"Perhaps, but we can't build on a foundation of politically motivated purges."

"I know," DeCarde sighed. "Fantasizing now and then helps me deal with my more reactionary impulses. An enlightened tyranny unafraid to remove society's toxic elements has its advantages."

"Until you're stuck with an unenlightened tyrant. No one thought even the most ambitious senator could upend succession rules that served the empire well for almost eight centuries, but here we are, refugees from the chaos his dynasty created."

"Here we are indeed." DeCarde inclined her head in defeat. "I concede the point."

Morane's communicator chose that moment to chime. He glanced down at it and grimaced.

"Gus Logran, right on schedule to complain about the latest batch of would-be settlers. Hi Gus. Brigid DeCarde is with me. What can the defense force do for our chief administrator today?"

"You heard about Rorik's latest scheme?"

"The Knowledge Vault Oversight Commission? I was informed of its unplanned birth an hour ago."

"Are you aware he strong-armed it through the council without consulting either the governor or me beforehand?"

"No, though I'm not surprised. He didn't breathe a word to Chancellor Reyes, Sister Gwenneth, or me, even though we're named as ex officio commissioners. We found out when a copy of the decision appeared on our communicator screens."

"As did the governor and I. Rorik likes to keep his cards close-held, but this was unusual even for him."

"I suspect Severin Downes has become one of his trusted advisers. This little surprise maneuver reeks of court intrigue. Thankfully, the speaker of the council can only nominate four of the eleven commissioners."

Logran cackled with derision.

"Just wait until you see how many of the commissioners named by the Estates General will be in his pocket."

"All four?" DeCarde asked.

"Perhaps, Colonel. But I'd put my next month's pay on at least two, so his people are in the majority."

"A fat lot of good it'll do them. His commission can only look at what we're doing and offer advice. It wields no real power."

"For the moment. Rorik has a longer game in mind. I don't know what that is, but I'm sure we won't like it, considering who he's named as commissioners, let alone as chair."

Morane's office terminal chimed for attention, indicating a call either from the operations center or through its node. He checked the routing and sighed.

"Mention the devil... Downes wishes to speak with me."

"I'll cut my link," Logran said.

"No. Stick around and listen in without saying a word. I won't tell Downes you're on my personal communicator."

"Understood. And thanks."

"You too, Brigid."

"I'll be as quiet as the grave I'd like to dig for Downes."

Morane touched the control screen, accepting an audio only connection.

"Severin Downes here," a dyspeptic, nasal voice announced. "Why aren't we on a video call, Admiral?"

"Because I'm indisposed, Mister Downes. What can I do for you?"

"I trust you received notification from the Colonial Council that it struck a commission to oversee this knowledge vault you're building."

"Yes."

"Then you're also aware they appointed me as its chair."

"That too."

"Good. I wish to inspect the vault so I may better acquaint myself with the commission's remit."

Morane turned a long-suffering glance on DeCarde, who repressed a mischievous smile.

"I'm sure we can arrange a visit, Mister Downes. Perhaps next Wednesday?"

"No. I mean to carry out my inspection forthwith."

"Today?"

"What else would forthwith mean, Admiral?" Downes tone seemed to question Morane's intelligence and genetic lineage. "I shall be there in thirty minutes."

"No."

"What do you mean, no?"

"You're not coming here in thirty minutes, Mister Downes. I will see that someone gives you a tour of the vault at thirteen hundred hours tomorrow."

"Why does this insistence on a delay make me suspect you're attempting to hide something?"

Morane pinched the bridge of his nose in exasperation, suppressing a reply that would only make things worse.

"I'd rather not intrude unannounced on those who devote their waking hours to make the knowledge vault a reality. An unplanned visit would needlessly disrupt a heavy work schedule and be discourteous to everyone involved. I'm sure you can appreciate how poorly that might reflect on a commission only a few hours old."

"And if I insist and show up anyway?"

"The vault is on a defense force installation, Mister Downes. You'd never make it past the main gate."

After a disdainful sniff, the former count replied, "We shall see how long the military keeps absolute control over humanity's heritage."

"If you can point at a civilian location just as capable of withstanding a kinetic strike from orbit as my underground warehouse, I'll gladly consider it. But since no such thing exists on Lyonesse, any discussion about moving the vault off Lannion Base is futile, and while it remains here, I am its sole custodian."

"As I said, we shall see. One of the main reasons for forming the oversight commission is to ensure we manage the vault for the greatest benefit of every citizen in this star system. Leaving its care in the hands of one man while hiding it behind armed soldiers is antithetical to that principle."

"Oh? And here I thought it was to give you and your closest friends the type of sinecure you used to enjoy on Wyvern."

Shocked silence greeted Morane's barb.

Finally, Downes asked, in a voice dripping with outrage, "I beg your pardon, Admiral? What did you just dare say?"

"If there's nothing else, Mister Downes, one of my officers will meet you by the main gate tomorrow at thirteen hundred hours sharp. Good day." Morane stabbed the controls embedded in his desktop.

"That probably wasn't the smartest way to handle Downes, sir," DeCarde said.

He gave her a rueful shrug.

"Probably, but unless I cut him off at the knees now, who knows what mischief he'll cause. This isn't one of those times to go along so we can get along."

"Mind you, his response was a thing of beauty," Logran said. "I almost thought he was about to choke on his wounded pride."

"You realize calling the commission a sinecure for exiled nobles means open conflict with Rorik Hecht, right, sir?"

"I do, Brigid, but the moment Hecht used Downes and the lordlings as tools to expand his political power, open conflict became unavoidable. If you ask Sister Gwenneth, I'm sure she'll say it was inevitable once Hecht understood the full import of my proposal. She warned us about him on our first day here.”

Logran chuckled. “Gwenneth had old Rorik pegged from the start, eh?”

“She’s the best judge of character I ever met.”

“They say Sisters of the Void can peer into your soul. Perhaps there’s a bit of truth to that.”

“Perhaps, but only those whose souls harbor darkness need fear a sister’s gaze.”

— 40 —

Yotai

Marta didn't cross paths with the admiral in the days after Heloise's death, a sign he was deliberately avoiding her. Regent Custis' behavior had remained unchanged from its habitual false solicitousness, but then she thought it unlikely Zahar would tell him about her transformation for fear of revealing his own sensitivity to a sister's mind.

But Custis was freezing her out of more and more meetings with star system and military officials in a barely disguised reminder her role was that of a figurehead. And without Heloise, Marta's isolation increased, especially after being gently told by her friends in the senior non-commissioned officers' mess it would be better if she no longer accepted invitations to enter. Worse yet, the handful of senior sergeants who'd made up her informal intelligence service were distancing themselves, no doubt after being warned off by Zahar or his minions.

The two Marines who'd accompanied Zahar into her office and took Heloise's body to the morgue seemed to have vanished altogether. Hopefully, they'd suffered nothing worse than a transfer off Yotai so they couldn't spread rumors of the incident. But after watching Zahar stab Heloise with such unalloyed rage, even if she'd used her talent to goad him, Marta wouldn't be surprised if they too were dead.

Though what disturbed Marta most was Custis rescinding her directive to withdraw naval units from Coalsack Sector star systems leading into what remained of the empire so they might be spared added devastation by Dendera's Retribution Fleet. He even ordered a task force back to Mykonos long after Commodore Sekine withdrew her ships to save them from almost certain destruction.

When Custis informed Marta of his decision, in an aside during one of the interminable social events he put on to raise her profile, she experienced her most intense and disorienting vision of fire and blood to date. It lasted only a few seconds and left her with no clear images, but the anguish she suffered for hours afterward drained both her energy and her patience. Whether he countermanded her to make a point or as an informed judgment call remained open to speculation. However, if it was the former, then she bore some responsibility for what might come thanks to how she'd exercised an empress-designate's limited authority.

Yet the most significant change to her daily routine since Heloise's death came via a Marine lieutenant colonel by the name Jacelyn Bram, assigned as her military aide-de-camp at Custis' orders. When Marta tried to refuse, the regent smiled and informed her she no longer had a choice. Sovereigns required at least one personal attendant and with Heloise dead, the position needed filling.

Marta, a woolen shawl wrapped around her shoulders, stood at the edge of the viceregal palace's observation terrace, watching mist born of the slow-moving river envelop Lena when Bram came through the open doors with her usual, energetic stride. Dark complexioned where Marta was pale, her short black hair framed an angular face more suited to the battlefield than the ballroom.

"Highness, news has come from the frontier systems. Regent Custis asks whether you'd consent to join him in the main briefing room."

Marta met Bram's dark brown eyes, searching for a deeper meaning to her words, but found none. The Marine guarded her thoughts well enough to the point where Marta wondered whether Zahar picked her for more than merely temperament and devotion to duty.

She'd not dared reach out so far, both in deference to the Rule of the Order and in case Bram was a wild talent capable of detecting intrusions. It wouldn't do for her to suspect Marta might be one of the proscribed mind-meddlers.

"Do you know what happened?"

"No, Madame. I was told to find you and pass along the regent's invitation. But for what it's worth, he apparently seems rather agitated, so the news probably isn't good."

"Let's hope we won't hear of civilian populations decimated because the Retribution Fleet's commanders condemned them as irredeemable traitors thanks to a handful of 16th Fleet ships patrolling the system."

In the days following her appointment as Marta's aide, Bram quickly learned the empress-designate held strong views and had few qualms about voicing them, including those deeply critical of the regent and his military commander. Yet even though part of her duties had to include reporting back on anything notable Marta said or did, she knew the Marine was staying silent. Something always seemed to hold her back.

"Let us hope indeed, Madame."

Though the aide never offered her own opinions, even in private, Marta sensed she shared the senior non-commissioned officers' mess dislike of Custis and their healthy suspicion for his plans to found a new empire. Bram turned on her heels and led Marta down the back stairs to the palace's office section.

While Marta swept into the room and headed for her seat while those present bowed their heads, Bram took her accustomed place along the wall with the other aides. Recognized as first among equals, just like Heloise, her high-collared, dark green uniform with gold braid aiguillettes dripping off the right shoulder nonetheless blended in better than the late Sister of the Void's black robes.

"Please be seated."

Custis' habitual smarmy expression was noticeable by its absence, replaced with an almost palpable aura of worry. He dropped into the padded chair across from her and leaned forward, arms on the polished tabletop.

"Thank you for joining us, Highness."

"My aide tells me we received news from our frontier systems. Since you seem concerned, I imagine it isn't good."

"No, Highness." Custis nodded toward Zahar, now sitting at one end of the table, as far as he could politely get from Marta. When she glanced at him, his cold, hard eyes conspicuously avoided meeting hers. "The admiral will brief us on the details."

"Your Imperial Highness, Regent. After weeks without sighting Dendera's Retribution Fleet anywhere in the Coalsack Sector or the adjoining wormhole junctions, Isabella and Mykonos became victims of quasi-simultaneous punitive incursions two days ago. The local task forces received no warning other than from their respective wormhole traffic control buoys when the attacking battle groups emerged. And I use the term battle groups loosely because the imperial units appear to have been larger than normal, which could indicate a concerted effort to destroy anything we place in their way."

"Why were we not warned?"

A faint grimace of irritation twisted Zahar's lips.

"Since none of the picket ships we sent to act as tripwires in adjoining wormhole junctions carry subspace transmitters powerful enough to reach Yotai without the help of retransmission arrays, we will never know, Highness. However, it seems likely they were destroyed before they could withdraw, perhaps through acts of treachery. We were fortunate the avisos posted in the Isabella and Mykonos systems made it back to report. Especially since both captains waited until they could confirm the fate of our forces before leaving by running silent while almost literally within enemy missile range."

Zahar touched a control, and the holographic tank in one corner of the room came to life with a schematic of the Isabella system and its wormhole termini.

"Approximately forty-eight hours ago, a thirty-five ship imperial formation, most of them heavy cruisers, came through Wormhole Isabella One. An almost identical formation of thirty-five ships simultaneously came through Wormhole Isabella Four."

Wormholes One and Four pulsed with a malevolent red glow and two swarms of red icons appeared, one by each of the marked termini.

"Of the first group, fifteen went FTL at once for Wormhole Two, which connects with Yotai, and fifteen of the second group headed for Wormhole Three, which connects with Ariel. The remaining forty ships jumped inward, aimed at Isabella itself."

Each of the red swarms in the holotank split in two.

"Rear Admiral Manard's escape routes were effectively cut off since the imperial units would reach Wormholes Two and Three before he could. With only fifteen ships in his task force, mostly frigates and light cruisers, the odds he could force his way through were next to nil. It left Manard with two options — flee through interstellar space under FTL drives in the hopes of reaching a friendly star system with a refueling station, or stand and fight. He chose to stand and fight."

A display came to life opposite the holo tank.

"The aviso's long-range video pickups took this in the moments before it crossed Wormhole Two's event horizon and fled under enemy fire. The wreckage orbiting Isabella is what remains of Rear Admiral Manard's task force, although he took an equal number of imperial ships down with him. As you can see from the flashes lighting up Isabella's night side, the imperials are carrying out an eradication-level bombardment."

"Which we could have avoided if you'd pulled Manard back one wormhole junction and left Isabella as an open system, ostensibly no longer under Coalsack Sector control." Marta modulated her voice to be soft and unemotional yet wrapped around a core of fiery hot anger no one could fail to notice.

"Maybe." Custis snapped. "We don't know that, Highness. Besides, no one expected the imperials to return with almost three times as many ships in a single system."

"A feeble excuse to offer the hundreds of thousands who are dead by now or will soon die through starvation and disease." Marta's tone held all the warmth of interstellar space. "Our responsibility is stopping the Four Horsemen of the Apocalypse, not helping them through vainglorious strategic miscalculations."

Appalled silence greeted Marta's declaration, then she heard Jacelyn Bram behind her murmur, "*So I looked, and behold, a pale horse. And the name of him who sat on it was Death, and Hades followed with him.*"

Though neither Custis nor Zahar could make out Bram's words, both gave her a poisonous glance before aiming wrath-filled eyes at Marta.

"If we're finished with Isabella, please tell me about the Mykonos system, Admiral," she said, her voice once more soft and unemotional.

Zahar cleared his throat before nodding.

"Of course, Highness."

The holotank shimmered, and a schematic of Marta's former home appeared.

"It was much the same scenario, with imperial formations emerging unannounced from Wormholes Three and Four, this time in groups of thirty starships. Each split in half to block Wormholes One and Two, and trap Commodore Sekine's Task Force. She also fought rather than attempt to escape FTL through interstellar space and risk running out of fuel before reaching a friendly harbor. Though she accounted for eleven enemy ships, the imperials destroyed all of hers and subjected Mykonos to orbital bombardment. If Your Highness wishes to see the video, I can put it on screen."

A new vision threatened to overcome Marta's senses for a fraction of a second, though as on previous occasions, she retained nothing other than blurry impressions of horror and destruction.

"Thank you, but that won't be necessary." She glanced around the room. "Would everyone other than Regent Custis and Admiral Zahar please leave?"

A few of the senior officers glanced at their commander as they hesitated.

"Now."

Marta's voice struck them with the force of a class five ion storm. When they were alone, she studied Custis with a gaze that made him visibly uncomfortable.

"Tell me, Devy, why am I here? You've frozen me out of decision-making fora since Admiral Zahar executed my lady-in-waiting because he has a superstitious fear of women who serve the Almighty. Why did you open yourself to the inevitability of my saying, in front of our most senior staff, *I told you so?*"

Custis paused while he chose his words.

"Events of such magnitude must be shared with you, lest people think you're a mere figurehead, a puppet, and I the puppet master. Many wouldn't look upon me as their ruler with equanimity. But I hoped you'd show more tact, Highness. Berating subordinates in the presence of others isn't a hallmark of good leadership, as your uncle, the Marine Corps colonel surely mentioned."

"When those subordinates disregard my direction and precipitate the deaths of countless thousands, perhaps even millions, they give up the right to treatment commensurate with their status. Especially if the true reason for said disregard is to show everyone who's the boss."

When Custis didn't react to her barb, a worm of doubt nibbled at Marta's certainty. After a pregnant pause, he smiled.

"You might see it like that, Highness, but none of the officers and officials in the room did," Custis replied in a calm voice while devilment danced in his eyes. "When you dismissed them, they left nurturing reservations about your fitness as our sovereign. A just empress doesn't demean her regent and the commander of her armed forces in front of lesser beings. Imagine how they'll feel after finding out you're an Order of the Void witch in all but name?"

"Meaning you found a better candidate to be figurehead empress and goaded me into what some would perceive as a show of unsuitability so you could more easily justify changing sovereigns midstream."

Custis' smile took on a mocking edge.

"Yes and no. Admiral Zahar's intelligence operatives found the trail of Corinne Ruggero, who hopefully won't have been tainted by the Void witches and I intend to follow up on their information. For the moment, you remain the chosen one, although this is your last war council. From now on, you will carry out only ceremonial and social duties, under my control. Publicly chastising your regent and military commander proved you shouldn't be involved in serious matters of state and diminished whatever influence you might have wielded. Be a good puppet, my dear Marta, and let your regent run things."

"Was any of this," she gestured toward the holotank, "real?"

"Sadly, yes. The imperial forces surprised us at Isabella and Mykonos and inflicted heavy losses, but only because of an intelligence failure, not because of — what did you call it again?"

"Vainglorious strategic miscalculations," Zahar supplied, a cruel smile creasing his ascetic features. "As if you witches know anything about such matters. The day Regent Custis' alternate choice for the throne lands on Yotai, I will make it my solemn duty to kill you myself, Highness. And I shall take great pleasure in doing so."

— 41 —

When the briefing room's door closed behind Marta, Admiral Zahar pushed away from the table, stood, and rolled his shoulders to release some of the accumulated tension.

"In retrospect, I wonder whether provoking her wasn't premature, Your Grace."

"The moment was perfect, Admiral. She showed herself to be another potential Dendera in front of our senior staff and aides. I would have been remiss in letting it pass after your discovery she'd been hiding a Sister of the Void as her companion. Who knows what mischief they were causing behind our backs? It was time to end the pretense."

"Perhaps, sir, but we merely have evidence from my recon team proving the 197th Imperial Battle Group, along with *Tanith*, reached Lyonesse where they revived the prisoners. My operatives brought no proof Corinne Ruggero was alive and well."

Custis shrugged irritably.

"Your people weren't able to account for everyone, yet when I left *Tanith* with my family, every single stasis pod was functional, except those whose destruction I ordered. She's somewhere on Lyonesse. Didn't you say they sent *Tanith*'s complement of common criminals to penal facilities, including one modeled on Parth's Desolation Island? If Corinne traveled as one of the latter, they might have released her under an assumed identity.

"Or better yet, they put her aboard under another noblewoman's name, and she's now living as her. No matter. Corinne is on Lyonesse. Your task force commander needn't be gentle with those separatists. They turn Corinne over or their nonsensical knowledge vault is history. That should motivate a monomaniac like this Jonas Morane who seems to believe we're doomed."

Zahar walked over to a sideboard and poured himself a glass of water.

"Maybe we should abandon the idea of a new empire instead, Your Grace, and break with a troubled past by making the Coalsack Sector into a republic. Then, you wouldn't need an empress, and I wouldn't be forced to send a badly needed naval formation five wormhole transits beyond our sphere just as the Retribution Fleet is starting a new campaign against us."

Custis scoffed. "A republic does not need a regent to work in the sovereign's shadow and any attempt to make myself first citizen for life would end badly. Besides, the people know nothing other than living under a constitutional monarchy and would rightly view a return to something like the despised Commonwealth's corrupt system with distaste. As for the Retribution Fleet, I can't see them coming back any time soon, not after the bloody nose we gave them. And as a bonus, we no longer need to station forces in the Isabella and Mykonos systems, since they're no longer of value."

Zahar drained his glass to hide a grimace of disgust at Custis casually brushing away those deaths. If Marta Norum weren't a Void witch under the skin, she would make a better ruler than the cold, ambitious grand duke. At least Norum understood there was more to governing than slaking one's lust for power.

"I want your expeditionary force on its way within the next seventy-two hours. They're to bring me Corinne Ruggero or incontrovertible proof of her death."

"As you command, Your Grace."

**

Once back in her apartments, Marta shrugged off her formal tunic and donned one of Heloise's black cloaks under Lieutenant Colonel Bram's curious eyes.

"Take me to Founder's Park, Jacelyn."

"I'll need a bit of time to arrange for an escort, Madame."

"No escort. I need to escape the palace's stifling atmosphere and breathe clean air for a few hours." She turned a wan smile on the Marine. "In fact, if you arrange for a car, I'll go alone, and you can do whatever aides do when they're not dancing attendance on their principals."

"Going without an escort might pass, but it could cost me my commission if I didn't at least accompany you whenever you leave the palace."

"After the dressing down I gave Regent Custis and Admiral Zahar?" Marta chuckled. "I'm sure neither would mind if I fell victim to a deadly accident that can't be traced back to them. Custis seems to have concluded I'm more of a liability than an asset."

"I'm sure that's not the case, Madame."

"You didn't hear the words we exchanged after I tossed the staffers out, Jacelyn. I think it's safe to say I no longer have any friends around here." Marta's hand unconsciously reached for the beacon nestled against her skin. "Perhaps I should leave the palace and vanish."

"Please don't force me to resign my commission, Madame."

"Why in Heaven's name should you do that if I went walkabout?"

"Because the regent would never forgive my losing track of you. Alternatively, if I accompanied you on this walkabout, I'd be absent without leave, and that is the same as resigning my commission."

Marta locked eyes with the older woman.

"Which of the two is your preferred course of action? Letting me go or accompanying me?"

Bram hesitated.

"If those are my only options, then I would go with you, Madame." A pause. "For what it's worth, I think you were right in telling Custis and Zahar what they needed to hear. Too many innocents died for nothing more than stupid politics. And it looks like plenty more will die before this is over..."

Her voice faded as she looked away. After a moment of silence, she said, "I had friends in both the Mykonos and Isabella task forces. Now they're gone, and for what?"

"Vainglorious strategic miscalculations."

A snort of laughter broke through Bram's solemn countenance.

"That was priceless. I've never seen so many flag officers look like someone pissed into their two hundred creds a bottle twenty-year-old Glen Arcturus."

"So I noticed. Tell me, how is it you can quote the verse about Death on his pale horse?"

"Quasi-eidetic memory. I received my early education in a priory-sponsored school on Zenia's World. If you've never heard of the place, then I'm not surprised. Zee-Dub, as we called it, didn't even qualify as a class one colony. The monastics provided us with much of our schooling and medical care. Since I was already a voracious reader at age nine, the friars and sisters gave me access to their library. I tore through every one of humanity's foundational books, among other classical works, before turning sixteen."

"Would I be correct in guessing your superiors, Admiral Zahar included, know nothing about your childhood? Because I can't see him appointing someone tainted by what he calls Void witches as my aide-de-camp, even if it was decades ago."

"You would, Madame. The details aren't in my personal file since I'm not a product of the Imperial Armed Services Academy. I enlisted as a private and made my way up the ranks. The Corps doesn't care about a mustang's pedigree, only how suited he or she is to become an officer. Pedigrees are for prospective Academy cadets, the fancier, the better. But unlike most of them," Bram put on a tentative smile, "I can quote every verse describing the Four Horsemen of the Apocalypse. And I'm with you in that respect, Madame. They're riding a deadly trail across the galaxy these days, and we shouldn't be helping them by being stupid."

Marta saw no falsehood hiding behind Bram's dark, guileless eyes and felt strangely heartened.

"You are an unexpected treasure, Jacelyn."

"I've been called many things, Madame, but treasure isn't one of them, and I won't tell you what the others were." The faint but unmistakable blush of embarrassment creeping up Bram's cheeks made her seem much younger. "With your permission, I'll arrange for a car and perhaps change into civilian clothes. My uniform will attract too much unwanted attention in Founder's Park. Or anywhere else. I'm the only officer in this star system wearing aide-de-camp braid on her right shoulder."

"Go."

**

Founder's Park was a hundred square kilometers of primeval Yotai forest and meadows along the Iriskaya River south of Lena, a short drive from the palace and almost directly under the Lena spaceport's main approach corridor. In other words, it was ideal for a quick, clandestine pickup by a shuttle from one of Galactic Dawn's armed merchant vessels.

Now she'd burned most of her bridges, Marta felt an urgent need to scout out possible landing sites under the guise of craving for fresh air, in case her talisman unexpectedly gave off a signal only an adept could sense. Whether a rescue ship would cross this system before Zahar carried out his threat was another matter altogether. But the Almighty would not bring her to this point only so she could die from a knife thrust into her heart.

"No problems about my leaving the palace without an escort?" Marta asked as she climbed into the unmarked staff car.

"Not a single raised eyebrow, Madame."

At Bram's gesture, the passenger door slid shut, cocooning them in a hull strong enough to ward off small arms fire.

"Perhaps word is already getting around that I'm a dead woman walking."

Bram glanced up from the controls as they took the ramp leading out of the underground garage.

"Or someone who shouldn't be crossed. Zahar and the regent don't enjoy universal respect, even among senior officers. And yes, I swept the car for surveillance devices, Madame. We can speak freely."

"You're one of those senior officers, aren't you, Jacelyn."

"I am. Zahar's actions turned many of us against the rebellion, but by then, it was too late. We saw how Dendera's supporters died and didn't want to join them. Not that she's any better. What's the old saying? Stuck between a rock and a hard place?"

The car rode up on its thrusters, changing from a ground vehicle into an aircraft.

"That would be the one. Truth is, it was too late when Stichus Ruggero threw away over eight hundred years of precedent and crowned himself emperor. Nothing we do will change the course of history. We can only try to preserve bits of it so that our species doesn't vanish from the face of the galaxy."

"A depressing thought. Where in the park should I land?"

"How about a few overflights so I can see what tickles my fancy."

Bram gave Marta a curious glance.

"As you wish."

— 42 —

Lyonesse

"Excellency, Admiral Morane and Chancellor Reyes." Wickham Sanford, Governor Yakin's secretary stepped aside and ushered them into her private day room.

She stood as they entered and offered her hand.

"Thank you for coming. I felt it would be better to discuss this new development in person rather than over a comlink. Please sit." She looked up at Sanford. "You can have the tea service brought in now. After that, I'm unavailable short of an extinction-level crisis."

"Yes, Madame. The tea is ready."

He made a hand gesture, and one of Government House's service droids trundled in, carrying a tray with three cups and a pot. It placed the tea service on the center table and, its mission completed, the droid left the room. Sanford followed it out and closed the doors behind him.

"Please, help yourselves."

When they'd done so, Morane took a sip of the rich brew before saying, "We're all ears, Madame. Whatever caused you to invite us here at short notice without either Rorik Hecht or Gus Logran in attendance must be worrisome."

"In fact, Rorik left me shortly before I called you. He came with advance notice of the Colonial Council's upcoming vote on the constitutional framework it will present to the Estates General when they meet later this month. And since Rorik always gets what he wants, the outcome of the vote is a foregone conclusion, which would be fine if the framework more or less matched what we've been discussing. But we're now facing something rather different."

"Let me guess," Reyes said with an impish smile. "Rorik wants to declare himself emperor and ascend the throne in a blaze of glory."

"No. The Estates General don't favor us becoming a monarchy. We're to be a republic under a leader named by the legislature, as planned. But that's where Rorik's framework diverges. Though the council will become an elected senate, under this new proposal, our legislature will not be unicameral. Besides the senate, Rorik wants an assembly composed of members nominated by the Estates General representatives."

"Unelected, then."

Yakin nodded at Reyes.

"Yes, and therefore open to all manner of political shenanigans, though its powers will be limited to acting as the senate's conscience by reviewing legislation and proposing amendments. My concern isn't so much with the idea of this assembly, but why Rorik came up with it. You'll understand in a moment."

Morane, eyes narrowed in thought, said, "The proposal is a bribe, to get the Estates General on Rorik's side as he puts forth constitutional provisions he knows we won't accept."

"Precisely. Here are a few of those provisions. The senate will not choose a leader who wasn't born on Lyonesse, and the assembly will likewise not choose a deputy leader who wasn't born on Lyonesse."

Reyes let out a frustrated sigh.

"Which conveniently excludes you, Jonas, Gus, and me along with most of the defense force members. Everyone who's been frustrating Rorik's ambitions. I can see why bribing the Estates General is necessary. How is that even legal?"

"There are plenty of historical precedents," Morane replied. "But Rorik is doing this for short-term political advantage rather than looking to Lyonesse's future. What else?"

"Legal responsibility for the knowledge vault will be taken away from the Defense Force and the Order of the Void and given to the Lyonesse Legislature, as the senate and assembly will collectively be known."

Morane's left hand clenched into a fist.

"I should have known he'd try something of the sort when his damned oversight committee wasn't getting anywhere. We can't allow politicians with a five-year time horizon to control something built for the distant future."

"Why do I think Rorik intends to become our first head of state?" Reyes asked in a soft voice. "With Severin Downes as his deputy?"

A smirk pulled up the corners of Morane's lips.

"Because you have a suspicious mind. Any other poison pills, Madame?"

"Several. The senate will not confirm the nomination of ministers, deputy ministers, defense force flag officers, and senior police officials. In other words, no legislative advice and consent for anything belonging to the executive. The same goes for supreme court nominations, though if the Estates General insist, he'll throw them a bone and give the assembly scope to question nominees, but not block them."

Reyes frowned.

"What is Rorik building? A republic or a dictatorship?"

"A republic that can easily become a dictatorship if the leader is so inclined." Morane put down his teacup and leaned forward. "There are enough historical precedents. None ended well. We need to stop this nonsense, Madame."

"I'm not sure we can. Even though Chancellor Reyes is a member of the Estates General—"

"For now. Rorik's been playing footsie with the Board of Trustees and is fanning the flames of dissension among the university faculty. Sorry for the interruption, Madame."

"I'm afraid most of her fellow members will see this as a chance to extract more advantages for their constituencies rather than set the foundations for a lasting civil contract."

Morane nodded.

"And Hecht will encourage horse trading, provided they vote in favor of the council's resolution. This stinks of Downes and his fellow former imperial court schemers. No doubt they're angling for ministerial positions under a Hecht administration. How long a term is he proposing for the head of state?"

"Six years, with no term limits. The head of state can only be removed for cause by the supreme court on a two-thirds majority vote of both the senate and the assembly."

"Meaning he can make himself leader for life." Morane jumped to his feet and paced the room. "Emma, you need to speak with your fellow Estates General members and impress on them the long-term risks for Lyonesse if they support Hecht's vision. I know a lot of them don't give a damn about the knowledge vault, so it's best you leave it out of your discussions."

"That was my intention."

He stopped as if struck by an idea.

"Now I know Downes is involved. This is a repeat of Stichus Ruggero's constitutional coup, only without the imperial trappings. Hecht doesn't need to be stopped, he needs to be shot!"

Yakin raised a hand.

"Please, Admiral. Not even in jest."

"It'll be a cold day in hell before I surrender the knowledge vault to a bunch of short-sighted politicians. And they have to be extremely short-sighted if they're voting in favor of this steaming mess."

"Rorik has his ways. If I order you to comply, as my last act before stepping down in favor of whoever will be the first head of state under our new constitution, would you refuse?"

"Yes. And I'd refuse the same order from your successor as ruler of Lyonesse."

"Then you'd be rebelling against the legitimate government of this star system and in no way different from many of your fellow admirals out there who forswore their oath to the Crown." Yakin pointed upward as if to indicate the galaxy at large. "And how will that help the situation? Would you order your troops to dissolve the legislature and executive at gunpoint so you can become a military dictator?"

Morane straightened his back under the lash of her words.

"Point taken, Your Excellency."

"Glad you see it my way. The solution to this conundrum is thwarting Rorik Hecht's ambitions without spilling blood."

"A shame the Order of the Void isn't part of the Estates General," Reyes said. "Sister Gwenneth is a master at the art of persuasion."

Yakin's eyes went from Morane to the chancellor.

"She is that. Do you think her late addition would help sway opinions against Rorik?"

Morane inclined his head.

"It can't hurt to try. And making her Order one of Lyonesse's community voices will tell Hecht we won't allow him to pervert the Constitutional Convention without serious opposition."

"Then it is done."

Yakin touched her brooch and Wickham Sanford entered moments later

"Excellency?"

"Draw up a proclamation adding the Order of the Void to Lyonesse's Estates General, with the leader of the abbey as representative."

"Yes, Madame. Shall I send it to the council for ratification?"

"No. Allowing the council to approve additions is a convention, not the law. Until Lyonesse has a new constitution, I remain its ruler."

Sanford bowed at the neck.

"As you command, Excellency."

"The gesture will infuriate Hecht and his entourage, Madame," Morane said once the secretary left them again, "but it's not nearly enough to trip the bastard up."

"Then think of more obstacles we can put in his way. I don't want Rorik to succeed, but your intemperate suggestion we kill him will only make matters worse. He is a duly elected colonial councilor and was acclaimed to the speaker's chair by his peers."

"Agreed, and I apologize for my earlier outburst. Perhaps Sister Gwenneth can give us sage advice."

"Or meddle with a few feeble minds," Reyes added. "That woman has scary insight. Pardon me for stating the obvious, but we shouldn't have let her focus on the abbey to the exclusion of everything else. Didn't you say she warned you about Hecht early on, Jonas?"

"She did. Excellency, I won't use main force to protect the knowledge vault just yet, but I would rather it be preserved intact for our posterity by a dictatorship than used as a political pawn by those whose vision doesn't extend past their own limited lifespans. Compared to what it means for future generations, the lives of Rorik Hecht, Severin Downes, and the rest of his nasty little cabal have no value."

Yakin caught his eyes and held them before nodding once.

"Understood."

"In that case, if there's nothing else, can Emma and I excuse ourselves? We have much to think about."

"Certainly. Thank you for coming, Admiral, Chancellor."

"We are at your service, Madame."

Once outside, in the afternoon sun's warm glow, Emma Reyes wrapped her arm around Morane's as they strolled toward the latter's staff car, patiently waiting by the Government House guard post.

"Would you really send out death squads if the Constitutional Convention falls for Rorik Hecht's slimy scheme?"

"Do you really expect me to answer such a question?" When she didn't immediately reply, Morane said, "The best time to stop an enemy is before he can make a move. Afterward tends to be messier."

Something in his voice caught her attention.

"Why do I sense a plan coming together in that fertile brain of yours?"

"Because I bared my soul to you."

"That's not the only thing you bared, and I'll point out it was reciprocal."

"Yet as much as I'd like to reciprocate right now, I need to spend time mulling over what Elenia told us."

"Alone?"

He stopped and glanced at her.

"We probably should talk this out, but in my quarters. Chances are a treacherous professor in the engineering department asked one of the brighter students to build him a state-of-the-art surveillance suite just for your home."

"Really?"

"Anything is possible these days. I can ask Major Barca to send one of her counterintelligence teams and check."

"Sure. If they find anything, what are the chances we can trace the components back to their origin?"

"Reasonably good. Why? Are you thinking of retaliation?"

"I hear revenge is sweet. If I'm to be ousted by the Board of Trustees in part because many among the most vocal faculty members don't have the foresight of a mewling infant, I'd like to leave as much pain and embarrassment as possible in my wake."

"If that's you want, my dear chancellor, I can arrange matters to your satisfaction before the trustees even meet. Several of the Rifle Regiment's part-time soldiers are university students, and they'll gladly carry out undercover work."

"Can I give you a list of names?"

"Please do."

Once they were in the car, Reyes said, "One thing puzzles me. Rorik is smart enough to know Elenia would summon us the moment he left Government House. Why give up the advantage of surprise by telling her about the council's, or rather his proposed constitutional framework before they vote on it? He didn't get to where he is by being a lousy political operator."

Morane was silent for a moment as they drove through the main gate and out onto Founders' Boulevard.

"No, he didn't. Hecht got to where he is by being a ruthless negotiator. This proposed framework is obviously his opening position, designed to wring concessions from us, something I might have figured out earlier if I'd kept my anger in check."

"Should we go back and let Elenia know?"

"It'll come to her within the hour. The sonofabitch knew we'd react this way. That's why he did it. Well, two can play this game."

"What are you plotting?"

"Buy me a drink, and maybe I'll tell you."

— 43 —

"Good evening, Sister." Morane, wearing a well-cut gray civilian suit, sketched an abbreviated bow as he ushered Gwenneth through the Lannion Base officer's mess lobby, one of many chambers dug into the towering granite cliff face. "Thank you for coming."

"After Speaker Hecht threw down the gauntlet, I'd not miss tonight for all the precious gems in the galaxy, Admiral."

"You look well."

"I look as I always do, but thank you for attempting to compliment me. The return to the quiet monastic life agrees with my Brethren, in spite of the occasional hostility at the university and working with new arrivals who know nothing about farming for a living. Though the latter generally tend to be happier and more grateful than the political prisoners we brought to Lyonesse."

Morane escorted Gwenneth to the main room, where most of the Lannion-based defense force officers not currently on duty were clustered around standing tables or the bar, enjoying friendly conversations. Colonel

DeCarde and Lieutenant Colonel Kayne broke free of their respective groups when they spied the Sister of the Void and came to greet her.

"I'll leave you in Brigid and Matti's capable hands. Our guests of honor should pass through the main gate at any moment now."

"And how would you know this? Did you develop a talent for prescience?" An amused smile danced on Gwenneth's lips. "It's not because of the time. Neither Speaker Hecht nor Commissioner Downes enjoys a reputation for punctuality, other than when they're expected at Government House."

"The admiral put surveillance teams from Major Barca's Security Company on both their sixes," DeCarde replied, a broad grin splitting her face. "Local youngsters who once belonged to Matti but decided they'd rather play secret agent than infantry trooper."

Kayne gave his commanding officer a tolerant smile.

"Talented, highly motivated people who'll go far whether they stay part-timers or make a full-time career in the defense force."

"I'm sure Adri is already dangling irresistible inducements before their eyes."

"No doubt."

"Keep Sister Gwenneth entertained." Morane returned to the lobby moments before the main gate announced Hecht and Downes' arrival.

When the speaker's official car pulled into one of the reserved spots near the ground level door, Morane stepped out and watched his guests disembark.

"Jonas." Hecht waved while he plastered on his hearty hail fellow, well-met smile. "Is this invitation a sign you might reconsider your position vis-à-vis certain matters of common interest?"

Morane waited until both men were near before holding out his hand.

"Welcome, Rorik. And yes, this invitation is a sign." After shaking with Hecht, he turned to Downes. "Severin, nice of you to come."

In contrast to the speaker's firm, domineering grip, Downe's hand felt like a cold, dead fish, with about as much muscle tone. Morane suppressed a smile at his sour expression, well aware the former noble detested anyone he considered an inferior addressing him by his given name. Especially one who'd long stymied his plans to take control of the knowledge vault. Downes might have been a successful schemer at the imperial court, but he was no master in the art of political glad-handing.

"Admiral."

Morane waved them into the lobby.

"Lest you think we threw this on just for you, the mess holds a get-together every second Thursday of the month. I just thought we might enjoy a companionable drink while discussing matters of mutual concern. Your money's no good here, by the way, so feel free to sample whatever tickles your fancy."

The buzz of conversation didn't dim when they entered the main room, and apart from a few curious glances, the assembled officers didn't pay their admiral's guests any attention. And it was by design, so Hecht and Downes understood the defense force wasn't about to give them a fawning welcome like their own social set.

"Good attendance," Hecht said when they reached the bar where a wide space had been cleared for them.

"These monthly events allow friends and acquaintances from different units to socialize and talk business in a relaxed setting. What can I offer you?"

"A glass of the Carhaix Barnburner will do me fine," Hecht replied, naming one of Lyonesse's better whiskeys from a distillery not coincidentally owned by the Hecht family consortium. "With a splash of water, if you please."

Morane signaled the bar droid and turned to Downes.

"And you, Severin? We offer a good Pinot Gris from the Dereux Vineyards in Trevena. One of Chancellor Reyes' favorites."

A grudging nod.

"It'll do."

Morane gestured at the droid again.

"And a Lannion Bitter for me."

"Funny," Hecht said, "I took you for a red wine man."

"I am when it suits the setting and the company." Morane winked. "And I've become rather partial to Lannion Brewery beer."

"Hah." Hecht's smile was as broad as it was insincere. "We might be rivals, but I'll be the first to admit Torvald has the best brewmaster on the planet, and he's not leaving Lannion for love or money, more's the pity."

The droid returned with their drinks and passed them out. Morane raised his foaming mug.

"Once again, welcome. I won't propose the traditional naval toast for a Thursday. Instead, let me just wish you good health."

"Good health." Hecht and Downes replied, the latter much less enthusiastically than the former.

After they'd taken a sip, Hecht asked, "I'm curious. Why didn't you want to propose the naval toast for a Thursday?"

"Because it goes, *to a bloody war or a sickly season.*"

Downes sniffed.

"Hardly cheerful. Glad you spared us, Morane."

"What's the meaning, if I may ask?"

"People die in a war or from disease, freeing up spots on the promotion ladder, something I'm sure Severin knows only too well from his time at court, though I understand wars and disease aren't the only way to clear spots in Dendera's shadow."

"How, um — macabre." Hecht took another sip. "Does every day of the week have its toast?"

"Indeed." Morane rattled them off. "The tradition dates back to the days of sailing ships on Earth, almost two thousand years ago."

"Fascinating." Hecht's eyes roamed over the assembly. "Shall we discuss business here, or perhaps somewhere quieter?"

"Definitely somewhere quieter. Considering the subject, I thought we'd talk in the vault itself, so you can see the progress we're making. I'll invite Sister Gwenneth to join us since she's not only an ex officio oversight commissioner, but her abbey is shouldering the brunt of the work."

"Is that necessary?" Downes asked in his nasal voice.

"I believe so."

"Let the man invite who he wants, Severin. It's still his show."

Downes gave Morane a hard glance.

"For now."

With uncanny timing, Gwenneth broke away from the group of officers around her and headed for the back door after giving Morane a quick nod.

"Perhaps we should finish our drinks," he said before downing the rest of his bitter. After a moment of hesitation, the others imitated him.

Morane led them through a rabbit warren of passageways until they reached a broad staircase shaped from the living rock by laser cutters.

"We're not taking the lifts like last time?" Downes asked.

"I thought I'd show you a bit more of the base this way. It's only five stories. We can use lifts on the way back."

The starship-grade airlock door protecting the knowledge vault was open when they reached the lowest level. Gwenneth was already inside, waiting with a blank expression on her face.

Morane, though a frequent visitor, never lost his awe at the endless rows of gray, armored cabinets, each holding books whose pages were printed on a quasi-indestructible polymer, along with various electronic formats. Though years of work still lay ahead, the amount of human learning represented by the books already stored in the vault boggled the mind.

Once inside, Downes looked around and sniffed.

"I see nothing different."

Morane pointed at the furthest row.

"We started storing some of the more important works of fiction produced by our species."

"Since you're not nearly done with technical subjects, isn't that premature?"

"Not necessarily," Morane replied in a pleasant tone. "As you might remember, Sister Gwenneth's people are preparing and storing texts on many important subjects concurrently, so that if they're interrupted, we have books covering a broad spectrum of human experience already safeguarded. Seminal works of fiction are part of that experience. For instance, are either of you familiar with Edgar Allan Poe?"

Hecht shook his head in silence though Morane could see growing suspicion in his eyes.

"Of course not. What is this nonsense?" An irritated frown creased Downe's high forehead.

"Humor me, Severin. It will become clear in a few moments. Poe was one of nineteenth-century Earth's most important English language writers. Or at least that's how we came to remember him almost sixteen centuries later. There might have been more prominent ones, but his works are among those that survived to the present day. A collection of Poe's works even now resides in the cabinets reserved for non-technical books."

"Please get to the point, Jonas," Hecht said in the voice of someone slowly losing patience. "We're here to discuss the vault's future under the new constitutional framework."

Morane raised both hands in a placating gesture.

"As I said, this will become clear momentarily. One of Poe's short stories is called The Cask of Amontillado. It describes the vengeance wreaked by a man named Montresor on his fellow nobleman Fortunato for what he terms a thousand injuries. Montresor carries out his revenge by playing on Fortunato's conceit and appetite for fine drink and lures him into his cellar where he gets him inebriated. The Amontillado in the title, a type of wine lost to us, was supposedly the best in Montresor's collection, and thus bait for his trap. He tricks Fortunato into an alcove, telling him the Amontillado is within. There, Montresor chains his victim to the wall and bricks the alcove shut, leaving him to die of hunger and thirst. At the end of the story, fifty years have elapsed, but Fortunato's body's remains entombed where Montresor left him."   At that moment, the knowledge vault's armored door swung shut with a loud clang, startling Hecht and Downes. "A fascinating tale, don't you think? Perhaps I'll forward a copy of Poe's book to your homes."

"What are you playing at, Morane?" Hecht growled.

"Can't you see the parallels with our current situation, Rorik?"

"Meaning?"

"That constitutional framework you forced on the Colonial Council is replete with injuries, many directly aimed at Elenia, me and others who've poured their heart and soul into making Lyonesse a last bastion against the collapse."

An air of exaggerated disbelief transformed Hecht's expression.

"My opening position in what I hope will be a fruitful negotiation, nothing more. I suppose that concept is foreign to the military mind."

"Didn't I tell you and Severin certain things are not negotiable?"

"Everything is negotiable. Besides, you're not well placed to oppose me publicly." He studied Morane through narrowed eyes before exhaling like an angry bull. "Please don't tell me your silly story was a way of threatening us."

"Very well, then. Here is my opening position, Rorik. Your proposed framework? Gone. The council will vote on what we initially agreed to, before this court jester," Morane jerked at thumb at Downes, "filled your mind with what he believes are Machiavellian tactics to gain power. No Assembly of the Estates General. That's an utterly stupid idea. It shows appalling short-sightedness. Did you even stop to think about how thoroughly a legislative chamber filled with people who solely represent special interests can be corrupted? Probably not."

When Hecht opened his mouth to speak, Morane raised a restraining index finger.

"I have the floor, Rorik. Place of birth will not be a restriction in qualifying for high office. And last but not least, the knowledge vault remains under full defense force and abbey control. Did I say that was my opening position? Sorry, I misspoke. That is my final position. Take it or leave it."

"You're mad."

"And you're in my cellar. Some say Poe's Montresor was insane, but he lived to a ripe old age while Fortunato didn't. Since Severin and you want the knowledge vault so badly you're willing to mess up Lyonesse's political institutions, and to hell with its citizens, I'll let you spend eternity here. I've prepared two cabinets as your final resting places."

Downes, struck speechless by Morane's matter-of-fact tone while discussing his and Hecht's murder stared at him with eyes the size of dinner plates.

"Bullshit, Jonas." Hecht tried to sound dismissive, but Morane could sense fear emanating from his every pore. "How will you convince Severin and me to cooperate with our own murders?"

"Sister?"

Hecht whirled around only to stare at the barrel of a large bore needler.

"I'm carrying non-lethal loads, Speaker. If you and Mister Downes are to become the admiral's Fortunatos, I can't use lethal ammunition."

Hecht turned back toward Morane. His face was rapidly taking on an unhealthy puce coloration while spittle foamed at the corners of his mouth.

"You're both rabid lunatics. I'll take your stars for this Morane, and your abbey, Sister? Done for. The Order of the Void no longer has a future on Lyonesse. You're both done for! I've been recording this conversation and once it becomes public knowledge..."

— 44 —

"Try not to suffer cardiac arrest, Rorik. I'd rather we finish this cleanly and not with an emergency medical team in attendance." A cold smile transformed Morane's face. "And if you've been counting on your personal communicators to make a record of our conversation, might I suggest you look at them."

The speaker of the council retrieved his device from an inner tunic pocket and glanced at it. After a few seconds, an incredulous expression replaced his anger as he touched every control surface with increasing panic.

"What did you do?" The words came out as a low hiss.

"Since I knew you'd try something of the sort, my people installed an electromagnetic disrupter. Any advanced electronics in this room are temporarily inoperative." He gestured at Downes. "Check yours, Severin."

"You'll pay for this outrage. With compound interest."

"Based on what evidence?" When Hecht didn't answer, Morane said, "Think about it, Rorik. What'll happen if you go out there and spin a tale claiming the Chief of the

Lyonesse Defense Staff and the head of the Lyonesse Abbey held you at gunpoint in the knowledge vault and threatened to entomb Severin and you in book cabinets? Never mind telling the world a Sister of the Void pointed a needler at you when everyone knows the Brethren never touch weapons. You won't take my stars or the abbey's freehold. But since you'll present evidence of mental derangement, the council will depose you as the speaker, and shortly after that, once Governor Yakin makes her views known, it will dissolve the Knowledge Vault Oversight Committee."

"Damn you." Hecht was quivering like a man on the verge of a seizure.

"See, Rorik, this is why we're preserving the classics. Without knowing about Poe's Cask of Amontillado, I might not have figured out how to put you between the devil and the cold of deep space. Best we allow future generations to discover the same thing, don't you think?

"Now then, it's quite simple. You and your lackey leave this place unharmed, and by the end of the week, the Colonial Council votes on the original framework. You finish your term as speaker and leave politics once Lyonesse elects a senate. Give Severin and the rest of the lordlings sinecures, if that's what you want, provided Hecht Industries pays their way. None of them will ever be employed in any capacity by the government, nor will they be allowed to stand for elected office above the municipal level. Yes, I know, it contradicts my earlier stricture that there will be no place of birth restrictions in qualifying for high office. But on second thought, we can't risk them polluting Lyonesse's body politic."

"What if I don't go along?" He growled through clenched teeth.

"Then you won't leave this place. Someone will drive your car into the wilderness, and by the time you're reported as missing, it'll look like the native wildlife did its usual job of cleaning up human garbage. Accidental death. Perhaps in a thousand years, someone will open your tombs and realize we left them not only knowledge but anatomical evidence of thirty-sixth century human males."

Morane turned his attention on Downes who still wore a stunned expression.

"I think your friend is about to suffer a stroke, Rorik. It won't save him from eternity in a book cabinet, but still..."

"Original framework?" Hecht's words came out in a hoarse whisper.

"In every detail. No more attempts to control the vault and you leave political life once the new constitution comes into force." When Hecht nodded once, Morane said, "If you renege or in any way try to change the deal, I will have you brought back here and entombed, no second chances, no discussions, no mercy. Understood?"

Another grudging nod.

"Understood."

"Just to keep you honest, I put surveillance teams on your and Severin's tail weeks ago. That will continue. And at the slightest sign of treachery, those teams will snatch you off the street, and we will meet again right here, for one last time."

"Got it."

"Take what you can. Become one of Lyonesse's founding fathers by sponsoring our original agreement instead of ending as a name in a missing person report."

"You leave me no choice, Morane, but this isn't over."

"It is." Morane reached into his pocket, and the armored door opened with a soft squeal. "Sergeant, please escort Speaker Hecht and Chief Commissioner Downes back to their car."

"Sir," a disembodied voice replied from the corridor.

Morane dipped his head.

"A pleasure to see you, as always, Speaker. Perhaps we could impose on Governor Yakin and discuss our arrangement with her tomorrow. I'll make sure Chief Administrator Logran joins us."

"Whatever you say, *Admiral*."

Gwenneth and Morane watched them leave. Once they heard the lift doors closing, the sister exhaled.

"I might almost believe you're blessed with the gift, Jonas. That went better than I expected."

He nodded at the inoperative replica weapon dangling from her right hand.

"Thanks to you. I wouldn't have been able to convince Rorik he was facing the real deal. And since no one will ever believe a servant of the Almighty could threaten another with a weapon of war, both Rorik and Severin understand speaking of what just happened would be worse than futile."

"Perhaps, but please remember, they will carry a grudge against you to the grave. Theirs or yours, whichever comes first. You not only thwarted intricate plans to become this star system's power brokers, you made them look foolish in their own eyes, and the latter stings worse than anything."

Morane shrugged.

"Fair enough, since I'll be carrying a grudge against them as well, perhaps not until death do us part, but something of it will always stay, like a blood stain that just won't wash out." When Gwenneth cocked an eyebrow in question, he made a dismissive hand gesture. "Not for what they tried. Just as a fish cannot shed its scales, people like Hecht and Downes cannot stop seeking power because they're unable to face the emptiness in their souls. No, I resent them for forcing me to threaten murder so I could protect what we built here from the same human folly that caused the empire's implosion."

After a few seconds of silence, Gwenneth asked, "Would you have carried out your threat if Speaker Hecht refused to back down?"

A wry smile tugged at Morane's lips.

"You know I can't answer that question, Sister."

"Just checking."

"Strangely enough, I suddenly feel an irresistible urge to wash out my mouth with strong drink. Can I buy you a dram of something that doesn't come from a distillery owned by the Hecht family conglomerate?"

"With pleasure."

Brigid DeCarde intercepted them as they re-entered the officers' mess main room.

"Please tell me you locked the slimy bastards into their very own Amontillado casks."

"Of course not. And you're confusing the title of the story with where Fortunato ended up."

"But Jonas branded their psyches with the fear of death."

DeCarde made a face.

"It'll wear off by sunrise tomorrow."

"Perhaps some of it, but Speaker Hecht and Chief Commissioner Downes firmly believe Jonas will kill them if the council puts forth anything other than what we previously agreed upon."

"The admiral is a good actor." DeCarde eyed her commanding officer with suspicion. "You were acting, right?"

"As I told the sister before we left the vault, you know I can't answer that question."

"Hah! I knew it. Remind me to never end up in your gun sights. Too bad the bastards backed off. I'll wager we haven't seen the last of their nonsense."

"I wouldn't be too sure." Gwenneth gave DeCarde a beatific smile. "Speaker Hecht knows a losing proposition when he sees one."

**

The next day, shortly after oh-eight-hundred, while he was scanning the operations center's overnight log entries, Morane's personal communicator chimed for attention. Governor Yakin. He placed the device on his desk and tapped its control pad. Almost at once, a small, holographic representation of Yakin's solemn face materialized in midair above it.

"Good morning, Madame. To what do I owe the honor of such an early call?"

"Good morning, Admiral. I just finished a most puzzling conversation with Rorik Hecht, and I'm hoping you can shed light on the matter."

"I'll try my best."

"Rorik showed up on my doorstep thirty minutes ago, after giving Sanford ten minutes warning of his arrival. He was white as the northern snows and for once without his constant shadow, that creature Severin Downes. Rorik said he'd held a heart-to-heart discussion with you last night during a social event at the officers' mess, and that you'd convinced him it would be better to stick with the previously agreed upon constitutional framework. The council will ratify it later today. When I asked how you'd changed his mind, the only thing he would say is you were frighteningly persuasive. He left me with a copy of the proposal he's putting before the council in a few hours as proof of his intentions."

"That is good news, Madame. I wasn't looking forward to protracted arguments with the Estates General."

"I've known Rorik Hecht since I took on my responsibilities as governor of Lyonesse. He has never, in all those years, walked away from something he wanted. He's a shrewd and tough negotiator. That incredible proposal was just Rorik's opening bid. He didn't expect us to concede on every item. Knowing the man, he would have tried to maneuver us into giving in on those important to him while letting us feel relief we didn't give everything away. And yet we're back to the original with no discussions, let alone negotiations. What happened last night?"

Morane fought to keep a guileless expression while he mangled the truth.

"We did, in fact, negotiate, Madame. I made a counterproposal Rorik found convincing enough to accept."

Yakin's lips compressed into a thin line.

"Please don't insult my intelligence, Jonas. You scared him, and he's not a man to take fright easily."

Morane repressed the urge to sigh.

"Very well. I invited Rorik and Severin Downes to visit the vault along with Sister Gwenneth. Once there, we discussed progress, and I mentioned we'd begun to store classic works of fiction. Rorik was dubious about doing so before we finished with the basic technical and scientific books. Therefore I gave him a practical demonstration of why fiction has its place in our vault. It sufficed to open his eyes on many things, including the wisdom of not reneging on his earlier commitments."

Yakin's eyes narrowed with suspicion.

"Pardon my crudeness, but stop feeding me bullshit."

"The practical demonstration involved a nineteenth-century piece of fiction by one Edgar Allan Poe called The Cask of Amontillado. I drew a thumbnail sketch of the plot for our guests, then pointed out the similarities between our situation and that of the tale's characters. It proved to be a winning argument. Perhaps reading the story will show you why. It is short. The university's virtual library has copies in both archaic English and modern Anglic."

"And that's all you'll say on the matter?"

"That's all I *can* say, Madame."

"In that case, I will read your Mister Poe's opus, and then we can resume this conversation."

"I'd be delighted."

"Yakin, out."

Morane slumped back in his chair and exhaled loudly. The governor would not approve of what he and Gwenneth did. She'd earned the respect of most Lyonesse citizens, even those who didn't like her personally, precisely because of her unimpeachable integrity. What he'd done to Hecht and Downes was criminal, even though few would blame him, and that wouldn't sit well with her. Perhaps he should prepare a letter of resignation, just in case. Yakin was smart enough to deduce last night's events after reading about Montresor's revenge upon Fortunato.

His communicator chimed again less than thirty minutes later.

— 45 —

Yotai

A soft rap on the office door pulled Marta from the fifth century Earth described by her book. After Custis excluded her from affairs of state and barred her from visiting any of the garrison's messes, she had little else to do but read in between excursions beyond the palace walls.

"Highness?"

"Come in, Jacelyn." Marta gestured at the room's other chair. "Sit. What's up?"

"Bad news. The Retribution Fleet is back. It pushed through to the Ariel system from Isabella and struck the resident battle group hard. Ariel itself wasn't touched, but we lost another ten ships to their eight."

Marta's lips compressed into a thin line.

"Fools. If they'd withdrawn Manard's task force to Ariel instead of letting him fight and die, the imperials wouldn't have dared go beyond Isabella."

"There's more."

"I guessed as much."

"An imperial formation entered the Parth system for the first time. Rear Admiral Ostrow, who commands the 164th, chased them off with minimal losses, but intelligence believes the incursion was nothing more than a reconnaissance in force, meaning they'll be back and in greater strength."

"The noose is tightening." She shook her head. "Sadly, I doubt Zahar will withdraw Ostrow and leave that planet of misery to our enemies."

"Agreed, Madame."

"Do you think Dendera concentrated her forces on the Coalsack because she sees it as her biggest rival for supremacy, or whether we're the last rebel sector still standing?"

"Intelligence figures it's the former."

"And for once, I concur."

"There's still more."

Marta smiled at her aide.

"Of course there is. Bad news always comes in threes, or so ancient lore tells us." She tapped the reader with her knuckles. "It's amazing what you can learn when you have nothing but time on your hands."

"I admire your patience. I'd be climbing up the walls with frustration by now."

"The third event?"

"Another incursion into the Mykonos system through Wormhole Three. This time the imperials jumped directly for Wormhole Two. The picket ship lying in wait by Wormhole One watched them transit out to the sterile system between Mykonos and Micarat. The formation's size would indicate another reconnaissance in force."

"Bracketing Yotai."

Bram nodded.

"That's my guess."

"They'll find Micarat more than strong enough to repel the battle groups they unleashed against Isabella and Mykonos."

"Which means they might probe Yotai itself next since they already enjoy local superiority in the branches ending at two of our four stable termini and won't try coming via the fifth, unstable wormhole. Why spend your strength against the sector's second most important system when you can leave it to wither on the vine by taking the capital? If they push Zahar's ships out of Ariel, that'll make it three. This won't end well, will it, Madame?"

Marta slowly shook her head.

"It can't. There was never more than a slight chance Grand Duke Custis' scheme to found a rival empire and save something from Dendera's mess might work. The best we can hope for now is an epiphany that will lead him and Zahar into surrendering and fleeing for the badlands before millions more die."

"And that won't happen."

"No. Custis will want his twilight of the gods. He's been invested in this scheme since the first rumblings of revolt in the Shield Sector. Dendera got wind of it, though she found no proof, which is why she exiled him and his entourage to Parth as both punishment and prevention."

Bram fell silent for almost a minute, visibly chewing on her thoughts.

"Madame, I'm a Marine. We're trained to face death. But getting bombarded from orbit by people who we once called comrades seems like an idiotic way to die. And for what?"

"I'm sure you'll find few around here who would disagree, yet even fewer brave or desperate enough to voice their fears."

For the first time since making Bram's acquaintance, Marta reached out to touch her mind. So far, the aide had proved herself to be honest, open, and candid to a fault, but before taking the final step of trust, she had to know.

"Admiral Zahar won't tolerate defeatists in his command. I've heard of senior officers who disappeared after voicing concerns too loudly. Ostensibly they were posted to frontier systems, but I doubt they ever made it off Yotai's surface." She shrugged with resignation. "Ours not to reason why, ours but to do and die."

Marta's third eye told her the Bram's hidden self wasn't much different from her outer shell.

"Words spoken by soldiers since the dawn of time. But I don't intend to stay around and find out what an orbital bombardment feels like on the receiving end if I can help it."

A frown of curiosity creased Bram's forehead.

"Madame?"

"If I told you at some point — I don't know when it might happen, if ever — that a ship is inbound to take me off Yotai, would you let me leave by myself? Would you go with me? Or would you denounce me to Zahar so I couldn't flee?"

Her answer came almost immediately.

"I'm your aide until relieved of duty, Madame. I'd come with you." Marta knew without the shadow of a doubt, Bram spoke the truth. "But why run away? You're the empress-designate."

"In no more than name. Since showing that I not only won't be a mere figurehead but appear to be blessed with more strategic acumen than Custis, I've become a placeholder. Once he finds and recovers his original choice or Zahar dispenses with a regent and makes himself emperor, I'll become one of those senior officers who vanished without a trace."

Bram fell silent again for several long heartbeats.

"A task force left Yotai three days after the incident in the briefing room, bound for Lyonesse. Would finding and recovering his first choice be its mission?"

"Perhaps. If he's willing to weaken his forces and risk sending ships far beyond Coalsack-controlled wormhole junctions, it has to be important. Zahar wouldn't let him waste precious ships on a side errand otherwise."

"If you'd like, I could try to find out more."

Marta shook her head.

"Don't. The less attention they pay us, the easier it will be to slip away when and if my ship comes."

"Can I ask who that ship belongs to and why it would come here?"

"Sorry, Jacelyn, but it would be advisable I keep that to myself until we're both safely aboard."

"Understood. I can't reveal what I don't know." She looked around the room. "Funny, but thinking about leaving all this doesn't exactly fill my heart with sadness, even if it means I'll no longer be a serving Marine Corps officer. In fact, now you've told me we might escape, I feel a lot more optimistic about my future."

"The operative word is might. No promises, no guarantees."

"I understand, Madame. How will you find out the ship is inbound?"

"To be honest, I'm not sure. Just as I'm not sure whether it will come."

A light went on in Bram's eyes.

"So that's why we've been roaming around Founder's Park, under the Lena spaceport's main approach path. We're scouting potential landing spots."

"In case we need one, yes. I couldn't say how we'll be picked up, only that a shuttle needs to land somewhere unobtrusive. Call it exercising the power of positive thinking. If I'm ready, my ship will come."

"From your lips to the Almighty's ear. May I make a suggestion?"

"Certainly."

"I assume you don't intend to leave with merely the clothes on your back."

"No. We should bring a modicum of clothing, and I'm sure you own a few personal items you'd rather not leave behind."

"I do, Madame. Since it would seem strange if we're seen leaving the palace at an unusual hour carrying travel bags once the ship arrives, I propose we find a suitable storage spot between here and Founder's Park where we can slowly accumulate our things."

Marta smiled at her aide.

"An excellent idea. Why don't we start today? I feel like fresh air and a few hours of freedom."

**

Custis and Zahar, standing on the former's office balcony, absently watched a staff car emerge from the palace grounds and lift off toward the city. Zahar's communicator buzzed at that exact moment. He quickly glanced at its screen.

"Lady Marta and her aide are headed for what I presume is another nature hike."

"So long as she stays away from anything important, I don't care."

Custis shrugged away his admiral's words with the irritation of someone whose long-cherished plans were slowly turning to dust. News of fresh reconnaissance intrusions by Retribution Fleet formations augured more death and destruction before he could consolidate his forces and present an overwhelming defense. That Marta was right only served to feed his simmering anger.

"Then why bother keeping her alive?"

"She's still a useful symbol. But once Commodore Bryner brings Corinne back to Yotai, you can stick a knife through her heart for all I care."

"If he finds her, and if he returns. I realized Your Grace doesn't wish to hear me say it, but we would be better off abandoning the idea of placing someone with imperial blood on a Yotai-centered throne. Call the current situation an emergency and make yourself first citizen for the duration. No one will object, not with Dendera's apocalyptic vengeance coming at us from every branch of the wormhole network."

"And what about those among your senior staff who've lost faith in our plans?" When Zahar didn't immediately reply, Custis turned a cold smile on him. "You thought I wasn't aware? I also have my informants. If we weren't facing immediate strategic problems, I'd order your headquarters purged of defeatists and doubters. But under the current conditions..."

"That is probably wise, Your Grace." Zahar fell silent for a full minute while the car vanished between Lena's glistening towers. "Perhaps you might arrange for Lady Marta to suffer a fatal accident, then proclaim an executive regency while we seek another suitable candidate instead of waiting for Bryner's return. That regency can last for however long you like."

"Why are you so damned keen on seeing her die?"

"She is tainted by the witches and their evil creed."

"I didn't know you were superstitious."

"Hardly, but that's neither here nor there. Marta hangs around us like an omen of destruction and watching her predictions come true is unnerving a lot of my officers. Her death would clear the air."

"Perhaps."

Custis kept his eyes on the horizon, wondering whether Zahar would simply take matters into his own hands and murder Marta without approval. His knife bore testament to a bloody disposition, which led Custis to ponder whether Zahar might not lose patience with him sooner rather than later and seize power, as he had done once before.

"Let me sleep on it."

"Don't sleep too long, Your Grace."

— 46 —

Lyonesse

"Madame?" Morane braced himself for the worst, but Yakin's composure seemed as perfect as ever.

"I just want the answer to one thing, Jonas. Who suggested that story? I doubt you stumbled on it by chance. I consider myself better read than most and never heard of Mister Poe."

Of all the questions she might have asked, he didn't expect this one.

"I'm sorry, Madame, but I've been sworn to secrecy."

The ghost of a smile touched her lips.

"Meaning the Almighty moves in mysterious ways. Fair enough. Please don't make a habit of using Mister Poe as reference material for your political skirmishes. I took a quick look at more of his oeuvre, and he strikes me as having been a rather strange man."

"I won't. My personal preferences tend toward Sun Tzu and Niccolo Machiavelli, among others."

"The latter isn't much of an improvement if you ask me."

"So noted."

"Yakin, out."

Moments later, Brigid DeCarde stuck her head through his office door.

"Was that the governor?"

"Didn't anyone ever tell you it's impolite to listen in?"

She shrugged, unrepentant.

"Sound travels when you leave your privacy settings at zero. All I heard was her lovely voice. The words eluded me."

"Elenia found Rorik's change of heart suspect, so I gave her something while leaving myself a margin of plausible deniability."

"And she figured it out. That lady is no addled noblewoman from Dendera's corrupt court. Lyonesse could do worse than keep her on as head of state indefinitely."

"True."

"That being said, I'm here not to spy but make a suggestion. After sleeping on last night's events, I think it might be wise if you asked Adri for a few of her irregulars as discreet bodyguards whenever you leave the base. I'd suggest a squad of Pathfinders, but even in civilian getup, they would stand out and give Rorik the idea you're afraid of retaliation, which might be counterproductive."

"You think someone could be daft enough to threaten my life?"

"Someone or rather several someones were daft enough to apply pressure precisely on your biggest pain point, the vault. The fact they couldn't predict you'd react by threatening their lives tells you plenty about the general intelligence level of Rorik Hecht's entourage."

"Point taken. I'll speak with Adri."

"Already done. Just make sure to let the ops center know whenever you leave the base."

Morane gave her a mock frown.

"And what would you have done if I'd rejected the idea?"

"Found someone in your office to warn the ops center whenever you leave the base."

"Might I infer from this solicitude for my health you're not interested in becoming chief of the defense staff?"

"Not anytime soon. Once the new constitution is in place, we can talk about my career aspirations again. Until then, it's best you keep running the show. I can't muster your level of patience when dealing with fools. If it were up to me, I'd have locked those two clowns in a cabinet for an hour. Or a few days, depending on how much they pissed me off."

"Don't think I wasn't tempted. Let Adri know I'm fine with the idea. If her irregulars want to give me a sign and let me know they're around, that's good too."

"Will—" The insistent buzz of a priority call from the operations center interrupted DeCarde's reply.

"Morane."

"Centurion Greff, sir. The wormhole traffic control buoy reported the arrival of a ship called *Dawn Runner*." Morane and DeCarde looked at each other in surprise. Another Order of the Void vessel? "Its captain, who goes by the name Korax sent a signal on the priority subspace channel moments later, advising he carries two hundred and five Void Brethren, refugees from the civil war, four mercenaries, and two children. He states he came across Captain Rinne of *Dawn Trader* several months ago. At that time Rinne informed him Lyonesse was now home to the Order's head abbey for this part of the galaxy. *Myrtale*, who has this cycle's wormhole picket duty, confirms *Dawn Runner* is, in every important aspect, *Dawn Trader*'s sister ship."

"Welcome *Dawn Runner* and tell them to report once they come out of FTL at the hyperlimit, then contact the abbey, so they know to set up another two hundred and five bunks. I'd also appreciate them interviewing the new arrivals and passing the results on to Major Barca's analysts."

"Yes, sir."

"Was that everything?"

"Yes."

"Morane, out." He looked up at DeCarde. "There has to be an interesting story behind those four mercenaries and two children. I wonder if they're connected."

"We should leave the kids to the abbey for now. But those mercs? I suggest we bring them here for debriefing. If they're the wrong sort, I'd rather not take chances. And if they're the right sort, perhaps they'd like a job with us. If you don't mind, since tomorrow is a training day for the part-timers, I'd like to use one of Matti's units as spaceport security when *Dawn Runner* lands, rather than a squadron of Pathfinders. Though at this short notice, it'll be A Company. They could use the practice."

"It's your brigade, Brigid. Deploy whoever you want."

**

"One Niner, this is One Three."

Command Sergeant Parmont Rehn's voice over the A Company push interrupted Centurion Antony Wolf's conversation with his first sergeant. Both stood by the arrival hall's inner doors watching as their soldiers funneled the newcomers through immigration before shipping them off to the abbey.

"One Niner."

"We're facing a bit of a situation outside. The four mercenaries are refusing to be separated from the children. They're armed and stubborn." Rehn was a

Lyonesse native with no military experience beyond serving in the Rifles ever since it was the embryo of a colonial militia with one officer, twelve troops, and half a dozen scatterguns.

"On my way. One Niner, out."

Wolf nodded at his first sergeant and crossed the hall to the tarmac doors, which opened at his approach. He immediately saw four men wearing the sort of black tactical clothes favored by private security operatives since time immemorial. They were clustered around two small children, neither of whom could have been older than ten.

A section from Rehn's Third Platoon stood at a respectful distance, weapons pointing downward while Rehn himself faced a large man whose features were seamed by decades of hardship. Their stances were relaxed, though an undercurrent of tension remained.

The man caught sight of Wolf.

"Finally someone with pips on his collar — no offense, Sergeant, but if your orders are to take the kids from us, then this is the man I need to speak with. And if he can't countermand orders, then it'll be your colonel."

"I understand, sir."

The mercenary's grin was friendly enough.

"I'm not a sir. I used to work for a living when I was on active duty." He turned to Wolf and opened his mouth, but the only words that came out before his voice died off were, "Now then, Centurion... Wait a minute. What the hell is going on here?"

Wolf came to a sudden stop as recognition dawned in both men's eyes.

"As I live and breathe. First Sergeant Hartwood Cahal, nicknamed Woody, F Company, 2nd Battalion, 77th Imperial Marines, isn't it?"

"Aye, and you're Antony Wolf, formerly of C Company, 1st Battalion, who retired here when the 77th bugged out.

What are you doing wearing centurion's pips and strange unit badges? Farming didn't suit?"

The men spontaneously reached out and grasped each other's right forearm in the traditional Marine Corps greeting between comrades.

"Long story, Woody. Welcome to the Sovereign Star System of Lyonesse. For my sins, I command the Lyonesse Rifle Regiment's A Company, based here in Lannion. Our regiment is one-half of the defense force's ground pounder element. Remember Matti Kayne?"

"Sure."

"It's Lieutenant Colonel Kayne now. He's my CO. And his CO is Colonel Brigid DeCarde formerly of the 6th Battalion, 21st Imperial Pathfinder Regiment which makes up the other half of our ground element, called 1st Brigade. These strange badges are our regimental and formation crests." Wolf pointed at the green flag with the gold, double-headed condor flapping lazily in the breeze above the spaceport entrance. "And that's our flag. We quit the empire."

"Did all you guys who retired here join this new military outfit?"

"Yep. Like I said, long story. Now tell me about the two wee ones. Why are you refusing to let them go with the Brethren? Our abbey is a safe place, full of good, kind people."

"It ain't the abbey, Tony. Your sergeant here says we need to come with you for a debriefing at Lannion Base, which I guess is where we used to hang our helmets back in the day."

"It's now the Defense Force HQ and home to the local garrison."

"Look, I don't mind going to the abbey, but I swore an oath to their mother I'd personally see them safe. Maybe your people can debrief us there."

Wolf thought for a moment.

"Here's what I propose. We'll drive you, your men, and your charges to the abbey where you can see that they're taken into care by the Brethren, then you come back with us to the base. Deal?"

Cahal scratched his chin before slowly nodding.

"Now that I know who's running the show around here, I guess I don't need to worry as much anymore. *Lieutenant Colonel* Matti Kayne, eh? Ain't that a kicker? Okay, Tony, you got yourself a deal."

"Let me call our ops center and make sure they know. Sergeant Rehn, see that Woody and his party go through immigration, then run them up to the abbey in one of your troop transports."

"Yes, sir."

"And Woody…"

"Yeah?"

"If you and your guys want a steady job, the defense force is recruiting. We will consider anyone who can provide a copy of their service records for enlistment at their previous rank."

"Got any private security companies around here?"

"Only rent-a-cops and that's not your style. The admiral won't allow anything else, especially not mercenary units."

"Then take us to your recruiting office after we sort everything out. Three squares and a cot still beat the alternatives."

**

"Captain Korax." Morane stood and came around his desk, hand outstretched. "Welcome to Lyonesse and Lannion Base. I understand you asked permission to stay on the ground for an indeterminate amount of time."

The two men shook.

"Aye, Admiral. If you don't mind. With darkness and evil spreading over the galaxy, it's been a physically exhausting and spiritually draining nine months crisscrossing the sector, hunting for survivors. My crew and I would do any penance asked of us for a few weeks of calm and contemplation among our brothers and sisters."

Morane waved him into one of the chairs in front of his desk.

"Would answering the questions of my intelligence section's analysts be considered proper penance? We're pretty much cut off from the rest of humanity here, which is both a blessing and a curse."

"We'd be glad to."

"How bad is it?"

"The Four Horsemen are abroad, Admiral. Dendera is scourging rebellious star systems with what is known as the Retribution Fleet. Since she lacks the strength to retake and hold breakaway sectors, she's giving individual planets the choice to either submit and lose all spacefaring capabilities for an indefinite length of time or resist and return to the Stone Age forever. Some of her admirals take the slightest hesitation in deciding as a sign of resistance and wreak incalculable ruin on peaceful societies.

"It's madness on a scale never seen in human history. We picked up four security consultants, two children, and five Brethren on Mykonos after it suffered a relatively minor bombardment, thanks to its government essentially dissolving, but they bore witness to the awful destruction that comes even with the meekest of submissions. It has since suffered a second attack, erasing most signs of advanced civilization. Why we do not know. Sadly, Mykonos isn't alone. Millions of souls are crying out, and I fear the worst is yet to come."

Suddenly, Korax seemed ancient, as if his short monologue aged him by a century.

"I won't guarantee you and those you rescued will be entirely safe here — we arrived just in time to help beat off a barbarian raid. But I doubt Dendera will waste what are surely dwindling resources on punishing an almost forgotten star system. If she's at the point of destroying what can't be retaken, then we're approaching the end."

"That is my assessment. I pray for the Almighty's mercy that he won't send us back out there. We escaped certain destruction more often than I care to remember."

"I'll put in a good word for you, but I'm not sure the Almighty listens to the likes of me."

A weak smile softened Korax's ascetic features.

"Every little bit helps."

"You mentioned four security consultants and two children. What's the story?"

"Another sad one in a universe replete with them. Perhaps you should speak with their guardian, Hartwood Cahal. He's a strong, honest man, loyal to a fault, a retired Marine first sergeant. I believe he would gladly give his life to protect his charges, orphans who saw their father executed and mother taken to an unknown fate."

"Then I will speak with him. My troops have orders to bring the mercenaries here for debriefing."

Korax smiled again.

"I hope they approach the matter with tact. Cahal won't allow himself to be separated from the children. I've observed his behavior aboard my ship for the last few months. No king or emperor ever enjoyed a more devoted bodyguard."

"Well, if he's a Marine, this Cahal will feel at home among us. It should help gain his trust."

Korax fought off a yawn and lost.

"My apologies. Now that I no longer need to worry for my ship, crew, and passengers, my spirit is calling for immediate rest."

"Then I won't detain you any longer. A staff car will take you to the abbey." Morane paused, pondering the wisdom of his next question. "Can I make a proposal concerning *Dawn Runner*?"

"Let me guess. You'd like to take her into naval service."

"Only until you or the Order need her again. Starships are built for a zero-gee, airless environment. Sitting on the ground, in an oxygen-rich atmosphere, inevitably speeds up aging. I could put a naval crew aboard and add her to the rotation as picket at the wormhole terminus, thereby relieving some of the pressure on my own four ships. It means reducing the size of the existing crews by a few each, but without the rigors of interstellar travel, we've come to realize the ships don't need a full complement."

"If you promise to take good care of her, she's yours until the Almighty calls for us to venture out again."

— 47 —

Yotai

Marta reared up in her chair with a suddenness that startled Jacelyn Bram.

"Madame?"

"I think our ship might be coming." She raised a hand to the hollow beneath her throat where Heloise's beacon pulsed with an otherworldly warmth. "Don't ask."

"A good thing we had time to fill our bags. When do we leave the palace?"

"Not yet." Marta couldn't explain to herself why she knew there would be a delay followed by a different signal.

"Should I ask for a car?"

After a moment's thought, Marta nodded.

"If you can do so without raising alarms."

"Good point. I'll go downstairs and speak with the motor pool noncom in person. If I ask nicely, he'll keep it off the books until we take possession. A little favor between old Marines stuck in this place of perdition."

Bram pulled on her tunic and left Marta to contemplate her mysterious connection with an Order of the Void ship via the talisman around her neck. Though she couldn't allow herself to feel relief until they crossed the event horizon of a wormhole leading away from Yotai, Marta nonetheless allowed her spirits to rise. The atmosphere in the palace had taken on an eerily dark edge in the last forty-eight hours, as if a menace was hanging over them.

Five minutes after Bram's departure, a familiar sensation pricked the edge of her consciousness. One of mortal danger. She only needed a few seconds to remember it from the day of Heloise's murder.

Zahar had finally convinced Custis she was expendable. And right before her escape.

The main door to her apartment opened without warning, and once again, the heels of military boots rang out on the foyer's marble floor. Moments later, Zahar, accompanied by two Marines, burst into her office.

Marta rose to her feet and glared at him with eyes colder than a miser's heart.

"What is the meaning of this, Admiral?"

"You're under arrest for treason. Do not try any of your tricks on me. These men are under orders to shoot you the moment I suffer from anything whatsoever — vertigo, headache, or seizures. Besides, this time, I'm ready, so good luck piercing my barriers."

"Treason? Surely your mind can't be that addled. How would I betray my own empire? A judge will laugh you out of court."

"It won't come to that, I can assure you. Regent Custis has declared an emergency. There will be no trials. Especially not for someone who, as our security services finally discovered, works for Dendera and has been impeding the war effort." When he saw realization dawn in Marta's eyes, a smile oozing pure evil twisted Zahar's mouth. "Yes, Milady, that's right. Your services as a figurehead empress are no longer required. I shall now enjoy executing another witch."

The same knife he'd used to kill Heloise appeared in his right hand as if by magic.

"Don't make this hard on yourself, Milady. You had a good run. And now, in the name of Regent Custis and the citizens of the Coalsack Sector, you will die for your treachery."

Marta probed Zahar's thoughts but ran up against a solid barrier which would require every bit of energy she could muster to surmount. Then, another, lighter set of footsteps came from the foyer.

"Colonel Bram, finally." Zahar kept his gaze locked on Marta. "Come in, please. I was about to impose the penalty applicable to traitors under martial law."

Bram slipped into the room and made as wide an arc as possible around the frozen tableau at its center. She'd drawn her personal weapon and held it against her thigh, barrel pointed at the floor.

"Perhaps you'd like to do the honors," he said. "Since this creature abused your honesty, your integrity, and your good name as a Marine officer by making you a party to her misdeeds. Execute her, and earn the thanks of the 16th Fleet."

Marta glanced at Bram, wondering whether she'd been wrong about her. When Bram met Marta's eyes, she seemed to plead for forgiveness.

"I'd be delighted to execute a traitor, Admiral."

For a fraction of a second, Marta stared into the barrel of her aide's blaster and composed herself to meet the Almighty in the Great Void.

Then, she saw Bram's aim change. A faint cough reached her ears as a bright dot of light seared her retinas. Zahar's face turned into a mask of astonishment, then he crumpled to the ground, dead, his brains flash-fried, leaving a stench of burned flesh in his wake.

"What's the proper expression for an occasion like this?" Bram asked in a hoarse voice.

Marta shook herself and answered, "*Sic semper tyrannis* might do in a pinch."

"You'll need to translate for me, Madame, but not right now." Bram turned her weapon on the Marines, who seemed rooted to the spot as they tried to process what just happened. "Her Imperial Highness and I face a problem, troops. I just shot your commander for attempting to murder Madame on trumped-up charges. The question is, what will you do now?"

"Colonel?" The senior of the two, a staff sergeant asked. "I'm not sure I understand."

"I have to take her highness away from here in case Zahar has backup assassins lying in wait. What will you do? What were you told?"

"Sir. Our orders were to escort Admiral Zahar and obey him without asking questions."

"If I tell you Zahar was the real traitor, not her highness, what would you believe?"

The staff sergeant hesitated, his eyes going from the admiral's corpse to Marta and then to Bram. After a moment, he straightened his back and came to attention.

"Sir. You're a Marine Corps officer."

Bram nodded once as if his answer told her everything she needed to know.

"Is anyone aware you came up here with Zahar?"

"No, sir. This detail was to be conducted under the utmost secrecy. All our CO got was a levy for two Marine noncoms. We didn't know it was for Admiral Zahar until we reported to the assigned rendezvous point. We sure as hell didn't know Her Imperial Highness was the target before now."

"And if you'd known?"

"I'm not sure what we'd have done, sir. The last time Admiral Zahar led Marines into this part of the palace, they were posted out the next morning and vanished to a frontier system."

Marta raised a hand to attract Bram's attention.

"For what it's worth, he is telling the truth. I sense no falsehood in either of them. But they are scared."

Bram bit the inside of her lip, eyes narrowed, before holstering her gun.

"Okay. Here's how it plays out. You two will return to barracks and tell your platoon sergeant the mission is over and you can't talk about it. And if you're smart, you'll deny you met Zahar tonight, let alone came to Madame's apartment with him."

"Yes, sir." The staff sergeant was visibly relieved. "Nothing happened here. We were never here. We never saw you or her highness."

"Dismissed."

Both noncoms stomped to attention and snapped off a salute that would do their regimental sergeant major proud before turning on their heels in a synchronized movement. Once their footsteps faded away, Bram nudged Zahar's corpse with her booted foot.

"We need to leave now, Madame, whether or not your ship is in orbit. Zahar will be missed within the next few hours, and even if he made sure no one could track his movements tonight, someone will eventually look here. While I change, grab any last-minute items you can't part with, and we'll head for Lena's riverside slums. Leave all electronics here, especially your communicator."

"Won't they track our car?"

"Sure, that's why we'll ditch it somewhere near Central Square and walk the rest of the way. I'm sure I can scrounge up transport for the run to the park when you receive that final signal."

Five minutes later, Bram drove them through the palace's main gate and down the steep hill on surface roadways, aimed at Lena's heart. Ten minutes after that, they left the car on a side street with orders for its AI to return home after a thirty-minute interval.

"Hopefully my motor pool contact will be smart enough to fiddle with the AI's log and wipe every trace of this trip," Bram said once they turned the corner and merged with regular foot traffic, still dense this early in the evening.

"Why would he do that without someone asking him?"

"I didn't exactly sign the car out, Madame. I gave him half of my remaining money to look the other way. He wipes the log, and no one will be able to tell we took it by the time they find the old bastard in your former lodgings."

"Understood. And from now on, it's Marta. I don't want to hear the word Madame or any other title, okay, Jacelyn?"

"Understood. And my friends call me Jace." Bram hesitated for a fraction of a second. "Marta."

She smiled at the Marine.

"That wasn't so difficult, was it?"

"No." Another moment of indecision. Then, "Why did he want you dead so badly he was about to do it himself?"

"You're aware he bore a deep hatred for the Order of the Void."

"I doubt there's anyone around here who doesn't. The bloodbath when he proscribed them was beyond anything I've ever seen. He justified it by calling them dangerous traitors and irredeemable Dendera supports, but I never believed it."

"Your predecessor, Heloise, was a Sister of the Void. She and a small band of Brethren saved my life and those of my children."

"Children?"

"They're alive, somewhere. A ship from the Order picked them off Mykonos after Jorge Danton captured me but before the Retribution Fleet's second, catastrophic attack."

Bram's pace faltered as she turned to stare at Marta.

"Oh. I was informed they'd been killed during the rebellion against your late husband."

"That's what I told everyone so they wouldn't be tracked. As I said, Heloise was a sister. It's why she died at Zahar's hands, and from the first day of our captivity, she trained me in the Order's disciplines. Zahar found out moments after he murdered her and has ever since considered me no different from any other witch of the Void, as he calls them. Once Custis decided I was superfluous, it's not a stretch to figure Zahar wanted the pleasure of killing me himself as revenge for any humiliations real and imagined I heaped on his head."

"I see." Bram fell into a thoughtful silence.

"Do you regret killing him to protect me?" Marta asked after they crossed another intersection and left the city center behind them.

Bram shook her head.

"No. I figure Zahar was a nasty piece of work who tricked many good Marines into committing atrocities. The friars and sisters educated me and opened my mind so it could encompass a whole universe. If not for them, I wouldn't have left home to become a Marine. When Zahar desecrated the Yotai Abbey, I promised myself I'd find a way of avenging them. And I did."

After almost an hour, they reached the anonymous storage depot where they'd stowed their bags and retrieved them. Forty-five minutes after that, they stood in front of a rundown inn close to one of the bridges leading across the river where Founder's Park loomed in the darkness.

"It won't be up to anyone's standards," Bram said, "but no one will ask for names, let alone IDs. And they won't remember we were there."

"How does a former Imperial Marine Corps lieutenant colonel know so much about vanishing?"

Bram winked at her.

"Friends in low places. Shall we?"

Marta took one step, then froze. The gentle warm pulse emanating from Heloise's beacon unexpectedly took on a more urgent rhythm.

"Um, I think we need to be in the park *now*."

Marta quickly explained about the beacon disguised as a talisman she wore around her neck, and that the ship she was expecting belonged to the Order of the Void.

"So they're inbound already? That was fast."

"I don't know if it's the case. Heloise didn't have much time to explain beyond trusting my instincts. But they're telling me our rescuers are in orbit."

"In that case, a shuttle might already be on the way, leaving us with perhaps forty-five minutes to reach the park. I hope you're not too tired."

"On the contrary. Set whatever pace you think best. I'll manage."

— 48 —

A soft tap on the briefing room's open door broke Custis from his contemplation of the sector's increasingly perilous strategic position. The only star systems in the holotank not pulsing in one of various baleful colors were Yotai and the two minor junctions between Parth and Micarat. Every other part of his shrinking realm had either seen off a reconnaissance in force by the Retribution Fleet or been attacked.

"Your Grace?" The voice belonged to one of Custis' military aides.

"Yes," he snapped, not bothering to hide his irritation at the interruption.

"We found Admiral Zahar. He's dead, shot by parties unknown in Lady Marta's apartments."

"What?"

Custis whirled around to stare at the aide.

"Admiral Zahar was killed by a small bore plasma shot to the head. Her Highness and Lieutenant Colonel Bram have vanished, leaving their personal effects, including communicators behind. The headquarters battalion commander has people trying to trace their movements as we speak. We know the vehicles in the motor pool are accounted for, including the one Bram usually signs out.”

Custis swung back toward the holotank so he could hide his growing rage from the hapless colonel standing in the doorway. Damn Zahar. Instead of letting Marta’s demotion from empress-designate to traitor unfold convincingly, he couldn’t even wait a day before trying to kill her. Yet she, or perhaps that hatchet-faced aide, had turned the tables on him.

Maybe it was for the best. With Zahar dead, Custis was no longer forced to look over his shoulder and wonder whether his soul would join that of the late Viceroy Joback in the Great Void. But where would Marta go? And did it matter? She was gone and could no longer cause mischief.

“Keep me apprised of developments as they occur.”

“Yes, Your Grace.”

“And send for Admiral Scerrix. He now commands 16th Fleet.”

Though unimaginative and an indifferent strategist, at least Scerrix didn’t nurture Zahar’s murderous ambitions. And he would be more amenable to Custis’ orders.

**

“How are you doing?” Bram asked once they were across the river.

“I’m fine, but the beacon’s pulse is getting faster. Something tells me we need to choose a landing site within the next few minutes.”

Marta called up her mind’s map of the park, built through successive visits. She realized that though its main entrance was a mere hundred meters up the road, the next isolated meadow big enough for a standard personnel shuttle was at least twenty minutes away. At this hour of the night, few if any of Lena's citizens would wander the park's winding paths, and chances were good the main parking lot by the information kiosk was empty. It would have to do.

"Then there's only one choice," Bram replied, coming to the same conclusion. "If late evening walkers are in the area, they'll witness our departure, but by the time someone in authority listens to the story of a mysterious shuttle pickup, we should be well away."

However, the lot was mercifully empty.

"It's near," Marta whispered. "The beacon is on a constant buzz now."

The moment she finished speaking, they heard a faint whine of shuttle thrusters slightly off the spaceport's main flight path. Then, a dark shape partially occluded the star-studded sky dozens of meters above them. The sound changed in tone while the shape grew in size as it descended vertically.

"Civilian model," Bram said when the craft finally settled on its landing gear. "The markings say Galactic Dawn Corporation. Never heard of them."

Marta stepped toward the craft and waited. After almost a minute, the aft ramp opened to the soft squeal of metal on metal, revealing a rectangle of dim red light. A man in a dark, unadorned spacer's uniform stepped out.

Though Marta couldn't see his eyes in the gloom, she knew he was staring at her. Or rather through her.

"Who are you, Sister?"

"My name is Marta. I am not a consecrated sister, but I was trained by one, the late Heloise of the Mykonos Abbey. She gave me her beacon moments before Admiral Zahar murdered her."

"Which explains why a Mykonos beacon drew us to Yotai. Your mind is strong, Marta. The beacon's signal was extraordinarily clear. Otherwise, we would not have come with such alacrity." He gestured at Bram, standing a pace behind and to one side of Marta. "She is not one of the Brethren. Who is she?"

"My friend and savior, Jacelyn Bram. She killed Admiral Zahar just as he was about to murder me a few hours ago. Where I go, she goes."

"Your friend is a woman of war, Marta. Her sort killed most of the Brethren in this sector."

"Jacelyn took no part in the massacres. Your brothers and sisters educated her as a child, and she holds the Order in great respect."

"What if I said I'm to retrieve Brethren only?"

"Then you may leave us to our fate. I am not a sister and I will not leave without Jacelyn."

When the man didn't immediately reply, Marta understood they were under scrutiny by a skilled female mind inside the shuttle, one capable of probing without leaving mental fingerprints. She opened her thoughts and waited.

Marta was proved right shortly after that. A low-pitched woman's voice said, "They come with us."

"You heard her." The man swept his arm toward the ramp.

Once inside, another crewmember, perhaps the sister who'd probed them, took their bags, then indicated side by side seats, and helped them with the restraints while the aft ramp closed. Moments later, the shuttle's thrusters spooled up, and it lifted vertically under full power. Marta's instincts told her she'd never set foot on Yotai again, that she and Jacelyn Bram were headed away from the Coalsack Sector for good.

No one spoke during the flight, and within an hour, the shuttle's apparent motion changed as it aligned its nose with a starship's open hangar doors. Marta sensed a slight change in ambient gravity, then a faint drop and the shuttle's drives died away.

"Welcome aboard *Dawn Seeker*." The sister stood and gestured at their seat restraints. "My name is Aello. You may free yourselves. I will bring you to our captain first, then find a pair of adjoining bunks. As you'll see, we are somewhat overburdened with Brethren and others whom we rescued, so don't expect comfort and our food, though still plentiful, is plain. But once away from Yotai, we head for sanctuary."

"Where would that be?" Marta tried to stretch muscles cramped by hours of tension as best she could in the confined space after climbing to her feet.

"Lyonesse. *Dawn Seeker* has not visited it yet, but we received word to head there once we finish our search for survivors. It is the Order's new and only home in this part of the galaxy."

**

Friar Bassus, *Dawn Seeker*'s white-haired, leathery-skinned master, sat back in his chair once Marta finished telling her story from the day of her husband's death until the shuttle landed. He studied her with eerily intense eyes.

"The late Sister Heloise must have been an exceptional teacher to instill such strength of mind and discipline in so little time."

"She was. I owe her my life, and that of my children, who I know are still alive somewhere."

"If a Galactic Dawn ship rescued them from Mykonos before the second great scouring, as your evidence seems to prove, then they will eventually land on Lyonesse. And that is our ultimate destination too, as Sister Aello probably told you."

"She did."

"We hold regular services and training sessions, should you wish to continue what Heloise started, though you'll find them a bit crowded." Bassus turned his searching gaze on Bram. "You are also welcome to attend. Even those without the talent benefit greatly from our training and spiritual practices."

"Thank you, Captain."

"Sister Aello will now show you to your bunks."

When Bassus climbed to his feet, Marta and Bram imitated him. Before they could reply, the intercom in Bassus' day cabin sprang to life.

"Captain, the Yotai Wormhole Three traffic control buoy just transmitted on the emergency subspace channel. Twelve ships identifying themselves as part of the Imperial Retribution Fleet came through the Mykonos branch."

"A reconnaissance in force," Marta said. "I think the end game for the Coalsack Sector's future is about to begin. And though I suspect the actual attack, when it comes, will break the Retribution Fleet's back for good, Custis' proto-empire won't survive."

Bassus' eyes searched hers while a frown creased his forehead.

"Is that an estimate born of strategic acumen, or did you sense something?"

"Perhaps a combination of both. I've seen images of fire and blood for months."

"Interesting. We should find time to talk once *Seeker* is FTL. There's long been a debate within the Order about whether such a thing as prescience exists, with strong supporters for both points of view and precious little evidence. But since things are about to become a little heated in this system, please excuse me while I get us away."

Bassus ushered them out of his day cabin and, after giving Aello tersely worded instructions, he headed for the bridge.

"I guess we escaped just in time," Bram said. "But I pity those who can't flee Yotai before the imperials come back to finish the job. They'll die for no other reason than a bunch of noble assholes and ego-maniacal flag officers playing their game of empires to the bitter end."

Marta laid a hand on her arm.

"Pray for them if you wish, but please do not indulge in survivor's guilt. We're on this ship for a reason."

"If you say so."

"I do."

— 49 —

Lyonesse

A recently promoted Major Haller approached Morane as he shared a glass of wine with Governor Yakin and Chancellor Reyes. Tonight was the Constitutional Convention's opening gala reception and everyone save Haller, who was on duty, wore their finery, officers in mess uniforms, scholars, and monastics in robes and civilians in formal suits. Soft music filled Warehouse A, turned into a ballroom for the occasion, courtesy of the Rifle Regiment's band.

"Could I speak with you, Admiral?"

"Certainly."

Morane knew she wouldn't pull him away from the reception without a good reason, so he excused himself, found a convenient horizontal surface for his glass, and followed Haller out of the cavernous warehouse.

"What's up?" He asked once the door closed behind them, cutting off both the strains of a classical composition and several hundred voices.

"The wormhole traffic control buoy fired off an alert on the subspace emergency channel a few minutes ago. Five ships, four of them tentatively identified as Kalinka class frigates and one as a Coromandel class light cruiser entered our system. They're not broadcasting on subspace bands, so we can't yet identify them. *Condor* has the picket duty and is observing, but remains under silent running."

Five warships, though older models, could only mean Admiral Zahar's spies reported back with enough information to convince Custis that Lyonesse had been *Tanith*'s final destination.

Vanquish could eat a Coromandel cruiser for breakfast and still chew up one or two frigates, but the strain *Myrtale* suffered during her wild chase through the Lyonesse wormhole branch made her more vulnerable.

And *Narwhal* was in transit to relieve *Condor* as picket ship. Which left two against five, if he didn't count *Dawn Runner*. Not great odds, even with the new orbital platforms they'd deployed over the last few months, but perhaps enough to convince the task force commander talking was better than fighting.

When they entered the operations center, Petty Officer First Class Leo Atreus, the duty noncom, swiveled his chair around to face them.

"The traffic control buoy went dormant after sending the alert, as per its programming. *Condor* is still making a small hole in space. I warned *Vanquish, Myrtale*, and *Dawn Runner*. They're watching the hyperlimit while waiting for orders. *Narwhal* is FTL and won't get the message until she drops out of hyperspace at the terminus."

"Thank you, PO."

Morane studied the main status display.

"My orders for Captain Mikkel are as follows. *Vanquish* and *Myrtale* are to shift their orbits beyond that of

Gwaelod," he said, naming the outermost of Lyonesse's three moons, "once *Condor* reports the intruders going FTL. They're to enter silent running in eight hours and wait for orders. If that task force makes a hostile move, I intend to ambush it. *Dawn Runner* is to stay at her current altitude and present a warship's aspect." He turned to Haller. "Please discreetly ask the governor, Chief Administrator Logran, Speaker Hecht, Colonel DeCarde, Sister Gwenneth and Captain Ryzkov to join me in the conference room. PO Atreus, patch Captain Mikkel in."

"Aye, aye, sir," both replied in unison.

Morane walked over to the operations center's holotank and touched the controls to bring up a three-dimensional representation of the star system.

Those ships could only belong to the 16th Fleet, and there was only one reason they'd come this far from the Coalsack Sector's sphere of control when hell was breaking loose thanks to Dendera's Retribution Fleet.

**

"Five emergence signatures," Petty Officer Atreus announced, "seven light seconds out. Four Kalinkas, one Coromandel. Still no beacons."

With the defense force at full alert, every station in the operations center was occupied, including the spare. Admiral Morane had taken the duty officer's command chair while Gwenneth, wearing a dark, single piece garment instead of a sister's robes, sat behind him.

For the first time in a long time, Morane felt in charge of a fighting force again instead of being a bureaucratic warrior. But he desperately wanted to avoid a battle that might harm Lyonesse's future.

An image of the intruders appeared on a secondary display, courtesy of the planet's geosynchronous surveillance satellites.

"Paint the Coromandel with our orbital subspace transmitter and demand they open a channel."

"What shall I call ourselves, sir?"

"Lyonesse System Command."

The spies undoubtedly took back word of Lyonesse's unilateral declaration of independence, but it wouldn't hurt to confuse the intruders' commanding officer by making it seem as if they might still owe allegiance to Devy Custis. Morane, who wore nothing more than rank badges on his uniform, like everyone else, took one last look around the room to make sure nothing would betray them, such as a double-headed Vanger's Condor insignia, then composed himself.

"The light cruiser *Savage* is responding, sir."

"On screen."

Seconds later, a tired-looking, middle-aged man with a commodore's single star on his collar visibly bit back his first words when he saw Morane's twin stars. Instead, after a brief pause, he said, "My name is Reginus Bryner, sir. I command Task Force One-Sixty Alpha, from the 160th Battle Group, with home port on Yotai."

"Welcome to Lyonesse, Commodore. I'm Jonas Morane, this system's military commander." He let a friendly smile pull at the corners of his lips. "You're the first patrol Admiral Zahar sent our way in a long time. It's good to see we weren't forgotten."

Bryner frowned.

"I thought this star system declared its independence from the Coalsack Sector, sir."

"We made a few political and military adjustments to account for our isolation now that several wormhole junctions no longer under 16th Fleet control separate us from Yotai. However, we remain loyal to Viceroy Custis and I am prepared to take Admiral Zahar's orders."

The frown deepened.

"Sir, if you'll pardon my impertinence, but that's not what my mission orders say."

"Really?" Morane's eyebrows crept up. "If you're not here on a routine patrol, then what is your objective?"

"Sir, I'm to find and bring back a person by the name Corinne Ruggero, who was held aboard the prison ship *Tanith*, probably under an assumed identity."

"Corinne Ruggero? As in Empress Dendera's younger sister?"

"That's what they told me."

Morane made a great show of turning toward Haller.

"Major, check the roster of prisoners we decanted from *Tanith* and see if anyone by the name Ruggero appears."

"Already ran it, sir. Negative."

"I don't suppose you know what assumed name she could have traveled under, Commodore?"

"No, sir."

"Hm." Morane tapped his fingertips on the command chair's arm. "Tell you what, we'll send *Tanith*'s manifest along with a list of every prisoner's current status. Perhaps you could narrow it down for us because we've not come across anyone who claims to be a Ruggero or bears a shred of familial resemblance to the deplorable Dendera. Major Haller?"

"Sent, Admiral."

"Shall I leave you and your staff to peruse it? You're still a few hours out from Lyonesse orbit. Perhaps we'll know more by the time you're here."

"Thank you, Admiral. I appreciate your cooperation. Most star system commanders aren't as amenable these days. May I ask where your ships are? My sensors can't spot anything other than what looks like a corvette in orbit."

"They're on patrol, practicing the art of concealment. You've been under observation since the moment your task force emerged from the wormhole terminus."

A light went on Bryner's eyes and he nodded.

"Running silent. Nicely done. We've not detected anything so far."

Morane smiled pleasantly.

"I find routinely running silent is good training. It toughens crews and forces them to hone their skills."

"Agreed, though we don't practice nearly as much as I'd like. Thank you for the list, sir. If there's nothing else, I won't take up any more of your time. Hopefully, we can call back with a few possible names under which Corinne Ruggero might be hiding."

"Hopefully. Until later. Morane, out."

When the image faded, Morane slumped in his chair and exhaled.

"Wasn't that fun?"

Someone out of visual range started clapping, and within seconds, the rest of the duty crew joined in. Morane turned around to see DeCarde enter from the briefing room.

"That was quite a show, sir. I knew you were a bullshit artist, but your performance surpassed our expectations."

"*Our?*"

"Didn't I tell you? Your entire command staff watched from in there, hoping to receive an education in the finer points of messing with an opponent's expectations."

Gwenneth, a tired smile on her lips, stood to stretch tense muscles.

"Brigid is correct. It was a fine example of talking instead of fighting."

"Just keep in mind this isn't over. We don't yet know what he'll do once he realizes no one can help him find Corinne Ruggero for the simple reason she isn't in this star system and never was, at least not alive. Neither Custis nor Zahar will be gentle with Bryner when he returns empty-handed, not if I'm right and Custis wants Dendera's sister as a figurehead for his own breakaway empire."

"Fat lot of—"

Petty Officer Atreus interrupted DeCarde with a muffled curse.

"Someone is trying to force a transmission through the subspace node using override codes."

"From where?"

"The routing tag shows it as coming from the speaker of the council's office, and those are Mister Hecht's codes. Good thing we suspended the overrides."

Morane's features turned to stone. Could Hecht be so stupid as to throw the game out of spite?

"Lock out all communication satellites. Nothing leaves the surface." He touched the controls in the duty officer's chair.

"Barca here, sir."

"Someone's playing silly bugger in the speaker's office and trying to contact the incoming 16th Fleet ships, Major. Send a troop of your finest, stat, and arrest whoever that is."

"Will do."

Morane saw Atreus raise a hand to attract his attention. "Yes?"

"The silly bugger is talking as if he doesn't realize the node's not letting him through."

A familiar and annoyingly nasal voice came through the control center's speakers.

"Hello, unidentified starships, I am Severin, Count Downes of Hallibrank. This is a warning. Lyonesse has declared itself independent of the empire and the Coalsack Sector thanks to a deserter called Jonas Morane. Beware his treachery. He is the sworn enemy of both the Crown and Grand Duke Custis and will try to destroy you with an underhanded stratagem. Many of my compatriots and I were held against our will aboard the Imperial Prison Ship *Tanith* and have been maltreated since arriving here. We need rescuing from this vile nest of dissident scum."

Morane slammed his hand on the chair's arm.

"That's it. He's for the Windy Isles before dawn."

"I'm sure Adri can arrange it, sir," DeCarde said. "A troop from the security company is on its way to Lannion."

"PO, connect me with Speaker Hecht." *Who will join Downes in the Windies if he was in any way involved,* Morane silently swore.

A minute passed, then Atreus said, "I have him, sir. He's at his residence."

"Not in the office?"

"Unless Mister Hecht is better at hiding his communicator's routing than anyone else I know."

"What do you want, Admiral?" The speaker sounded like a man rudely awakened from a deep sleep.

"Why would Severin Downes be trying to call the newly arrived starships from your office, Rorik, using your codes? A good thing I ordered the subspace node overrides suspended. Otherwise, who knows what trouble he might cause? A troop of military police is on the way to your office and will place Downes under arrest for treason against Lyonesse. I'll see that he heads to the Windies once a court finds him guilty. Now give me a reason why I shouldn't charge you with dereliction of duty. The override codes we gave a select few on Lyonesse were not to be shared with staff, let alone ordinary citizens. How did that idiot Downes get a hold of yours?"

Silence greeted Morane's diatribe. Then Hecht replied in a tone fraught with anger.

"He must have filched them. Listen, Morane, I may be guilty of many things, including letting my ego interfere with good administration. I am not, however, a complete idiot. You and I still disagree on major issues and always will. Yes, I still resent the way you made your point in the vault, and yes, I'll hold a grudge against you to the grave. But I'm a man of Lyonesse, loyal to my birth planet and my star system. I would never open it to outside attack."

"You know we'll investigate, right?"

"Understood. I'll throw myself on Governor Yakin's mercy in the morning and take responsibility for Downes getting unauthorized access to secure governmental facilities. If she decides my time's up, then so be it."

"That is your choice. In the meantime, I'm taking control of all communications satellites, not just the subspace nodes. Once our visitors leave, we will discuss who exercises control in the future."

"Trying to turn Lyonesse into a military dictatorship, Morane? That's not what it sounded like when you were offering me — what was it again? A cask of Amontillado?"

"Don't push your luck, Rorik. Morane, out."

He slumped back in his chair and sighed. When he noticed the duty crew's furtive looks, Morane realized they'd overheard everything. Wonderful.

"Folks, that discussion between Speaker Hecht and me doesn't leave this room."

"Of course, sir," Haller, replied. "Everyone here gets that."

Their vigorous nods didn't give Morane much comfort his conversation with the hapless Hecht wouldn't become gossip fodder. The man wasn't popular. But there was nothing for it now.

"Open a link with *Vanquish*."

"You're connected," Atreus announce a few moments later. Iona Mikkel's face swam into view on a secondary display.

"Working an ops duty shift, Admiral?"

"Needs must when the devil drives."

She chuckled.

"Now where did I hear that before? I listened in on your conversation with Bryner. Nicely played. If he came here ready to fight, you threw him off kilter."

"My problem is I don't know what he might do once it becomes clear we cannot produce the person he's looking for. His superiors aren't likely to tolerate failure and that is worrisome. When his ships cross Gwaelod's orbit, I want *Vanquish* and *Vanquish* alone to go up systems. *Myrtale* is to stay silent, though I want you and her to track the Coromandel class cruiser on passive fire control. If Bryner decides to fight, we'll get one chance at a first shot."

"Who calls it?"

"I do, Iona."

She nodded.

"That's what I figured. Here's to hoping we don't expend ammo."

"From your lips to God's ear."

"Did you ask the Brethren for help? Maybe they could spend the next few hours beseeching the Almighty on our behalf." She caught sight of Gwenneth and waved. "Hi, Sister."

Morane gave his former executive officer an exasperated look that was only half feigned.

"It doesn't work that way, and you know it."

Mikkel repressed a grin.

"Since the good sister is at your side, we should be okay. I'll wait for your order to fire. Was there anything else, oh commander of the faithful?"

"A bit of respect for my stars if you can't respect the man wearing them?"

"I've always held you in high regard, Skipper. Otherwise, I wouldn't have followed you to the back of beyond in the forlorn hope of staving off the long night."

— 50 —

An hour later, Petty Officer Atreus stuck his head in the briefing room where Morane was enjoying a quiet coffee with DeCarde and Gwenneth.

"Sir, Commodore Bryner is asking for a link."

"Coming." He drained his cup and glanced at the sister. "Time for act two. Shall we?"

DeCarde raised a clenched fist. "Knock 'em dead, Admiral."

"Thanks."

Moments after Morane took the duty officer's chair from Major Haller, Commodore Bryner's face materialized on the main display.

"Hello again, sir. My staff and I went through your list of *Tanith* prisoners and compared it to the one they gave us. Both match perfectly. Since we can provisionally rule out the known nobles, the criminals you kept incarcerated, and those who were killed in the Parth system, we're left with one name, a Taylar Noe, marked as deceased."

Morane turned to Haller. They'd expected this development, and she was prepared.

"Imperial household servant. Condemned for embezzlement. She died because of a stasis pod malfunction at some point during the trip, but we only found out when we tried to decant her. The body was overripe by then. Cremated and ashes scattered since there were no relatives to claim them."

"Seems rather convenient, sir. If you'll pardon my skepticism."

"What can I say, Commodore. These things happen. If you want to interview the former *Tanith* prisoners, I'll gladly welcome your landing parties and facilitate their work. We have nothing to hide. The simple fact is, Corinne Ruggero was never aboard that prison ship."

An air of indecision crept across Bryner's seamed features.

"Sir, my orders are to return with Corinne Ruggero or with irrefutable evidence of her death. You're not giving me much hope of doing either."

"Wouldn't recorded interviews with the former prisoners be evidence?"

"Except for this Taylar Noe, sir. She's the problem. Without proof she wasn't Corinne, I have nothing to satisfy Grand Duke Custis or my admiral."

"And the punishment for failure would be severe, so you can't just go back empty-handed based on my word."

"That's the extent of it, sir."

"What pressure tactics were you told to use?"

A pained expression replaced Bryner's earlier indecision.

"I'm to threaten the destruction of your knowledge vault."

"Are you aware of what it represents?"

When Bryner shook his head, Morane launched into an impassioned explanation and saw the man's expression change as he grasped the vault's significance and what it would mean to lose it.

"The chamber itself is beneath almost a hundred meters of granite and encased in starship-grade alloy. Destroying it would require a kinetic bombardment of sufficient intensity to eradicate everything within a hundred-kilometer radius and potentially cause a rift in the planet's crust. Half a million humans would die."

"Then I'm damned if I do and damned if I don't. My crews wouldn't allow me to imitate Dendera's Retribution Fleet and wipe out entire populations even if I were inclined to commit genocide, which I'm not. Too many of us lost relatives and friends on worlds subjected to her vengeance." He sighed. "Nor will my senior officers want to face Admiral Zahar and report failure."

"An unpleasant dilemma," Morane said in a sympathetic tone. "I don't envy you."

Bryner let out a soft snort.

"Perhaps I should turn rogue and offer my services to the highest bidder instead of going home."

Morane smiled. "Now that you mention it..."

"I beg your pardon, sir?"

"You've seen what's happening out there, Commodore. What chances do you give Custis for holding on to the sector and keeping it from collapse and ruin? How many ships has he sacrificed on the altar of his vanity? And more importantly, how long do you expect your ships and crews to survive even if you suffered no penalties from returning empty-handed."

Bryner didn't immediately reply, but understanding seemed to dawn in his eyes.

"Stay here. Join my command. Lyonesse is just about the safest star system in this part of the galaxy. No one crosses interstellar distances in hyperspace anymore, and since we have only one wormhole terminus, no one will randomly pass through looking for a chance to raid. The last bunch to come here deliberately hoping for cheap spoils suffered one-hundred percent casualties in the space of a few hours."

The commodore stared at Morane in silence for a long time, jaw muscles working.

"I'm not sure how to react, sir," he finally said.

"Here's my proposal. Put your ships in orbit beyond the outer moon, then come down to Lannion with whoever you want. We can talk. I'll show you around, including the vault, so you know I wasn't kidding. I'll introduce you to the governor and leading citizens, let you see what we're doing. Once you're satisfied, return to your task force and ask your crews what they think."

When he saw Bryner hesitate, Morane added, "I went through the same thing with what was left of the 197th Imperial Battle Group a year ago and a lot of light years away. And I didn't even have the benefit of being able to show them their new home. Three-quarters joined me. The rest took one of my surviving frigates with the intention of returning to our home port. I suspect most of them fell victim to the fighting since then, if they even made it back in the first place. Give it some thought and call me back."

Another moment of hesitation, then a nod.

"Yes, sir."

"Morane, out."

"I didn't quite expect you to go down that route," DeCarde's voice said from the briefing room's open door. "But I suppose trying to recruit them beats trying to outshoot them."

"Economy of effort is still among our principles of war, Brigid. Besides, normal people experience difficulties ordering the deaths of those they know personally, so I hope that by introducing Bryner to as many of us as possible, it'll further deter him from doing something awful."

"Sneaky."

Morane smiled and nodded at Sister Gwenneth.

"I learned a thing or two about human psychology from my friend here."

**

"Half of my crews are already declaring themselves in favor of staying," Bryner said after he exchanged salutes with Morane on the Lannion Base tarmac. He gestured at the hulking chief petty officer first class standing at attention beside him. "This is Chief Aaron Kolat, *Savage*'s coxswain and the task force senior enlisted spacer."

"Welcome, Chief."

"Sir."

"If you don't mind, I'll pair you with Regimental Sergeant Major Bedros Havel of the Lyonesse Rifle Regiment." Morane indicated the neatly attired non-commissioned officer standing one pace behind him and to his right. "My senior chief is aboard *Vanquish*, somewhere up there, watching your ships. RSM Havel is a Marine who retired here and became one of the Rifle Regiment's plank owners."

The two grizzled noncoms eyed one another as they shook hands. Morane sensed each liked what he saw in his opposite number because the handshake quickly became a contest of strength which lasted just long enough to produce white knuckles before they let go by unvoiced common accord.

"RSM, why don't you and the chief head off? I'll take good care of Commodore Bryner."

As the two noncoms headed for a staff car parked by the cliff side base's main entrance, Bryner chuckled.

"I've known Kolat for a long time, sir. I think he likes your sergeant major. Otherwise, he wouldn't bother testing his grip. That'll count for a lot when it comes time to ask my ratings what they want to do. Kolat's one of the 160th Battle Group's wise old men. It was my fortune Zahar gave me *Savage* as flagship."

Morane gestured toward the cliff.

"Why don't I show you the vault first?"

After they'd taken a few steps, he asked, "How bad is it really out there, just between you and me?"

Bryner grimaced.

"Some days it feels like the end of times, sir. I'd give anything to go back and stop the rebellion. The empire might have been a corrupt, failing police state, but at least we didn't massacre each other in job lots."

**

By the time Lyonesse's sun kissed the western horizon, painting a riot of colors on towering clouds over the Middle Sea, Morane and his guest were talking like two old friends contemplating the future.

Morane led Bryner to the clifftop observation platform, high above Lannion Base's tarmac, grabbing a bottle of Carhaix Barnburner and two glasses from the mess along the way. Once there, he poured them each a healthy dram, then set the bottle on a recessed stone shelf.

"They distill this stuff not far from here. It's no Glen Arcturus, but as whiskeys go, I'm not complaining." Morane raised his glass. "May the future be less dire than we fear if it can't be better than we hope."

Bryner took a sip, swirled it around in his mouth, and swallowed.

"That's actually better than the Yotai rotgut they distribute to wardrooms and officer's messes."

"Lyonesse isn't just a pretty place with plenty to live for. What do you think?"

The commodore's eyes were drawn to the lights of Lannion, coming to life one at a time, and the distant dark line of the Middle Sea. He inhaled deeply, relishing the faint salt tang in the air.

After another appreciative sip, he said, "I'd rather serve Governor Yakin than Devy Custis. She has an irresistible innate dignity."

"You and me both. What else?"

"The vault — your project — it stirred something within me. Capturing the best our species produced and preserving it from our worst instincts? I can't conceive of a nobler endeavor." A pause. "Forgive me if I sound a little strange. You've opened my eyes to so many things today, I'm not sure where to look, but I'm beginning to understand your passion for protecting this place. It's a nobler undertaking than Regent Custis trying to create his own doomed empire."

The sound of footsteps coming up the staircase burned out of the living rock stilled Morane's reply. Kolat and Havel appeared moments later.

"Figures we'd find our flag officers having a drink up here. Best damn view for a hundred kilometers." Havel held up a bottle and two tumblers. "Great minds and all that."

"What's the word, Chief?" Bryner asked once Kolat held a glass filled with amber liquid.

"Good land, good people, good troops, and no chickenshit. Bedros took me to meet the Lyonesse Abbey's head sister, Gwenneth, who I knew on Yotai before Zahar murdered most of the Void Brethren and flattened the abbey. She figures we could do much worse than make this our home port, sir, and I believe her. A lot of our people would rather swallow the anchor in a place with a future. And that's here, not where we came from."

Kolat raised his glass and turned to Morane.

"I say we take the admiral's offer and don't look back. Screw Custis, screw Zahar, and screw the whole damn crap show out there. I don't want to die for sweet fuck-all, and neither does anyone else in the 160th."

Bryner gave Morane a wry smile.

"I think you heard our answer. What's the drill? Do I genuflect in front of Governor Yakin and swear an oath of fealty?"

"The plan is to drop nonsense like that when the new constitution comes into force. What I suggest, after a good night's sleep in our guest quarters, is return to your command and lay it out for your crews. Offer those who don't want to stay a ship and let them go. I doubt your entire complement is made up of folks without close relatives. If they want to find their way back here after fetching loved ones, they'll always be welcome."

"Maybe we can arrange something a little more formal, like send one of my frigates to retrieve families."

"Absolutely. If that's what you'd like to organize, feel free. In the meantime, I'll send orders pulling you into a tighter orbit so your ships can rotate their personnel through shore liberty while we work on the logistics of sorting the leavers from the remainers and integrating the latter into the Lyonesse Navy."

"A good plan, sir." Bryner drained his glass. "If there's more of this divine nectar available, I'd like to raise a toast and seal the deal. What do you think, Chief?"

"Sounds about right, Commodore. And if we can distribute samples to each ship, it'll help show Lyonesse will make one hell of a better home port than Yotai."

"I know you're only halfway serious, Aaron, but I'll see that a dozen cases are loaded aboard your shuttle tomorrow morning anyway," Havel replied with a satisfied smile. "Try not to hoard them."

—51—

"Major?"

Eve Haller glanced over her shoulder, then back at Captain Ryzkov, who was using the operations center conference room as her temporary office while the Defense Force Support Group worked double shifts to integrate Commodore Bryner's task force with the Lyonesse Navy. Or at least the three ships that stayed behind. One of the frigates had taken those with no interest in remaining back to Yotai, while another was on its way to recover families, accompanied by *Dawn Runner.*

"Sorry, sir. Duty calls."

"We can pick up the conversation later, Eve."

"Sure thing." Haller returned to the duty officer's command chair. "What's up?"

"Another Galactic Dawn ship just popped through the wormhole terminus. *Dawn Seeker.* A Captain Bassus is on the subspace link and wishes to speak with someone in authority."

"If this keeps up, we'll have the whole damned Void fleet here. Let me speak with him."

As Bassus appeared on the main display, Haller couldn't help but think Galactic Dawn captains came from the same mold. They all seemed older than the universe, with faces so lined they looked like topographic maps. And the eyes? Intense wasn't an adequate description.

"I'm Major Eve Haller, the Lyonesse Defense Force operations officer. Welcome. What can I do for you?"

He nodded gravely.

"Bassus, of the Void Brethren, master of *Dawn Seeker*. Rinne, who has *Dawn Trader*, told us Lyonesse was my Order's new home, and so I bring two-hundred-ninety rescued from this damnable war."

"They are most welcome. The abbey will be overjoyed. Sister Gwenneth, formerly of Yotai, leads the Brethren here."

"So I understand. One of my passengers is not of the Order, and it is on her behalf I speak with you now instead of waiting until we're on our last leg inbound. Did a Galactic Dawn ship perchance deliver two small children, they would be nine years old by now, along with a party of guards and Brethren from the Mykonos Abbey?"

A pulse of excitement ran through Haller's veins.

"Yes. They arrived aboard *Dawn Runner* and are in the abbey's care. Sigrid and Stefan, children of Marta Norum, last seen surrendering to rebel troops on Mykonos. Both are healthy, though they miss her."

Bassus' severe features softened.

"Marta Norum is aboard my ship, Major. She will be overjoyed beyond words."

An idea formed in Haller's mind.

"If you'll delay going FTL for thirty minutes or so, I will send for the children and they can speak to their mother now, instead of waiting another agonizing ten hours."

The friar inclined his head.

"A true kindness, Major. Of course, I shall wait as long as needed."

"Then keep this link open. We'll call back to you once they're here."

"Thank you, Major. I shall ensure Marta is in my day cabin."

"Operations, out."

Haller turned to Sergeant Rodion Kuryakin, the duty communications tech.

"Contact the abbey and tell them. If they don't have a car available, we'll send the duty runner."

"Already done. Sister Averyl is bringing them herself."

She gave him a big grin.

"I knew there was a reason I've been keeping you around despite that questionable thing you call a sense of humor."

"I aim to please."

**

Marta rapped the bulkhead beside day cabin's open door with her knuckles.

"You called for me, Captain?"

Bassus looked up from his reader and smiled.

"I did, Marta. Please come in and sit. You too, Jacelyn. I've been in contact with Lyonesse."

"And the news?" Marta's heartbeat surged when she met Bassus' sparkling eyes.

"See for yourself."

He gestured at the main display, which sprang to life as if by magic.

Two achingly familiar faces replaced the Galactic Dawn logo and Marta felt the universe enter into a spin. Bram grabbed her by the shoulder and kept her from falling into a dead faint.

"Mom?"

Tears erupted from Marta's eyes with unexpected force, veiling her sight. She fought both sobs and an overwhelming urge to laugh with joy and couldn't get out a single coherent sound.

"Your mother is fine," Bram said. "She's just incredibly happy to see you."

But neither Stefan nor Sigrid heard the former aide because they too were crying.

Bassus and Bram glanced at each other with slightly damp eyes.

"You should check your environmental systems, Captain. Suddenly, there's a lot of dust in the air."

"Don't hold back on my account. The Almighty commands us to celebrate joyful occasions."

"I prefer to raise a glass, Captain."

Marta finally regained a modicum of control and wiped away the worst of the waterworks to clear her sight.

"My darlings, safe and sound." Her voice, turned raspy by emotion, nevertheless touched Bram deeply.

"Our journey wasn't without its challenges," a woman's voice said. Then, another familiar face joined the children. "But I've never seen braver little humans than these two."

"Averyl!"

"Lady Marta. All of us made it. Hartwood Cahal asked that I tell you he kept his word. He's now back in service with the Lyonesse Defense Force, as are his three men."

"It's just plain Marta now."

"Understood. And Heloise?" Marta gave Averyl a quick summary of their time together, ending with Heloise's violent death. "You said she was touching you when she died?"

"Yes."

"Then a spark of what was once her consciousness survives within you."

"I know."

A small voice piped up.

"When will you get here, mommy?"

Marta glanced at Bassus, who said, "We should be on the ground in just under twenty hours."

"Did you hear, Stefan?"

"Yes, mommy. Sister Averyl says we'll be waiting for you at the spaceport."

Another upwelling of tears threatened to overwhelm Marta.

"I can't wait."

**

"Minor miracles like this give me hope for the future," Morane said, watching two little people run into the arms of their mother on the Lannion Spaceport tarmac.

"We should savor every one of them, Jonas because they'll likely be far and in between from now on," Gwenneth replied. "But I agree, joy brings hope, and there's a lot of joy here today."

Both stood on the spaceport terminal's observation deck, curious to meet the woman who'd seemingly returned from the dead. Based on what little Bassus relayed to Gwenneth after *Dawn Seeker* dropped out of FTL at the hyperlimit, she'd lived through an extraordinary adventure and was not just a mother reunited with her children in an unpredictable twist of fate.

"More than I've seen in a long time, Sister."

"I know you're keen on hearing her speak about Grand Duke Custis' court and his plans, but give it a few days, please. Let them enjoy each other's company undisturbed on the abbey's peaceful grounds."

"Of course. I'll have enough to keep me busy talking with Lieutenant Colonel Bram. She's not turning into one of you, is she?"

"The exact opposite of Marta. Not a shred of talent, but according to Bassus, filled with compassion. She should make a good addition to your staff."

"Glad to hear it. Otherwise, the Brethren might end up outnumbering the defense force, and though you're capable of doing much to protect Lyonesse, sometimes the use of military might is unavoidable."

Gwenneth, eyes still on mother and children, now walking toward the terminal, arms around each other, said, "I wonder how history might have turned out if Admiral Zahar had welcomed the Brethren as friends instead of enemies to be destroyed."

"Perhaps he did, in a parallel universe, though we'll never know. And neither will he. Colonel Bram appears to be handy with a gun."

A wry expression softened Gwenneth's severe face.

"That bit of military might which can't be avoided? Perhaps, but she made this reunion possible, and I thank the Almighty for guiding her hand."

Morane nodded toward the stairs.

"Shall we welcome Marta Norum?"

"In a moment."

He noticed her hesitation. "What is it?"

"I've been speaking with Bassus and his people since they came out of FTL at the hyperlimit."

"And?" Morane gave her a curious look.

"How can I put this without appearing...?" Gwenneth seemed to search for her words. "Overly esoteric, I suppose."

"Try me."

"Marta isn't a consecrated sister, yet she's one of us, religious rites notwithstanding. Furthermore, she exhibits the most powerful talent in living memory, one developed over an impossibly short period. I don't understand how, or why, nor does anyone else. But Bassus and I are in agreement. Her arrival here, at this juncture, is no happenstance. She has a role to play in this planet's future. In the knowledge vault's future. What that is, no one can tell. Marta is not even aware she might be called to serve a higher purpose."

"But you are?"

"Signs and portents, Jonas. When Kal, first of his name, founded the empire, the head of our Order received a vision, a prophecy if you like. It spoke of a sister with unusual ability appearing out of nowhere shortly after the Four Horsemen begin their apocalyptic ride across the galaxy, a sister charged with protecting the spark that saves humanity from eternal darkness."

"And you think Marta is this sister?"

"I can't discount the possibility." She looked down at the tarmac again. "Bassus said Marta might have the gift of prescience, as foreseen by the prophecy."

Morane surprised himself when he didn't automatically discount Gwenneth's words as mere religious nonsense. Instead, he said, "I'm not sure what to make of that, Sister. Mysticism isn't one of my strengths and belief is an on and off thing, depending on how the universe is treating me."

Gwenneth smiled fondly at him.

"Few have the sort of faith that encompasses thousand-year-old visions, Jonas, even among the Brethren. You're a good man, with a self-imposed mission that transcends space and time. Let it be sufficient. Whatever the Almighty intends for Marta is not ours to question. We should merely be aware she may have a purpose as well, one none of us can see for the moment, and leave it at that."

Morane inclined his head.

"As always, I bow to your wisdom in these matters. I'm just a naval officer who reads too much history, not one of humanity's great thinkers, let alone a philosopher."

She shook her head with amused indulgence.

"You're more than that, Jonas Morane, as you well know but refuse to admit." She nodded toward the stairs. "Shall we?"

— Nightfall —

"What is it now?" Emma Reyes muttered as she turned the lights on. Then, in a louder voice, "Who's calling?"

"Lannion Base Operations Center for Admiral Morane, Chancellor," Carson, the butler AI replied in a smooth, almost affected tone.

Reyes nudged a half-asleep Morane.

"Wakey, wakey. Your office is looking for you, and if they're doing it at two in the morning, it won't be because Rorik wants to renegotiate some obscure part of the constitution."

"Bugger Rorik," he replied with visible irritation. "The man's given me a piece of his mind so often, it's a damn wonder he has anything left. At least with Downes on a timeout in the Windies, I can tolerate his presence again."

"Something major is brewing if they reached out to you here, Jonas."

Morane grumbled inaudibly but sat up and grimaced at Reyes.

"The night is ruined anyway since we're both awake."

She grinned at him.

"That's the spirit, O Great Warrior. Carson, please accept the connection, audio only."

"Yes, Chancellor." A pause. "I have the Lannion Base Operations Center for the Admiral."

"This is Morane."

"Centurion Greff, sir. You asked to be informed at once when *Dawn Trader* showed up. She just transited through the wormhole. Captain Rinne would like to speak with you or, I quote, whichever lost soul is in charge nowadays."

"He obviously didn't check what time it was in Lannion," Reyes grumbled.

Morane, now fully alert, shrugged.

"It doesn't matter. I'm just glad he made it home. Centurion, please tell Captain Rinne I said welcome and to stand by."

"Will do, sir. Does that mean you're coming in?"

"I'll be there in twenty minutes. Morane, out."

"You can always return once you've spoken to him." She gave Morane a seductive smile. "At best speed, he won't arrive until late tomorrow, no?"

"What's my inducement?"

"Breakfast." She ran her fingers down his bare chest. "A two-course meal, starting with me."

**

"Captain Rinne! Sister Gwenneth and I were wondering whether you'd come home. It's been over a year."

"Aye." His voice had lost none of its gruff undertones. "I was wondering myself whether I'd ever make it back. Admiral, eh? Congratulations. That must mean your scheme is working."

"So far, so good. But I get the feeling you're about to inject my dreams with a dose of unwanted reality."

"Things are dreadful out there, Morane. I can't count the number of close scrapes we had evading rogue navy units, reivers, and assorted pirates. It's to the point where you can barely tell those three species of scavenger apart. Word is Wyvern was devastated by rebel units that snuck in while most of 1st and 2nd Fleet's remaining ships were away on one of Dendera's genocidal retribution missions. Kinetic strikes from orbit."

"You could almost call that punishment of biblical proportions."

A bark of laughter came over the subspace link.

"Almost? An eye for an eye *is* biblical. No one knows whether Dendera survived or whether such a thing as an imperial government still exists. Wild rumors about Shrehari invading the Rim Sector seem to be running rampant, though with the boneheaded buggers caught up in their own version of Armageddon, I'd take that with a grain of salt. As you might expect, tales of woe are coming from every direction."

"Sounds like the end of days has finally arrived."

"If not that, then something close. Perhaps there's still a functioning sector government in the Coalsack, though it'd be news to me. Mind you, we stuck to the backwaters of the wormhole network where there's nothing but anarchy, piracy, and death. Perhaps Yotai still controls itself and a handful of nearby systems, but I wasn't about to check."

"Did you find many of your Brethren?"

"Enough to fill every spare bunk. We also rescued the survivors of a merchant ship left for dead by reivers a few wormhole transits back. Thirty-nine of them. They'll need more care than we can manage, especially the little ones. If you could arrange for the Lannion hospital to take them when I land…"

"Of course. You'll be glad to know four Galactic Dawn ships are in orbit. Between them, they brought over a thousand Brethren to Lyonesse. The abbey is busy establishing priories throughout the settlement area."

"Thank the Almighty! Which ships?"

"*Dawn Runner, Dawn Seeker, Dawn Glory,* and *Dawn Mercy.* The last two showed up less than a month ago."

"More than I expected but less than I hoped for in my heart of hearts. Still, we take what is given and do our best with it."

"And that's all anyone can ask of you, my friend. Welcome home."

Ashes of Empire continues with
Imperial Night

About the Author

Eric Thomson is the pen name of a retired Canadian soldier with thirty-one years of service, both in the Regular Army and the Army Reserve. He spent his Regular Army career in the Infantry and his Reserve service in the Armoured Corps. He worked as an information technology specialist for a number of years before retiring to become a full-time author.

Eric has been a voracious reader of science fiction, military fiction, and history all his life. Several years ago, he put fingers to keyboard and started writing his own military sci-fi, with a definite space opera slant, using many of his own experiences as a soldier for inspiration.

When he is not writing fiction, Eric indulges in his other passions: photography, hiking, and scuba diving, all of which he shares with his wife.

Join Eric Thomson at: http://www.thomsonfiction.ca/

Where you will find news about upcoming books and more information about the universe in which his heroes fight for humanity's survival.

Read his blog at:
https://ericthomsonblog.wordpress.com

If you enjoyed this book, please consider leaving a review on Goodreads or with your favorite online retailer to help others discover it.

Also by Eric Thomson

Siobhan Dunmoore
No Honor in Death (Siobhan Dunmoore Book 1)
The Path of Duty (Siobhan Dunmoore Book 2)
Like Stars in Heaven (Siobhan Dunmoore Book 3)
Victory's Bright Dawn (Siobhan Dunmoore Book 4)
Without Mercy (Siobhan Dunmoore Book 5)

Decker's War
Death Comes but Once (Decker's War Book 1)
Cold Comfort (Decker's War Book 2)
Fatal Blade (Decker's War Book 3)
Howling Stars (Decker's War Book 4)
Cahal Sword (Decker's War Book 5)
No Remorse (Decker's War Book 6)
Hard Strike (Decker's War Book 7)

Quis Custodiet
The Warrior's Knife

Ashes of Empire
Imperial Sunset (Ashes of Empire #1)
Imperial Twilight (Ashes of Empire #2)

9 781989 314142